CW00688064

THE
HONOUR
AND THE
GLORY

Also by Douglas Boyd:

THE EAGLE AND THE SNAKE

THE
HONOUR
AND THE
GLORY

Douglas Boyd

LITTLE, BROWN AND COMPANY

A *Little, Brown* Book

First published in Great Britain in 1994 by
Little, Brown and Company

Copyright © 1994 Douglas Boyd and Atarah Ben-Tovim

The moral right of the author has been asserted

All characters in this publication are fictitious and
any resemblance to real persons, living or dead,
is purely coincidental

A CIP catalogue record for this book is
available from the British Library.

ISBN 0 316 91030 9

Typeset by M Rules
Printed and bound in Great Britain by
BPC Hazell Books Ltd
A member of
The British Printing Company Ltd

Little, Brown and Company (UK) Limited
Brettenham House
Lancaster Place
London WC2E 7EN

To Cathy and Richard

ACKNOWLEDGEMENTS

Once again I am privileged to thank past and serving members of the French Foreign Legion – from retired colonel down to *simple soldat* – for revealing to me while I was working on this book something of their combat and peacetime experiences. As is always the case with legionnaires, they remain anonymous.

I thank also Russian friends both old and new for helping me learn their language and understand something of their way of life. Except for the few public figures who appear in this book, none of the Russian or any other characters is based on a real person, although many of the events described have actually taken place.

The biggest debt here acknowledged is to an old comrade-in-arms: Ron Sharp, the best buddy I ever had.

PART I

THE INCIDENT

May 1986

. 1 .

In the moonlight the outline of the ruined caravanserai on the low hill in the valley below Mount Ararat stood out like a plywood silhouette in an old Hollywood musical. Genghis Khan was reputed to have camped on the spot and Marco Polo had once slept safe from bandits inside its crenellated walls.

On the night of 1 May 1986, as the blazing Number Four Reactor at Chernobyl was spewing radioactive dust around the globe, the valley below Ararat was lit by a full moon intermittently veiled by puff-ball clouds that scudded across its face, driven by a bitingly cold wind blowing off the Anatolian desert.

The immense dark bulk of the sacred mountain loomed up into the sky, its distinctive twin peaks still capped with winter snows. To the east lay the lightless expanse of Armenia. Between Ararat's flanks and the caravanserai the ground was barren and stony, littered with the wind-dried carcases of trees that had been cut down when Kemal Ataturk's men pushed back the eastern frontiers of their country in 1924 and cleared the area of inhabitants. It was a process that cost a million and a quarter Armenian lives. Six decades later, Turks and

Armenians still watched each other across the uneasy border as warily as only hereditary enemies know how.

A jeep of the Turkish border patrol drove in low gear along the stony track that ran parallel to the line of the frontier. The driver braked sharply, switched off the lights, stopped the engine and sat listening for several minutes before driving on.

When the sound of the muffled exhaust had died away, two dark objects that resembled fallen trees moved slightly in order to ease cramped muscles. The man and the woman who lay in a shallow, disused irrigation ditch were dressed from head to toe in sand-coloured cotton fatigues that matched the arid soil. Their faces were concealed in knitted khaki ski helmets. Their hands and faces were smeared with dark green and brown camouflage make-up.

Van raised her head from the ground. Nervous perspiration was cold on her skin and grains of sand clung to her sweat-moist cheek. 'Peter,' she whispered, 'do you think they saw anything?'

Bergman had used a branch torn from a thornbush to smooth away the marks of their passage across the tell-tale strip of raked sand, but the jeep had stopped within a few metres of where they had crossed. Coincidence was a word he did not use.

'One thing's sure,' he grunted. 'If they did, they'll be back, so let's get outta here fast.' His accent was Canadian with an overlay that came from years of living in Africa, south of the Equator.

By the time he let her take a break, two hundred metres further on, Van's neck muscles were screaming for relief from the unaccustomed strain of holding her head up while alternately snaking on her belly and crawling on hands and knees over the rough ground.

Bergman rolled onto his back to rest a moment. To save his night vision he avoided looking at the moon; towards the eastern horizon the stars shone crisply through the clean dry air like tiny diamonds scattered on black velvet.

He could smell his own tension. It was not just the naked fear that always went with a clandestine frontier-crossing. From the beginning of this job everything had smelled wrong; he should have backed out long before. So why was he here? The girl was a part of the reason. She stopped him thinking straight. Correction, it was his own obsession with her that stopped his brain working properly. And maybe bravado, he accused himself. Was he trying to show her how tough and clever he was, by pulling off an impossible job? If he were alone, it wouldn't be so bad. He had wriggled out of the way of certain death so many times, but if this operation backfired, she would pay the price too . . .

Bergman's train of thought was interrupted by an involuntary sigh of relief beside him as Van rested her head on her forearms. 'What is it?' she asked.

'Your bosses in London must be out of their cotton-picking minds,' he said to distract her. 'What the hell are they doing, sending a woman all the way to an RV on the wrong side of this, of all borders? It's insane.'

Van grinned to herself. 'I'm not "a woman", Peter. I'm an officer of the Service. That's why I'm here. There's no way London would sanction handing an irrevocable letter of credit for one hundred thousand dollars to a freelance like you.'

She felt the breast pocket of her fatigues to make sure it was still there – payment to a bent KGB officer for the arrangements made on the other side of the border.

Bergman grunted disparagingly.

'I suppose it would flatter your male ego to have me sitting safely back there in the Land-Rover,' she teased. 'Perhaps you'd rather I was daintily nibbling sandwiches and drinking coffee from a flask while the men did the hard work?'

'I'd have you any way.' Bergman rolled towards her. He pulled his helmet clear of his mouth and lifted Van's to kiss her on the lips. His hand slipped down her spine to feel her tightly-muscled buttocks and squeeze them through the thin cotton material. The adrenalin of a clandestine border crossing always made him feel randy afterwards, but this was the first time he had ever brought along a girl on the job itself. He wanted Van right there and then.

She felt his surge of desire. An old school-friend had once boasted to her at a reunion dinner that she had qualified for membership of the Mile High Club, composed exclusively of air hostesses who had made love to other crew members while in the air. She had said the experience had added zest, mainly because of the high risk of discovery.

If danger heightened the pleasure, Van thought, then going all the way in this lethal setting would be mind-blowing, not that one could ever talk about it afterwards . . .

Bergman pushed away the thoughts of lust. It was crazy to be thinking about making love while playing a game that made death so easily . . .

He snaked ahead over the hard and stony ground without waiting for Van. Time and again she admired the way he used what little cover there was, waiting always for a cloud to pass across the moon before starting on each patch of completely open ground.

Seeing him in action, she understood what Roscoe had meant when he said, 'Bergman's the ultimate pro at this game. He's quite simply the best *passeur* in the world.'

'*Passeur*?' She had queried the unfamiliar word.

'Smuggler,' Roscoe had explained. 'My old buddy Peter Bergman has moved people and packages across frontiers in five continents. You name it, he's done it.'

He sounded to Van proud of Bergman and proud of being able to call him a friend.

'A smuggler?' Van had a fleeting image of a moonlit cove and men in three-cornered hats using muffled oars to row small boats under the noses of the sleeping Revenue men. Brandy for the parson, baccy for the clerk . . . 'Drugs?' she had asked, prepared to believe the worst.

'He doesn't handle them,' said Roscoe. 'Nor arms. Moving people is his speciality. But I suppose you'd call him a soldier of fortune. He'll take on most jobs – so long as they're dangerous.'

Back to the present, Van thought. Why has Peter stopped?

In front of her Bergman was using a couple of stunted thorn-bushes to disguise the outline of his body. Five metres ahead of him lay the wire. He lay methodically scanning the Armenian side of the valley through night glasses until he was certain that the guards on the other side really had been withdrawn.

When Van asked for a look through the glasses he refused with a curtness that made her wonder again what was on his mind. It seemed to her they were all alone in the empty valley.

Cautiously scanning 180 degrees from Ararat to the caravanserai she could see no sign of life anywhere.

She lay with her face on the ground, resting her neck muscles
while Bergman used his wire-cutters to make a small hole in the
wire. The succession of loud snicks made her jump each time.

He jabbed her in the ribs with a terse: 'Wake up, we still have
a way to go.'

Her pulse racing, Van wriggled through the gap in the wire
and followed Bergman on to Soviet soil, staying two metres
behind him as he had ordered and exactly in his tracks. She
thought of the mines on either side of them, ready to shred an
incautious limb or hurl her mutilated body high in the air if she
deviated from the path he had checked. Her confidence in the
man she followed was total, so that she did not even think of the
other possibility – that he might trigger a mine which could cost
her a limb or her life.

In the darkness she bumped into him, lying still and listening
to the night sounds, near and distant. Satisfied after a couple of
minutes, he pulled her forward until his mouth was against
her ear: 'We're well into Soviet territory now. Check our position. But first cup your hand over the compass to shield the
glow.'

Van flicked the cover back from the luminous dial and took
bearings on the higher of Ararat's two peaks and the gate of the
caravanserai. By her reckoning Bergman had navigated them to
within a hundred metres of the rendezvous point.

As a cloud cleared the moon she gave him a nudge. 'That pile
of rocks at two o'clock must be the RV.'

He gave a low throaty chuckle at her use of the clock-
compass. 'The rocks stand out a mile,' he said slowly, thinking
aloud. He had often complained of inadequate briefings but
this one was too good, too complete . . .

'And?' she prompted.

'Everything stinks.'

The tension inside him uncoiled into sudden fury that
focused on Van. She was one of them, an insider, an officer in
the goddam Service, as she had just reminded him. Therefore,
they must have told her more than he knew . . .

He gripped her shoulder painfully tight and hissed, 'If the RV is so fucking obvious, why in hell did Jack Roscoe give us a grid reference and bearings as well?'

'I don't know, Peter.' She winced with pain. 'He didn't set this up. Roscoe was only passing on the details that came from the other side. They insisted on making all the arrangements as to place and time – everything down to the last detail.'

Bergman released her without comment. It was himself he was angry with, not her. As a sliver of cloud slashed the moon in two, he tensed his muscles and waited for the rest of the cloud to give a full blackout and then took off into the darkness. She caught up with him among the rocks where he was crouching half-erect to get a higher angle of view over the terrain ahead. The landscape was not so bleak and desolate on this side of the frontier; isolated trees had been allowed to grow, with a few low bushes in between.

Van felt a sharp pressure on her wrist from Bergman's fingers – not anger this time but a warning. They had a simple code: one tap meant freeze; two meant that it was safe to move.

In the moonlight, she saw a Turkish foot patrol on the edge of no man's land behind them. The cold wind carried the quietly grumbling men's voices clearly across the empty ground, growing gradually fainter.

Two taps on her wrist and Bergman pointed ahead. 'The Soviet sentries' path through the minefield runs between the two olive trees dead ahead,' he whispered, 'to the left of that ruined farmhouse.'

He squatted with his back against one of the rocks and pulled the cuff away from his watch. After checking the time, he folded the cuff back and grunted, thinking aloud: 'I've got twenty minutes to spare.'

Van slumped down beside him. It was sheer pleasure to resume a normal posture once again after all the crawling.

'Roscoe said . . .' She hesitated, unsure of herself. She outranked Bergman on paper but here in no man's land, he was the boss.

She began again: 'Jack said that the other side insisted we arrive here no more than ten minutes before the rendezvous time.'

Another low chuckle from Bergman. 'Fuck what the other

side, quote, insist on, unquote! If I wanna do a recce before the other guys arrive, I damn well will. Now you stay here and don't move till I get back.'

'Peter!' Van caught Bergman's sleeve and hissed urgently, 'It's absolutely against Roscoe's orders to go any further into Redland.'

'Roscoe's orders?' he mocked her authority. 'Out here, I'm the captain of the ship, honey. Nobody gives orders to me. Not here.'

His face was close to hers. Van could see the devil of laughter in his eyes. Was it all a game to him? she wondered. Was he so high on his own adrenalin that he didn't feel any fear? Wasn't his spine wet with perspiration like hers? Wasn't his pulse racing and thumping like a trip-hammer in his ears?

'Peter . . . ' she whispered. Desperately not wanting him to leave her alone, she clutched at the cloth of his fatigues.

'What?' He spoke without looking at her, his mind already ranging ahead in the darkness.

Ashamed of her intuition which seemed as childish as a fear of the dark, Van let go of him. 'Nothing,' she muttered.

With a last pressure of his fingers on her arm Bergman wriggled into a small hollow, using a fallen tree for cover. Van blinked and he was gone. Straining her eyes in the direction where he had been heading, she could see nothing. It was eerie, as though the bare, stony ground had swallowed him whole, leaving her in an empty nightmare landscape surrounded by menace on all sides.

.2.

Alone in the darkness with all his senses sharpened by the adrenalin pulsing through his body, Bergman felt more alive than at any other time. The controlled elation he experienced on jobs like this was more powerful than the kick he got from flying blind above mountainous terrain in bad weather or inching his way solo up a sheer rock face with only finger- and toe-holds above a drop of hundreds of feet and no rope to save him. Other people could fly blind and climb mountains solo, but for a clandestine border-crossing Peter Bergman was the best in the world! Why else would the British bring a wild colonial boy like him halfway across the globe to do this job?

Despite the whisper of doubt that was growing to a scream inside his head, he smiled grimly. Whoever was dealing the cards in this game was going to get a surprise because he, Peter Bergman, knew they were playing with a marked deck. He just did not know who was dealing.

Using knees and elbows, he lizard-crawled past the roofless farmhouse, moving faster now that he was alone. According to his briefing from Roscoe, the mine-free path used by the Soviet sentries led between the two dead olive trees ahead of him.

However, he took no chances and moved with a curious swimming motion, feeling the soil all around before each move as well as the air in front of him in case there were tripwires.

To the right and left of the narrow passage between the two trees his questing fingers found the spikes of anti-personnel mines. He flared them lightly and left them alone. The path itself was clear. Bergman made good time until his fingers touched the cable that should not have been there.

Abort! Abort! The scream of suspicion became alarm bells in his head and the scent of danger that had been teasing his nostrils, was suddenly overpowering. He felt the cable and weighed it in his hand before deciding that it was too thick and heavy to be the detonation circuit of a Claymore mine or a line to a field telephone. No, a cable like this must be for high voltage, which made him curious. Anything unusual made Bergman curious; only a cat-like curiosity had kept him alive so long.

Changing his plan of action, he followed the cable to a powerful searchlight mounted on a tripod by the corner of the farmhouse. It was pointing back to where Van lay in darkness among the rocks. The cable severed with one stroke of his knife, Bergman squatted, back to the wall, thinking. From the direction of the concrete blockhouse where the Soviet guards sheltered in bad weather he could hear the hum of a silenced diesel generator.

Question: was the searchlight a permanent fixture or had it been set up especially that night?

Observing the Armenian side of the border the previous night from a hidden vantage point inside the caravanserai, he had watched Soviet foot patrols with dogs passing at regular intervals. Tonight no movement at all had been visible on this side of the valley.

Question: was that because the guard commander had been bribed? Or was there another explanation?

Bergman checked his watch again and tried to work out how long it would take him to reach the blockhouse. There was no time for caution; speed was the priority now. He estimated that the next cloud would give him ten to fifteen seconds of darkness, and started counting as it hit the rim of the moon.

On 'two' Bergman launched himself in a noiseless crouching

run, using the scattered thornbushes for cover and gambling that the mine-free path was a straight line between the trees and the guard-house. Each time the cloud thinned he froze in mid-step, curbing the instinct to drop flat. Moving only his eyeballs, he checked out the ground ahead.

He flattened himself against the wall of the blockhouse and peeked inside. It was empty. Bergman controlled his breathing and thought: so far, so good – the guards must have been paid to keep out of the way, after all. Maybe I was imagining things . . .

Then he heard low voices from behind the blockhouse. They were speaking not Armenian, not even Russian but English!

Bergman dropped to his knees and eased one eye round the corner of the building. After one glance into the small pool of light in the sunken mortar pit he slowly eased his head back out of sight.

From the mugshots which Roscoe had shown him, he identi-fied one of the two men who were talking. The small, hawk-nosed Armenian in the mortar pit wearing the uniform of a KGB major was Anastas Lirian. Once a brilliant State chess-player, he had changed games to become one of the most successful KGB officers of all time, largely because of his hand-ling of one agent inside Downing Street itself.

Bergman eased his eye round the corner of the blockhouse for another look. The man to whom Lirian was talking was an obvi-ous Brit from his Sherlock Holmes tweed cape and deerstalker hat to the brown brogue shoes on his feet. Seated on a shooting stick, he looked as calm as on a grouse moor waiting for the beaters to get in position. Sir John Bowles-Haddon had been Intelligence Secretary to the Cabinet Office for fifteen years before running for cover with the help of his case-officer, Anastas Lirian. Now, according to Roscoe's briefing, he had changed his mind and wanted to come home. Oh boy, thought Bergman, did London get that wrong! But what the hell was going on?

The face at which Bergman was staring did not resemble the mugshot Roscoe had used at the briefing, but it was known that Sir John had undergone plastic surgery. Bergman watched as the man in the mortar pit took an inhaler from his pocket and drew on it deeply. Sir John was known to be asthmatic, so that was confirmation of a kind.

His senses all heightened, Bergman could smell the smoke of the cigarette that Lirian was smoking. American tobacco, he guessed. Camels? No, Marlboro. Yes, even that little detail had been in the briefing.

He blinked to clear sweat from his eyes. There was no way that the two men at whom he was looking were about to scramble through a minefield.

'*Yeshchó pyát minút.*' The announcement came from a uniformed MVD border guard lieutenant who was using a shielded torch to count time off his wristwatch out loud for two soldiers crouched beside the tube of a 30 mm. mortar. 'Five minutes to go,' he repeated.

Lirian stubbed his half-smoked cigarette out nervously. Sir John stifled a yawn as though mildly bored. The server picked up the first mortar shell from the crate beside him and positioned it above the tube, ready to drop.

A quarter of a mile away, Van crouched among the rocks. Getting more anxious with each second that passed, she was trying not to stare directly at the derelict farmhouse. At night it was better to look off to one side, she knew, and let the rods – or was it the cones of the eye? – pick up movement first. Only then did one look directly at . . . At what? There was nothing to see. Bergman had been gone ten minutes, maybe more, and there was no sign of his return. She had no watch but was sure he should have been back by now.

In the hostile landscape, nameless terrors of the dark crept up on her. If something had happened to Bergman, could she find her way back through the minefield? She had not consciously memorised the way, but just followed him blindly. The thought of what would happen to her if she were caught here on the wrong side of the wire suddenly became real. Prison, interrogation, torture and death all stared her in the face.

Peter! Don't leave me like this! She beamed the thought into the unresponding night. Peter, where the hell are you?

It seemed to Bergman also an eternity until the next cloud covered the moon and he could risk retracing his steps to the farmhouse, running in the same painful crouch.

He was nearly there when instinct more than any sound made him look over his shoulder in time to see the dog as it hurled itself through the air at him. He threw himself sideways and rolled twice to put some space between them, ending the roll on his feet with his right hand grabbing the Smith & Wesson .38 from a holster in the small of his back.

No, that was too noisy . . . He stooped, scooping the knife from its sheath on his calf to hold it left-handed, blade horizontal and steady. The dog was a large black Alsatian crossbreed, trained for silent killing. It scrambled round five or six metres distant and came at him again, launching itself through the air, aiming for Bergman's neck.

There were several ways of dealing with the attack, of which only one guaranteed that the dog would make no noise. Bergman braced himself and gave it his right arm to fasten onto. He felt the sharp flesh-tearing teeth pierce skin and muscle to grate against the bones of his forearm as he was carried backwards by the animal's momentum.

They fell together, the man on his back underneath the dog. He had tensed his belly muscles to avoid being winded. Calmly, the razor-sharp matt black blade went in once, then a second time to make sure. There was a whimper from the dog and Bergman's face was bathed in a hot, pulsing shower of sticky blood from the Alsatian's carotid artery. Another whimper. The rear legs twitched and lay still.

Two hundred metres away, Van heard the scuffle. She took the risk of standing up to scan the apparently deserted landscape in front of her. Blinking rapidly from tension and with her breathing out of control, she licked dry lips and wiped the sticky palms of her hands on her trousers to dry them. She was sure that the twenty minutes were up – and there was still no sign of Bergman or of the two men they were supposed to be meeting at the RV point.

Damn Peter! she thought. What the hell was she supposed to do? Go after him or go back? How could she move either way? There was metal-clad death all around, its fingers poking through the soil, waiting to trip her and rip off a foot, a leg, an arm. Without Bergman to guide her safely out of this nightmare, she felt paralysed by fear.

Lying in the darkness, Bergman kept his injured arm jammed in the beast's mouth until the huge body went limp on top of him. He counted the seconds, forcing himself to ignore the pain and listen to the night sounds. There was no reaction from the guardhouse that he could hear. He supposed that all the men in the mortar pit were too busy concentrating on the countdown to have heard anything. And, keeping their heads down, they would not have seen anything either . . .

Gingerly he prised the heavy jaws open to remove his arm from the dog's mouth. It took all his self-control not to groan out loud with each stab of pain. Alarm signals threatened to swamp the brain's switchboard and his right hand would not obey any commands.

No time for pain, Bergman told himself. No time either to waste looking for the handgun which had dropped from his inert fingers, somewhere among the stones.

He rolled from beneath the dog's dead weight and scrambled to his feet using just the good arm. There were no excited voices coming from the direction of the guardhouse. And there was no jet of blood pumping from a punctured artery in his arm, just a steady warm oozing; things could be worse.

A large cloud obscured the moon just when he needed it. He folded the injured arm to his chest and ran upright this time – for that was faster – to the shelter of the farmhouse. There he paused to get back his breath and check the time on his wrist-watch. Miraculously, it was still working. There were only seconds to go until the shit hit the fan with a vengeance.

Scheiss! Bergman swore under his breath, angry now more at himself than anyone else. It was too late to play If Only . . . In the few seconds he had left, there was just one thing he could do. To shout a warning would cost his life, but it might save hers.

Yet would Van act on it fast enough? At a time like this, a woman might argue or need reasons. He could try calling something like: *There is a mortar trained exactly where you are, so* . . . No, that was too long. A simple order would be better – and hope to God that she had the discipline to obey without thinking.

Standing upright, so that his voice would carry better, Bergman filled his lungs and called in a loud, clear parade-ground voice: 'Van, move your arse! Get out of there, fast! That's an order! So move it! Go! Go! Go!'

His voice echoing away down the valley *go – go – go – go – oh – oh!* Bergman strained his ears for any sound that would tell him she had understood and was moving fast away from the rendezvous point and back to the hole in the wire. But the darkness stayed silent, although he thought he saw one patch of black that moved.

He never prayed for himself but he prayed now: *Please God, let her get away!*

And then the noise started.

First – but everything followed so fast that it seemed simultaneous – came the observer's shout: '*Osveshchénie! Davái! Davái!*' Gimme light!

And the mortarman: '*Nichevó ne vízhu!*' I can't see a thing!

A third voice joined in. It was the officer, screaming at them both: '*Yob tvóyu mat! Ogón, durák! Ogón!*' Fire, you motherfucker!

A .50 calibre machine-gun opened up on the left, very close. Then another began firing from the right. Their tracers intersected on the crumbling wall less than a metre from where Bergman lay flat on his face, bathed in a hail of stone chippings. A second and a third machine-gun opened up further away, scything the bare earth from the farmhouse right up to the Turkish border. If the floodlight had been working to give them visibility, Van would not have stood a chance.

With his good arm, Bergman covered the back of his head and his ears. He prayed that she had heard and obeyed, that she was fast enough – and lucky enough – to get away. They were firing blind, so she might just make it . . .

Then came the *whoof-crump* of the mortar.

Bergman was so close he could hear the propellant exploding in the tube. He felt clods of hot, chemical-smelling earth and stones falling on his unprotected back and shoulders as the rock-pile was blasted to fragments. When the mortar started walking its earth-shaking way towards where he lay, he knew his number was up. All the jokey metaphors mocked him now: *the golden bullet, buying the farm, the PX in the sky, the one you never hear . . .*

Like all fliers he had told a thousand stories of hair-raising incidents, ending: 'I thought I was gonna die that time, for sure.' But somehow he had always envisaged going out with a bang at the centre of a fireball on a mountainside or in a heap of tangled metal that had been a flying machine until shortly before. He had never thought it would all end with a whimper, cowering like a beaten animal, trying to dig himself a protective hole in the earth with his bare hands.

A white-hot piece of shrapnel sliced into Bergman's injured wrist and a hundred tiny particles of metal lashed his back and buttocks, flaying the skin like a cat-o'-nine-tails in hell, pumping pain into his brain through a hundred nerve-endings laid wide open.

This time, the pain was too awful to control. He screamed, a wild pre-human noise lost in the explosions and the whine of ricochets. In a final attempt to fight the searing, burning, throbbing ocean of agony that was engulfing him, Bergman concentrated his fury on the man who had set him up that night.

His last conscious thought was: You bastard, Jack Roscoe! You bastard, I'll kill you for this!

.3.

'Go! Go! Go!'
Van had been raised to obey orders. Bergman's shout was an order, so she was up and running before the echoes had died away. Only afterwards did she flinch in retrospect at the thought of the mines. With every pace her pounding feet must have touched the ground within inches of one.

'Go! Go! Go!'

There was no time to think of anything except the mortar shells crumping behind her and the machine-gun bullets sweeping closer and closer towards her in the darkness, chasing her and pacing her. The only important thing was to put as much distance between her vulnerable flesh and blood and the noisy machines that were trying to pierce it, tear it, spill it open, maim it and destroy it.

Like invisible claws, thornbushes reached out to catch her clothing and slow her down. She fell several times after tripping over low rocks in the darkness. One fall saved her life; she lay winded in an old ditch while a storm of super-heated shrapnel zizzed overhead like a swarm of angry hornets. She was cut by sharp, hot fragments of rock and felt blood running down her face and a burning pain where the back of her left hand was torn open.

At the wire she stopped, panicking. Which way to turn: right or left? Like a miracle, the flash of an exploding mortar shell revealed the hole in the boundary fence only a couple of metres away. She scrambled through and on to Turkish soil where the frantic stumbling run continued as she headed by blind instinct for where the Land-Rover was concealed.

When the firing stopped, Van's hearing threshold took several seconds to adjust. Then she heard a wild animal panting, sobbing and moaning with pain and fear. Realising that the animal was herself, she slowed down and stopped. The only way to silence the involuntary noises was by clapping her unwounded hand over her mouth until the sobs and moans had died to a few whimpers. As the next step on the path to self-control, she took control of her wheezing lungs as they fought for oxygen and forced herself to take deep, slow breaths.

Where was Bergman? She turned and looked desperately back at the border, feeling sick at the mental picture of him lying out there wounded or, more likely, dead. She started back to find him but stopped after a few paces. There were men running and calling to each other in the direction from where his shouted warning had come. Indistinct figures moved across the now dark landscape with powerful hand-held lamps. How strange, she thought remotely: it's only a few minutes ago that Peter laughed and kissed me and touched my arm . . . and now he's lying out there, dead.

She grabbed control of her thoughts. On this side of the border, she knew that the Turks would swiftly come to investigate the firing. Being caught by them would be only marginally better than being captured on the 'wrong' side of the frontier. Although a political ally of Britain and a member of Nato, the government in Ankara did not take kindly to illicit activity on its territory. If she were picked up in these circumstances so near to the border, the least she could expect would be a long stay in a Turkish gaol.

Van started running again, but moving purposefully and no longer in panic. Whenever possible she kept to the hollows and the shadows where the moon did not reach.

Its motor screaming in low gear and headlights full on, a border patrol jeep came bouncing across the rough ground towards her. There were headlights of other vehicles ahead, to the right and left, all converging on her. Van threw herself flat and lay immobile as the jeep passed within a few metres. Then she was up and on her feet and moving again, trying to work out a plan.

She had heard the marathon runners' phrase: *going through the wall*. She fixed that image in her mind and kept running, ignoring the urgent messages from tortured muscles, her wildly pumping heart and straining lungs. The salty taste of blood and sweat trickled into her mouth and still she ran. At last she broke through the wall and it was almost peaceful; now she felt she could run all night and all day if necessary.

As she ran, she improvised a plan. One, simple was best. Two, sooner or later the Turks would find the hidden Land-Rover and send out search parties, so she had better keep away from it. Three, she could not walk back to safety. Four, since she could not avoid the search parties indefinitely, she would take advantage of them . . .

With only a few brief pauses to check her direction by Bergman's luminous compass, she kept moving obliquely away from where the Land-Rover was hidden, at the same time putting more and more distance between herself and the frontier. By the first flush of daybreak she reckoned that she had covered ten or twelve miles across country. That was enough; being too ambitious could blow her chances of success.

She found the spot to put her plan into execution where a single-track road crossed a rocky gully by means of a ramp of earth that had been bulldozed over a concrete storm drain. She crawled inside the drain just before a convoy of army trucks drove slowly over it. Half an hour later she awoke, wondering how long she had slept. Sheer exhaustion made her limbs so heavy that she could hardly move them.

A drink! She would do anything for a drink. A few paces from her hiding place were some pools of muddy brackish water between the rocks in the gully. Van took the risk of crawling down to the nearest pool and gulping a few mouthfuls of brown water.

The cut on her hand needed stitching but the scalp wound that had bled so much when she was running, seemed to have staunched itself. Her face, reflected in the water, was scratched by thornbushes, cut by stones and filthy from the camouflage make-up.

It took an effort of will to remove the warm anorak and bury it in the stream-bed. She smashed the compass and buried the pieces in a different place. The knitted ski helmet and her cotton fatigues she buried elsewhere. Then she washed her face and hands, hoping that what remained of the grease-paint would pass as ordinary grime.

Wearing just a shirt of Bergman's and a pair of jeans, she shivered in the dawn cold. It was time to empty her pockets of everything: handkerchief, a lipstick, cigarettes, matches and the waterproof plastic envelope that contained the letter of credit. She stripped naked despite the cold and turned each garment inside out, tearing off any labels before she put it back on. Then she lit a small fire in the bottom of the gully and fed everything into it, item by item, until there were only two things left: a torn photograph and the piece of paper which bore the letterhead of a bank in Zurich. *This irrevocable Letter of Credit . . .* it began.

She read the amount in words and figures several times as though it were some mystic code whose meaning was unclear at first sight. When Roscoe had handed her the LC she had thought that $100,000 was a lot of money for bringing one man over a border. Now it did not seem nearly enough to pay for a man's life. Was Bergman dead? Would she ever know, either way? She felt no grief yet; that would come later.

The fire had gone out. Van realised that she must have dozed off, squatting beside it. There was a sound of men's voices nearby from a search party on foot, coming her way. She scooped water over the ashes and stamped them into the mud. Then, acting on a last-minute impulse, she scrambled back to where the track crossed the gully. There she put the letter of credit and the photograph inside the plastic envelope, which she stuffed as far as she could reach into the crack between the drainpipe and the bedrock against which it was laid.

Now hurry, she whispered to herself. The voices were very near.

She had left this part of the plan until last. It was surprisingly hard to pick up a knife-sharp flint with a serrated edge and use it like a knife on her own flesh, but it was important to have an injury that would have stopped her walking far, never mind running twelve miles.

She gritted her teeth and ordered herself aloud: 'Do it!'

And after the first cut: 'Do it again, Van! Go on, do it!'

By the time the soldiers found her lying in the gully apparently unable to move, she was whimpering from the new pain and there was blood on her clothes. She groaned a lot when they helped her to sit up.

An officer arrived in a radio jeep. He asked questions in English, politely at first. Then, when she did not answer, he barked a command and two soldiers pulled Van to her feet. They tore her shirt half-open and pulled it down from the back, pinioning her arms against her body. The other men gathered round, staring and grinning as the officer dealt her a series of hard backhand blows across the face, shouting in Turkish.

It required no acting ability on Van's part to dissolve into helpless, hopeless tears.

.*4*.

Two Turkish sentries armed with sub-machine-guns presented arms as the black Rover flying a Union Jack on the
bonnet drove out of the gateway of the prison hospital just
before midday.

'All's well that ends well.' The Consul sitting beside the driver
heaved a sigh of relief. The last thing he ever wanted was to have
to ask HE to intervene. His most fervent prayer was that the
two men sitting behind him would now fly back to London and
not return to Turkey until he had been posted elsewhere.

He turned to them and announced, 'Johnny Turk's being
lenient to your girl because of her injuries. She'll be released in
a day or two with a stiff fine for being in a military zone without a permit. Then she'll be expelled from the country. I'll put
her on the plane to London myself. End of story.'

It's enough, thought Roscoe.

'Bright gal, isn't she?'

Roscoe grunted agreement.

'I mean,' the Consul continued, 'they haven't any specific
charge against her. She was picked up a dozen miles away from
that fracas on the border – must have travelled like a blue-arsed

fly to get so far, so fast. And her story that she had fought off a rape attempt, been beaten up and thrown out of a moving car was spot-on. It's a plausible explanation for those injuries. Worse things have happened to girl hitch-hikers in Turkey before now.'

He stopped, realising that relief was making him talkative in front of the driver. Neither of the men in the rear seat had said much since they left the Embassy at breakfast time. The Rover was approaching the new motorway bridge over the Bosporus when Roscoe tapped the driver on the shoulder.

'Pull over and stop,' he ordered.

They cut across two lanes of traffic to the accompaniment of loud hooting from other drivers. Leaving the Consul and his driver in the car, Roscoe and Dawson got out and strolled onto the bridge itself where they stood at the balustrade looking across towards the old city.

The two men could not have been more different physically. Roscoe was thirty-two, fit, tall and dark with the sort of smouldering good looks that made women look twice at him – plus the physical confidence not to bother how he dressed. He was wearing an open-neck shirt, anorak and jeans with grubby trainers on his feet. That morning, his face was ashen and he looked as though he had not slept for several nights.

Beside him, George Dawson was ten years older than Roscoe but looked a hundred. He was flabby and out of condition. With thinning mousey hair, he stood less than five-eight and always managed to look crumpled as though he had slept in his cheap off-the-peg suits. Under his breath he was humming the tune of the old Count Basie hit, 'Istanbul'.

It was getting on Roscoe's nerves. He felt like hitting Dawson in the teeth to shut him up; the blow would have relieved some of the guilt he had felt on seeing Van with a cut and bruised face limping painfully back to her cell, dressed in an ugly grey prison dress and escorted by two grim-faced wardresses.

Unaware, Dawson took a deep breath of the fresh morning air and stretched. 'Could be worse, Jack,' he said. 'Thank God that Van managed to destroy all her false papers before they picked her up. There's nothing to link her with the incident on the border, unless . . .'

'Unless what?' Roscoe snapped.

'Unless she left any fingerprints in the Land-Rover they were using.'

'She won't have been so stupid.'

Dawson shot Roscoe a questioning look. 'Let's hope not. As to how she managed to walk or run so far in her condition, Jack, I just don't know. She looked pretty cut-up to me. Must have a lot of stamina, despite the pretty face.'

'She does.' Roscoe's hands gripped the handrail savagely as though he were contemplating wrenching it free for use as a weapon.

'Of course, she's her father's daughter,' mused Dawson. 'It runs in the blood.'

'What are we going to do about it?' Roscoe interrupted. He had a strong suspicion that he already knew the answer.

Dawson was thinking that things could have turned out a lot worse, with the Ambassador summoned to the Sublime Porte to be handed a Note. He winced at the thought of the repercussions it would have caused in Whitehall and the heads that would have fallen. His own would probably have been one. It was more humane than being stitched inside a silken bag and thrown into the Bosporus, of course.

He pointed at the golden domes of the Topkapi palace on the opposite bank. 'From here, Ottoman decadence delights the eye, as they say in the travel brochures. Istanbul from a distance is still one of the great tourist sights of the world.'

Two hundred feet beneath them a grey-painted frigate flying the hammer and sickle was sliding slowly across the slate-grey waters of the Bosporus. Roscoe could have spat on the jack-tar hats of the sailors in the deck-party below.

He spoke slowly, his mind far away in the valley below Ararat. 'I meant, what the hell are we going to do about Bergman?'

Dawson stopped humming and made a grimace of distaste. 'There's not much we can do, Jack. You were at the caravanserai with me next morning. You saw the three bodies being carried away from the scene: Lirian, Sir John and your pal Bergman.'

'Even using binoculars we weren't near enough to identify them positively.'

'Oh, come on, Jack,' Dawson objected. 'The Soviet guards carried three stiffs away. Bergman must have been one of them.'

'Must have been?' Roscoe's voice was harsh. 'What kind of a fucking epitaph is that?'

Dawson was tamping tobacco into the bowl of his pipe with an old .303 cartridge case he carried for the purpose. 'Well if he is dead, we can't do anything about it. And if he isn't, we can't do anything either, Jack. London doesn't want any waves made about this little cock-up, that's for sure. Too embarrassing for our masters.'

He turned his back to the wind and struck a match to light the pipe. 'I know Bergman was a pal of yours but – let's face it – that's why we used a non-Brit freelance for the job in the first place. So that we could write him off if worse came to worst and no questions asked.'

How long he spent in the danger ward of the military hospital outside Yerevan, Bergman would never know. The only clear memory of that time was one he clung to afterwards with every ounce of psychic energy he could spare. It was of a visit before he had properly recovered consciousness.

There was the feel of a drip needle itching in his left arm and another in the crook of the right elbow but they were as nothing to the agony of his shrapnel-torn back which was a raging surf of pain battering him down and down, with each undertow threatening to drag him away into the eternal depths where the intolerable punishment would end in blessed nothingness.

The orderlies turned him every half-hour. It was sheer chance that he was lying on his side, face to the wall, when the visitors arrived so that they did not see his eyelids flicker open for one unguarded second. They were talking English; it was the sound of the language that fanned the spark of consciousness deep in Bergman's mind.

'It's remarkable the chap's still alive . . .'

Sir John's words and the languid upper-class drawl in which they were delivered were imprinted for ever in Bergman's memory. An orderly turned him in the bed so that the visitors could have a view of the prisoner-patient's face.

That hurt.

Somehow Bergman mustered the strength to stifle a groan. He kept his eyes closed, squinting between the lids to photograph the face of the tall, fair-haired Englishman and fix it in his memory for ever.

He heard Lirian, the swarthy little uniformed KGB major with the snake-like eyes, ask the army surgeon about the prognosis for the patient if the drips were removed.

The patient . . . thought Bergman. The word was the same in Russian. It seemed remote and abstract, as though the three men were talking of someone else – not the flesh and blood and consciousness that made up Peter Bergman.

The woman in the white coat kept her face an expressionless mask. She was an army captain, outranked by Lirian and the tall foreigner who was equally obviously KGB.

'*Dva íli tri dnyá, mózhno,*' she shrugged a reply: two or three days perhaps.

The two visitors conferred briefly in English. The prisoner heard his death sentence translated into Russian for the surgeon's benefit. She gave a terse command to the orderly and Bergman's drips were removed.

He felt the needles being pulled from his veins and curled his psychic body into a foetal form, concentrating all his will on two ideas only: survival and revenge!

PART 2

AFTERMATH
June 1986 – November 1991

.1.

After thirty years as a detective in the large, sprawling industrial city of Smolensk, Captain Oleg Glasov had few illusions about himself or his job. The archetype of Soviet civil police officer, his sole long-term ambition was to retire on a full pension, on the first possible day. A more immediate hope was that his keen young assistant, Lieutenant Akhmatov, would drop dead or get promoted somewhere else long before then.

Glasov had recommended Akhmatov for several postings; the trouble was that the lieutenant was what his boss called a pushy wog, and it showed even on paper. Akhmatov was a Moslem from the Caucasus who worked hard and put in long hours in the belief that effort was rewarded.

Glasov did not like wogs, especially pushy ones. He had warned Akhmatov a hundred times that people like him upset the system. Akhmatov nodded politely, but still came to work early and stayed late in the evening, even after seven years of Glasov's good advice. Day after day he attacked the double workload on his desk with a vigour and tenacity that made his superior feel tired, just to watch him.

When Glasov arrived in his office unshaven and bleary-eyed

at ten o'clock one Monday morning in June 1986, he was suffering from more than his usual post-weekend hangover. He
and two like-minded pals had been celebrating Boris Yeltsin's
election victory on a platform which they understood to mean,
among other things, that people like Akhmatov would soon be
sent back where they belonged.

On being greeted with the news that the body of a whore had
been found badly carved-up on the wooded bank of the
Dnieper, Glasov yawned with boredom.

'A party of Young Pioneers who are camping by the river
went looking for firewood to make breakfast,' Akhmatov
announced. 'I took a statement from the youth leader . . .'

Glasov tipped the bent tin lid full of dog-ends into the
wastepaper basket that had not been emptied. He lit his first
cigarette of the day and stared gloomily out of the window.
The sky was clouding over; it had been humid for several days
and thunderstorms were forecast. Through the dirty pane, the
office had an excellent view of the urinals across the yard.

'Two boys discovered the corpse, Captain.' Akhmatov
coughed to regain Glasov's attention. 'Immediately the youth
leader despatched a runner to the nearest militia post. Their
report was timed at 08.45.'

'So?' Glasov took a deep drag. He smoked *makhórka* – black
Russian tobacco so strong that it made bystanders cough even
in the open air. Akhmatov waved the fumes away from his face
and continued filling in the details.

In Glasov's view, there was nothing to get excited about.
Whores got themselves killed all the time; it was an occupa-
tional risk in their line of business. Since they were classed as
socially unproductive elements, like the vagrants and other
drifters who slept rough in the woods during the summer
months, nobody bothered much about one of them getting
topped. Certainly no one would get promoted for wasting
police time chasing the killer of an old bag who worked the
woods because there were no streetlamps by which a client
could see her face.

For cases like this Glasov opened a file which stayed on his
desk a few months to show how busy he was. After a year or
two it would get shoved into a drawer in one of the periodic

weeding-outs. Finally it would end like everything else in the incinerator beside the urinals.

'Happens a couple of times every summer,' he said. 'No sweat.'

'Not like this, Captain,' Akhmatov disagreed politely. 'This time, there's a witness. A woman who owns a beer stand down by the river has volunteered a name for the john with whom the deceased was drinking last night.'

The mixture of *the john* and *deceased* in one sentence was real wog-talk, thought Glasov. He gave a guffaw that ended in a paroxysm of smoker's cough.

'I've detained her in the interview room,' said Akhmatov. 'I thought you'd want to talk to her.'

Glasov vaguely recognised the woman. Something to do with the black market, he thought. That was it, an accusation that she was selling illicit booze, a few years back. Presumably she had done the right thing, dropped him a little present on the side and been released without being charged – he could not recall the details. Akhmatov had already checked that she had no previous record. All he had come up with, was that the woman's husband had done seven years in a labour camp under Article 58, paras 6, 8 and 9. That meant nothing; Article 58 covered everything from complaining about food shortages to blowing up the Kremlin.

Accustomed to vague denunciations which usually had more to do with a desire for personal revenge than the interests of justice, Glasov half-listened to what she had to say.

'Better than just a name,' she said with the air of self-importance that people wore when making denunciations. 'I can tell you more about the murderer than that. Like what he does for a living, for example.'

'What does he do?'

'He's a colleague of yours,' she smirked. The idea seemed to amuse her.

They took a detailed description. Name: Ossetin, Nikolai Ivanovich. Age: forty-two or -three, she thought. Physical description: less than average height, chubby build, baby face, thick eyeglasses, slight stammer. Occupation: Senior Archivist at the State prison in Butyrki, outside Moscow.

Glasov winced. He had a feeling they would not be able to wriggle out of this one.

'You know the type,' the woman ended. 'A flabby cut-balls – a eunuch.'

'How come you know the guy so well, if he's from out of town?' Glasov did not believe in Father Christmas and was wondering why the old crow in front of him was so keen to drop Nikolai Ivanovich Ossetin in the shit.

'He used to work here in the Smolensk prison,' she explained. 'I was a cleaner there. He was always complaining the floor of his office wasn't clean. You know the type.'

Petty revenge, thought Glasov – at least, that's normal. 'Did he recognise you?' he asked her. 'I mean, last night when you were serving him?'

The woman laughed. 'You're kidding? That sort doesn't look at a woman's face. I could have been a piece of furniture.'

'I asked: did he recognise you?'

'No,' she said.

'Where is he now?'

'You're the bloody detectives,' she laughed again, revealing a dental battlefield of missing and dead teeth. 'How the fuck would I know?'

They picked up Ossetin at the main station where he was waiting for the Moscow train. It was Akhmatov's idea to go there first. In answer to Glasov's questions in the station master's office, the nervous, rather overweight little man in thick glasses said he had been staying in Smolensk with his stepfather for a couple of days.

'Purpose of visit?' Glasov asked.

'To attend my mother's funeral.'

The burial, they learned, had taken place the previous day. Ossetin looked upset at the memory. Now, if they didn't mind, he had a train to catch . . .

The stepfather he had mentioned was a well-known local Party high-up, which could complicate things. For that reason, plus the nature of Ossetin's job, Glasov would have let him go. It was Akhmatov who asked politely to look in Ossetin's briefcase as the Moscow train was pulling into the station.

Ossetin neither objected nor resisted. He seemed frozen to

the spot in indecision. Akhmatov thought afterwards that perhaps he was relieved to be caught. Inside the case, wrapped in a pair of pyjamas, was the set of scalpels which had been used to carve up the whore's breasts, a bloodstained towel and the knife that had killed her. It was as easy as that.

Back at the precinct house, after formally arresting Ossetin, Glasov asked as a matter of routine, 'Are there any other crimes you wish to be taken into consideration?'

He was watching Lieutenant Akhmatov pack away the shining instruments that lay on the table in the interview room. Ossetin had demonstrated to them how he had carried out what he called the breast surgery. He had been co-operative most of the time at the murder site, answering all their questions except about the missing pieces of the body.

From the glance Akhmatov gave his boss, Glasov reckoned they were both thinking the same thing: Ossetin had eaten them. There had been fresh traces of a fire near the body and a sharpened twig that looked as though it had been used as a skewer to cook some pieces of meat in the flames.

Glasov did not really expect the nervous little man who was under arrest to offer any other information at this stage. As a prison officer, Ossetin would know enough about the system to keep silent. He had already told them a surprising amount.

Both detectives were surprised when Ossetin coughed apologetically and said in his prissy little voice, 'There is something else I'd like to tell you about.'

They had been lucky with the weather on the first trip across the Dnieper; the rain had held off. But during the time it took to charge Ossetin, a cloudburst had soaked the ground and turned the woodland paths into muddy streams.

The small procession of uniformed militia and the two detectives trailed after Ossetin through a forest that was steaming in the sunshine. Nobody had thought to bring rubber boots. Their shoes were soon muddy from squelching through puddles and their trousers dirty from slipping and sliding on the wet ground, clambering over fallen trees and pushing through thickets. Akhmatov and Ossetin were in the lead. At the rear, Glasov was sweating and feeling the need for a beer.

The woods along the banks of the Dnieper were all about the same age. Not a single tree was more than forty years old. The whole area of Smolensk had been laid waste twice during the war: once when the Red Army retreated behind scorched earth in 1941 and again when the *Wehrmacht* retreated westwards in 1943. Any trees that had survived the passage of armies, had been hacked down and used as fuel by the desperate survivors and returnees, to keep themselves from dying of cold during those first bitter winters after the war. Then houses were roofed with tarpaulins or open to the sky, there was no central heating, no food in the shops. The only clothes to be found, were those taken from dead bodies.

Glasov could remember that time. He had walked to school each morning, with no overcoat but layers of newspaper roughly stitched into his jacket and trousers for warmth. Like the other half-starved kids of his age, he had not even spared a second glance at the naked corpses laid out at the roadside for collection by the municipal refuse-disposal team – two men with a horse and cart.

The column bunched up behind Ossetin who was apologising to Akhmatov for losing his way: 'It must be twenty-six years ago. The woods have changed since then. I was only eighteen at the time. It's difficult to be sure this is the right path.'

Much of the time, they had to go in single file, so the handcuffs had been taken off Ossetin who was carrying his suit jacket neatly folded over one arm. He mopped his brow with a clean handkerchief as they broke through thick undergrowth into a hidden clearing.

'If this is a wild-goose chase . . .' Glasov puffed, out of breath. From smoking so much, he was very short-winded.

'Oh no, Captain.' Ossetin was confident. 'As a boy I used to know this woodland very well. I'm sure this is the place, give or take a few metres.'

Glasov smoked his last cigarette watching Akhmatov and the uniformed men dig out the shallow grave in the thick leaf-mould. The pile of displaced earth steamed in the sunshine that shafted between the leaves. The photographer shot a roll of film of the grave, including close-ups. Then, moonlighting, he put another film in the camera and wandered around the clearing, shooting pictures of leaves and cobwebs bejewelled with raindrops.

In the grave was a skeleton with a cheap necklace of glass beads round the neck vertebrae. Apart from a belt buckle and some buttons, the clothes had rotted away. When touched, the beads of the necklace rolled away into the moist, disturbed earth like so many children's marbles.

Nobody talked much. The long walk through the forest in the heat and humidity had sapped their energy. Akhmatov and the militiamen worked in silence, turning the leaf-mould over with a couple of borrowed garden rakes, not expecting to find anything else.

Glasov was watching Ossetin, who was staring into space. He had folded his jacket inside out and used it as a cushion to avoid getting moss stains on his trousers from the fallen tree-trunk where he sat, handcuffed once again to one of the uniformed men.

Akhmatov hurried across the clearing and showed Glasov the remains of a handbag in which were some outdated coins – a few roubles and some copecks – and a wad of long-rotted paper which could once have been an internal passport. There was also a cheap wristwatch in some corroded green metal.

'What do you think?' he asked his boss.

Glasov was thinking he needed a smoke and a drink at one of the riverside beer stalls. The uniformed sergeant had offered him a cigarette but nothing milder than *makhórka* would still the craving.

'There's a statute of limitations, even for murder,' he grunted. 'That fat-arsed little creep sitting over there knows perfectly well that we can't do him for this one.'

'That's not what I meant, boss,' Akhmatov kept his voice down so that only Glasov could hear. 'We're less than a kilo-metre from where the other body was found this morning.'

'So?'

'If a man commits two murders in more or less the same place, twenty-six years apart, don't you think it likely . . . ?'

Glasov did not want to listen.

When the uniformed men had finished putting the remains

into a plastic sports holdall, Ossetin said several times to no one in particular, 'I've wanted to tell someone for a long time.'

It was Akhmatov who understood what he meant.

'What do you want to tell us?' he prompted.

Ossetin fixed his piggy little eyes on the younger detective. He looked grateful for the help.

'About the others,' he said.

'*Bózhe mói!*' Glasov swore. 'How many, for Christ's sake?'

Ossetin looked nervously from one detective to the other and giggled nervously. 'I'm not exactly sure, but there's a map on the wall of my office in Butyrki prison.'

'And?' Glasov prompted.

'You'll see there are a lot of drawing pins stuck into it,' said Ossetin. 'Each one marks –' His eyes drifted from their faces in the direction of the now empty grave. '– another of those.'

. 2 .

Because Ossetin's confession included murders of women that had taken place in more than fifty police districts all over Russia, the case was designated federal and taken over by the Serious Crimes Squad from the State Prosecutor's office in Moscow. Captain Glasov was delighted to hand the file over to them and could not believe his luck when the harassed investigators from Moscow asked for his keen young lieutenant to be seconded to work on the case.

For Akhmatov, it was the stuff of dreams. The investigators did not arrive at work late or drunk. They did not knock off early like Glasov. They did not lose files or exhibits, which was always happening in Smolensk. They worked not five but seven days a week and seemed tireless in their devotion to exposing the inefficiency and corruption of the crumbling Soviet system. They were the sort of first-rank colleagues with whom Akhmatov had always hoped to work. Twice Akhmatov saw in the canteen his hero, a senior investigator who had risen to the top despite being a member of the persecuted Ingush race and a Moslem like himself.

Hints were soon dropped that Akhmatov was the kind of man

they were looking for to make up the numbers of the Serious Crimes Squad, which was always short-handed because of the hours they had to work and the months on end they spent living in cheap hotels, away from home. A bachelor, Akhmatov did not mind that; he travelled with the investigators to one after another of the sites marked on the map in the records office of Butyrki prison to discover that some of the bodies were still *in situ*, while others had been found years before.

The Serious Crimes men showed a detached professional respect for Ossetin's method of avoiding detection. It was based on the huge map of the Russian Federation which hung on the wall of his office and showed the seventy-odd districts into which the criminal police system was divided for administrative purposes. Until the slip-up in Smolensk, Ossetin had always stuck rigidly to two principles. One: he killed only whores because he knew very little energy was put into chasing their killers. If not solved swiftly, their deaths were classified 'non-serious crimes' in order not to distort the statistics. Two: he never killed more than once in any administrative district.

For non-serious crimes, as he knew, there was no cross-referencing between districts, so Ossetin had been able to kill two women each year for over a quarter of a century using exactly the same methods, without anyone realising that all the women's deaths were the work of a serial killer.

As part of his research, Akhmatov checked Ossetin's *stazh* or work record. Never once had the bespectacled little murderer been drunk on duty or even late for work. Never had he missed a political meeting or failed to return a form by the due date. He was a model employee with a record that had earned him five outstanding service medals.

As the case got bigger, Akhmatov grew steadily more awed at the implications. The most embarrassing aspect of all was that eleven of the murders to which Ossetin was confessing, were already officially classified as 'solved'. Other men had been sentenced for the crimes – mostly drifters or drunks who had agreed to collaborate after being beaten up in the cells. Three of them had been executed in the usual cost-effective way by which capital punishment was meted out under Soviet law: one 9 mm. bullet fired into the base of the skull.

For the lieutenant from Smolensk, the sense of anticlimax was crushing when, after two months' investigation, the team was disbanded and re-allocated to other work overnight. When he met the investigators in the canteen, they refused to talk about the case and seemed surprised that Akhmatov was still in Moscow. So on his own initiative the young lieutenant spent the next days in long conversations with Ossetin who was always polite, standing up when the lieutenant came into his cell, or waiting for permission to sit down if the interview were taking place in the office Akhmatov used – the one where the files and evidence were still stored.

'Tell me about your mother,' suggested the young detective. Nobody else had bothered to follow up what he felt was a powerful connection between her death and Ossetin's first and only mistake, on the evening after the funeral.

'She was so strong,' said Ossetin wistfully. His baby face crumpled at the memory of the pale, waxen face in the coffin.

'Did you get on well with her?'

'Oh yes.'

'But your stepfather said you hadn't visited her for several years. Why was that?'

'I was afraid she'd be cross.'

'What about?'

'You know.' Ossetin sniggered and looked down at his pudgy hands which were clasped on his lap. He motioned with his head at the map which was leaning against the wall in one corner, the pins still in place.

In a moment of inspiration Akhmatov said, 'I'm going to give you some paper, Nikolai Ivanovich. Perhaps it would help if you could write down how all this . . .' He nodded in a similarly vague way at the map. 'How it all began.'

'How far back do you want me to go?' Ossetin asked.

'As early as you can remember.'

Ossetin had no memory of the first years when his mother fled from city to city – one of millions made homeless by the war – looking for surviving relatives, for shelter or work. His mother had said often enough that this had been a terrible time, but Ossetin was convinced that he had been happy then, alone with her, before that day . . .

He picked up the ball-pen and started writing:

The first memory I have is of when my mother took me to the apartment of my stepfather. He was a Party functionary at the factory where she worked. She married him because he had an apartment where we could live. I was five at the time. I remember she said: 'Say hallo to Tatiana.' That was my stepsister.

He stopped writing; it was too painful: the end of something nice and the beginning of the nightmare.

'What kind of child were you?' asked Akhmatov, to get him going again.

'I was small for my age, with poor eyesight. I stammered badly.'

'You don't stammer much now.'

'I cured it.' Ossetin looked smug for a moment. 'I'm coming to that.'

He bent over the paper, wanting to please this young lieutenant whose eyes did not have the hardness of the older investigators. He sensed that Akhmatov knew what it was like to be an odd man out. With the lieutenant standing over him and the sheet of paper waiting to be written on, it was like being back at school.

At school I was praised by the teachers for conscientious work, but my stepsister used to get into trouble often. It served her right, she was always baiting and teasing me. Tatiana never used my proper name, nor Nikita which is what my mother called me. She had an armoury of nicknames . . .

Akhmatov was reading over his shoulder. 'What were the nicknames?'

Ossetin shook his head.

'I want to know,' the lieutenant insisted gently. He had an intuition that, by pushing now, Ossetin would crack wide open.

'She called me Four-eyes, Stammerer, Spindle-shanks and sometimes Cry-baby because I was so fearful of other boys, even those younger than myself. When we reached adolescence she called me other awful things.'

'What sort of names did she call you then?'

Ossetin shook his head. Even thirty years later he could not bear to utter the names Tatiana had thrown at him as they got ready for bed in the small, damp, unheated room which they shared. He would try to hide his body while she flaunted herself, taunting her puny stepbrother with her fully developed womanhood.

'She was a disgusting creature,' Ossetin said. 'She used to tell me which of my classmates had fondled her here.' He touched his chest.

'Touched her breasts?' Akhmatov supplied the word.

Ossetin nodded. 'And she took special pleasure in telling me which boys she had allowed to touch her *there*.'

He touched his crotch. With eyes shut, the memories rushed back, as vivid as yesterday. Tatiana's promiscuous sex-life obsessed her shy, under-developed stepbrother. A pale-faced, pimply youth, Nikolai followed her and the other girls into the woods along the Dnieper on summer evenings to spy on their petting sessions. There was so little privacy in the cramped one- and two-roomed apartments where they all lived that the woods had to serve as courting grounds.

'Shall we break for lunch?' Akhmatov asked, cutting through the memories.

He sent a guard to the canteen, paying out of his own pocket for both the meals that were brought on a tray. He ate in silence, standing by the barred window that looked out onto a blank light-well. Behind his back, Ossetin sat primly at the table, knees together and elbows tucked in. He cut the gristly meat from the stew into small portions before putting it into his mouth and chewing everything very thoroughly before swallowing. He had a mannerism of licking his rather full lips with the tip of his tongue after each mouthful which reminded Akhmatov of feeding-time at the zoo.

It was getting dark. The small square of sky at the top of the light-well had clouded over early. Akhmatov switched on the light. The table was covered with sheets of paper bearing

Ossetin's neat handwriting. Some were covered from top to bottom, with alterations and insertions in the margin; others had only a couple of lines on them.

Read in any order, they were disjointed without the conversation that had linked one revelation to the next. Akhmatov wished he could have used a tape recorder, but so far as he knew, there was only one that worked in the entire building.

'That first time in Smolensk,' he said. 'Tell me about that.' Ossetin took a clean sheet of paper and started writing again.

I began hanging around the beer stands on the banks of the Dnieper. On summer evenings, there are always whores there. I chose one of the older ones because she had large breasts that reminded me of Tatiana's. Few women wore bras at that time – I'm talking of 1960. Then there were more important priorities than the manufacture of lingerie. It's a scandal now what unnecessary rubbish is produced by our society. Evening after evening, I bought a single beer and stood for hours watching that woman's breasts move beneath her blouse like two animals clinging to her chest, wriggling with an independent life of their own as she laughed at the dirty jokes of the men at the beer stall.

Akhmatov saw for a moment the shallow grave, the bones, the few pathetic souvenirs of the woman Ossetin was talking about. He waited a few minutes before leading with a Glasov-type question: 'Did you fuck her?'

Ossetin sniggered. 'It wasn't as easy as that.'

It had taken a couple of weeks before he built up the courage to offer her a drink. She made him buy two more before she agreed to walk off into the woods. Ossetin felt both afraid and excited that something terrible but pleasurable was going to happen to him but . . .

'So what happened?' Akhmatov prompted.

'Nothing.'

The evening had ended with him running away after throwing some money on the ground, and leaving the drunken, half-naked whore shouting abuse after him.

'I felt so ashamed that I ran away and hid in the woods. I wanted to cut my wrists with my mother's kitchen knife.'

'You had the knife on you?' Akhmatov asked.

'I carried it everywhere in my briefcase for protection because I was afraid of being picked on by people.'

It was customary in Russia, where shortages were a way of life, for women to carry empty shopping bags wherever they went. They were called maybe-bags. Passing any shop with a queue, they would join the long line of waiting people without even asking what was on sale. Whatever was left when they reached the counter, was bought and stuffed into the maybe-bag, to be resold or exchanged later if unwanted. Men carried empty briefcases for the same purpose.

'I took the knife out of my case,' continued Ossetin. 'But an inner voice argued with me that I should not be the one to suffer. It was the women like Tatiana and that whore who deserved to be punished, not me.'

The incident had obsessed him for days until he realised what had to be done to procure for himself the relief that other young men of his age seemed to find so easily with a few thrusts of their hips.

'The woman was a little wary when I turned up again and started chatting her up a second time.'

'Didn't she just tell you to piss off?'

'I paid her in advance and promised a bonus afterwards. That kept the greedy cow happy.' Ossetin lowered his eyes and started writing again.

She followed me into the woods but grew uneasy as I led her way beyond her normal haunts. I was a very feebly built young man, so I don't think she was afraid. Anyway I quietened her suspicions by explaining that I couldn't perform the previous time because I was nervous of being interrupted.

It was all surprisingly easy. I said something like: 'You'll have to look away while I take it out and get ready. I'm afraid I'm very shy.'

The woman laughed at what she thought was his modesty and

turned her back for a moment. Ossetin undid not his trousers but the maybe-case. What he took out was not his penis but a hammer, which he used to stun her with one blow on the back of the head. She dropped to the carpet of leaves with a small grunt that reminded him of the noises his stepsister made in bed when she was dreaming.

I turned her over onto her back and stabbed her beneath the ribcage with the kitchen knife. There was less blood than I would have thought. I tried to pull the blade out, but it would not come.

I was frightened of what my mother would say, if I didn't return the knife when I got home. Then I recalled a war story, read aloud in school, in which the partisan hero had to twist his bayonet in a Fascist soldier's body in order to release the suction in the wound. The technique worked. I plunged the knife in several more times because it was so satisfying.

I didn't hate the woman any more. I felt like a priest, purifying her of evil. Or maybe like an eagle crouched over its kill. I felt I could fly. It was a mystical experience. You who have not killed cannot understand what I mean.

Ossetin waited until the forest was silent again. When he opened his victim's blouse her huge, sagging breasts taunted him. He touched them, took hold of the symbolic flesh and readied it for the sanctifying knife, like a high priest of old. Carefully excising what he saw as the power foci of the whore's body, Ossetin experienced the first sexual release of his life. He took all his clothes off and lay for a while on the now flat-chested body, feeling very peaceful. Then he rose and washed himself in a stream.

The experience was so powerful that within a month my acne cleared up. I began to put on weight and the stammer that had troubled me all my childhood grew less bothersome. In atheism lessons we had been told of the Christian rite of Communion, eating the body of Christ. It's the same thing.

Ossetin's prim functionary's mannerisms, the cringing look, the baby face, the apologetic giggles were all gone.

'What are you telling me?' Akhmatov asked hoarsely. 'That you ate her flesh?'

Ossetin looked up at the detective. His eyes were shining brightly, not hidden in the folds of flesh, nor hiding anything. He smiled pityingly at Akhmatov and stood up.

'Now I shall return to my cell,' he announced with an uncanny air of authority. 'Call the guard, please.'

The following day when he presented his ID card at the entrance to the Attorney-General's building, Akhmatov was not handed the usual day-pass and the key to the office. Instead he was refused admission and given an envelope which contained instructions to report back to duty in Smolensk within twenty-four hours.

Baffled, he hung around the official car-park until he spotted a twenty-year-old Zhiguli saloon that belonged to one of the younger investigators. The man had been friendly, even inviting Akhmatov to go swimming with his wife and children in the Moskva River on a free Sunday afternoon. They had eaten shish kebab together and drunk beer in a rest area, half an hour's drive outside the city. Akhmatov had danced in the evening with the man's wife and shown her pictures of his own girlfriend.

'What's going on, Vassily?' Akhmatov asked, as the investigator got out of his car. 'I've been taken off the Ossetin case.'

The other man did not look pleased to see him. 'That's wrapped up,' he said. 'The investigation has been binned, old son.'

'There's been no date set for the trial?'

'There isn't going to be one.'

Akhmatov was half-running to keep up as the investigator hurried into the building. 'This doesn't make sense, Vassily,' he said. 'Just yesterday I cracked Ossetin wide open. He's telling me everything.'

'Congratulations. Now go home.'

Incredulously Akhmatov asked, 'You're not telling me we're going to sweep fifty-odd murders under the carpet for some reason?'

The investigator laughed hollowly. He could remember feeling the same bewilderment and anger, the first time it happened to him.

'Where the hell do you think you are, Akhmatov?' he asked. 'I'll tell you. You are standing in the capital city of a country where nobody knows how many died during the Civil War. Twenty million is a conservative estimate.'

He started counting on his fingers. 'Next, in the mid-thirties, at least five million peasants died during the collectivisation programme. That's official. Nine million more people were executed by the State during the purges before 1939. And thirty million died during the Great Patriotic War.'

He paused to let the numbers sink in. 'Sixty or seventy million people, Akhmatov, have died unpleasantly and violently in Russia during this century and you have the fucking gall to get excited over fifty whores who got carved up by a madman. You gotta be joking!'

'But what happens next to Ossetin?' Akhmatov persisted. He was genuinely puzzled. 'Is he going to be executed or locked away in a nuthouse? It has to be one or the other. He's quite mad and very dangerous, you know that.'

The investigator laughed wryly. 'Someone at the top of our admirable prison service has decided that Ossetin is just the man for a very hush-hush job, so our fat little friend with the glasses is getting promoted. Keep that to yourself, Akhmatov. Don't drop me in the shit.' He flashed his ID card at the doorman and passed through the barrier

'I don't believe this,' Akhmatov gasped. 'You must be crazy, Vassily! After all the work we put in . . .'

The investigator came back to the barrier. He leaned over it and grabbed Akhmatov's lapels. 'When are you going to grow up, young man? You had a nice holiday, playing detectives with us. Now piss off back to Omsk or Tomsk or wherever you came from. And take my advice: if you ever want to make captain, just forget you ever heard the name of Ossetin, Nikolai Ivanovich. Ain't no such person, OK?'

. 3 .

Bergman's tortured body clung to life. For three days and nights it hovered on the borderline *in extremis*. Then sheer physical toughness and the will that went with it took over and a slow recovery began.

The precise wording of the order given by the snake-eyed little KGB major was crucial in what happened next. The army surgeon had not been told to kill him, but just to let her patient die by withdrawing all medication. When Bergman's condition stabilised and showed a spontaneous upturn instead of the predicted swift decline into coma and death, she was professionally intrigued and gave orders for him to be given liquid nourishment. Up to that point, she had not disobeyed the order. His continued improvement kept her awake for two nights as her professional conscience wrestled with the fact that no sane person would try to thwart a major in the KGB. On the third night she slipped into Bergman's room in the early hours while the night staff were asleep to give him surreptitious injections of antibiotics and vitamins in places where the needle-marks would not show. She did the same the next night and the next. Two weeks after the incident on the border, Bergman was normally conscious and no longer losing weight. One week after that he was up and walking around his room, holding onto the furniture for support.

The surgeon's nightly visits were now for conversation. She was intrigued by this mysterious patient who spoke Russian so badly and who had refused to oblige the KGB by dying when he should have done. She pretended not to understand Bergman's questions as to how long he would stay in the army hospital and what would happen next.

It was in July, nearly three months after the shoot-up in the valley under Ararat that a captain from Yerevan KGB came routinely to collect Bergman's personal effects and erase from the hospital records any trace of his stay there. Amazed to find the dead man still alive, if somewhat weak, he immediately called Moscow for instructions.

Next morning, the surgeon hurried into Bergman's room with a hastily packed bundle of foodstuffs. 'Get ready,' she warned him. 'You're being moved.'

'Where to?'

She grimaced, 'The order has arrived for you to be transferred to the custody of the Ministry of the Interior. There's nothing more I can do for you now.'

'What does that mean?' Bergman asked.

'You disappear,' she sighed. 'You disappear into the Gulag, my friend. You know what that means?'

'I think so,' said Bergman.

The surgeon looked away. 'I don't think anyone in the West has the remotest idea what it means.'

'While there's life, there's hope,' said Bergman. 'It's an old English saying.'

The captain was not smiling. 'I'll trade you an old Russian saying: where there's no hope, you might as well be dead. And that's where you're going.'

Hauled out of bed and kicked into the back of a canvas-topped truck, Bergman began a nightmare journey, each stage getting worse. The first day he was given no food or drink but managed to eat a few biscuits from the surgeon's food pack before it was stolen from him by the guards. He spent the night in a rattling ancient Ilyushin propeller-driven cargo plane that bucked its way through a storm above the Caucasus Mountains. While the guards clung to their seats and ate his food, guffawing with laughter, Bergman rolled like a sack of potatoes from side to side of the hold, unable to help himself because of the handcuffs that now pinned his arms behind his back. The wounds on his shoulders broke open from the repeated bruising and twice he fainted from the pain.

For the final stage of his journey into hell, he was thrown bodily by a new set of guards into an equally ancient Mi-4 piston-engined helicopter and double-handcuffed to a tie-down bolt on the floor. The new guards were, if possible, more uncouth than the old ones: Bergman spent the flight half-suffocated by a black sack which had been tied over his head as a blindfold. Above the noise of the motors he could hear the men around him making jokes at his expense as they got progressively more drunk. It was hard to follow their slang precisely but the meaning was plain, reinforced by kicks and blows. Bergman heard one, two and then three empty vodka bottles clattering round the metal floor until they fell out of the open doorways.

There had been a leering menace on the stupid, brutal faces of the MVD guards when they were blindfolding him which reminded Bergman of the two days he had spent captive of a band of SWAPO rebels in Angola, on the wrong side of the Caprivi Strip. Every hour, on the hour, the door of the mission schoolroom had been thrown open and another white had been taken for a so-called trial that lasted two minutes. The charge was always the same: the half-drunk SWAPO irregulars accused them all of being mercenaries. The remaining prisoners heard shouts of abuse, the sound of beating, a few screams and then a ragged fusillade.

Bergman had a gut-feeling that he was in for a similar experience at the end of this helicopter ride, with the difference that this time it would not end in a hail of well-aimed bullets and a grinning black South African special policeman leaning out of the gunport of his Casspir armoured car and thrusting a can of warm Castle beer into his hand . . .

'How come you're not dead already, man,' one of the guards asked, poking the blindfolded prisoner with a booted foot. The others laughed at their shared joke, of which only they knew the punchline.

Bergman thought that the voice was that of the hard-faced young KGB lieutenant who had signed for him at the airfield. He was a Tartar hardly able to speak Russian, with the dispassionate face and dead eyes of a hired killer.

'Because I'm a survivor,' Bergman grunted through the sacking.

'Up to now,' someone said. They all laughed again.

It was hard to hear anything through the black sack. An experienced helicopter pilot himself, Bergman tried to listen to the Mi-4's worn-out engines. They seemed to be straining in thin air, which meant that he was being taken over more mountains and farther to the north. He shivered in his thin cotton hospital pyjamas that were caked with blood across the shoulders. The gale of wind blowing in through the open doorways was cold. The only part of his body that was not frozen was his head and that was so hot inside the suffocating bag that he thought he had a fever. In a particularly bad area of turbulence he thought he was going to be sick and panicked, fearing that he would drown in his own vomit, trapped inside the bag.

The turbulence ceased, as though in answer to a prayer. Crouched sweating and shivering on the floor of the helicopter and listening to the guards getting steadily drunker, Bergman wondered, What happens next?

The answer came when the helicopter went into a hover. The guard undoing the second pair of handcuffs that secured the prisoner to the tie-down bolt was so drunk, he was having trouble getting the key into the lock. Bergman was hauled to his feet and the Tartar lieutenant shouted, 'This is where you get off!'

Men laughed in the background and Bergman's arms were tightly gripped from both sides as he was manhandled to the doorway.

'You got any last message for humanity?' one of the guards shouted.

'Fuck you!' Bergman yelled back. There was no point in trying to fight half a dozen men with his hands cuffed, blindfolded and half-suffocated by the sack over his head. Struggling would just give them added satisfaction.

He decided to jump out of the door, not wait to be pushed, both to get it over quicker and to cheat them of the last small pleasure. Blinded by the sack, arms pinioned behind his back, he tore himself free from the grasping hands of the guards and leaped into space.

For a split-second he was weightless in mid-air. Then he crashed with a bone-jarring thump onto the rocky ground three metres below. Unable to save himself, he sprawled winded and half-stunned, not certain for a moment whether he was alive or dead. Then he realised the trick that had been played on him and lay gasping, lashed by a storm of grit and pebbles in the whirlwind of the rotors' down-draught as the helicopter settled onto the ground beside him.

The pitch of the engine noise fell away and the rotors slowed to idling speed. Bergman lay still, trying to get his breath back. Two of the laughing guards unlocked his handcuffs, which had cut red welts into the swollen skin of his wrists. They removed the suffocating black sack from his head and climbed back into the helicopter, leaving Bergman gulping fresh air into his lungs. As the Mi-4 lifted off, he saw the Tartar's sweaty, boozed-up face grinning down at him. Pushing him out of the 'copter had been a great joke.

'Fuck you!' Bergman yelled.

A gobbet of spit landed on his upturned face. It was the right introduction to the Gulag.

The skinny, rat-faced camp guard with bad breath who had signed for the prisoner seemed drunk. Bergman was grateful for that small mercy: the first two badly aimed kicks did not connect with his ribs, which gave him time to scramble to his feet before the guard's aim improved.

Ignoring the scream of abuse mixed with orders to keep his head lowered at all times, Bergman looked around the bleak and hostile environment, wondering where in hell he was. As he would soon learn from the other prisoners, the answer was: in hell – or as close as it was possible to get while still alive.

Bergman squinted up at the departing helicopter, which was circling above the camp to gain height in order to clear the surrounding mountain peaks. He noted the long-range tanks which would give it a flying range of perhaps three hundred miles. Even if he could get his hands on the controls of such a machine, it would be no good to escape from a camp which, he guessed, was fifteen hundred miles or more from freedom.

The blow of a pick-handle behind his knees brought him literally back to earth. Another guard had arrived on the scene. The two took turns hitting and kicking the new arrival while Bergman tried to stand to attention, as ordered. From their blank, disinterested faces, he did not think there was anything personal in the violence; it was just the routine way of softening up a new arrival to teach him who was in charge. Twenty metres distant, a line of prisoners shuffled past with heads down and hands clasped behind their backs. No one looked up at the everyday spectacle of a man being beaten by the guards.

The camp was a cluster of unpainted wooden huts at the bottom of a disused quarry. The single-track road by which the rock had been trucked out, had been swept away by a landslide years before, so that the only way into or out of the camp was by helicopter. The quarry was open to the sky on the north side, where the view was of an identically bleak rock face on the hillside opposite.

High in the Ural Mountains that divide Europe from Asia, the heat in the quarry was stifling in mid-summer. Winter, as Bergman would discover, was six months of frozen misery. Officially designated Perm 39B, the camp was a long way from the city of Perm. Like army PO box numbers, postal addresses in the Gulag were intended to confuse. Perm 39B was a *spét-slager* – a camp with a special regime of discipline that was harsh even by the universally grim standards of the Gulag. The guards were all criminals who had been sent there from other camps all over the Soviet Union as an alternative to serving a long prison sentence. All were guilty of some major crime. They included Russians and Balts, but also Kalmucks, Uzbeks, Georgians, Tartars and Cossacks. Rapists, robbers and murderers, they began their service in the camp mean, drunk and vicious, growing steadily meaner and more vicious as the hopeless years went by. Beatings were routine. Withdrawal of food was the worst punishment for the prisoners, whose drawn faces, staring eyes, thinning hair and missing teeth all betrayed the signs of semi-starvation.

Like the rest of the Gulag, the camp had once been crammed to overcrowding. However, by the summer of 1986, most of the Russian dissidents and criminals had long since been moved elsewhere, and it was a ghostly holding tank for a small number of foreign prisoners whose names not even the commandant was allowed to know.

In the Gulag it was normal for a prisoner addressed by a guard to identify himself with his number, followed by name, the article of the Soviet penal code under which he had been sentenced and the length of his sentence. In Perm 39B the only identity a prisoner had was his number. Names were forbidden, nobody knew under what law he had been sentenced and no one expected to be released. The prisoners were men who had ceased to exist.

The day of Bergman's arrival was unusually eventful. The weekly ration helicopter – another antiquated Mi-4 – clattered in at midday, bringing the new commandant, Nikolai Ivanovich Ossetin. He was replacing a predecessor who was the fourth in a row to die of alcohol poisoning.

While Bergman lay low and tried to work out how to escape from this grey hell, Ossetin was lapping up every detail of his new job. In Perm 39B he was the absolute ruler of his very own small kingdom of misery. Immaculately clean – he showered each morning and rarely needed to shave – Ossetin wore well-pressed and starched uniforms that fitted tightly when he sucked his flabby belly in, in front of the bedroom mirror. Strutting round the camp, he seemed both physically and metaphorically to be bursting out of himself as he asked a thousand questions about the decaying buildings, the bad food, the inadequate clothing and the general hopelessness of everything in sight. For several weeks he sustained a prolonged sub-orgasmic glow of sheer joy. He was in paradise, in a world where there were no women and where he had total power over everyone in sight.

Most of the food in the camp that was fit to eat was consumed by the guards. Ossetin ate well. With the sense of well-being that came from at last having a job he had been born for, he put on so much weight that he became obese. In contrast, the low-nutrition daily ration per man of between 1200 and 1500 calories kept most prisoners too weak to cause problems, which accounted for the rarity of any kind of trouble in the camp. Most of the prisoners' thoughts were of food. The only outside exercise they got was half an hour a day shuffling round the circuit between the high wire fences in a line of men who moved like sleep-walkers, heads down and hands clasped behind their backs. Any deviation from this posture was met with a hail of blows from the guards' fists and rifle-stocks and boots.

In their desultory conversations the prisoners referred to themselves as *zaks*. The word was short for *zaklyúchonniye*. Everything was abbreviated or given a special name in the *blátny yazyk* – the thieves' slang of the camps – as though normal Russian were a foreign tongue in the hell where they lived. Most were too far gone in hopelessness to answer Bergman's questions about the camp security routines. Two who were less zombie-like than the others reported that he was trying to escape. Their reward was an extra portion of *shchee* – the watery cabbage soup which was served twice a day – and Bergman was sentenced to two weeks on reduced rations in solitary confinement. It was the first punishment Ossetin had awarded personally and it gave him great pleasure.

Still weak from his injuries, Bergman developed a racking cough from being locked up twenty-four hours a day in the damp solitary block. Sometimes the phlegm he spat out was flecked with blood. The coughing fits left him shivering from cold and covered with sweat. They also stopped him sleeping at night and earned him blows from the guards and curses from the prisoners in neighbouring cells.

It was on the fourth day that the prisoner-orderly doling out the watery regulation bowlful of *shchee* at midday slipped a second ration of dark, stale bread onto the open *kórmushka* – the food-flap in Bergman's cell door.

'You need,' he whispered. 'Otherwi' you get sick an' die.'

Amazed at the gesture of friendship in such a place, Bergman crouched down and peered up at the man standing outside by the soup trolley. He was short and thin. In the gloom of the unlit corridor his face looked Chinese.

Bergman grabbed the bread, took a bite and hissed, 'How d'you fix this?'

The Asiatic looked round to make sure there was no guard in sight. 'No fix,' he said in a low voice. 'That my bread. So ration-count is OK, no trouble with guard.'

Bergman shoved the second hunk of bread back. 'You need it.'

'Me, no,' the Asiatic grinned again. 'I can live, two bowl rice each day. Two bowl rice, you die sometime quick. Two week cough like that, you die also. You take bread.'

Arguing was pointless. Bergman grabbed the bread. Before the food-flap was pushed closed he stopped it with his hand. 'What's your name?' he hissed through the gap.

'Ah!' There was a moment's hesitation. 'Here pris'ner have no name.'

'Tell me.'

The man looked nervous. 'OK. My name Wu. What yours?'

'Bergman.'

'Ber'man? OK, we buddy now, I think.'

The food-flap was slammed shut as the sound of a guard's boots came nearer.

The extra food did not warm Bergman's body half so much as the knowledge that he was not alone. In all the weeks he had been drowning in the unplumbed hopelessness of Ossetin's camp he had not figured out any way of escape. That day his spirits soared; knowing that one other man in Perm 39B was courageous enough to share his food and tell a fellow-prisoner his name, had given back to Peter Bergman the most precious of all emotions – hope.

.4.

Jack Roscoe parked his car outside the Spaniards Inn on Hampstead Heath, positioning it behind a hedge so that he could see the traffic without being seen. After being explicitly ordered to have no further contact with Van, he was taking the same precautions as for an agent meeting on hostile territory.

He waited while a couple of dozen vehicles passed before going into the lounge bar which was empty. Most of the customers had chosen to drink outside in the garden on such a hot, humid August evening. After swallowing two double whiskies without even tasting them, he left the pub to walk along Heath Road and into the grounds of Kenwood House.

A poster for an open-air symphony concert that evening gave him the reason why Van had chosen the rendezvous. There were vehicles parked on the verges of the road in both directions. Roscoe checked his watch again and lit a cigarette, strolling in leisurely fashion around the corner of the house, past the tea rooms and onto the lawn that sloped gently down to the lake at the bottom. Inside the roped-off enclosure the audience was already seated, waiting for the concert to begin.

A few late-comers were hurrying from the car-park. He looked among them for Van.

In the brief phone call he had taken in the pub where he habitually lunched, she had said only, 'Jack? Remember our first date? Same place. 7.30.' Then she had rung off before he could say anything.

It was 7.35. Roscoe scanned the audience for a sight of her long blonde hair, wondering whether she had changed her mind about coming. Then he saw her. Jogging across the mock-Chinese bridge that spanned the far end of the ornamental lake was a figure in dayglo running gear. Even at a distance, Roscoe recognised the easy, relaxed running style. During their affair, they had run together on the Heath every Sunday morning.

Breathing deeply but not out of breath, Van halted, leaving a couple of paces between them.

'You're drinking again,' was the first thing she said. 'I can tell by your eyes. You look terrible.'

'Thanks.' Roscoe slipped off his lightweight cotton jacket and draped it over her shoulders, to make the shiny green running top less eye-catching. The jacket covered also the brief black running shorts she was wearing and made her look disturbingly naked.

Van pushed her sunglasses up onto the top of her head and gave him a false smile and 'Happy Birthday!' for the benefit of people nearby. A chaste kiss on the cheek and she stepped away.

Roscoe led her towards the edge of the audience area, outside which people were sitting on the grass to hear the concert without paying. They sat down at a reasonable distance for privacy from the nearest couple but near enough to look like a part of the crowd.

Close to, he thought that Van's face had changed. It was partly the effect of her hair being dragged back into a pony-tail for jogging, which revealed the bone structure, but there seemed also to be a hard set to her features that had not been there before. The bruises and cuts on her face had healed. On the back of her left hand was a long white scar.

The applause for the leader's entrance covered Roscoe's question, so that he had to repeat it: 'Why did you call me?'

With a minute shake of her head the pony-tail swept the skin on the back of Van's neck. 'I returned from convalescent leave to be de-indoctrinated this morning. I have now officially left the Service.'

'What are you going to do?'

'I'm going abroad tomorrow,' she murmured.

'Where to?'

'Don't ask. But there's something I've got to know, Jack . . .'

The orchestra was retuning to the leader's A note. Roscoe ached to touch the woman beside him. The jacket sagged open, revealing the shiny green material clinging to the perspiration on her breasts and emphasising the nipples. Her long bare legs were stretched out on the grass beside his own.

He forced himself to look at what was happening on the platform, and spoke out of the side of his mouth: 'For you, resignation is quite a step.'

'Not for me.' Van sounded brisk. 'For my father's daughter, maybe – but I've grown up at last. I'm my own woman now.'

'Is it as easy as that,' he wondered aloud, 'to kiss goodbye to the career you were raised for?'

'I've had enough,' she snapped. She had not come here to be questioned by Roscoe, but to put one question to him. 'I've had enough of all the lies and the pain. Enough of the stupid, point-less, bloody dangerous games you all play.'

Roscoe saw now that it was not anger which had marked her face, so much as bitterness. Daughter of a dead hero and grand-daughter of a couple who had risked their lives spying for Britain in Hitler's Germany, the woman beside him had renounced her family vocation . . .

The expression on her face, he thought, was that of a nun who, escaping back into the world, has only the sour taste of failure in her mouth, instead of the sweetness of the Blessed Sacrament.

'Don't stare at me,' she said.

'Sorry.' Despite the crowd listening to the music, Roscoe felt alone with Van for the first time in a long while and the dagger of desire stabbed deep.

To his surprise, she took his hand and squeezed it. Whatever had really happened, she thought, was not just Roscoe's fault; they were all soiled in one way or another.

'I didn't mean to be bitchy,' she said. 'It's been rather an emotional day, that's all.' She removed her hand to join in the applause for the conductor's entrance.

'Who de-indoctrinated you?' Roscoe asked quietly.

In the hush of waiting for the music to begin, people nearby were giving them disapproving looks.

'Dawson, of course,' Van whispered. 'I know he's a drinking pal of yours, Jack, but I wouldn't trust that two-faced lush as far as I could spit on him.'

On the platform by the lake, the conductor raised his baton, gave an up-beat and began the music.

'What are they playing?' Van asked.

'Dvorak,' he whispered in her ear. The smell of her shampoo triggered painful memories of intimacy. With his eyes closed, he recalled waking to that smell and the softness of her hair on the pillow beside him.

'I know the music,' she said.

Roscoe opened his eyes. 'It's used in a TV commercial for bread. The symphony's correct title is *From the New World*.'

Her blue eyes bored into his dark brown ones. 'Like Peter Bergman? From the new world?'

There were so many things Roscoe wanted to say to her, but all his thoughts were blocked in a log-jam behind the unspeakable words *I still want you.*

Van leaned closer to him and lowered her voice still more. 'Jack, I've got to know one thing.'

The rest of her question was lost beneath the music. He waited for her to repeat it.

'That day in Turkey when you came to the hotel where Peter and I were staying –'

Her blue eyes locked on his. It was hard for him not to blink and look away.

'– you were breaking security,' she said. 'Why?'

A lifetime would not have been long enough to explain everything to her. 'I was jealous,' Roscoe said. 'I knew you and I knew Peter. With all the delays, I knew the two of you would be having an affair. I couldn't . . . just sit on my arse inside the Nato base at Izmir, only twenty miles away from where you and he were . . . Don't you see? I had to come.'

He tore his eyes away and concentrated on the grass between his feet, counting the bars in the music. For several minutes Van did not speak.

'That's all?' she asked.

He nodded.

She looked from Roscoe to the white line on the back of her hand which was the only physical scar she bore from that night on the border. Should she believe him? She was good at picking up nuances in people's conversation. There had been a clue of something else in Dawson's debriefing, she was sure of that. But he – the crafty old sod – had covered it so swiftly that she wasn't sure whether she had imagined it.

'Jack,' she said, and waited until he looked at her. 'Do you swear that's the only reason?'

Do you swear . . .? Roscoe remembered an oath chanted in unison on a rainswept parade-ground when he was a young man whose head was full of dreams. 'Yes,' he said.

Thinking that the music was coming to an end, Van started to get up. Roscoe pulled her back with a muttered, 'I'm going to get Peter back, you know.'

'You're crazy,' she said. 'He's dead.'

'Listen,' Roscoe insisted. 'Bergman has the luck of the devil. I've seen him step out of a burning car and two wrecked air-craft, Van. Each time he walked away laughing. That guy has flown through hostile ground-fire that would have shredded a fly, never mind an airplane. Somehow, somewhere he's still alive – take it from me.'

'You're like all the others,' she said. 'After a few years work-ing in Intelligence, people don't know the difference between reality and fantasy. I tell you: Bergman . . . is . . . dead.'

Roscoe shook his head.

Van placed her mouth close to his ear. 'I heard about the trouble you've been causing. You're wasting your time. If you go on pestering the Service to make some kind of spy swap for Bergman – never mind making enquiries off your own bat – they'll sack you for unauthorised activities.'

'Who says so?'

Her mouth tightened. 'I picked up hints from a couple of the girls this morning.'

'The ladies' toilet grapevine?' Roscoe shrugged disparagingly.

Van read the cross-currents of emotion on his face. It had always been like that with Roscoe, as though he were two men. From the beginning of their relationship he had alternated between being a sensitive, romantic lover and another man altogether different: dark and brooding, out of touch with reality.

'Have it your way,' she hissed. 'But carry on as you are, and you'll be on the street pretty damn quick. The Service won't stand for it.'

'Well, I don't happen to believe that Peter's . . .'

'Listen,' she cut in on him. 'I was there, Jack. I saw it all: there were mortar shells exploding, machine-gun fire, men all over the place with dogs and guns.'

A sudden crescendo and a menacing roll on the timpani made her shudder at the memory of the moonlit valley of death which she had revisited a thousand times in her dreams.

'There's no way anyone could have lived through all that flak,' she said, eyes closed. 'I swear to you he's dead.'

Roscoe would have liked to explain that he was bound by his legionnaire's oath not to leave a comrade – even a dead one – on the field of battle. He had sworn it like a Crusader's vow, his head filled with dreams of honour and glory. And beside him in the ranks of young men wearing their white *képis* for the first time that day, had been Peter Bergman.

'You're trying to assuage your conscience,' said Van with finality. 'Everyone else *knows* Peter is dead.'

As the First Movement ended, she took advantage of the pause to stand up, shrugging off Roscoe's jacket which fell to the grass. She stepped over people's outstretched legs and stood looking back for a moment at Roscoe from the edge of the crowd.

Roscoe, she thought, was like all the other men in the Service – a cross between an overgrown Boy Scout and a mafioso. Why should she care about him or Bergman? They had both screwed her life up in different ways. Men didn't care about women they had used for sex, so why should she forfeit her peace of mind for these two?

The audience's coughs and shuffling died away. The conductor dipped his baton for the long-drawn funereal chords on the brass which begin the Second Movement. Van slipped the sun-glasses down over her eyes and walked a few yards before breaking into a run, back the way she had come.

Roscoe watched the dwindling black and green blob on the expanse of green lawn until it vanished into the sunset as the long cor anglais solo of Dvorak's music echoed Van's words: *You're alo-one. Ros-coe, you're all a-lone . . .*

.5.

Ossetin's passion for poring over files, which his superiors in the prison service had taken for conscientiousness, was rooted in his voyeurism and the pleasure he derived from spying on people who knew nothing about him.

The only aspect of life as commandant of Perm 39B which irked him was the lack of any personal records in the camp for him to poke and pry into. As the months passed, he took to hanging around the solitary confinement cells and pestering prisoners when the guards were out of earshot with questions about their identity, their crimes, their sentences. Even proferred bribes – small pieces of bread dangled in front of the desperately hungry men – got him nowhere. Some prisoners had forgotten who they were; the others knew it was more than their life was worth even to utter in sleep the name by which their mothers had called them.

As winter slowly gave way to the summer of 1987 Ossetin worked out a way to satisfy his visceral need to know about the men in his power. A three-month-old copy of *Pravda* blew out of the rations helicopter on its weekly trip. He smoothed it out, ignored the stink of the rotten fish that had been wrapped in it and lay in bed that night, ploughing through every turgid paragraph of the boring speeches by delegates to conferences on agriculture and Marxist Theory and the development of proletarian solidarity in African countries. The page three photograph of Margaret Thatcher on her recent walkabout in the Soviet capital made Ossetin think: if she can go to Moscow, so can I . . .

It cost him the equivalent of two months' salary to bribe the helicopter pilot and cargo-kicker on the next rations delivery. Set down illicitly at the nearest train station, Ossetin travelled to Moscow, where he used *blat* – the peculiar Slav mixture of bribery and influence – to persuade a former colleague from Butyrki to let him spend Sunday afternoon poring over the personal files of his charges.

It was almost a sexual pleasure to learn that the toothless, half-demented wreck No. 4179986 had been a brilliant Israeli physicist, caught in the prohibited area at Baikonur in 1980. No. 8590584, who wet his bed each night, was a former American aid official, kidnapped at a Vietcong roadblock in the Mekong delta in 1974. No. 79555416, the tall black man who wept so easily when picked on at roll-call, was a West African prince, arrested while a student at Moscow's Lumumba University and taken hostage so that his father would allow a pro-Moscow opponent to win an election.

The more he learned, the deeper became Ossetin's sense of intimacy with his prisoners. It was both more sustained and far more intense than anything he had ever felt for his female victims. They had been just *things*, mysterious and menacing until dealt with, but things all the same, whereas these men in his power were sentient beings like himself who would feel every pain, every humiliation and every punishment he meted out to them. Now that he knew who they were, his pleasure would be doubled.

The greatest joy for Ossetin was to find that all the files were marked *No Release*. For reasons of state, his prisoners were officially dead. They would never leave the camp except to take their places eventually in the row of unmarked graves that lay between the twin fences of the perimeter. He and they were wedded together until death did them part.

The knowledge made Ossetin impatient to get back to the

camp. In the departure lounge at Moscow's Vnukovo Airport an expensively dressed woman sat down on the bench beside him. She looked like the wife of some Party functionary in her smart high-heeled boots and with an expensive sable fur coat over her arm, despite the stifling midsummer heat – the air-conditioning was not working.

Momentarily Ossetin thought of how she would look and the noises she would make if he had her alone in the woods, gagged and tied to a tree, conscious but helpless, watching him fondle the soft flesh of her breasts, pulling it, kneading it and bruising it carefully – that was a tip he had got from a cookery book, borrowed from the prison library at Butyrki.

She was checking her make-up in a compact mirror. In the glass he caught a close-up of one mascara'd eye glancing sideways at him. He imagined the eyelashes opening wide in horror, unable to look away as his scalpel sliced the flesh of her nipple. He groaned involuntarily. The woman gave him a wary look and moved further away along the bench.

There were no available seats on any eastbound passenger flight for two days. Ossetin solved the problem by buying a bottle of black market vodka from a taxi-driver outside the terminal and using this to bribe the pilot of an Ilyushin freighter to give him a lift so that he could get back to Perm 39B with the minimum delay.

There, revelling in his forbidden knowledge, he saw the prisoners in a new light as his children whom he could – indeed, should – humiliate and punish at will. It was his duty as commandant to drive them to the edge of madness and keep them there for a long, long time. He took an especial interest in the few prisoners who were physically fit. They should live the longest and give him the most pleasure – especially the latest arrival, Prisoner 51044712 whose name, he now knew, was Peter Bergman.

'Bergman is dead!' George Dawson had no doubt about it. 'We saw the three bodies carried away between the taped paths through the border minefield, Jack.' It was an argument he had had many times with Roscoe during the year since the fiasco in Turkey.

Roscoe subsided into the one Civil Service armchair in Dawson's sparsely furnished office. He had been dozing off the effects of a liquid lunch in his own office when the summons reached him. The August sun beat through the tinted double-glazing, burning the back of his neck. He felt in his pockets for a cigarette and realised that he must have left the packet on the bar in the pub.

Dawson sat on the corner of his desk. The wall safe was open, full of dusty files; he had never got the hang of playing with keyboards and preferred to wander down to Registry and ask for pieces of paper. He tamped tobacco into the bowl of his briar with the old cartridge case and lit the pipe, studying Roscoe through the smoke.

'The business in Turkey has become an obsession with you, Jack,' he said in his low, gravelly voice. 'I understand how you feel about your first operation as control going so badly wrong. I also understand the way you feel about your old buddy getting the chop – especially as he once saved your life. But I can't cover up for you any more. Your illicit enquiries have caused waves once too often.'

'I'm sorry about that!' Roscoe's sarcasm fell flat. He burst out: 'Christ, George! All I'm asking is that we do what the other side does. Moscow moves heaven and earth to get back one of their guys who has fallen into our hands.'

'Of course they do,' Dawson agreed calmly. 'In order to debrief the poor bastards and then shoot them!'

He talked over Roscoe's objection. 'We nearly had a PQ on our hands, Jack – thanks to your latest indiscretion. If the DG hadn't been able to head it off through the Opposition Whip's office . . .'

'It's a pity,' said Roscoe. 'A question in Parliament might have got something done.'

A rare gesture of irritation escaped Dawson. 'I don't know why I bother,' he snarled. 'You're fired.'

'You haven't the authority to sack anyone,' Roscoe laughed sourly.

'For Christ's sake, Jack! It's not me that's firing you. The DG made the decision herself. I shouldn't even be telling you about it. Your termination interview has been arranged for three-thirty.'

He checked the watch in his waistcoat pocket. 'That's in fif-teen minutes' time. I'm just giving you an off-the-record chance to collect anything you want from your office. You'll be escorted from the building by Internal Security and not allowed to come back. I suppose they're searching your flat right now, recovering all Her Majesty's ball-pens and toilet rolls you've nicked over the years.'

Roscoe had known it was coming but it was still a shock. He felt dazed by Dawson's words: '. . . but since I brought you into the Service, Jack, I want to give you a warning.'

'You left it a bit bloody late, George,' he muttered.

'I'm not talking about losing your job,' said Dawson. 'I'm talking about your drink problem, Jack. You ought to get pro-fessional help. Talk to Establishment during the termination interview. They have a tame shrink who dries people out in a nice quiet farm down in Devon. It costs a packet but the Service will probably pay for everything, if you ask now.'

Roscoe laughed hollowly. 'Coming from you, that's rich!'

Picking up his reflection in the window glass, he saw himself briefly through Dawson's eyes. For a man of thirty-three he looked in poor shape, thanks to too little exercise, pub food, late nights and too much booze.

'Oh shit,' he slammed a fist against the toughened window glass. 'I've really fucked up now. Once I'm outside, there's no hope of getting on Bergman's trail, is there?'

He turned back to Dawson, enshrouded in smoke on the cor-ner of his desk. Anticipating the question on Roscoe's lips, Dawson shook his head.

'It was your last chance,' he said.

The rock-strewn gulley was hot as an oven in the mid-morning sun. Van lifted up the ankle-length skirt of her baggy cotton dress, holding it above her knees as she scrambled over the rocks. The granny glasses slipped down her nose, moist with perspiration. She grabbed them with her other hand and swore. The glasses, no make-up and the straggly, unwashed mouse-coloured hair were all part of her cover personality for this illicit trip back to eastern Turkey.

She had made a big decision at Antalya Airport while the

immigration officer was staring hard at the passport photograph in which Van's natural blonde hair was freshly cut and washed and she was wearing make-up. To calm her nerves Van chatted to another woman in the line of tourists. The passport was her own and had never been used in Turkey before, but inwardly she was trembling as the official asked her to remove the spectacles for a moment. Then he had stamped the back page and handed the passport back without comment. As she walked past him, Van knew that her days of wanting to play spooks were over for good: the surge of adrenalin that had once been such a trip now simply made her feel sick.

On the circular tour of eastern Turkey she was posing as a vegetarian animal-lover and had caused problems from the start by insisting on frequent stops for pretended travel sickness. She also complained loudly about the lack of women's toilets and the food and the way the natives treated their dogs and mules. After a couple of days, most of the other members of the tour group avoided her when they could, which suited Van fine.

This morning she had pretended to have an intuition about an accident on the road they should have taken. After hysterical insistence on her part the guide had agreed to depart from the usual route. Then Van had pleaded an attack of diarrhoea to persuade him to stop the tour bus in the middle of nowhere and give her a few minutes' privacy, out of sight behind the rocks.

'Bloody sandals!' she swore again as a strap broke.

She stuffed both of them into her home-spun shoulder bag and continued to pick her way down the gully, feeling like a refugee from the Hare Krishnas in her velvet jacket and the Indian dress that reeked of patchouli.

At last she reached the drainpipe where she had sheltered from the search parties fifteen months before. She thrust her hand into the gap between the concrete drainpipe and the earth ramp and felt something move against her searching fingertips. European scorpions were not lethal, she knew – just extremely painful. But were Turkish scorpions European or of some more malignant Asiatic species?

Careful not to make any sudden movement, she slid her hand very slowly out of the crack, nearly fainting with the involuntary reaction as a light brown snake, almost two feet long, wriggled out and slid away between her bare feet to vanish among the rocks.

It was impossible to see into the hole. Van looked for a stick long enough to poke into it in case there was another snake inside. In this arid part of Turkey any dead vegetation was collected by nomads for firewood; there was not even a small twig in sight. She forced herself to slide her hand into the hole a second time. It went in up to the elbow and nearly as far as the shoulder. Nothing. Had someone found . . . ?

Then she felt the plastic bag. She pulled it free and stood looking at the irrevocable letter of credit that was worth $100,000 to the bearer.

The coach driver was repeatedly blasting the echoes of the rocky valley with his air horn. Van hurriedly crammed the plastic bag into her shoulder bag and scrambled back up the gulley the way she had come. She was planning to make some embarrassing remark about feminine hygiene to her fellow-tourists in order to cover her long absence. Then she would sit out the rest of the tour and leave them in peace. Ahead lay another five days of heat and dust and bad food. It seemed a small price to pay for $100,000.

Her name was being called. The guide and the driver were clambering over the rocks, looking for her, calling, 'Vanessa! Vanessa!'

'Cooee!' She stood on a boulder and waved her floppy hat for them to see.

'Are you all right?' the guide shouted.

Right . . . ight . . . ight. The sound echoed among the rocks – like *Go! Go! Go!* on the night of the full moon.

'I got lost!' she cried, waving her hands helplessly. 'Sorreee, Mehmet. Didn't know which way to go. Thanks awfully for coming to look for me. My sandal's broken and . . .'

There was a short exchange between the two men in Turkish. She could imagine what they were saying, and voiced it for them: 'Isn't this just like a woman? Oh, thanks, Mehmet. Can you carry my bag? You are an angel.'

When the coach pulled up outside the caravanserai below Mount Ararat, Van wandered away from her fellow-tourists taking photographs of each other sitting in the crenellations.

On the stony, grassless slope below the caravanserai two ragged and dirty little girls in hand-me-down dresses far too large were herding a dozen brown-fleeced sheep. A middle-aged woman from Bradford was giving them money and sweets, against the guide's advice, and taking photographs. A motherly type who insisted on feeding Van with travel sickness pills for her pretended crises, she looked up and waved.

Van waved back. She was startled by the voice of Mehmet the guide, speaking from close behind her: 'I hope you are feeling better now, Vanessa.'

She turned and saw his angry eyes, pale skin and the heavy, dark moustache which reminded her of the Turkish army officer who had slapped her face in the gulley.

'Yes,' she said, fighting the memories. 'Much better, thanks. Mrs Shipley gave me a pill.'

He smiled thinly. 'I hope it did the trick at long last.'

'I think so.'

'Well, don't get lost again,' he said, tight-lipped. 'Thanks to you, the expedition is now half an hour behind schedule. We leave in five minutes.'

When he had gone Van took the plastic envelope out of her bag. Tucked behind the letter of credit was a torn black-and-white photograph. She had to colour it in mentally to see the blond hair, the steely blue eyes that matched her own and the tanned skin. But even in monochrome there was no mistaking Bergman's mocking gaze and the arrogant way he held himself, as though challenging the world.

She had tried to forget him but it had not worked; each time another man touched her, she remembered how it had been with Bergman.

She slipped the photograph back inside the envelope and returned it to her bag. Down in the shimmering heat of the valley before her, lay the desolate landscape that haunted her dreams.

With a good head for terrain, Van worked out exactly where Bergman had cut the hole in the frontier wire. Beyond it she could see, dancing in the heat-haze, some kind of concrete blockhouse with a sandbagged pit behind it. And between the two lay the tumbled pile of rocks which had been the RV point.

In the mid-morning light it looked like a memorial for the man whose touch she could still feel on her skin.

The coach driver kicked the engine to life, releasing a cloud of diesel fumes that drifted down the valley.

Van stood up. 'Goodbye, Peter,' she said.

.6.

In the summer of 1990 the whole machinery of the USSR began to seize up cog by cog like an obsolete machine for which spare parts and lubricants were no longer available. Mikhail Gorbachev's makeshift repairs kept it running at half-speed for a while longer and then the greatest empire of the twentieth century – 150 million Russians ruling the same number of subject peoples – ground to a halt.

Ossetin spent the summer months in his quarters, hunched over an illicit transistor radio, listening anguishedly to echoes of the shock waves emanating from the epicentre in Moscow. For days on end he never went into the prisoners' compound. He bribed the crew of the rations helicopter to smuggle in newspapers each week and read with horror of the hundreds of thousands of detainees being released from camps all over the former Soviet Union. His great fear was that *his* camp was to be closed down like so many others, that *his* men would be taken away from him. Yet winter came and went and still no orders were received from Moscow to release a single prisoner from Perm 39B.

At the end of the Gulf War in March 1991 came a summons

to Moscow which Ossetin obeyed in fear and trembling. The new orders he received there made all his fears groundless. Yeltsin's slimmed-down Gulag administration had decided that the entire personnel of the camp – prisoner and guard alike – should be moved to a new location where the secrets locked up in Perm 39B would be safe from the unrest that had broken out all over the newly independent Caucasian republics.

Apart from the move it was decreed that life in the camp would continue in every respect as before. Even the guards' drab olive uniforms with the red star on their caps were to stay the same, so that the prisoners gained no inkling of the enormous political changes which were taking place in the outside world. Despite the geographical relocation, Perm 39B was to be an island where time stood still. Transported to the nearest railhead and herded into locked and sealed cattle trucks under armed guards who were forbidden to speak to them, the prisoners were shunted slowly thousands of miles across Russia.

Through a crack in the planking of the truck that carried him, Bergman logged the names of the stations they passed. The first ones meant nothing to him, but Perm did. And after Perm came the slow progression from Kirov to Kotlas to Vologda, confirming what he could tell from the sun and the stars: they were travelling westwards. Why? With no knowledge of the break-up of the Soviet Empire, he could find no answer except the insane hope that for some reason they were all being taken westwards to be released.

He fought the hope, on guard against the despair that it could engender but found himself dreaming of meals he would eat back in the West, of being seated on the flight deck of a plane again – and of the girl he had left lying in the darkness below Ararat.

'*Peter . . .*' she said in his fantasy.

'*What?*'

'*Nothing.*'

He played their last exchange over in his mind again and again, wondering whether Van was still alive. Each time the warm and comforting embrace of the dream was broken by a sick prisoner moaning in delirium or by a fight breaking out over some pathetic scrap of bread that had been stolen or a man intruding on a piece of floor that was claimed by someone else. The only sanitation in the carriage was a stinking old fifty-gallon oil-drum in one corner that overflowed long before each stop, so that the prisoners nearest to it had to stand day and night or lie in a lake of excrement. At each of the infrequent stops in remote sidings far from the nearest town, the slop can was emptied, a corpse or two were buried and rations were distributed.

After three weeks, they had left Moscow well behind and were travelling northwards. Bergman could no longer delude himself and had to face the bitter truth that the journey would not end in freedom. He told himself that the anticlimax served him right, that in future he should hope only for what he could achieve by himself. Face glued to the crack in the planks to keep Wu from reading on his features the new despair that was eating at him from within, he recognised fewer place names than before but some were in a language that could only be Finnish, which told him they were in Karelia, the province of Finland that Moscow had kept as a buffer zone at the end of World War Two.

The sight of a ship's superstructure apparently ploughing through the flat, endless tundra hundreds of miles from any natural waterway, made Bergman think he was hallucinating. He grabbed Wu's arm and dragged him across the tangle of inert and stinking bodies.

'Do you see what I see?' he asked. They had to be careful never to use names in front of the others.

'I see ship,' Wu confirmed.

It was one of the Russian prisoners who explained the impossible sight: the railway was running parallel to the line of the Belomorsky Canal, dug fifty years before at enormous human cost to realise Stalin's dream of a waterway linking the Arctic Ocean to the Baltic Sea.

At last the train stopped and the prisoners were driven outside, to stand blinking at their new home. A handful of decaying wooden huts was surrounded by a new double wire fence, punctuated at intervals by *ptichniki* — bird-houses, as the watchtowers were called in prison slang.

The new Perm 39B was the remains of a prison factory built in the thirties when hundreds of thousands of men and women were banished to the Karelian sub-arctic to construct the White Sea Canal. Tormented by mosquitoes in summer, maimed by frostbite in winter, underfed and worked like machines until they dropped, they died by the thousand from dysentery, injury, starvation and sheer hopeless misery. Half a century later, history was repeating itself as Ossetin watched his flock settle into their new home.

The strict regime of discipline that had reigned in the Caucasus had to be relaxed for a few months while prisoners and guards worked alongside each other to rebuild the derelict huts before the savage northern winter set in. The pace of work was slower even than was usual in the Soviet Union because the guards were too drunk and idle and most of the prisoners too weak to put in more than a couple of hours' labour without a break. They worked the long days of the brief northern summer stripped to the waist and eaten alive by clouds of mosquitoes as they collapsed unwanted hovels outside the wire in order to remove enough timber to repair the huts in which they would be locked throughout the long dark winter.

As an incentive, those prisoners who could do a full day's work received extra rations. Of these the two fittest were Peter Bergman and Wu. They alone had somehow managed to cling to their mental faculties and stay physically healthy as well. Watching them at work on the jobs that required both strength and intelligence, Ossetin was intrigued. They were thin, as were all the prisoners, but these two had bodies like whipcord and steel, while the others resembled broken stick-men. The commandant gave orders that Bergman and Wu should receive the same rations as the guards, to replace the energy they used doing construction work. He wanted to keep them alive for a long time.

Because of the shortage of accommodation, the prisoners spent the white nights of the summer months padlocked into crates and packing-cases; it was impossible to sleep in the open air because of the swarming clouds of mosquitoes. Bergman and Wu shared a crate near to the fence that girdled the camp. Their shelter was a two-metre cube of plywood with CATER-PILLAR stencilled on the sides in faded ink, indicating that it had once contained spare parts for an American bulldozer.

Provided they kept their voices low, they could talk. What

they talked about most of the time was Bergman's obsession: escape. He estimated that they were less than two hundred miles from the Finnish frontier.

'Two hundred mile of swamp,' observed Wu. 'No man can get through, my friend. Some try, they die. We mi' as well be maroon' on island.'

'But we're not on an island,' argued Bergman. 'Sure, you could say we are in the summer, but in winter the swamps are frozen over. Then we could walk to Finland.'

'More like we freeze to death.'

'No. There's a time-window when we can make it,' Bergman whispered. 'If we can manage to continue getting extra rations until the end of the summer, we'll be at our peak of fitness just at the right moment.'

'When is that, my friend Ber'man?'

'When the first snow falls, the ground will freeze and if we're fast, we can make it to Finland. Between us, we can carry enough food for three weeks. That should be enough.'

'First snow followed often by thaw,' Wu objected. 'Then we stuck in swamp and die when food run out.'

'It's a quicker death than dying here, Wu,' Bergman argued. 'You've seen the way that fat pervert Ossetin looks at us, like we're the Thanksgiving turkey. He's keeping you an' me alive for something special.'

'If no thaw,' said Wu, 'we freeze to death without warm clo'.'

'So we kill two guards and take their clothes.'

'Can you kill man just to take clo'?' Wu wondered.

'Couldn't you?'

There was a sigh from Wu. 'I was scholar, not soldier like you, my friend Ber'man.'

'I was a flier, not a foot-slogger, so what does that prove?'

'And what happen when we reach frontier?' Wu wondered. 'No one live so far north. No shelter there, no food. We die same-same.'

'No, we live off the land.'

'In cold of arctic winter?' Wu queried.

'We trap animals for food, make clothes from the skins. Once we're in Finland, we don't have to hide. If our fire is seen, so much the better.'

Wu thought Bergman's plan was madness but did not say so outright. To survive in the Gulag, a man needed hope. Killing hope, to Wu's way of thinking, was the ultimate injury one could inflict on a fellow-prisoner.

'What do you think?' Bergman asked. 'If we can time it right . . .'

'Ah!' Wu quoted a saying from the *Tao-te Ching*, the teachings of Lao-tzu: '"In action, look to your timing. With correct timing, all may be achieved."'

If philosophy had kept Wu sane in Perm 39B, it was the idea of escape that had kept Bergman sane through five years in the claustrophobic nightmare of Ossetin's private hell. He fixed his mind on the idea as a high-wire artiste fixes his gaze on the mark at the far end of the rope. It burned in his mind, day and night, like a twin star whose partner was revenge.

He lay now listening to Wu's regular breathing. The slightly built little Asiatic was not the partner he would have chosen for a desperate escape attempt; he lacked both the temperament and the training to kill a man with his bare hands, should it be necessary. Against that, Wu was physically fit and totally trustworthy. What he lacked in violence he made up for in a rock-hard integrity of spirit. Bergman had come to respect him as he had respected few men in his lifetime. That he had to take at least one companion with him, Bergman had no doubt. In the onset of the sub-arctic winter another man's body-heat could make the difference between freezing to death on the first night and surviving long enough to reach freedom. Of the available choice, Wu was the best man to take along, by about ten million miles . . .

Bergman lay planning how they could manage to steal enough food and hide it in one of the old buildings outside the wire. As Wu said, everything hinged on the timing. Would it be possible to coincide their optimum health, the freeze-up that would make the swamps passable and the confusion of the guards when the first *púrga* or blizzard swept down from the frozen Arctic?

Bergman swatted some of the mosquitoes gorging themselves on his face and dozed restlessly, planning, always planning . . . He never thought, If I escape: It was always, When I go . . .

And when he was free again, back in the West, he would go hunting Jack Roscoe. He would track the man who had betrayed him – to the ends of the earth if necessary – and bring him to bay.

If Bergman had to kill a few guards in the course of his escape, he would do so with no more emotion than a farmer snapping a chicken's neck. But when he caught up with the man who had been his best buddy for eighteen years, it would be different, Bergman promised himself that. Then he would take pleasure in killing.

.7.

A long-term prisoner in a *spétslager* either became an expert thief or died sooner than necessary. Bergman found the choice easy, although it seemed ironic that he who had once smuggled gold and diamonds, was now reduced to stealing sugar lumps or a piece of stinking, badly salted fish. Week by week, the cache of provisions stashed away in a ruined machine-shop outside the wire grew larger.

Of all the items on Bergman's list of things vital for the escape, a compass was the hardest to find. Yet without one they would surely lose their way in the first white-out and die. As the brief summer gave way to autumn he had to admit, after scouring the camp high and low, that there was no compass to steal anywhere in Perm 39B.

It was like the answer to a prayer when, towards the end of August, a light aircraft used for surveying ran out of fuel near the camp due to a combination of a faulty gauge and bad maintenance. As the single engine coughed away the last drops of petrol, the pilot and surveyor were relieved to see, appearing out of the endless forest and swamp, the only road in a hundred kilometres – and on it the distant figures of a working party.

Using the last drops of fuel to gun the sputtering engine into lifting itself over the last line of trees, the pilot smashed through the topmost branches to make an emergency landing on the road within a hundred metres of the group of prisoners that included Wu and Bergman.

Euphoric at their escape – for to have crashed in the swamps would have meant a slow death from starvation even if they survived the impact – the pilot and passenger failed to guard their craft for the few seconds that it took Bergman to clamber into the cockpit and remove, not the dashboard instrument but even better, a hand-held compass from the surveyor's kit.

Once inside the cabin, it was torture for a qualified pilot like him, who had flown both fixed-wing and helicos, to know he was so close to escape. The temptation to try just once to start the engine was almost irresistible. He flicked a switch. The needle of the fuel guage twitched but stayed on zero. To remain in the cabin one second longer risked losing everything, so Bergman scrambled out fast, clutching his treasure. By the time the camp guards had run up to beat the prisoners back to a safe distance, Wu and he were standing at the back of the small crowd of filthy human scarecrows around the plane.

Watching it take off again, running on petrol siphoned from the guards' lorry, Bergman stood beside Wu, a great sickness in his stomach. Ignoring the guards' shouts to get back to work, he said dully, 'Those two guys in that plane could be you an' me, Wu. We could be up there, flying away to freedom.'

Wu's left hand had an axe cut that had gone septic. It was bandaged with a dirty rag, neatly retied to hide the compass. 'Their misfortune was our good fortune,' he said, nursing his throbbing arm. 'Think that way, my friend Ber'man.'

The cut worried Bergman; it would not heal. Two of the prisoners, unable to take the over-work, the mosquitoes and the sheer unrelieved hopelessness of it all, had used an axe when the guards were not looking to chop three fingers off their right hands, each one doing the same favour for the other. Self-mutilation to escape work was a tradition in the Gulag. There was a shortage of the brown and brackish water that was used for drinking and the only water for washing was swarming with insect larvae. The camp had no disinfectants or medicines, nor even soap for the prisoners. Within a week both men had died in agony from tetanus.

'Do not worry,' said Wu calmly. 'Those men die from wrong thoughts. That not happen to me.'

That night the autumn rains began. Huge drops drummed relentlessly on the weathered plywood of the packing-case and made it impossible to sleep. Bergman lay thinking of the compass, secure in its hiding-place in a ruined building outside the camp perimeter. The luminous needle seemed to glow in the dark above him like the cross before a believer praying. The noise grew worse as the rain turned to hail. Unable to sleep, the two men listened and tried to avoid the worst drips. Water ran into the base of the case. At first it was an inch deep, then two and three – and still it kept coming until they stood shivering, knee-deep in muddy water.

Wu groaned, despite his self-control. He was shaking with fever.

'Listen to that music,' said Bergman, meaning the rain. 'These are the autumn rains we've been waiting for. In a coupla weeks we'll have snow and then . . .'

Wu's good hand reached out in the darkness and squeezed Bergman's arm. 'You never give up, Ber'man,' he said. 'For that I admire you.'

They spent the rest of the night talking. As usual Bergman listened most of the time. It seemed to him afterwards that Wu had known what was coming and used the time they had together to equip his friend for the trials which lay ahead, by offering a distillation of the Eastern learning that had kept him alive. It was not easy to convey philosophy in pidgin Russian or the *blátny yazyk*. When Bergman interrupted to ask for clarification, Wu refused to waste time in explanation.

'All thing acquire meaning at right time,' he would say quietly. 'That is Tao. That is the Way.'

Some nights – like tonight – this infuriated Bergman. 'I'm a man of action,' he snapped. 'Not a thinker like you. I need straight answers.'

Wu chuckled, 'What is difference between man of action like you and scholar like me? Which is better general – he who win hundred battles by fighting or he who avoid thousand battles by thinking?'

'What kind of a philosophy is that, Wu? You talk in riddles half the time.'

A piece of poetry came into Wu's mind. He had learned it many years before and translated it now for Bergman's benefit, slowly and hesitantly in his sing-sing voice:

'You ask me . . . what kind of scholar I am, and I reply:
My thoughts have travelled no further than my feet.
You ask me . . . what is true happiness and I reply:
It is to hear a young girl singing along the road after she
has asked me the way.'

There was a long silence inside the crate, broken only by the drumming of raindrops on the plywood. Then Bergman heard Wu's body sliding down the rough wooden wall against which he was leaning. He reached out a grimy hand in the darkness and touched Wu's cheek. It was wet, not with cold rain but warm tears.

Bergman knelt down in the liquid mud and took the other man in his arms. He held him tightly for a long while to calm Wu's trembling, and kept repeating, 'It's gonna work out all right, old buddy. You'll see, Wu. Everything'll be OK.'

The first snow melted in minutes. Bergman watched it go, flake by flake. He had a good flier's feeling for weather. Like a dog sniffing a bitch in heat, he rammed his nose against a crack in the crate and inhaled the outside air, smelling more snow on the way.

Next morning, the dusting of white powder on the ground did not melt and there was a rime of ice on every puddle.

'Not long now,' he whispered, waking Wu up.

Wu's almond eyes took in Bergman's excitement. 'Relax,' he warned. 'You look like runner on starting block. Someone will see.'

For weeks Bergman had fretted that a guard or prisoner might stumble by chance on their pitifully small cache of provisions, acquired at such risk. They still had nowhere near enough food but all Bergman's instincts told him that the first blizzard was heading their way that day. Once the weather had definitely broken, no working parties would be allowed outside the wire. He and Wu had to seize that one crucial moment or lose the chance of escape for a whole year, perhaps for ever.

Wu's hand was still swollen, although he said it had started to heal and his nightly fevers seemed to have lessened. He had slept that night without moaning, which seemed a good sign to Bergman. As the padlock was removed from the crate in the grey light of dawn, he grinned at his cell-mate and said one word: 'Sevódnya!'

Wu heaved a deep sigh and asked his ancestors for strength. During their time together he had tried to make Bergman something of a philosopher. Now it was time to see whether Bergman's attempts to make him in return a man of action had worked or not. He looked at the camp buildings which were still not ready for the winter. He looked at the other prisoners with whom he and Bergman seemed to have so little in common, for they were men who had abandoned hope. He looked at the guards shouting and hitting the last arrivals, harrying them into the linéika for roll-call. He looked at Ossetin's fat figure waddling through the mud to the camp office with a slice of black bread in one hand and a glass of steaming tea in the other. He looked at the watchtowers and the endless hostile swamp and forest outside the wire.

'Sevódnya,' he agreed: today!

They had rehearsed every move a hundred times in midnight whispers although Bergman knew that telling Wu what had to be done was no real preparation for the reality of killing a man. That was a job he would have to do.

When the púrga struck out of a clear sky in mid-afternoon, they were in a working party with two guards several hundred metres from the camp. Frightened by the primeval violence of the storm, the guards were shouting at the line of prisoners to drop their load of planks and run for the gate. Visibility was down to a few metres and getting worse.

Bergman grabbed Wu out of the line of men shambling towards the camp and shouted, 'Stand still. Don't move from there or I'll never find you!'

The nearest guard aimed a blow at Bergman's head with the stock of his rifle and was amazed when the weapon was grabbed and pulled out of his grasp.

Bergman heard a yell of sheer animal rage escape his throat. It was a declaration of war by one man against the system that had deprived him of life for so long. He felt adrenalin course through his body. He had acted! After five interminable years of inaction, he had made a decision and acted on it. He was determined that nobody and nothing would stand in his way.

The guard's reactions were slow. He was a squat Georgian with a scarred face, bad teeth and foul breath, neither better nor worse than the others – just the one that happened to be nearest when the world turned white. He opened his mouth to scream with mingled rage and fear as the rifle was wrenched from his hands.

Bergman reversed the rifle and struck the side of the man's face hard with the stock of the rifle, snapping the spinal cord. Like a beast in an abattoir, the guard slumped to the ground, dead.

They were alone in a world of white: he, Wu and the dead guard. Bergman felt drunk with oxygen and adrenalin and the exhilaration of having struck the first blow back after receiving so many.

Nothing could be heard above the noise of the storm. Bergman left Wu to strip the dead guard naked and exchange clothes with him while he groped his way through the savagery of the *púrga* to find a second source of clothing for himself. Another blow. Another body in the snow but this one refused to lie still. It tried to reach for the gun beside it until Bergman delivered a second lethal blow from the rifle butt. He would have liked to continue smashing, battering the guard's face to a pulp, in order to assuage all the rage he had bottled up inside himself since arriving in Perm 39B. With difficulty he kept control of himself; there was no time to waste on revenge.

Indistinct figures stumbled past only a few metres away with noses muffled against the snowflakes that threatened to suffocate and eyes closed against the stinging, sharp, icy fingers of winter. Bergman crouched over the second body, wrenching off the vital *bushlát* or padded winter coat, the padded trousers and the felt boots called *válenki*. The wind and the snow fought him for possession of the garments. Desperation gave him the strength somehow to struggle into them.

Leaving the naked body with snow already piling up in its lee, Bergman went looking for Wu, praying that he would not have panicked in the white-out and gone looking for him. If he had, they might never meet in the nightmare of wind and snow – and it would be his fault.

He took a few steps in one direction, then a few in another, always coming back to the body in the snow as his only point of reference. Minutes were wasted until he blundered into Wu in near-zero visibility.

Bergman nearly killed his friend, now dressed as a guard. Only the lack of a rifle in the other man's hands stopped his instinctive blow halfway. He threw his bloodied weapon away – the weight made it a liability – and grabbed Wu's arm. Together, like a pair of drunks, they staggered through the white-out.

This first hundred metres would be the greatest navigational test of the whole escape, Bergman knew. If he got this part wrong with no compass to guide him, they were both dead men. In Siberia countless guards and prisoners, all sense of direction lost, had frozen to death during blizzards within a few paces of the camp gate where their bodies were found after the storm had blown itself out.

There was, in the heart of the *púrga*, no sense of direction except down. Bergman's body wanted to give up the awful, unequal struggle against the elements and fall to the soft bed of snow, there to curl up and rest. Beside him, Wu was feeling the same.

Bergman's only clue to direction was the line of planks dropped by the prisoners as they ran for shelter. When that was gone, he ploughed grimly ahead, hoping that he was keeping in a straight line. He could have wept when a dim orange moon in the grey whirling murk overhead turned out to be one of the perimeter floodlights.

Stumbling and reeling, forced sometimes to their knees by the violence of the wind, he and Wu groped their way along the perimeter fence. The gale threatened to tear them from each other's grip. A guard dog, half-husky and half-wolf followed snarling on the other side of the wire until it smelled the guards' clothes and backed away whining in the expectation of a kick.

The cache in the ruined machine-shop was intact. Bergman felt weak with relief as he clutched the compass in numb fingers. It was several days since he had checked the secret hiding-place, not wanting to give away its location by too frequent visits. Hurriedly Wu and he shared the food between them, stuffing it into pockets and the slits in the lining of the quilted overcoats. There was a panic as their entire stock of sugar – ten lumps – was missing, followed by a wave of relief as Wu's calm probing discovered them camouflaged by snow that had drifted in through the gaping holes in the roof.

It took a ruthless determination on the part of both men to leave the poor shelter of the ruined building and venture into the naked elemental fury of the *púrga*. Then they were away, heading south and west, with the blizzard at their backs. For the moment it was a friend helping them along in more or less the right direction, but both men knew that the arctic winter made a treacherous ally who might yet claim their lives in return for this brief help.

.8.

The first day after their escape, they made good timing by Bergman's reckoning. He kept beneath the tree-cover whenever possible, even if it added distance. From his long-past experience on winter warfare courses in the French Alps he remembered how obvious from the air was the track of even one man across an expanse of virgin snow. Only when it was snowing or when he was sure that a fresh snowfall was imminent did he take short cuts across open snowfields.

The caution paid off when a light aircraft flew slowly overhead on the second morning, no more than a hundred feet above the treetops. It banked and flew round in a circle as the two fugitives clung to tree-trunks, trying to merge into the bark. They both sighed with relief when the plane flew slowly away to the south, the pilot following tracks left in the snow during the night by some large animal.

Since daybreak Bergman had been heading slightly north of west in the hope that the main search would assume they were aiming south-west – the instinctive direction for a prisoner to take, because it was the shortest distance to safety in Finland. He wished it had been possible to glance even for a second at a map and plan a specific and logical route that would avoid the worst of the unknown hazards ahead.

They waited until the sound of the aero engine had died away and the awesome silence of the snow-covered wasteland pressed in on them once again from all sides. Wu had spoken little since they rose after a night pressed together for warmth in a hole dug in the snow. But he was keeping up with Bergman's hard-driving pace and said he had no pain in his swollen and useless left arm.

'Liberty is strong pain-killer,' he explained. It sounded as though he was smiling behind his snow-mask made from a rag with two small holes poked in it for the eyes.

By nightfall, Bergman estimated they had covered twenty miles from the camp. It was a superhuman effort to have travelled so far in deep, powdery snow but he had insisted on pushing them to their limits, knowing that the distance they could cover each day would get less as they exhausted the scant energy reserves in their bodies. For dinner they ate some mouthfuls of bread and drank snow melted by holding it inside their clothes in their one chipped enamel mug. Bergman refused to touch the small reserve of sugar which, with a half-full box of matches and the compass, constituted their most precious possessions. After eating they curled up together in a snow-cave to sleep.

The second day was also good travelling weather, with light snowfalls to disguise their tracks and hamper any search parties on foot. They heard aircraft twice but saw nothing in the empty grey, lowering sky that seemed to sit just above the treetops.

On the third day they hit a wide area of swamp. There was a crust of ice on the water of the pools, some of which were big enough to be lakes. But the ice was not yet thick enough to risk walking on, so they lost a lot of time and much irreplaceable energy in finding a way through and round the wetter places. That night it was impossible for them to get warm, even burrowed deep below the snow on a small dry hillock. They lay shivering in sodden clothes until Bergman decided it was time to share a couple of sugar lumps just before dawn. The effect was partly psychological and partly physical – like alcohol suffusing the whole body with heat.

He told Wu to rest for a while longer while he invested half an hour of daylight in weaving two pairs of *lyzhi*, crude snow-shoes fashioned from some willow shoots he had cut in the swamp with a rusty, broken pocket knife found hidden between the walls of a building they had demolished. It was unlikely that the *lyzhi* would last for the whole journey but they made progress much easier for the moment. At least their legs no longer sank into the snow up to their thighs with every step.

They seemed to have left the swampy country behind for a while. That day Wu talked a lot, as though to make up for his silences of the previous one. He chattered about many things, as though the easier terrain, the snowshoes and the sugar had combined to lift his spirits.

On the fourth day they hit another area of swamp, worse than the first. Here they proceeded like two men in a mine-field, Wu in the rear carrying the now useless snowshoes while Bergman advanced one step at a time, prodding the ground ahead with a branch to feel where it was safe to tread. Time after time, what had seemed solid to his probing gave way beneath the weight of his body. He became soaked, first one leg and then the other, until he was wet through up to the waist. From the exertion, his chest was heaving, sweat froze on his face and his vision kept blurring over.

He felt like crying when Wu pulled his arm and said softly, '*Smotrí tam, Ber'man! Smotrí!*'

Bergman looked. He stared disbelievingly at a hole where he had fallen through the crust of ice and peat an hour before. The brown water was already icing over anew. But there was no mistake: their footsteps led up to the hole and past it. There was even the clear imprint of the snowshoes where Wu had put them down to help him scramble out.

He shook the compass. It was working; the fault was his. After only five days, his attention was wandering and the world had shrunk to a nightmare small circle of white in which he was going round and round.

'Give compass to me,' said Wu quietly. 'You break trail. That is hard work, so I be navigator.'

The new division of responsibilities worked better. They ate two more sugar lumps at midday and came out of the swamp as the light was failing.

'How far still to go?' asked Wu.

'Not far,' Bergman lied.

The snow was not so thick here, for whatever reason. He scouted around in the last few minutes of grey gloom and found a shelter excavated by some large animal among the tumbled rocks. It was part-cave and part-overhang but it was the best resting-place they had found so far.

Bergman stripped off the sodden quilted trousers and tried to get some feeling back into his legs. It was Wu who insisted on using one precious match to light a fire of moss and twigs and dead branches from trees nearby. Bergman was afraid the flames might be seen but Wu overruled him on two grounds. The cave, he said, could be a bear's den to which the animal would return during the night; also he feared that Bergman was getting frost-bite.

They crouched close to the fire, Bergman trying to rub circulation back into his legs which refused to respond. It was Wu who one-handedly massaged blood and warmth back into them. Because Bergman's trousers were still damp, despite the fire's heat, Wu insisted on taking off his own and making his comrade wear them, together with his own dryish boots.

At some time in the small hours, Bergman half-woke, an instinctive awareness of danger fighting the lethargy of his body. He blinked his sore eyes open to see another pair of eyes glowing in the gloom a few metres outside the light of the fire. He shouted and threw a burning branch at the animal which vanished with a sound midway between a grunt and a bark. Wu slept on, exhausted. Bergman spent the rest of the night fighting sleep, propped against a rock, tending the fire and keeping watch.

When Wu awoke, it was daylight. Bergman was slumped against a rock, his eyes closed. The fire had burned down to the embers. Wu puffed some life into them and roused the sleeping man with the luxury of a mugful of hot tea. Only a *zak* would have called it tea; it was *kipyátok*, boiled water with two small brown leaves floating in it. Wu refused to share the brew, saying that he had already drunk a whole cupful himself while Bergman was asleep.

He insisted on inspecting Bergman's painful legs and feet before starting out. There was some discolouration in the feet but at least there was feeling in them, which Wu said was a good sign. When Bergman wanted to examine Wu's arm in return, the offer was refused, Wu saying that he had already dressed it that morning and arguing that they had already lost enough travelling time.

They made good progress that day and the next and the next, but on the morning of the eighteenth day, Wu did not waken. He lay in the crude bivouac of intertwined branches beneath the snow in which they had spent the night, breathing alternately very shallowly for a few minutes and then very deeply. His face was grey, there was a frosting of snow on his wispy moustache and eyebrows and his sunken eyes appeared frozen shut.

Bergman shook him and rubbed snow on the grey cheeks. When that failed, he breathed on the frozen eyelids, trying to warm them. At last one eye opened and Wu looked up at him.

It took him a huge effort to focus on Bergman's filthy, ice-encrusted beard and eyebrows. Then Wu's good hand lifted and touched the face above him.

'My friend Ber'man . . .' He spoke so quietly that Bergman could hardly hear. 'I hope you now better thinker than I was man of action.'

Bergman shook his friend and slapped his face. A great sigh went out of Wu. 'It is good thing,' he said, 'for man to die free.'

The almond-shaped eyes looked peaceful. As Bergman watched helplessly a tiny spark of light went out of them and left him alone in the immensity of lifeless winter. For a while it was tempting to lie down beside Wu and just give up. In the sunless gloom he could not tell how long it was until he roused himself to go on and forced himself to empty Wu's pockets in search of the remaining food he had been carrying.

In doing this, Bergman discovered what he had suspected against all his friend's denials. For the last several days, knowing that he was dying, Wu had not eaten anything. And far from getting better, the injured arm was swollen to treble its normal thickness. The soggy skin was already frozen in places, a dark purple colour right up to the shoulder. Uncovered, it stank like a corpse. Wu must have been in agony from gangrene for days. Only his superhuman mastery of his own pain had made it possible to even stagger onwards. This silent heroism was a sacrifice which brought tears to Bergman's eyes. He brushed them away before they could freeze and swore to Wu's already stiffening corpse that he would honour the sacrifice that had been made by escaping to freedom, so that a brave man could survive in at least one person's memory.

Bergman stumbled on day after day through the white nightmare, walking as long as it was light and resting during darkness. Sleep came to him now only in fitful bursts. He did not want to lie still too long in case he froze to death, with no one to wake him up. For two whole days he lay in a snow-cave during a *púrga* that was longer and more murderous than any of the previous ones. Every hour or so he roused himself and massaged blood back into cold muscles. When the light diffusing through the hard-packed snow told him that the blizzard had blown itself out he tried to rise but could not break through the crust of ice made by snow melted by his breath and then refrozen. He panicked and struck blindly at the white death all around until his strength gave out and he lay whimpering, curled up – a filthy foetus in a white womb of death.

'Get up, my friend Ber'man! You mus' get up!' The whisper was Wu's voice; he had never been able to pronounce the g in the middle of Bergman's name.

But which way was up? Completely disorientated like a buried avalanche victim, Bergman had no idea. He tried dribbling to see which way the saliva ran but had too little moisture in his dehydrated mouth. There was little urine in his bladder either but just enough to wet himself and find that the moisture ran over his emaciated leg in the direction he thought was left.

He summoned up all his energy and punched hard at the ice wall on his right. It gave way and cold air rushed into the snow-cave. Bergman sobbed with triumph, breaking his way through the snow-crust and rising into the grey daylight like some creature of the snows emerging from its lair. He stumbled on, heading west, always west. Mistrusting the compass, he checked direction by the moss on trees and by infrequent glimpses of the sun through the overcast.

Bergman knew he was slowing down. Despite his will, his body was slowly dying on him. Each step hurt, each breath of frozen air was agony – but that did not matter. All that mattered was that he honoured Wu's sacrifice . . .

When the last snowshoe broke, Bergman knew he could not go much further, honour or not.

It was then that he saw Wu again – not the whole man but just his face, suspended in mid-air, gently chiding Bergman for giving up.

'Of course you can go on,' Wu whispered. 'Are you poor weak scholar like me or man of action who goes on until end? Which are you, Ber'man?'

Wu's face receded as Bergman's vision widened to perceive a Chinese landscape. It was like a silk painting of limestone crags with stunted pine trees perched on the tops. Below the crags there was a river where some women were washing clothes in the clear blue water. On a small humpback bridge a man dressed in a white-and-blue striped robe sat peacefully fishing.

It was Wu! Bergman wanted to run to the bridge and greet his friend but something held him back. Instead, the fisherman levitated and floated through the air towards him. The phenomenon was puzzling to Bergman but not frightening. Wu came close but did not speak, merely pointing to the west with a faint I-told-you-so smile.

Bergman blinked and shook his head as the vision cleared and vanished. This was not a hallucination from snow blindness. There really was a man standing in the middle of the snowfield, dressed in blue and white. Beside him stood another man wearing a striped robe – dark green and red.

No . . . Bergman looked again, forcing his burning eyes to focus through the holes in his improvised snow-mask. These were not men, but man-size liquorice sticks planted in the snow, one painted with blue-and-white stripes and the other red-and-green. There was a copper plaque on the top of the red-and-green one bearing the Cyrillic initials of the Soviet

Union: CCCP. The blue-and-white post marked the beginning of Finnish soil.

Bergman pulled the mask away from his eyes and squinted northwards and then south. The twin lines of boundary posts stretched away across the snowscape as far as the horizon in each direction, the only colour in a world of white snow and grey sky. Thanks to Wu, he had reached the border.

· 9 ·

Colonel Ivan Ivanovich Plotnik was a soldier's soldier from the crown of his close-cropped head to the combat boots which he wore even on visits to Moscow – which were as rare as he could make them. Politicians and civilians thought him mad, which was par for the course: Special Forces officers in any country are expected to be crazy.

The *Voiská Spetsiálnovo Naznachéniya* or Spetsnaz troops were organised on the basis of one brigade per military district. Strictly speaking, Plotnik and the 1250 men and women in his brigade were subordinate to the general commanding North-west Military District (St Petersburg) but Plotnik despised chairborne soldiers and rarely sought his superior's approval.

The lifestyle which their tall, lean, commander imposed on himself did a lot to reinforce his reputation of being crazy among the elite soldiers, male and female, that he commanded. He used none of the privileges taken for granted in Soviet society by members of the *nomenklatúra*. As officer commanding the strategic area between St Petersburg and the Finnish border, he was expected to live in the Villa Orlova – a fifty-roomed wooden folly that had been built as a present for his mistress, the Baroness Orlova, by a nineteenth-century Swedish fur merchant. It was a kitsch Russian-style palace fit for Disneyland, with belvederes, turrets, verandahs, gilded cupolas and heavily carved gables and window frames. As the largest and most luxurious dwelling inside the high-security border zone, Plotnik inherited it from his predecessor by right of office.

He paid one visit shortly after his appointment and stomped in muddy boots from one elegantly decorated room to the next, incredulous at the style in which the outgoing colonel was living. Discovering that the man kept three nubile recruits at instant readiness in the three en-suite master bedrooms, Plotnik dubbed the place *publichniy dom* – the whorehouse – and departed to more congenial surroundings in the camouflaged Spetsnaz barracks which were concealed in the forest, half a mile away.

There he ate in the canteen among his troops and rose each morning at 5 a.m. Obeying his own Standing Orders, Plotnik began each day with a thirty-minute programme of strenuous physical exercises in the open air. His workout ended with an orderly throwing over his naked CO a bucket of cold water. In mid-winter when the air temperature plummeted to minus forty-five centigrade the water froze instantly on body hair and eyebrows and left even Plotnik gasping with momentary shock. Showered, shaved and bursting with energy, he was then ready to put in a sixteen-hour day running his command as well as taking what he considered a legitimate interest in everything else that went on in the strategically important border area between St Petersburg and the Finnish frontier.

There are some officers who like to delegate and others whose favourite command is: 'Follow me!' Plotnik was definitely in the second category. It would have been more than his avionics operator's job was worth to have failed to monitor on the multi-channel receiver the brief VHF transmission which came up on the local frontier patrol frequency. He relayed it immediately to his commander, whose response was to grab the controls of the command helicopter in which he was overflying a foul-weather training exercise. It was a Huey, left behind in Vietnam in 1965, which Plotnik had been given as a personal present on a trip to Hanoi.

With a shout of, 'I've got it!' the colonel grabbed control
from the pilot in the left-hand seat. He threw the thirty-year-old
craft into a power dive, the engines screaming in protest as the
colonel wound them up to their maximum power output and
headed northwards through thick cloud at speeds indicative of
the high quality of the Spetsnaz maintenance bay.

Picking up what the pilot estimated to be the line of the invisible frontier below, Plotnik plunged through cloud to emerge
below the extremely low cloud base. The pilot gritted his teeth
and muttered a prayer as the colonel zoomed through the last
wisps of cloud to clear the treetops by less than the 45-foot
span of the rotors. Plotnik went over to visual, picked up the
line of the twin rows of frontier posts and flew northwards
above them, cutting corners even when it meant overflying
Finnish territory.

He landed within twenty metres of the Mi-8 frontier patrol
helicopter which had originated the monitored transmission,
scrambled out of the Huey and sprinted through the deep snow
to the other craft before it could lift off.

Pulling open the sliding door of the Mi-8's rear compartment, Plotnik screamed at the pilot, 'Cut the engines!' He was
ignoring the fact that frontier guards were MVD troops and, as
such, not under his command. It was the sort of detail that did
not worry a man like him.

As the twin turbo-shaft engines slowed to idle, the colonel
scrambled aboard. The crew chief – a sergeant – saluted to be
on the safe side. Plotnik brushed the sergeant aside and knelt on
the metal floor beside the heap of filthy, snow-encrusted rags
that was a comatose man.

Uncovering Bergman's hollow face with its three-week beard
coated with icicles, he whistled. 'Are you telling me that this
poor bastard just walked two hundred and fifty kilometres
through the snow, in the weather we've just had?'

'*Da, továrisch polkóvnik!*'

Plotnik felt for Bergman's pulse. It was hardly perceptible
and very irregular. Even through the clothing, he could feel
Bergman's ribs, and the arm and leg bones sticking out from the
wasted flesh.

He rocked back on his heels, clicked his tongue and smiled

admiringly. '*Bózhe moi!* This guy must have balls. He's no more than a fucking skeleton. What I could do with a dozen men that have his kind of drive!'

He looked up. 'Where are you taking the poor devil now?'

'We have orders to deliver the prisoner back to the camp designated Perm 39B.'

Plotnik never forgot a detail on a map, but Perm 39B meant nothing to him.

'Where's that?' he snapped. 'I never heard of it.'

'*Eto spétslager* – a special camp, not marked on maps.'

'Do they have a hospital there?'

The crew chief laughed at the idea of a hospital for *zaks* who were going to die anyway.

The colonel's backhand, delivered from a kneeling position, would have scored at Wimbledon. It left the frontier guard flat on the floor, seeing stars and with a ringing in his ears.

'*Ne povtoryáyu vopróca!*' Plotnik said quietly. He never repeated a question.

The crew chief scrambled to his feet and stood at attention. 'No, sir! Comrade Colonel, I beg to report they do not have a hospital.'

'Then this man is coming with me.' Plotnik had taken off his own padded combat jacket and was wrapping it around Bergman's limp body.

He lifted Bergman effortlessly off the floor, marvelling that a man who weighed no more than fifty kilos could have kept going in the appalling weather conditions of the past week, which had put several members of the Spetsnaz units into hospital suffering from exposure. Jumping down to the ground with his unconscious burden, he strode through the deep snow towards his own machine.

The aircraft commander, a lieutenant whose blue-grey greatcoat bore the green collar tabs of the frontier patrol, leaped out of the helicopter and ploughed through the snow after him.

'That man is our prisoner,' he shouted, pulling at the flap of the holster on his belt. 'I protest!'

Plotnik turned. He lifted Bergman, swaddled in his own jacket, level with the lieutenant's face and thrust him at the startled man.

'Smell that!' he said grimly. 'The poor bugger's shit himself and peed himself. This man is nearly dead of hypothermia, you stupid pig's arse. I'm taking him with me to the Spetsnaz recovery unit. It's the only facility outside Moscow where he stands a chance.'

'Fuck off!' The lieutenant's face was white with anger. 'I don't take orders from the bleeding Army.'

He drew his automatic, slipped the safety off and pointed it deliberately at the colonel's face.

'Listen to me, sonny,' said Plotnik. He kept his voice deliberately calm. 'If you look at the open doorway of my helicopter you will see two of my men covering you with Kalashnikov AK 74s. They're good. They could shoot your balls off without damaging either leg. Think about it, Lieutenant. Then make your decision very clear to them. You've got two seconds to stop annoying me.'

'You're making this very difficult, *továrisch polkóvnik*,' the lieutenant stammered. His gun hand dropped, shaking visibly.

'If you didn't have a pig's brain to match your pig's arse face,' hissed Plotnik, 'you'd realise that I'm making things easy for you. Now get back to the controls of your machine and follow my craft back to my base.'

He turned away, contemptuously throwing over his shoulder, 'And listen, pig's arse! If you break radio silence during the flight, I shall regard it as a hostile act and shoot you down in self-defence. *Ty pónyal?*'

'The prisoner . . .'

Plotnik leaped aboard his own helicopter and handed Bergman to the radio man.

'Pig's arse,' he shouted, his voice carrying over the noise of both helicopters 'Get this straight. There is no prisoner here, just a brave man who's dying, minute by minute. Any guy who does what he did, deserves a break. When I'm personally certain the poor devil's going to live, he'll be returned to you motherfuckers, but not before.'

Bergman floated in a vast sea of pain. At the top, like white flecks that flickered and vanished on the heaving crest of the ocean swell, were the small pains from the needles stuck in his body, the alternate heat and cold of the treatment, the chemicals they were pumping into him and the nausea which they caused. Deeper were the pangs of frostbite in his hands and feet and the agony of returning circulation. Further down was the ache in every one of the overstressed, abused organs of his body in crisis. At the very bottom, in the lightless depths, was the greatest pain of all: he had failed Wu by accepting his friend's ultimate sacrifice and not making it all the way to freedom.

Colonel Plotnik's decision that Bergman was to be cared for by the best team in the Spetsnaz recovery unit was not purely emotional; he knew that there would never be a better test of their ability to bring a man back from the threshold of death by exposure. He was taking a personal interest in Bergman's progress and when Plotnik took a personal interest in anything, people tried very hard to get the right result.

After three days during which his body was massaged, manipulated, drip-fed and interfered with in a hundred other ways by Plotnik's doctors and nurses, Bergman was dimly aware of the team of women around him, caring and performing all the intimate functions he could not handle himself. It was the timbre of their voices that directed the rambling of his mind and made him see again the face of the girl he had left in that moonless moment on the Turkish border.

'Peter . . .' she breathed. The sound echoed away down the dark and lonely valley below the looming mass of Mount Ararat. 'Peter . . . Peter . . . Peter . . .'

Bergman knew that she was in danger. If he did not warn her that there was a mortar trained on the very spot where she lay, she would die. He tried to lift himself up and yell at the top of his lungs: 'Go! Go! Go!' But he could not open his mouth or lift a finger to help her.

.10.

Ossetin lived in fear that he would be put before a firing squad for allowing two prisoners to escape. He lay awake night after night, feeling the leather straps tie him to the post and the blindfold placed over his head. He heard the click of the bullets in the breech, the orders: 'Load! Take aim! Fire!'

Night after sleepless night, he felt a thousand imaginary bullets tear into his bulging flesh. Yet the days turned to weeks and no orders came for his arrest or execution. As 1991 drew to a close, there were too many more urgent problems in Moscow for anyone to devote much time to Perm 39B. It might have been different, had Bergman not been recaptured and Wu dead. As it was, all that happened was a second reprimand on Ossetin's personnel file; he was ordered to forfeit leave for one whole year as a punishment. His luck, it seemed, had held good once again.

Two hundred miles to the south, Bergman lay in the Spetsnaz recovery unit. As soon as he was conscious and lucid, Colonel Plotnik came to visit him for a few minutes each day, taking as detailed an interest in the patient's progress as any doctor. He was fascinated by the way Bergman's tough body sorted itself out, with help from the team of physiotherapists and doctors, faster than anyone would have imagined possible when he was brought in as good as dead on board the colonel's old Huey.

During Bergman's long weeks of convalescence in the adjacent sick quarters, Plotnik came less often but stayed longer. At first the conversations were quite impersonal, but imperceptibly a relationship of mutual respect grew up between the prisoner-patient and the colonel who had saved his life.

For that act, Bergman owed a debt that could never be repaid. He also genuinely admired what he was able to see of the way Plotnik ran his private army, demanding and getting unquestioning devotion from every member of the Spetsnaz forces. To them he was God in boots, a Russian version of Colonel Patton – a hard-driving, hard-living, hard-fighting man – but unfettered by the constraints of democracy that had been Patton's undoing.

Able to give as well as accept respect, Plotnik in turn admired Bergman for driving his body so far beyond all reasonable physical limits, for touching base with death and coming out, if not smiling, at least with his will and determination to live still intact.

Both men swiftly realised that they were – in Plotnik's words – from the same stable.

'The Aegean stable,' the colonel said one day, pouring into Bergman's tooth mug some vodka he had sneaked into the sick bay illicitly inside an ammunition pouch on his mud-spattered combat fatigues. 'We're Bronze Age warriors, you and me, Bergman. Two thousand years ago we'd have died young and gloriously, surrounded by a pile of enemy dead. Beautiful women would have wept and blind poets would have sung songs about our deeds of valour for generations to come.'

He raised his glass in an ironic toast. 'Today, we're an anachronism. We're like the last dinosaurs, the end of a line of evolution. Perhaps it's just as well, when you think of the weapons we've got to play with now.'

It was the first time in five years that Bergman had been addressed by his name, except by Wu. Cautiously, he asked, 'Where d'you get my name, Colonel?'

Plotnik grinned, relaxing his normally flint-hard features and looking for a moment like an overgrown schoolboy, pleased with a trick he had scored. 'You know what Spetsnaz forces are all about, Bergman? Our role is to penetrate far beyond the scene of conflict to take out specific targets and assassinate people important to the enemy's war effort. Today that brief includes ferreting our way fast into Western computer facilities, injecting viruses, accessing data etc.'

'And suddenly I'm a state secret?'

Plotnik's grin faded. 'Actually you are, Bergman.'

He was wondering how much to tell the man in the bed, and changed the subject to give himself time to think that one out.

He nodded at the window. 'If I let you walk around my base, you'd find two types of soldier. There are the tough guys like you and me but also weedy little runts with glasses and females with big brains and small tits that I'd never want to hump in the sack.'

Bergman laughed outright for the first time in a long while. Russian was a coarse language, but in Plotnik's mouth, it sounded right.

'They're my boffins,' Plotnik continued. 'Electronic warfare experts, computer geniuses – you name it, I've got 'em. I don't know what the hell they do all day, Bergman. Give some of them a rifle and they'd take it to bits, looking for the transistors. In combat, I wouldn't even trust them with a sharpened pencil – they'd probably stab themselves. But they're clever bastards in other ways.'

He poured the last of the vodka equally. 'And when I want some information I'm not allowed to have, they get it for me – whether it's in Bonn or Washington or Moscow. It took my boys half a day to find where your file was and get a print-out on my desk. You've used up more lives than a cat, my friend.'

My damned tongue, thought Plotnik. I'd have made general if I could keep my mouth shut. But this guy deserves a bit of hope to take back with him into hell . . .

He stared out of the window at the vehicle park, the drivers, the sentries, the mechanics going about their business of perpetual readiness. With his back still turned to Bergman he said, 'I don't know what rumours you get to hear in places like this Perm 39B.'

'Not much, Colonel. In the rest of the Gulag there's a rumour machine, even newspapers. In a *spétslager* there is never any news from the outside world.'

'That's what I figured. And that's why Moscow is hustling me to send you back there – in case you get to hear things you shouldn't and tell the other poor bastard *zaks* the good news when you get back.'

'What good news?' Bergman's heart leaped. 'An amnesty?'

'Not that good.' Plotnik swung round and faced the man in the bed. 'All I'm going to tell you is this, Bergman. There are changes going on you wouldn't believe. The whole USSR has fallen to pieces in the last couple of years while you've been incommunicado.'

He pointed south across the Baltic. 'Latvia, Estonia, Lithuania are all independent states now. And in the east, Georgians, Azeris, Armenians . . . everyone's got a gun in his hand, shouting *Svobóda!* – or whatever damn word they use for freedom from the Russian yoke.'

'So that's why they moved Perm 39B two thousand miles to the west!'

Despite his caution, the questions spilled out of Bergman. He felt his pulse quicken with the promise of freedom. 'You mean the whole Gulag is about to be wrapped up after all these years? Is that what you're telling me, Colonel?'

Plotnik gripped Bergman by both shoulders. 'I've told you too much already, son. Fact is, officially the Gulag doesn't exist any more. Perm 39B doesn't exist and neither do you. All the world-shattering events I'm talking about won't help you or the other poor bastards in that camp.'

Bergman grabbed the colonel's arm. The sweat stood out on his brow.

'Come on,' he said. 'I'm not a criminal. There must be an amnesty soon for prisoners like me. It's happened before now – even under Stalin.'

Plotnik shook his head.

'What's that mean, Colonel?' Bergman was half-out of the bed, demanding answers. 'If you've seen my file, tell me how long I was sentenced to. No one ever told me.'

'It means . . .' Plotnik broke Bergman's still feeble grasp and stood back. 'It means that all the files of prisoners in Perm 39B are marked *No Release*, Bergman. Your only hope of ever going free is if you can manage to hang in there until not just the people who put you in that place, but the whole fucking Moscow-based regime goes up in smoke.'

And that's no exaggeration, thought the colonel, recalling his own surprise at the endorsements of that grim *No Release* on Bergman's file. Andropov, Gorbachev and Yeltsin had each confirmed the decision of their predecessors. Whatever games Bergman and the others had once been a part of, the stakes must have been sky-high . . .

Bergman sank back on the pillows. He felt a chill steal over his body as the nervous sweat cooled on his skin.

'I guess you're not kidding, Colonel,' he muttered.

Plotnik's cold grey eyes bored into his. He spoke in American-accented English, 'I shit you not, son.'

Bergman's hands were cuffed and there was a short piece of chain between his ankle irons that made it impossible for him to take steps of more than a few inches at a time. He shuffled slowly out of the sick quarters to the helicopter pad in front of the building.

Plotnik, dressed in his usual combat fatigues, was standing by the border patrol helicopter, ignoring the noise of the engines and the down-blast from its five-bladed rotor as he waited to say goodbye.

Pointing to the chains, he grinned at Bergman. 'I see you've still got the bastards scared,' he shouted, nodding at the two escorting MVD officers and Ossetin, who had come to sign for the prisoner. Dressed in a fur coat belted around his fat belly, the camp commandant looked like a pig-faced teddy bear.

'They're taking no chances you'll beat them up and run away again.' Plotnik was deliberately shouting loud enough to make sure he was heard.

Bergman nodded noncommittally. It was fine for the colonel to mock the heavily armed escort, but no sensible prisoner would join in the laughter; he had survived his years in the Gulag by keeping his head down, both literally and metaphorically.

The colonel stepped forward and embraced him Russian-style with a kiss on both cheeks, '*Do svedánya!*'

Then he stepped back and saluted. '*Vsyévo khoróshevo!*' Good luck, Bergman, you'll need it . . .

As Plotnik's aide-de-camp handed to Bergman a large kit-bag stuffed with vitamin pills and high-nutrition food, the colonel grabbed the teddy bear sleeve before Ossetin could clamber into the machine.

The border patrol lieutenant was the same man that Plotnik had threatened to shoot out of the sky on the day Bergman was found. A slow learner, he pulled Plotnik's hand away and found himself flat on his back in the snow, covered with automatic rifles, held by two impassive Spetsnaz guards.

The colonel did not even look round after shrugging him off. He was leaning into the cabin where the other border guard was shackling Bergman to a tie-down bolt, and shouting at Ossetin who had scrambled inside and was huddled against the far side of the compartment.

'Listen, cut-balls,' Plotnik yelled. 'If any of you bastards take that food away from the prisoner –' A thin, razor-sharp knife appeared in the colonel's right hand as if by magic. '– I'll creep up on you one dark night and cut off whatever it is you have between your legs. And then I'll slit your goddam throat. That's a promise.'

Ossetin nodded wordlessly.

'*Peredácha pónyata?*' yelled Plotnik: Got my message?

Ossetin licked his lips and nodded nervously. '*Ya pónyal, továrisch polkóvnik!*'

As the helicopter lifted off, Plotnik turned his back to the storm of rotor-driven ice particles. To his aide-de-camp he muttered, 'I should have let that poor bastard Bergman die in the snow. It woulda been kinder than sending him back there.'

. *11* .

Bergman squinted through the snow goggles that Plotnik had given him. Thanks to the lingering effects of snowblindness, bright light still hurt him like a spike stabbing right up the optic nerve and into the brain. Pushed roughly out of the helicopter and unable to save himself, he rolled on the snow-covered ground and manoeuvred himself awkwardly upright. Back on his feet, he looked around in amazement, unable to orientate himself at all. The fences and watchtowers of the camp were roughly as he remembered them but everything else inside the perimeter of Perm 39B was different.

Since his escape the camp had been transformed into a small high-security prison. Determined to avoid the possible embarrassment of a successful escape from this *spétslager*, Moscow had given priority to the job of razing all the ramshackle wooden huts and replacing them by a hexagonal brick-and-concrete bunker. There was only one doorway and no windows at all that Bergman could see. A separate block of admin offices and guards' quarters was joined to the bunker by an above-ground tunnel. The rest of the compound inside the wire was open snow, raked smooth each day to show footprints and harshly lit against the dusk by powerful flood-lights on each watchtower. Guard dogs ran loose between the twin fences.

The border patrol helicopter lifted off and clattered away into the murk of snow-haze, leaving Bergman alone with Ossetin.

'What do you think?' the commandant asked the handcuffed and shackled prisoner beside him. His eyes were moist with expectation as he watched Bergman's face for reactions.

Ears adjusting to the silence after the noise inside the heli-copter, Bergman could hear what sounded like the noises of a kennel: a muffled animal howling and yelping. He shrugged his shoulders, keeping his head down, eyes fixed on the ground in the approved Gulag slouch.

'Look around,' said Ossetin. 'Take a good look, 712.' He came close, wanted to touch Bergman but was frightened, despite the handcuffs and shackles, to get too close to the man who had killed two of his guards with such savage fury.

He pointed to the hexagonal bunker and giggled. 'These are your new quarters. Four-star accommodation for such impor-tant prisoners as you, from now on. Moscow intends to make sure you do not leave us again.'

Bergman kept his eyes on the ground. At the risk of being beaten up for insolence he refused to talk to Ossetin, who dis-gusted him. Where were the guards? he wondered. There was not a man in sight. Behind the glass of the watchtowers indis-tinct figures watched him through binoculars. A movement caught his eye on one of the corners of the bunker as a televi-sion camera scanned the compound. Bergman wondered what other changes had taken place since his escape. He was shortly to find out.

Ossetin was hammering on the steel door of the bunker which opened to reveal a guard post like an airlock. Behind the two grinning guards armed with AKMS automatic rifles, the stocks folded back to make ugly machine-pistols, was a second identical solid steel door blocking access to the interior. A third door led off sideways to the guards' quarters in the next block. Here the noise of howling was louder. With a shudder of appre-hension Bergman realised that he was hearing not dogs but men. At the involuntary expression of unease on his face, Ossetin's pink tongue darted out and licked his fleshy lips. He wanted to savour Bergman's horror in every detail.

The heavy outer door closed itself hydraulicall. One of the guards knocked Bergman's snow goggles off with a sneer. 'You won't be needing these again.'

The other swung a lazy backhand blow that connected with the back of the prisoner's skull and then proceeded to knee him in the kidneys. Prostrate on the rough concrete floor, Bergman realised that some things had not changed in Perm 39B . . .

A word from Ossetin and the guards stepped back. The commandant, peeling off his teddy-bear coat, had had a flash vision of Plotnik rappelling down a rope from the sky with the knife gripped between his teeth. 'Stop it!' he screamed to the bewildered guards.

Bergman scrambled to his feet. Unable to pick it up, he had to leave Plotnik's kit-bag on the ground at his feet. To his surprise it was opened, the contents examined and thrust back inside, the bag returned to him. Then he had to undergo the indignity of the routine body-search of any prisoner arriving or departing from a Gulag camp, including the painful squeeze of the scrotum and the dirty finger inserted in the anus, and afterwards the same finger forcing his mouth open, lifting his tongue, searching for no one knew what – except the prisoner's humiliation.

Eagerly Ossetin pressed a button on the control desk and watched Bergman's face as the inner door swung open. A stench of caged animals wafted out which made even the guards, who were used to it, catch their breath.

'*Voydí*,' smiled Ossetin. 'Walk inside, 712 and take a look around your new quarters.'

Picking up the kit-bag with difficulty, Bergman hobbled into the bunker, moving a few inches at a time. On each of five walls, three cells faced him. On the last side, where he stood, were only two cells, the entrance taking the place of the third. Fifteen of the cells were occupied by prisoners, some in Gulag pyjamas, some naked. The air was hot and steamy.

The cells were simple cages with concrete walls on three sides and the fourth completely taken up by a grille of thick steel bars which permitted not even a square centimetre of privacy to the occupants. Most of the prisoners were clinging to the bars, staring out at Bergman.

Recognising him, one of them called above the din. 'You see what you have done to us, 712? We were in hell before but now it is even worse.'

Other prisoners shook fists at him and mouthed curses. One or two, as he could see now that his eyes had adjusted to the dim light, were crying or gazing blankly into space. The din audible outside even through two steel doors, was a compound of men coughing, their lungs full of fluid, and of the noises made by two prisoners who had gone mad. One crouched in a corner of his cell, howling like a wolf and the other was curled into foetal form on the floor, eyes open and legs twitching like a dog dreaming of rabbits as he uttered periodic yelps. Amplified by the shape of the concrete and metal bunker, the resultant cacophony was appalling.

Built like a nightmare bank vault, the bunker had walls, ceiling and floor dripping with moisture oozing from the still drying concrete. Already the damp air was clogging Bergman's lungs and his first cough was lost in the chorus of baying, coughing and yelping.

The stench came from the open slop cans – there were no lids because they could be used as weapons and hurled between the bars by a desperate prisoner. The man howling was smeared with excrement, his cell completely bare and empty with filth everywhere. The other cells were furnished with a bed fixed in one corner and a shelf which had to serve as table, storage and washbasin. Apart from the lidless slop cans there were no other furnishings.

Bergman heard Ossetin's voice close to his left ear: 'Well, 712, what do you think of my private zoo?'

A guard had opened the door of one of the two vacant cells. Bergman did not reply but shuffled inside. While the second guard covered the prisoner with his machine-pistol, the first one removed Bergman's cuffs and shackles, retreated to the door and threw the kit-bag inside before slamming the grille.

Ossetin watched Bergman's face for reactions as the key turned in the lock. He took it from the guard and waved it at his prisoner. 'The next time you pass through that door, 712 – you'll be carried out in a box.'

Bergman sat on the welded steel bed, rubbing his wrists. The mattress and blankets were clean. An electric bulb behind a shatterproof glass panel in the wall above the door gave a dull glow while the main lighting came from a ceiling panel in the centre of the bunker where a battery of television cameras scanned the cells constantly.

'Take your time,' purred Ossetin. 'How long will you live here? Ten years? Twenty, maybe? You look thin. I think we should feed you up and put some flesh back on your bones. That way, you'll last longer.'

In the stench and din, Bergman's spirits sank to a new low. *No Release*, Plotnik had said. Was it possible that he had endured all the agony and hardship of the escape, caused Wu's death and nearly killed himself, only to spend the rest of his life locked up like an animal in the private zoo of a madman?

Ossetin was taking no chances of Bergman suffering a relapse before his body-weight was back to normal for a prisoner of his height. Each time the food trolley was pushed into the bunker, Bergman was surprised to find on his plate some unheard-of luxury like a few shreds of meat, some vegetables or even the occasional small portion of fruit. All these things were noticed by the other emaciated prisoners and the tide of hatred grew deeper until none of the prisoners who could talk coherently would address to the man they saw as the cause of all their current miseries anything but insults. Eventually Bergman gave up trying to talk to anyone and lay on his bed, hour after hour for days on end.

Ossetin's daily enquiries about his health had a ring about them of the witch in the gingerbread house who fed the children tidbits to fatten them up before eating them. For a while Bergman thought of taking action by refusing to eat. It would not have taken long to starve to death. But dying was giving in, he reasoned. He owed Wu and he owed Plotnik, so he decided to ignore the insults and catcalls of his neighbours and retreat into a world of silence, eating everything he was given until he had made a full recovery.

Kennelled like a dog in the bunker, with the din of coughing, yelping and howling that went on day and night, Bergman knew moments of depression when he wished he had died in the snows at the Finnish border. Then he felt ashamed of himself. What right had he, Peter Bergman, to write off Wu's sacrifice and Plotnik's friendship by giving up and letting Ossetin win? Hadn't Plotnik said that the whole Soviet system was crumbling to pieces? If he could somehow keep fit and sane for long enough, release might come one day.

Plotnik . . . now there was a man, thought Bergman. If Ossetin was the kind of scum that rose to the top of the perverted world of the Gulag, the tall Spetsnaz colonel with the crew-cut hair was an example of another side of the Russian character – romantic, obstinate, crazy maybe. It had been the Plotniks who died in their hundreds of thousands to save Russia during the Winter War, fighting Hitler's invincible *Wehrmacht* with their best generals all dead, murdered in Stalin's paranoid purges of the thirties. Just knowing that a man like Plotnik existed and would take a risk for someone who could never repay it, made Bergman feel better. It meant that the entire world was not made up of crazed, filthy prisoners and debased, sadistic guards.

Able to take only five steps in any one direction, he decided to start getting fit again in the only possible way – by working out a daily programme of exercises based on what he remembered of the karate and t'ai chi that Wu had taught him. The most obvious advantage for a man in a cell was that it required very little space.

In time the gentle routine known to Europeans as shadow-boxing surprised Bergman in its effect on his body. A sense of well-being grew in him, despite the horror of his physical surroundings. He heard Wu's faintly sing-song voice explaining, 'T'ai chi is not system of physical jerks like you Westerners impose on the body. Is more of way to explore body's tensions and release them before they damage us.'

And Wu had said, 'T'ai chi is balance. You must seek balance, my friend Ber'man.'

And: 'Symbol of trinity is little understood, Ber'man. Three in one means: man have three brains in one body. There is brain which control our physical functions and brain which Westerners call subconscious. And there is conscious brain, which try to tell us that it is most important of all. Not true; if any one of the three try to dominate, man is like vessel where one helmsman fight his comrades for control. It drift at mercy of every adverse storm and current in life. No, in our body each of three brains must be in harmony with others. From that state of being, everything flows.'

The pidgin chatter – for Wu had never mastered Russian or the *blátny yazyk* – were forgotten now; the important thing for Bergman was that the little Asiatic of whom he thought so often had somehow communicated to him the essence of keeping alive and sane in a world of death and madness. But Bergman was no philosopher. Fretting at his confinement he worked day after day in the gingerbread cell at following Wu's precepts but the harder he strove, the further away seemed the state which he was seeking. Again Wu came to the rescue: the same remembered voice saying, 'No, Ber'man. Striving is not the Way. Striving is not balance. Striving undoes what you seek to achieve.'

Like all Wu's other riddles, it made no sense at first – until Bergman ceased to strive consciously. Then the progress began. The first sign was an improvement in his physical sense of balance. As that got better, so Bergman felt his conscious brain become more sympathetic to the body he had always taken for granted and often driven ruthlessly in pursuit of conscious aims and desires. From that achievement, as Wu had foretold, everything flowed.

Sadly Bergman realised that he knew almost nothing about his dead mentor. He was not sure that Wu was ethnic Chinese, had no idea where he had grown up, whether he had been married or had children. He did not even know for certain what had been Wu's mother tongue. Mandarin, Mongolian or some Turkic dialect of central Asia? The little Asiatic had used words from all those languages from time to time, mixed in with the *blátny yazyk*.

And what chain of misadventure had led to Wu's banishment to the lost world of Perm 39B, with a file marked *No Release*?

Before the escape, Bergman had looked upon the other

prisoners simply as potential accessories in a desperate endeavour. Out of them he had chosen Wu because he was the fittest, mentally and physically. Of Wu the person he knew nothing at all. Now he felt a great loneliness for the man who had endured such agony on his behalf.

It was not just that Wu was dead, his body lying somewhere in the frozen wastes of the tundra, food for any hungry predator during the spring thaw. In his globetrotting life Bergman had lost other comrades. The difference this time was that he had been so single-mindedly intent on planning his escape that he had never really taken the time to get to know Wu. So the friend was twice lost, his death marking a double bereavement.

These were thoughts the old Bergman would never have had. Hated by the other prisoners, he was as good as alone in his cell for twenty-four hours a day with only himself for company. There he became aware of profound changes taking place within his psyche. It was as if some part of Wu's mind had osmotically seeped into his own brain cells during their agonised communion in the snows . . .

That was it! With a start, Bergman remembered the last few hours before he had reached the border. He had run out of food the day before, or maybe the day before that – memory was unclear. In a trance-like state of hunger, cold and exhaustion, his body was an automaton heaving one leg and then the other clear of the drifts and stumbling forward a few metres at a time before collapsing again in the snow – the treacherous, seductive snow that promised warmth and oblivion. After each fall he would lie a few minutes resting, then force himself to get up and take a few more painful paces before he collapsed again.

The pain eased as abruptly as though a switch had been turned off, leaving him free and pure, beyond the reach of such fleshly sensations as cold and hunger. Standing up without effort, Bergman realised the reason for the change when he saw his body still lying on the snow beneath him. He was not the body; the body was something else.

As the spirit-self continued rising to the level of the treetops, Bergman knew intuitively that he could go on floating higher and higher for ever if he wanted to, but that after a certain point he would not be able to return. So he stayed close to watch his body lurch upright, stagger a few laboured paces and fall again. He wondered how long the husk of flesh could go on before abandoning the struggle and becoming just another unmoving part of the white death all around.

Minutes passed, maybe hours. Time had no meaning or relevance.

When he saw Wu fishing on the bridge, there was a decision that had to be made. Bergman wanted to run through the dream landscape and on to the bridge, to laugh and hug Wu and shout out loud with joy. But he knew that taking those few steps meant crossing a borderline more eternal than any geographical frontier and which, once transgressed, could never be recrossed. He made his choice, slipped back into the struggling body, felt the pain and the cold and the hunger – and knew with great sadness that he was losing sight of Wu for ever.

Later, at the border itself, Bergman's spirit again floated free of his body, away and upwards from the pain and cold. He watched his body clinging to the blue and white Finnish boundary post until the first helicopter landed and the frontier guards pulled him away. It took the strength of both men to undo the dying man's frozen grip around the post. Bergman looked for Wu but found the dream landscape, the bridge and his friend no longer there. There was a message – graven in stone or whispered on the wind, it was all the same – that Wu had travelled on.

It was the loneliest moment of Bergman's life.

PART 3

MEMORIES

1973 – 1986

.1.

Bergman shifted on his bed, aware of some slight change in the usual pattern of noises in the bunker. Ossetin was standing outside his cage, looking in through the bars. His sharp feline tongue darted out and licked the fleshy lips. There was a sensual half-smile on the commandant's face as he took his daily promenade around the human zoo.

Bergman turned his head away, more interested in the changes within himself than anything happening around him. Plotnik had played a part in this new man as well as Wu, he reflected. The few weeks of being treated as a human being by the rock-hard Spetsnaz colonel after five years of being just a number in Perm 39B, had given his morale a powerful dose of self-respect.

From his own experience of escape-and-evasion simulations, Plotnik knew what the Gulag could do to destroy a man's will and even his sense of identity. He had been intrigued to know how any man could stay sane enough to plan and execute an escape after five long and debilitating years in a *spétslager*.

Bergman had confided how the idea of revenge had become his motive for keeping alive and fit and ready to escape. It had served him as a compass, forever indicating the direction of reality, while the other men locked up in Ossetin's kingdom of pain had lost their bearings and drifted into a brain-numbing limbo.

'I gotta stay alive, colonel,' Bergman had said. 'I've got a job to do on the guy who put me in the Gulag. I want the pleasure of killing him.'

But that had been the old Bergman talking. Somehow the man he now was, found the simple idea of tit-for-tat revenge too facile, too easy, too shallow – unless given substance by an understanding of how and why Roscoe had betrayed him. If that required going over everything that had ever happened between himself and Jack Roscoe . . . well, time was something he had plenty of.

Polishing boots! That's a hell of a way to remember a guy, but it is the first memory of Jack that comes to mind, so let's begin there – with him an' me a couple of raw recruits, polishing boots in the barracks of the Foreign Legion's 4th (Training) Regiment at Castelnaudary in south-west France.

It was May of '73 when Jack and I first met up. I guess that the conversation back home in Toronto or at smart dinner parties in Washington DC must have been about the Senate hearings into the Watergate conspiracy and how Nixon's days in the White House were numbered. At the Quartier Lapasset – that Foreign Legion man-factory where a whole generation of young men was processed into finished legionnaires – the smart conversation on that or any other night was all about pressing creases, cleaning weapons and polishing boots.

At 3 a.m. God incarnate marched into the dormitory where we engagés volontaires *were asleep, exhausted after an eighteen-hour day. Within two minutes we were dressed and standing at attention beside our beds. The snap inspection lasted half an hour of screaming abuse and individual humiliation.*

By the time that our sharp-tongued, beady-eyed little Belgian drill-instructor switched out the lights and left the dormitory, kit that had been neatly folded and laid out

ready for inspection the next morning lay hurled all over
the floor in disarray. Five beds had been kicked to pieces by
the screaming maniac with the stripe on his sleeve.
Blankets, mattresses and parts of the frames lay in tangled
heaps.

Our kit had to be refolded in the regulation creases and
the beds rebuilt without putting on the room lights. With
two weeks' training behind us, we were getting good at
doing the job in the dim glow of the emergency lighting.
Even beds were re-assembled in seconds.

Ten minutes after Corporal De Wilde had gone back to
his own billet to sleep the sleep of the just, our dormitory
was quiet again apart from a few snores. One of the first
lessons we learned as recruits was the importance of
grabbing every minute of slumber we could.

But two beds were empty: Roscoe's and mine. We were
squatting on the tiled floor of the shower room because it
was the only place where the light was left on all night. A
pair of dog-tired nineteen-year-olds who looked like
convicts with our hair shaved clean to the skull in the
Legion's regulation billiard-ball haircut, we had work to do
before reveille – polishing boots!

Why did De Wilde pick on me an' Jack? Why were we
vertical in the showers when all the other guys were
horizontal? Because we had played right into that evil little
bastard's hands on the first day, is why. Jack an' me were
two cocksure kids who thought we were tough. Truth was,
we didn't know a goddam thing . . .

At Aubagne, in the headquarters depot, us new boys had
been given the runaround, drawing our kit and getting so
many jabs from the medics that some men's arms swelled
up as thick as their thighs. We were shouted at, sworn at in
several languages and hustled by everyone in sight.

We thought that was a rough introduction to the Legion,
but it was nothing compared with the tricks that toothless
little DI of ours would pull out of his immaculately pressed
khaki sleeve during our six months' basic at Castelnaudary.
I can still hear his ratty little voice with its Belgian accent as
he chased us off the canvas-topped trucks that brought us

*into the Quartier Lapasset. We started running as our feet
hit the concrete and for the next half-year we never walked
at a normal pace.*

*Before we had even unpacked our brand-new kit-bags
completely, De Wilde was harrying us off on a five-mile run
across the broken terrain outside of town. We ran with
rifles held above our heads, helmets bouncing on our
shaven skulls and full packs slamming against our spines
with each step. De Wilde kept us running in the midday
heat of early summer until, one after another, all the men
dropped to the ground and could not get up again – except
for me an' Jack.*

*We stood there, chests heaving, streaming with sweat and
ready to drop – but somehow still on our feet and bodies
rigidly in what we hoped was the position of attention. De
Wilde came close and looked into our eyes for a long
moment. He was shorter than us by a long way, but had
that DI's knack of tilting his head back and looking down
his nose at even the tallest recruits as though we looked and
smelled like something a dog had left on the sidewalk.*

*I guess he saw in Jack's eyes and mine a brief flash of
pride that we had proved ourselves tougher than the others.
Was that a mistake! We should have dropped with the
others and taken a break. By staying on our feet we singled
ourselves out for De Wilde and as good as volunteered
ourselves for his special treatment.*

*'You think you're tough guys, don't you?' he hissed
through the gap in his teeth. He had bad breath, I recall.*

*The message he was laying on us was that Roscoe an' me
were going to find out just how tough we really were . . .
which, when I think about it, is why we had joined the
Legion in the first place.*

*Hold it there, Bergman! It was why you joined the Legion
maybe but Jack's motives were more complicated. Truth is,
I don't know exactly why Jack volunteered. Oh, I know
why he said he did it, but that's something else . . .*

*So there we were, being eyeballed by De Wilde. Standing
just five-eight in his polished boots, he did not like tall
recruits! Even if Jack an' me hadn't been a lot taller than*

him, the dice in De Wilde's game was loaded against us
because of our mother tongue. The little runt loathed
Anglo-Saxons – a title under which he lumped together all
the English-speakers in the Foreign Legion. Britishers, Irish,
North Americans, Australians, New Zealanders – we were
all the same to him because we tended to band together and
look after each other. Which is why in the Legion we're
generally known as the English Mafia.

De Wilde gave a chuckle of anticipation, as though
taking apart the tall English boy standing beside me was
going to be a real pleasure. At age nineteen, Jack did look
kinda pretty like a rosy-cheeked choirboy.

De Wilde stepped right and faced me. I gave him my
street stare. I was tough. I'd broken my nose boxing when I
was fourteen and refused to have it set because I was proud
of the evil look it gave me.

'I'll have your balls for breakfast,' De Wilde hissed at me,
like someone else might have said, 'Nice to meet you,
Bergman.'

Our corporal had been a drill-instructor with the Fourth
Regiment for seven years. His job was essentially to break
the men who could be broken and toughen the ones who
could take it. The technique was not original. It had been
used in Caesar's legions and the impis of Chaka the Zulu
and still is used wherever young men have to be
transformed fast into disciplined soldiers. I didn't know it
then, but the first step is always to cut the toughest recruits
out of the herd for a contest of wills which the DI must
win. After that, the rest follow like lambs to the slaughter.

'What's your name, shit-face?' De Wilde stepped close
and deliberately thrust his face within an inch of mine.

'Bergman, mon caporal!' I shouted.

One pace left and De Wilde repeated the treatment on
Roscoe.

'Raven, mon caporal!' he shouted.

That was the first odd thing I found out about Jack. He
had joined the Legion under an assumed name – but I'll
come back to that later.

Menacingly De Wilde took his time walking all around

us, hoping we would turn our heads or move our eyes to follow his movements so he could bawl us out for not facing front. We won the first round by staying rock-still. He turned to the other recruits who were sitting up and watching as they got back their wind.

'Raven and Bergman,' he sneered. 'We have a Ravenburger in the squad, gentlemen. These two tough guys are gonna be the meat in your corporal's sandwich, you'll see.'

From that moment Roscoe and I could do nothing right – which was why we were still awake at four o'clock in the morning, polishing boots in the shower room. Oh, like all the other recruits', our boots had been clean and polished when we went to bed – we'd removed the last grains of mud with our toothbrushes. But at every inspection we had to lift our feet like horses at a forge, to show that the soles of the boots were as clean and polished as the uppers. That night, there was one stud missing on Roscoe's left sole which De Wilde spotted in a second.

As punishment, he ground the heel-plate of his boots into Jack's toe-caps and mine, removing in one practised movement the near-metallic sheen which had cost us so much work. He ordered us to repolish not just the damaged toe-caps but the whole boots. 'Soles, studs and all, must gleam,' he ordered. 'Even the laces must shine!'

The air temperature at 4 a.m. that night was a stifling twenty-five degrees centigrade. We were wearing only our cotton issue skivvies, but even so sweat ran down our spines – and God, were we tired!

.2.

Bergman closed his eyes and leaned back against the tiled wall to cool his skin. His head dropped and he fell asleep in a squatting position.

'Don't nod off,' warned Roscoe.

He blinked and perspiration dripped from his long eyelashes onto the polished leather. Still damp from unarmed combat practice in a mud-pit the previous afternoon, his boots refused to shine any better, despite all his efforts.

'Reveille,' said Roscoe, 'is less than an hour away. If we go to sleep now, we'll feel worse than if we stay awake.'

There was no reaction. Roscoe prodded his buddy with the boot he was holding. Bergman sprawled sideways without waking and lay full-length on the tiles, fast asleep. Roscoe slapped his face a couple of times and tried to pull him upright.

'Quit shaking me, will ya?' the Canadian groaned.

'You've got to stay awake, man,' said Roscoe urgently. 'Stand up and walk around, you'll feel better.'

Bergman stood, hardly able to keep his eyes open. He walked up and down for a couple of minutes, complaining: 'I think I'm still asleep, Jack.'

'Here!' Roscoe thrust out the boot he was working on. 'Polish this. You're better at it than me. That'll keep you awake.'

With a groan of protest the Canadian hunkered down again beside Roscoe, took the boot from him and spat on the leather. He rubbed the sputum in with a piece of bone, using small circular movements.

'Secret's in the bone,' he confided sleepily. 'It's gotta be dog bone to get that DI shine.'

Roscoe had heard about the trick before but pretended it was news to him, just to keep his buddy talking and awake. 'Where d'you learn that, Peter?'

'My pop,' said Bergman. 'He gave me the bone.'

'I thought he was a trapper.' Roscoe was puzzled. 'A trapper who polished his snowshoes, maybe?'

Bergman grinned. 'That was just a yarn I spun for the other guys. We didn't live on Hudson Bay. I never grew up with a rifle in my hand or walked a trap-line in the snow, either. I went to school and Cub Scouts just like the other kids in Etobicoke. That's a suburb of Toronto.'

'What's your father do?'

'He's dead.'

'So what did he do?'

'Pop was a soldier.'

'He fought in Korea?'

'Nope.' Bergman shot a wary glance at his friend. 'World War Two.'

'Army?'

'Yup,' Bergman laughed shortly, then relaxed. 'But not in the uniform you're thinking, Jack. He was on the other side – a *Feldwebel* in the good old *Wehrmacht*.'

'How could a Canadian serve in the German Army?' Roscoe was thinking of old black-and-white newsreels, the torchlight processions, the hands raised in salute . . .

'At the time he was German,' Bergman explained. 'Canada is a land of immigrants, remember?'

That accounted for a lot, thought Roscoe. With that blond hair and clear blue eyes he could see Peter Bergman in a high-collared German uniform . . .

'So where did he fight?' he asked.

'The Eastern Front. You know, the Russian campaign.'

Roscoe whistled, 'That must have been tough.'

'Tough?' Bergman laughed again. 'You shoulda heard the way my old man told it. Death or Victory! was the slogan. That was OK, except the guys on the ground didn't get to choose which option. The decision was made for them by Uncle Joe. Two of Pop's best buddies lost both feet from frostbite at Stalingrad – all because they had no socks and their boots were worn through with holes in the soles.'

'Jesus!' Roscoe winced.

'Pop said those guys were the lucky ones.'

'Lucky?'

'The *Führerbefehl* from Berlin was simple: there will be no retreat! You are all heroes! So the heroes without socks became heroes without feet to put 'em on.'

'And how come they were lucky?'

'Because they died, Pop said. The ones who survived and sur-rendered didn't make it back to Germany for ten, twelve years – some of them even longer.'

'Jesus! Did your old man go through all that?'

'Yes, sir. He did. You know, Jack, there were over four hundred thousand German soldiers in von Paulus's Sixth Army when he surrendered to the Reds at Stalingrad. Think of it . . . nearly half a million guys taken prisoner on one day! They died like flies. There was no way the Ivans could clothe or feed that many, even if they felt like it – which they didn't. Most of those men died in Russia because the Reds used them as slave labour in Siberia.'

Roscoe whistled quietly. 'He must have had a few tales to tell, your dad.'

Bergman nodded. He liked the picture he had just painted. It did the old man more credit than the painful last memories of a grey-faced, prematurely aged cripple gasping for breath in his wheelchair.

He passed back the boot. 'Here y'are, Jack. This'll do for that toothless little bastard De Wilde.'

'I wonder who knocked them out,' Roscoe mused. 'I'd like to have seen that.'

'If we ever meet the guy, I'll buy him a beer or ten.'

'Thanks for my boot,' said Roscoe. He was still thinking

about the man whose dog bone had put such a good shine on the leather. 'Did he have a pile of medals, your dad?'

'Not one,' said Bergman. 'Not that I ever saw.'

'So he wasn't a hero?'

'There are different kinds of heroes, Jack. Some win a medal and some lose their feet. Anyway, what the hell's a medal?'

'It proves you're brave.'

'Nah,' Bergman gave a streetwise laugh. 'Do you know what's the most important thing, if you want to get a medal?'

'Bravery, I suppose.'

Bergman remembered saying the same thing, an eager six-year-old asking his father what it had been like in the mystery time before he was born.

He relayed his father's answer now to Roscoe: 'The most important thing is (A) a witness (B) of superior rank, (C) who survives and (D) who knows how to write a clever commendation. Without the alphabet, no medal.'

'I hadn't thought about it like that.' From sheer bone-weariness, Roscoe was dozing off despite his interest. To rouse himself, he slipped off his green cotton pants and stepped into a shower cubicle, pulled the chain and let the cold water sluice over him from head to feet. It was refreshing, delicious. He stopped the flow of water so that he could hear what Bergman was saying.

'I guess Stalingrad was one of those battles where somebody said that uncommon bravery was a common virtue. My old man was supposed to have been awarded the Iron Cross, First Class two days before von Paulus surrendered.'

'What for?'

'Carrying his two crippled buddies back under fire when they abandoned a position.'

That impressed Roscoe. He stepped out of the shower. 'The Iron Cross was some big deal!'

'You don't know my pa.' Neither did I, thought Bergman. He felt better now about the old man than he had for a long time and wanted to explain to Roscoe things that he had not understood himself until that moment.

'You know, Jack . . .' He paused. 'People have this image of the German soldier from war films that portray him as an unthinking kraut-head with a stick-grenade in both hands who shouted, "*Zu Befehl, Herr Leutnant!*" as he threw himself under the treads of a GI tank. Well, I'm telling you it wasn't like that. Pop and his buddies who died three weeks after their feet were just like you and me, to start with. They didn't want to die, any more than we do.'

'So what happened to the Iron Cross?' Roscoe persisted.

There was the ghost of a smile on Bergman's normally immobile features. 'You'll like this, Jack. *Feldwebel* Bergman turned down the offer of the medal and asked if the Führer would send him a coupla pairs of gloves instead – before his buddies lost their hands too.'

'Crazy!' Roscoe laughed.

'That was Pa's sense of humour,' Bergman grinned at the memory. 'He was making a point the only way he could. Right up to the last day when von Paulus's men were already surrounded by the Reds with not a chance to break out and no food left, consignments of Iron Crosses were parachuted into the pocket. Did you know that?'

Roscoe shook his head.

'It's true. Germany was short of pilots and plans but men were being shot down and dying daily in the attempt to fly loads of propaganda leaflets and medals through the blockade! A lot of the *Frontschwein* – that's what Pop's buddies called themselves – reckoned that it would have been better to drop a few cases of ammo or bales of food and clothing, rather than meaningless bits of tin and paper.'

Roscoe nodded agreement.

'Trouble was, Pop's CO was a fanatical Nazi who decided to court-martial him for rejecting the Führer's honour. Pop told him that a useless medal wasn't honour; it was just glory. Honour, he said, was something much, much bigger than a piece of tin on a pretty ribbon.'

'Was your dad court-martialled?'

'Nah, Stalin changed the timetable.'

There was a pause in which the only sound was a tap dripping somewhere in the showers.

'If your old man was so pissed off with army life,' said Roscoe, 'what are you doing, joining the Legion?'

'You're full of questions, Jack, you know that?'

'I'm curious, that's all.'

Bergman stood up and padded around the showers. He felt tired but strangely peaceful, talking to Roscoe. 'Pop died when I was twelve. I always felt that I'd have known him better if he'd lived a few years longer. Maybe then we could have talked properly – you know, man to man. I guess I gave him a lot of aggro the last couple of years, him being an invalid and living on handouts and all.'

'What kind of aggro?'

It was Bergman's turn to cool down. He kicked off his pants and stood under a shower, letting the cold water shock him awake.

He spoke over the noise of the water. 'Nothing big-time. I used to hustle the old guy for pocket money, clothes, vacations – things like that. But it must have made him pretty sick, the way things were. So I guess I thought, joining a tough outfit like this, I'll maybe come to understand a bit better what an *ehemaliger Frontschwein* like my pop went through and how his mind worked – even though it's too late now.'

He stopped the water and stood dripping on the tiled floor, taking deep breaths and trying to convince himself that he had just had a good night's sleep.

Roscoe grunted sympathetically.

'And there's another reason, Jack,' Bergman finished. 'My mother just remarried. I guess it'll make things a whole lot easier for Ma if I'm not around for a while.'

The night-time revelations had changed the way Roscoe saw his buddy. It seemed that, behind the streetwise scowl, Bergman was not all just muscle and guts.

'Will you go back to Canada,' he asked, 'after we've completed our five years' engagement?'

'Jesus!' yawned Bergman. 'That's a long way off, Jack. First we gotta survive the mad corporal.'

'Hitler?' Roscoe queried sleepily.

'Nah, De Wilde!'

'Oh yeah.' Roscoe stretched and groaned at the stiffness in his leg and arm muscles.

'Fuck De Wilde!' said Bergman. 'It's you an' me against him,

Jack. We'll show the toothless little short-arse we can take everything he can hand out and still come back for more, right?'

He stuck out his hand which Roscoe shook solemnly. The two tired and naked young men were startled by the sound of a bugle playing the first notes of morning call on the barracks PA system. Both men grabbed their boots and polishing kits.

'Move it,' said Roscoe urgently. 'We've got about ten seconds to get flat on our beds before the corporal walks into the dorm.'

. 3 .

There must have been hundreds of times in my life when lessons I learned in the Legion have enabled me to stay one jump ahead of the mob. Even here in Ossetin's zoo I know I'll survive what makes other guys go mad or die.

When I'm exercising naked that fat little creep of a commandant sits out there watching me on the television screen, I know. I see the camera panning round and locking onto my cage when I'm sitting on the can. Right now the lens is aimed at the black guy jerking off under his blanket in the cage opposite mine.

It doesn't bother me. I got used to the lack of physical privacy back in basic training; in the recruits' barracks the shower cubicles had no curtains and the toilets were without doors. I didn't mind guys walking past when I was taking a shower but I never got used to someone on the pot opposite talking to me while I was taking a crap. It seemed like he was poking his finger up my arse. At least here nobody talks to me when I'm crapping – or any other time, come to that.

The weirdest thing about the Legion was the contrast

between the lack of physical privacy and the traditional
respect for personal privacy: a man's background and
reasons for joining up were his own business. Anyways we
recruits were too goddam tired at the end of an eighteen-
hour day to ask each other questions more intrusive than:
'Can I use the iron?' or 'Have you finished with the floor
polish?'

On three nights out of four, De Wilde would crash into
the dormitory at 3 a.m., stomping his feet, hollering and
banging on a dustbin, for a snap inspection that shattered
sleep patterns. Night after night, he picked on Jack and/or
me, handing out yet another unmerited punishment to keep
us short on sleep.

I'd been pushed around all my life since I was a kid, so
I could take it but the victimisation was really getting to
Jack. He needed sleep. He had a whole crop of
giant boils on his neck that were infected from rubbing
against his uniform collar. Each time the medic lanced
them, they swelled up again. I could see he was near
breaking-point, physically and mentally. De Wilde piled
the pressure on more and more. A coupla times I stopped
Jack doing something stupid like running away or taking
a swing at our toothless tormentor – for which he would
have gone straight into the stockade, which we called le
gnouf.

Four weeks into basic training, Roscoe could not recall what it
was like to spend eight consecutive hours in bed. He could
hardly keep his eyes open during the day, never mind at night.

He felt nauseated and dizzy a lot of the time, from the after-
effects of a severe blow behind the ear from another man's
rifle-butt on the *parcours des combattants* – the battle simula-
tion course. It was an accident, but that did not make it hurt
any less. His throat was raw from having to scream at the top of
his voice each time he rammed his bayonet into a man-size
sandbag. And every muscle in his body ached.

His main worry was that, if he became sick enough to be hos-
pitalised, he would be put back into the next intake and thus be
separated from Bergman.

Apart from badly blistered feet that were painted daily with gentian violet, and a festering sore on his right hand where gun oil had got into a deep cut, Bergman's tough body was taking the treatment better than most. All the recruits had eyes blood-shot from lack of sleep. Each man had lost fifteen pounds in weight, thanks to the relentless training schedule and missing a meal most days.

It was the third night running that Roscoe and Bergman had spent squatting in the showers, polishing boots after De Wilde's 3 a.m. inspections. This time, Bergman was the one who was trying to keep his buddy awake until reveille at 5 a.m.

'Say, Jack, what is all this mystery about your name?' he asked, rubbing the polish in. Spit and polish. Spit and polish. He felt he could do it in his sleep.

'We're not supposed to ask questions like that,' Roscoe objected.

'Aw, come on!' Bergman snorted. He spat again and mixed in some polish. 'That stuff was fifty years ago. We're not criminals on the run with Beau Geste riding across the desert on a camel to rescue the beautiful girl from the clutches of the wicked Arab chieftain. They shot that scene way back, man.'

Neither he nor Roscoe dreamed that before their service was finished, they would take part in an action as heroic as any dreamed up by Hollywood or P.C. Wren, risking their lives to rescue hundreds of women and children held hostage under threat of rape and murder.

'So?' queried Roscoe.

'So what's your real name?'

'Jack Roscoe.'

Bergman stopped polishing and stuck out his blackened, swollen paw. 'Nice to meet you. So why choose Raven?'

'It's the name of a character in a novel I was reading by Graham Greene the day I joined up.'

'Never heard of him.'

'You don't read much?'

'You mean books? Nah, I never went for that stuff. No time, I guess.'

Roscoe took a deep breath. The pre-dawn chill was creeping down from the mountains to the north of Castelnaudary. It was

a relief after all the heat, but meant that dawn was close, herald-
ing another day of punishment.

'I'm a deserter,' he said. 'That's why I had to use a false name.'

Bergman rocked back on his heels and guffawed with laughter. Roscoe's story didn't mesh with his innocent looks: the long
lashes, the soft skin and rosy cheeks. 'You're putting me on?' he
said, getting his breath back.

Roscoe was blushing. 'I was in the British paras.'

'No shit?' Bergman was puzzled. He looked at Roscoe with a
new respect. 'Why'd you keep it a secret? Most of the guys
would sound off about a thing like that.'

'Because I thought the Legion would hand me back to the
British and I'd go inside a military prison.'

'You are a very weird person.' Bergman shook his head. 'I
mean . . . Don't take this wrong, Jack, but you look like a fucking cherry choirboy.' He had been going to say *like a fairy*.

He slapped his thigh in a gesture of amazement and admira-
tion. 'And now you're telling me that you're a goddam para.
How 'bout that?'

'I *was* a para,' Roscoe corrected him.

'Why'd you desert?' Bergman's question was part-disbelief,
part-curiosity. 'It can't have been worse than what we're living
through right now. If you can take this, why'd you run away
then?'

Roscoe grimaced. The real answer was: *because I didn't have
a buddy like you to watch my back*. 'It wasn't worse than here,'
he agreed. 'In fact, 16 Para was OK, but I wanted to show my
mates I was tougher than they were, so I volunteered to join the
SAS. You know what that is?'

'Sure,' Bergman said eagerly. It crossed his mind that the
whole story was a fantasy, a yarn to impress him.

'I went on what the SAS call "selection", spelled R-E-J-E-C-
T-I-O-N. They give you the runaround, night and day.' Roscoe
grinned tiredly at the memory. 'At Bradbury Lines in Hereford
we didn't sleep much, either.'

'Why'd they chuck you out?'

'I stuck it until Day Three of Week Three,' Roscoe recalled.
'We were climbing up and down an ugly mountain called Pen-
y-Fan in the Brecon Beacons. It was raining all day, I recall. As

I climbed into the transport to go back to camp, the instructor who'd been beasting us up and down the hill all day, clapped me on the shoulder and said, "That's it, chum. Piss off back to the paras and tell them what real training is like."'

'He didn't give any reason?'

'They don't have to,' Roscoe made a face at the memory. 'But I knew. I slugged a timekeeper who said I was two minutes late at a checkpoint.'

'You hit the guy?'

'Too true.'

'That was just plain stupid.'

'It was,' Roscoe agreed, 'but I couldn't help it, Peter. You know how I am when I lose my temper. I'd have slugged De Wilde a couple of times if you hadn't been there.'

'When was all this SAS stuff, Jack?'

'Two days before I joined the Legion.'

Bergman gave a low whistle. 'How 'bout that! So you joined this mob on the rebound?'

The memory of failure did not hurt, now that Roscoe could talk about it: 'I sat on Platform Four at Hereford station and tore up the travel warrant back to 16 Para at Aldershot. I couldn't have gone back there to face my mates, with them knowing I hadn't made the grade in the SAS.'

Bergman thought about it. 'I reckon I'd feel the same. So what'd you do?'

'I hitched a lift to Dover and asked a French trucker on the cross-Channel ferry whether the Foreign Legion still existed. He talked to his mates and got me a ride all the way to Marseille – where Jack Raven was born, on the spur of the moment.'

'The Legion wouldn't have handed you back,' said Bergman. 'You didn't kill anyone.'

'I didn't know that at the time. I thought it best to play safe.'

Bergman grunted. 'What did your old man say, when you decided to desert?'

'Nothing,' said Roscoe.

'Nothing? He didn't say nothing? Or you didn't tell him?'

'That's right.'

Without warning, Bergman slammed a fist hard into Roscoe's arm, knocking him flat on the floor.

He scrambled to his feet, fists balled and ready to return the blow as Bergman stood up slowly.

'What the hell was that for?' Roscoe snapped, standing over him.

Bergman was looking equally angry, his face only inches from Roscoe's. 'You know something, Jack Roscoe, or whatever your fucking name is? We've been buddies for more'n a month and you've asked me plenty of questions, but you never tell me anything about your folks or where you're from.'

He poked an accusing finger in Roscoe's face. 'You're a secretive bastard, but why? What've you got to hide?'

'There's not much to tell,' Roscoe knocked the accusing hand away and stepped back. 'I never knew my dad.'

'How come?'

'Ah, divorce.' Roscoe turned his head to avoid the stare of Bergman's pale blue eyes, walked to the far end of the shower room and hit the tiled wall hard with one clenched fist. 'He pissed off when I was four years old. I was brought up by my mother – just the two of us alone.'

Roscoe's memories of that time were confused. If there was one image that predominated, it was of his mother weeping, holding him tightly in her bed all night long – and the mutual promises in the warm, claustrophobic darkness: *Promise you'll always love me, Jack? Yes, Mummy. Always and always? Yes, Mummy. And you'll never leave me like Daddy did? No, Mummy. No!*

'So your old lady never married again?'

'No!' Roscoe's voice was harsh, echoing the small boy's anguished protestation. 'She didn't.'

'And you never saw your old man after he took off?'

'He was a shit,' Roscoe said. 'I wouldn't have wanted to know him.'

'Maybe,' said Bergman softly. 'Or maybe he had problems too.'

'Maybe you can mind your own fucking business!'

Bergman walked the length of the showers and stood close behind Roscoe. 'Take it easy, Jack. You're too quick on the draw.'

'Who says?'

Bergman placed a hand on Roscoe's shoulder. 'Relax, Jack. Go with the flow. If we stick it out and do our five years in the

Legion, we don't have to prove anything to anyone for the rest of our lives. So take it easy, huh?'

Roscoe half-turned to face him. His eyes were shining. He nodded, 'Thanks.'

Bergman defused the intensity of the moment with a chuckle. 'I'm not kidding, old buddy. *Ne craque pas*, as they say around here. Don't take a swing at De Wilde, whatever you do. He'd just love that.'

He placed the other hand on Roscoe's other shoulder and pulled him round until they were face-to-face. 'Reckon you can hack it, man?'

Roscoe let out a huge sigh that had been a long time coming. His eyes met Bergman's levelly. 'Don't worry, Peter. This time I'm going to stick it out all the way.'

De Wilde did the job he was paid for. Unable to take the pressure, three out of four recruits dropped out before the end of basic training. Those who remained were tempered by pain and fatigue, their bodies tougher and leaner and stronger than they had ever been, by a long way. Thanks to the Belgian drill-corporal's calculated insanities, the whole squad drilled and exercised as one man. Even the oddballs who had been cynical loners at the beginning now took pride in being cogs in De Wilde's machine.

They were proud of having survived the tough training that had weeded out the weak sisters, proud to be fighting fit, proud to be masters of the soldier's arcane skills, and proudest of all to belong to the small but legendary fraternity who had worn with honour the *képi blanc* – the distinctive white forage cap of the Foreign Legion.

They could recite the history of battles in Mexico and North Africa, in the trenches of the First World War, in Vietnam and Algeria in the fifties and sixties and in all the wars during a century and a half where other countries' men had shed their blood and died for France. The recitation of regimental and Legion history was more than a repetition of cold facts learned in a classroom; it was an evocation of heroism. Ardent for glory, they yearned to measure themselves against the valiant ghosts of yesterday's warriors.

The passing-out parade took place on a cold, wet, windy November morning. Fully fledged legionnaires at last, Roscoe and Bergman ceremonially donned their white *képis* for the first time. As he felt the hard rim of the cap settle around his head there was a lump in Roscoe's throat. He wondered whether Bergman and the others standing there felt the same.

As part of the ritual, they chanted in unison the Legionnaire's Code, swearing to serve France with honour and fidelity, to be brothers to every other legionnaire, to be courageous and loyal, to be dignified but modest, to look after their weapons and their bodies, to carry out their mission at whatever cost, to fight without passion or hatred and never to abandon a dead or wounded comrade.

As they marched across the parade-ground of the Quartier Lapasset for the last time, the sound of their voices echoed back from the blank façades of the barrack blocks on three sides of the square. Not a man on that parade-ground felt the rain slanting down on him, or the evil wind from the frozen Pyrenees which curled round his body.

For the hymns at this group baptism they sang the nostalgic slow marching songs of the Legion. The parade, with its shouted commands echoing off the walls of the barrack blocks, the drill movements executed at the funereal tempo of eighty-eight paces to the minute and the striding march of the Legion with hands outstretched, was a quasi-religious climax to a half-year which they would never forget.

There was a handful of relatives clustered behind the reviewing stand, braving the wind and rain. Among them was Roscoe's mother who had travelled from England especially for the ceremony. She felt bewildered by the tall, fit young man who had been her son a few months before and was now a stranger – a member of another family with its own traditions and its own peculiar language. The mixture of French slang, German and Arabic was all but incomprehensible to her, although she had taught French language for thirty years in school. As with all jargons, those who talked Legionese were 'in' and anyone else was 'out' – as she sensed more deeply than relatives who did not speak French.

The colonel of the regiment invited the parents and friends to a *vin d'honneur* in the mess. He kissed Mrs Roscoe's hand and offered her a glass of red wine, congratulating her on her excellent accent when she spoke French. A lifelong pacifist, she found it unnerving to be surrounded by men in immaculate uniforms, trained to kill. She looked at her son standing beside his Canadian buddy and saw two legally licensed murderers. To her eyes Roscoe's face had lost its innocence and his body had thickened with a man's muscles. He even walked differently, with a confident step that made him seem older than his years.

With an ache in her heart she wondered: *Why, Jack?* Why are you doing this to me? What are you trying to prove?

The bewilderment and hurt showed on her face, making Roscoe angry that she had come and angrier with himself for inviting her. The family news she had brought – about relatives back in England who had been ill or got married – meant nothing to him now.

I thought I had gotten to know Jack pretty well during our six months' training. That day he gave me a whole bunch of surprises, starting with how uneasy he was around his old lady. He hardly talked to her, leaving me to suggest we show her around the town. There isn't much to see in Castelnaudary, so I led off with the church of St Michel because Jack's mom taught the piano as well as French and I'd heard there was a famous organ there.

There was an old guy tuning the pipes, or whatever they do with organs, when we walked in. As a favour, Jack's ma asked him to allow her son to play for a few minutes. The tuner seemed surprised that a shaven-headed, muscle-bound hunk of legionnaire should be able to play an organ but he got off the bench and let Roscoe sit down.

I was standing in the church doorway, scratching my head and wondering where else we could take Jack's old lady, when I was . . . stunned, is the only word. A cascade of chords was pouring out of those huge pipes as my buddy's fingers rippled over the manuals. He said later that it was some favourite Bach toccata he was playing from memory, but the name of the music didn't register with me. Standing in the doorway of that church listening to Bach's

*music fill the building, I realised that I didn't know the half
of Jack Roscoe.*

*His mother had tears running down her cheeks when he
stopped playing after a couple of minutes. Roscoe grunted
some excuse that he was out of practice and refused to play
any more, despite her pleas. I told Jack he was crazy not to
have volunteered for the regimental band, if only to escape
De Wilde's worst excesses.*

*As we were leaving the church, his mother said, 'You
shouldn't let your musical talents go to waste, Jack. Really
you shouldn't.'*

*The kind of remark that proud mothers make, to me it
seemed harmless enough. But the look Jack gave her from
those dark eyes of his was like a slap in the face. She
stepped back, visibly hurt – and I thought: You arsehole!
What'd you do that for?*

*We'd agreed to take her for a meal of cassoulet – the
delicacy of beans and home-made charcuterie for which
Castelnaudary is famous. Jack's mom had never eaten it
before. Instead of going to our usual restaurant, Jack
insisted on taking the three of us to the town's smartest
restaurant. I suppose it was his way of saying sorry, but
during the meal he sat silent and withdrawn, leaving all the
talking to me.*

Watching his mother's train draw out of the station, Roscoe
felt that his childhood and adolescence – all his life before joining the Legion – was like a play in which he had tried first one
role and then another, hoping in each to find an identity that
was not within. None of them had fitted like the uniform he
now wore. Walking back through the town towards the barracks, he caught sight in shop windows of himself and Bergman
striding along together. They looked good and belonged to
something even better.

He wanted to share the revelation with his buddy and yell
out, 'I have an identity now!' but the thought was naïve when
put into words, so he walked in silence, making a conscious
effort not to march in step which had become second nature.

They celebrated the end of basic training in a bar called Le

Camerone, full of Legion mementoes. It was after a few beers, that Roscoe threw out a challenge which Bergman accepted. The next day they volunteered for parachute training.

The élite *Deuxième Régiment Etranger de Parachutistes* was referred to in the Legion as the *deuxième REP*. Like Britain's SAS, it rejected most of the men who volunteered but Roscoe and Bergman got through the selection. The training was tough and not dissimilar from what Roscoe had sampled during his brief spell with the SAS. The storm-lashed terrain on which they trained in the Corsican mountains during the winter of 1973 had more in common with the Welsh mountains than the golden tourist beaches only a few miles away where winter hol-idaymakers were sunbathing.

The *deuxième REP* pushed men to the point of exhaustion and beyond in the hope that, if they were going to snap, they would do it in training and not later, on the battlefield where it could cost lives. The schedule was arduous and would have given an Olympic athlete some bad moments but Roscoe and Bergman got through it and won the right to wear the blue shoulder-flashes of the *deuxième REP* with the Annamese dragon harking back to the Legion's deeds of valour in Indo-China. After that came the anticlimax that all peacetime soldiers know. At the peak of fitness and training, Jack Roscoe and his Canadian buddy had to wait for some far-off event to call for the exercise of their hard-won skills.

The Legion was founded to conquer and police the French Empire without spilling French blood but France no longer had an empire to fight for. True, there were some small-scale actions in former French colonies like Chad or Guyana, but the num-bers of volunteers required were small. Growing increasingly disillusioned as the end of their five-year engagements drew near, Roscoe and Bergman were ticking off the last days on their demob calendars and making hazy plans for civilian life.

Then came Kolwezi . . .

.4.

On 12 May 1978 the name meant nothing except to a few thousand people in the mining industry who had worked there. The following day, the world's media knew all about Kolwezi, a typical African mining town in the Shaba Province of Zaire, where the giant Gécamines complex employed several hundred European technicians.

With their dependants, the white population of Kolwezi was approaching three thousand men, women and children. On that Saturday morning they woke up to find themselves at the wrong end of Operation Chicapa. They were de facto hostages of several thousand Katangan rebels who had taken over the town after a forced march through two hundred miles of bush from their training camps across the border in Angola.

The Katangans were led by Cuban advisers under whom they had trained in Angola, but the operation was planned in Moscow. As often happened, the KGB was keeping a low profile, using the Cubans as front men to fool world opinion. Castro's men running the rebel training camps in Angola were themselves under the guidance of Soviet officers.

At Camp Raffali on Corsica the *deuxième REP* sat up and

took notice. Maps were requisitioned and men found who knew the country; in the Legion that was almost always possible. The current situation in Kolwezi was unclear. While officers clamoured for orders from Paris, the barrack-room rumour was clear enough. Three thousand white hostages under threat of rape and death in a French-speaking African country? Only the *deuxième REP* was trained and equipped to intervene fast enough to save all those lives.

Men returned early from leave all over the world, without being ordered to. Then it was a case of Hurry Up And Wait.

Five days later, the paras were still sitting on their kit-bags in Camp Raffali while the politicians in Kinshasa, Paris and Brussels haggled and manoeuvred. Men, women and children died in Kolwezi. At last the government in Paris – alarmed at the scale of the massacres already reported and the large number of French citizens at risk – ordered the *deuxième REP* to go at zero notice.

Even then, the problems were not over; there was a shortage of suitable military planes. Paris could find only one transport aircraft with the necessary range, so three DC8s were hired from UTA, a French airline that flew the African long-haul routes. A Boeing 707 had to be hired from Air France to make up the numbers. Even so, most of the *deuxième REP*'s equipment – including their parachutes – had to be left behind, for lack of space.

After a ten-hour flight the transports landed six thousand kilometres from Corsica, at Kinshasa, the capital of Zaire. There the men realised the size of the country: they were still a thousand kilometres away from Kolwezi itself. After more delays and technical hold-ups they found themselves in the air in strange aircraft, buckling on unfamiliar American parachutes. After three days and nights without sleep, they were to drop into a war situation where Intelligence on the ground was zero.

Bergman could hardly believe his luck, sitting in the rattling Zairean C 130, waiting to jump. Only a few days short of demobilisation, he was getting the chance of a lifetime to find out just how good a soldier he really was. Beside him on the wooden-slatted seat, Roscoe listened hollowly to the last-minute boasts of what men were going to do to the Katangans on the ground below.

Some men were even asleep. Roscoe had been awake ever since they climbed into the trucks at Camp Raffali for the four-hour drive through the mountains to Solenzara Airport. Every time he closed his eyes he saw an image of himself sticking his bayonet into a stuffed sandbag on the combat training course, but this sack turned into a black man whose belly split open at the first stab to spill an infinity of warm, moist, stinking entrails all over him.

'What was it like,' Van asked me when we were getting to know each other. 'What was it like to make a combat drop into an alien country where several thousand black rebels were on the rampage – where being captured meant death by torture?'

I don't know what the other guys felt as we went into action that day. There was a Mexican radio man in our squad, name of Espinosa, who kept crossing himself and muttering Hail Marys. Some guys vomited and blamed the turbulence. Me, I just wanted to get my arse back on terra firma before some guy down there used his Kalashnikov to drill me a second anus, diameter 7.62 mm. Further than that I didn't think.

Modern combat drops are low-altitude – around a couple of hundred metres – to minimise the time when you're a helpless target in mid-air and there's damn-all you can do about it. Forget that stuff from old war films where the 'chutes all blossom prettily between the clouds and float gently down for minutes on end. Fact is, you don't have much time to think – just a few seconds from leaving the aircraft to the moment you hit the ground.

And yet I do recall one thing. It didn't last long but I remember hanging beneath the canopy of my 'chute, briefly enjoying the silence! For days we'd been in noisy machines. Just for a couple of seconds as the transport planes disappeared high above us in the dull coppery sky, we floated in silence. It was like sipping a cool milk-shake on a hot day.

Then we heard the dry pop-pop-popping of AK 47s as the ground rushed upwards fast. It was a uniform burned-out straw colour with the odd splash of green where a tree or a bush managed to find some moisture. Maybe a kilometre distant were the outskirts of the town: low white buildings in the khaki landscape with the heaps of rust-coloured tailings from the mines dominating everything.

I didn't know we were dropping into elephant grass taller than my head. I hit the ground to find myself alone, with no reassuring sight of the next guys in the stick to right and left of me and no familiar figure of the sergeant waving a hand-signal to home on him. The world had shrunk to a wall of head-high grass in all directions.

The equipment I was carrying was so heavy and awkward that I was still struggling to get rid of the 'chute harness when this black guy leaped out of nowhere brandishing a Kalashnikov and jabbering something. I could see from his rag-tag uniform that he was a Tiger. That's what they called the Katangan élite forces after the silver tiger embroidered on a blue ground which was their emblem.

I didn't know what language he was using, but I knew he was saying, 'I'm gonna shoot your balls off, whitey!' – or words to that effect.

Luckily he was in no hurry because he could see I was tangled in a mass of webbing. And possibly he didn't recognise the neat little 9 mm. machine-pistol I was carrying. The folding stock was bent back for the drop. To him, used to the heavy Kalashnikov AK 47 which he was pointing at me, my weapon probably looked like a toy. Also, I was holding it awkwardly in my left hand because my right hand was tangled up in the harness.

Through lack of space in the transports we'd had to leave our own 'chutes back in Corsica, so at Kinshasa we'd been issued American T 10 'chutes from Zairean army stores. They were a type that didn't mate with our equipment buckles. As a result, we dropped with items of gear tied all over us with bootlaces, bits of wire and string. The release button of my harness was caught on a short piece of bent

*coat hanger – a small inconvenience that could have ended
in a little wooden cross in some military cemetery, marked
P. Bergman 1954–1978.*

*The Tiger could see my problem. He laughed, showing a
fine set of teeth and didn't find out until too late that in the*
deuxième REP *we practised shooting both right- and left-
handed. I'd moved the fire selector to short burst as my first
act on landing, so all I had to do was forget the effing
harness for a moment and drill the guy through his head
with three 9 mm. rounds. He really did die laughing! It was
a combination of luck and training – I hadn't time to aim.
A coupla inches higher and my bullets would have just
parted his crinkly hair and he'd be remembering this now
instead of me.*

*I'd just got clear of the tangled shrouds and the collapsed
canopy when I heard someone forcing his way through the
elephant grass behind me. Finger on the trigger, I spun
round to meet this new threat and found myself staring
through the grass at Roscoe's white face. He stood looking
down at the dead Tiger with his mouth open. I had to grab
Jack's arm and shake it hard to get him moving.*

The sounds of combat were all around as the *deuxième REP*
skirmished their way into the town. Blinded by the head-high
elephant grass, they fought their way forward against odds of
ten to one. Now the discipline and training paid off. This was
real. This was what it was all about.

Every legionnaire was high on adrenalin. They liberated their
first objective – the low brick-built Impala Hotel – to find it a
charnel house. Mutilated bodies of black men, women and children were strewn everywhere. Every single object in the building
had been smashed to pieces by the Katangans in a senseless
orgy of destruction. Afterwards even the broken pieces had
been literally ground to powder underfoot with an inhuman
fury. It looked as though some rabid beast had been unleashed
from hell.

There was no sign of the European hostages who should have
been there, or of the five-man French military mission based in
the motel, whose bodies were never found.

The *deuxième REP* fought their way into the outskirts of the European quarter of the town against increasingly stiff resistance. They came to the first massacre site in the office of the Baron Levêque company. Here the bodies were white. They lay – men, women and children with their arms and legs intimately intertwined in the last desperate thrashing. The corpses were piled a metre high and more in a blood-smeared tangle of death, at the bottom of which one woman was still alive.

The fog of war is a metaphor for the confusion of the battlefield in which only discipline and drill make the execution of orders possible. At Kolwezi, progress was hampered by a real fog as well as the metaphorical one. The real one was a mixture of choking red dust kicked up by the explosion of mortar shells, mingled with eye-smarting smoke from the fires started by the rebels, who were retreating despite the heavy odds in their favour and busily destroying everything they could not take with them.

The paras made good progress through the streets of the residential area, lined by well-tended bungalows where European families cowered behind makeshift barricades. Roscoe was high on the potent mixture of adrenalin and sleeplessness – and had been since the first exchange of fire. So far he had only seen the enemy at a distance. He had fired in their general direction and men had fallen but he could not be sure that his bullets had killed them. As the hours passed he began to hope that his vision of bayoneting a man was just a bad dream and not a foretaste of a real event.

Coughing his way through the smoke, Roscoe saw an African child coming towards him from a garden across the street. It looked as though the toddler had been wounded and had some kind of field dressing taped on his chest. He was clutching to himself one-handed what looked like a fruit and screaming something incomprehensible against the background of automatic fire from all sides. Tears were streaming down the bewildered little dust-streaked face. A line of .50 calibre bullets from the machine gun mounted on a Katangan armoured car at the nearby intersection punctuated the dust within inches, missing the child by a miracle.

Roscoe cradled his MAT 49 machine-pistol in his left arm and reached out instinctively, calling, '*Ici. Viens ici.*'

The child saw him and turned in his direction.

Roscoe was just about to slip out of cover from behind a stone wall in order to grab the toddler and pull him to safety, out of the armoured car's line of fire, when he was deafened by Bergman's MAT 49 firing a short burst hard by his left ear. He jumped to the right by instinct and saw the 9 mm. slugs impact on the child's chest, slamming him back against the stone wall opposite.

Horrified, he twisted in a crouch to scream at Bergman. 'What the hell . . . ?'

Before he could finish the sentence, Bergman had launched himself through the air in a rugby tackle. He knocked his buddy to the ground behind the wall just as the grenade that had been strapped to the toddler's chest exploded, showering them both with small globs of pink flesh. Roscoe sat up feeling sick.

During a lull in the firing, someone sprinted across the street to where they lay. It was their red-haired sergeant from South Africa, Jan Coetzee, clutching an Fl sniper's rifle in one hand and a two-way radio in the other. He threw himself flat beside Roscoe and took in the scene from their side of the street. '*Ça va, les gars?* You guys all right?'

Roscoe was sitting, back against the wall, looking dazed. Bergman explained what had happened.

'I grew up among Kaffirs,' Coetzee spat. 'But I never saw one pull a trick like that, genuine.'

'Maybe the Cubans taught them,' Bergman suggested.

'Could be.' Coetzee rolled over and squinted down the street. 'They're the bleddy bastards who stirred all this up, not the blecks, you can take it from me.'

He patted the telescopic sights on the rifle. 'I'd like to get a few of those bastards lined up in the cross-hairs.'

Coetzee's simple summary of the situation was accurate. Chicapa was Spanish for Dove. It was the code-name of a Soviet/Cuban plan to annex by force the world's largest single source of diamonds and the sixth-largest source of copper before the newly founded Zairean Army of President Mobutu could react.

After the Communist victory in Vietnam and the turmoil in South America, the men in the Kremlin believed that such a prize could finance the long-awaited worldwide revolution.

While the politicians and media pundits of the West argued what should be done in response to the Cuban invasion of Zairean territory, only a few hundred Foreign Legion paras stood in the way of that grand design.

Roscoe's horizons were more immediate. He was frightened that he was going to be sick in front of Bergman and Coetzee. He could not stop trembling and the feeling of nausea would not go away. He took a drink from his canteen, which made no difference, and stared at the small pieces of flesh turning dark on his bare arms.

However many he picked off, there seemed to be just as many left.

Twice Coetzee requested orders by radio but was told to keep the section where it was, observing the road junction from where the armoured car had been firing. Occasionally the firing was near but most of the fighting seemed to be taking place closer to the mine buildings in the centre of town.

The sound of overrevving engines announced two jeeps heading out of town with the Katangan silver tiger pennant fluttering on their radio aerials. The first had a German World War Two machine-gun mounted on the bonnet – the famous MG 42. The other was literally festooned with men clinging on to each other – a dozen or more rebels trying to make good their escape.

The Legion's light mortar section in the next block already had the co-ordinates of the intersection. Cued by Coetzee over the radio, the first shell stopped the front jeep dead. It came to a halt right in the centre of the junction, slewed across the road. Several men leaped to the ground and ran to cover, leaving their wounded comrades behind. As they ran, they sprayed the houses and gardens all around with a panicky hail of 7.62 mm. bullets from their Kalashnikovs.

A rapid correction of aim by Coetzee over the radio and another mortar shell exploded beside the second jeep, setting on fire the petrol tank. In the heat of the fireball, hair flared and skin peeled off the popping, crackling bodies of the men on board. The driver and a front-seat passenger struggled out, fell to the ground and rolled in the dust, desperately trying to extinguish the flames that were fuelled by their own body fat.

'Beautiful!' Coetzee was grinning with pleasure as he radioed the mortar section to cease fire.

Roscoe could not look. He was traumatised with the filth of war, epitomised by the pink blotches on his skin and the ditches full of decomposing corpses among which they had had to take cover when under fire on their way into the town. They had burrowed into the stinking flesh, using decomposing human bodies like sandbags. Now, his nostrils full of the smell of meat roasting in the burning jeep, he wondered how one could ever wash so much filth off one's skin and feel clean again.

.5.

The three men lay in the dust, waiting for orders as the sun rose higher in the sky.

It was Bergman who called Coetzee's attention to a movement by the first jeep. They squinted through the hedge of red bougainvillea that grew above the garden wall. There was no firing nearby and in the lull someone in one of the bungalows had let a pet spaniel dog out for a leak. It trotted to a lamppost on the opposite pavement and lifted its leg. The peaceful suburban banality of the scene was unreal.

'I can't see anything now,' said Bergman. 'But I know something moved.'

'Keep your voice down,' rapped Coetzee. 'It's one of the Katangans from the leading jeep, trying to crawl back to his mates under cover of the smoke.'

Bergman lifted his weapon and rested it on the top of the wall beside Coetzee, careful to make no sudden movements in case some sniper was watching.

The sergeant adjusted the telescopic sight of the F1 and squinted through the haze of smoke and dust by the stranded jeeps. Through the lens he could just make out a white face with a black moustache. A pair of angry eyes seemed to be staring straight at him.

Coetzee put out a hand and grasped the barrel of Bergman's weapon. 'Hold your fire, man. We're in luck. That's no bleck. We got us a Cube out there, boys. Even better – we got ourselves a couple of the bastards.'

'What are they doing?' From his slightly lower position Bergman could see some movement but was unable to make out what the two men on the ground by the still-burning jeep were up to.

'Good question, man,' Coetzee muttered, concentrating all his attention on the scene alternately revealed and then hidden by drifting smoke.

He panned the rifle slowly from side to side, to compensate for the narrow field of vision. 'One of them's wounded. He's dragging a leg, so what the hell is he going back to the jeep for? Must be important.'

'To get a weapon?' Roscoe suggested dully from the ground where he was listening to the commentary.

'Negative,' Coetzee muttered. 'They both have Kalashnikovs. No, they're after something inside the jeep.'

There was a pause.

'Hold it,' Coetzee's commentary continued. 'One of the blecks on the jeep is alive. He's asking the Cubans for something! . . . a drink, by the look of it. The Cube . . . Christ! He's just bashed the poor Kaffir in the face. There's fraternal solidarity for you. Oh, Jesus . . .'

There was a brief scream from the jeep and then silence.

'The bleddy Cuban,' said Coetzee quietly, 'has just slit the bleck's throat.'

Roscoe lay in the dirt and dust. He picked a piece of the child's flesh off his trousers as the low-voiced commentary went on, wishing that he could clamp his hands over his ears and shut his eyes until it was all over . . . but that would be letting down Bergman and Coetzee. On the parade-ground at Castelnaudary he had chanted the Legionnaire's Code. He had sworn *to carry out the mission at whatever cost*. So what right had he to feel this way?

'Ah,' breathed Coetzee. 'He's found what he was after, *nuestro amigo cubano . . .*'

'What is it, Coot?' Bergman asked. 'I can't see from here.'

Coetzee slid down from his vantage point and pulled Bergman with him. Noticing Roscoe still slumped against the wall, his machine-pistol lying in the dust, the sergeant said roughly, 'Get a grip on yourself, Jack. That's an order. Shape up.'

Roscoe did not move.

With the stock of his F1 Coetzee hit him hard in the chest. 'You're wearing the flash of the *deuxième REP*, soldier.' He pointed to the dragon device on Roscoe's sleeve. 'Either pick up your weapon and look like a legionnaire or take that badge off your arm.'

Roscoe looked at the two other men. Hunkered down and looking at him, they were like two strangers talking to him from far away. He touched the dragon patch on his sleeve, feeling the texture. The two strangers both had Annamese dragons tattooed on their left forearms; his was just stitched onto a sleeve. That was the difference between them.

'Jack,' said Bergman softly. 'Come on, fella.'

With a huge effort, Roscoe picked up his weapon and checked the action.

'Good guy.' The sergeant gripped Roscoe's arm for encouragement.

He turned to Bergman with a raised eyebrow.

Bergman shook his head slightly, meaning: he'll be OK . . .

'Right, let's get on with it,' said Coetzee briskly. 'We know which way those two Cubes are going. They're heading out of town, so if we cut through the back of these gardens behind us, we'll head 'em off. If we can, we'll take them prisoner, for interrogation. But don't take any risks, eh? The Cubes are pros. Don't give them a chance to fire first.'

He led them at a crouching run through the garden of a bungalow, the radio bouncing heavily on his back. As the three pairs of boots pounded along a gravel path past the house a nervous woman's voice called out from inside, 'Who's there? Who's there?'

Roscoe skidded to a halt and hissed in French through a bullet-shattered window. '*C'est nous, la Légion.* Keep your heads down. We'll be back.'

There was an outburst of excited chatter in children's voices which the woman shushed. Roscoe hurried on after the other two men.

They stood, concealed behind the trunks of mature trees, watching a wall of greenery at the bottom of the garden. Coetzee held up one hand, giving Roscoe the signal to get behind a third tree.

There they waited, moving only their eyes, trying to see through the luxuriant foliage ahead of them. There was the sound of someone forcing a way through the undergrowth and one, then two voices speaking rapid Spanish.

One of the Cubans burst through the screen of greenery no more than ten metres away. There was blood streaming down his face from a scalp wound. His reply to Coetzee's challenge was the coughing of a Kalashnikov AK 47. Chips of bark flew in all directions as a magazine of 7.62 mm. ammunition shredded the side of the tree-trunk that shielded the sergeant's body.

Left-handing his rifle, Coetzee waited for the AK 47's magazine to be exhausted, then stepped calmly out from the other side of the tree-trunk to put a single round into the Cuban's chest. It impacted on the breastbone, converting it into a miniature fragmentation grenade of bone slivers which transfixed every organ of the chest cavity, hurling the instant corpse back into the greenery, where it crumpled out of sight in the undergrowth.

The second Cuban lurched through the wall of green, hidden from Coetzee's line of vision by the tree that had saved his life. Blood from a leg wound was soaking this man's trousers right down the left side. He took one look at his fallen comrade and swung his Kalashnikov round in the direction of the first man he saw, which happened to be Roscoe.

A short burst from Bergman's MAT 49 saved Roscoe's life for the second time that day, stitching the Cuban across the abdomen with 9 mm. slugs and spinning him round like a rag-doll. The body flopped to the ground so close that Roscoe could have touched him with his boot.

Coetzee walked up to the body and fired a single shot into the head. The body jerked and lay still. Roscoe stood staring at it, mesmerised.

'What's the matter with you?' Bergman shook his friend savagely as the echoes died away. 'What the hell were you waiting for, Christmas?'

'I'm sorry, Peter.' Roscoe's eyes focused on the man lying dead at his feet. He was cold with shock and trembling, aware that he had looked death in the face and lost. But for Bergman, it would be his body lying there.

He could not take his eyes off the dead Cuban on the ground. He told himself that the twisted corpse had been a soldier like him, who had known the odds. That was OK. That killing was legitimate. It was the death of the toddler that had unmanned him.

Bergman placed an arm round Roscoe's shoulders and hugged him. 'You're OK now, man. You're OK. Take it easy.'

Roscoe swallowed bile.

'*Faîtes gaffe, les gars!*'

The shout was from Coetzee. Feet braced apart, he was taking aim at a tall Katangan, in a bizarre mixture of Palm Beach shirt, tiger-skin jacket and fatigue trousers, who was coming at him from the side, running fast over the low stone-built garden walls with long, powerful hurdler's strides.

Coetzee squeezed the trigger a fraction of a second before the Katangan raised his AK 47 on the run. Nothing happened. There was a jam in the chamber of Coetzee's weapon. By reflex, Roscoe shouldered Bergman out of the line of fire, pressed the trigger of his machine-pistol and sprayed red over the Katangan's chest and belly.

The running man stopped in mid-stride, his momentum counteracted by the impact of the 9 mm. rounds. His face looked surprised more than hurt as his knees crumpled and he sagged to the ground where he stood, the Kalashnikov clattering away from his hand on the gravel path.

'Nice shooting, Jack,' grinned Coetzee. His voice was as calm as though they were on the firing range at Camp Raffali.

A long, low, shuddering moan came from the man Roscoe had shot. The three paras watched as he stretched out a bloody hand and started to crawl towards the first Cuban – the one Coetzee had taken out – leaving a glistening red snail-trail on the gravel of the garden path behind him. A babyish mewling sound came from between his teeth, gritted with pain.

There was no way the crawling man could live long. The jam cleared, Coetzee chambered a round and walked up to him.

Roscoe wanted to shout, 'Stop!' although he knew there was no point.

The sergeant fired one shot into the back of the man's head. The Katangan jerked and rolled over with a final spasm, grasping his belly with hands that shone bright red with blood. A sound halfway between a belch and a groan came from his mouth. A gobbet of blood came with it and trickled down his cheek.

'Was he going for his weapon?' asked Roscoe uselessly.

He looked from Bergman to Coetzee and wondered how they could be apparently so calm and in control of themselves. They looked as peaceful as if they had been practising on sandbag dummies, not sentient human beings like themselves.

Roscoe retched again. With the sour taste in his mouth came the awareness that he had soiled his trousers.

'Oh Christ!' he groaned.

Coetzee's eyes were flickering busily from the body to the wall of greenery from which another threat might emerge. On a hand-signal from the sergeant, Bergman walked into the undergrowth and put another single shot into the head of the first Cuban. Then he came back to Roscoe, sniffed and took in the stain on the other man's trousers.

He put his free arm around Roscoe's shoulders and muttered, 'It's OK, Jack. You're doing fine, man.'

Coetzee held up one hand for silence. He listened. Satisfied that there were no other sounds of movement nearby, he dropped to one knee and picked up something that had fallen from the first Cuban's hand.

'Lookit,' he said to Roscoe. 'This is what he went back to the jeep for.'

He held up a small and bloody leather pouch.

Bergman was walking back to them after picking up the Kalashnikov which the running man had dropped.

'You know something, Coot?' he grinned at the sergeant. 'This is your lucky day. That poor dumb bastard had his fire selector on Safe all the time.'

The two men grinned at each other.

'That's the way it goes,' chuckled Coetzee.

'I didn't need to kill him,' said Roscoe hollowly. 'I killed a man whose weapon would not have fired anyway.' He turned his head away, clutched a tree for support, and vomited.

Coetzee slung his rifle and loosened the draw string of the pouch he was holding. From it he poured into his large palm a stream of small glassy pebbles like badly made marbles. The big South African had a grin all over his freckled face.

'I don't know how much you guys know about diamonds,' he said to Bergman in an awed voice, 'but I'd say there's enough here to keep us happy for a long while to come. Genuine.'

.6.

Like most of the guys who dropped that day, I looked on
Kolwezi as a job we'd done – and done pretty well, by all
accounts. It's true that a few gun-freaks went around
boasting about how many Katangans they had blown away
but the rest of us just felt good that we had performed a
difficult task for which we'd spent five years of our lives in
training. Under-resourced and lightly equipped, the
deuxième REP's officers and men had achieved a
remarkable feat of arms, saving three thousand lives at the
cost of only five of our own men dead and twenty
wounded.

But Jack came back from Africa a changed man. I
thought he'd get over whatever was bugging him in a day or
so but instead it seemed to get worse. He didn't sleep, he
hardly talked and he hit the bottle every night. Oh, we'd
sunk plenty of glasses of beer during our time in the
Legion. Young men with time on their hands and money in
their pockets tend to drink too much but this was different:
Jack was drinking now to get drunk fast and stay that way
as long as possible.

> *Thinking to help by voicing what was on his mind, I asked him once whether he felt bad about having to change his pants that morning. He stared at me like a stranger.*
>
> *'You weren't the only one by a long way,' I said.*
>
> *'Jesus!' He looked like he was going to slug me between the eyes. 'D'you really think that's what's gnawing my guts out?'*
>
> *I couldn't get through to him at all. I realise now that Jack was a romantic who had dreamed dreams of martial glory whereas I had always known from my old man that war was shit. Still, whatever Jack's problem, I felt responsible for him because if it hadn't been for me, he'd have crapped out during the first six months' training and never made it into the paras. Then he'd never have dropped at Kolwezi and been bitten by the black dog.*
>
> *I wonder now whether Jack worked all that out for himself – in which case he had good reason to hate me. But would he then go on being my pal for eight years, waiting to get his own back by dropping me in the brown stuff that night in Turkey? No, it doesn't figure. Of course by then he had a different reason to hate me. It was the most basic of all the many reasons for which men kill each other: sexual jealousy.*

Roscoe's depression after Kolwezi was a complex made partly of guilt for all the bloodshed he had seen and taken part in and partly of the awful discovery that once again he had been acting a part. What he had originally thought would be an identity for life as a legionnaire had turned out to be yet another role he was playing. The costume had fitted, rehearsals had been fun, the props had been great to play with, the company had a reputation second to none, the lines had been written by Homer and Shakespeare – but the performance had found him wanting.

After Kolwezi, he knew beyond any shadow of doubt that it was not his destiny to be a soldier. Although tough enough when it came to taking punishment, he had no will to hand it out; a soldier must be able to do both.

Even before they returned to their base at Camp Raffali on Corsica, Roscoe's face showed the changes within. There were lines of tension which were out of place in a man of twenty-four. The haunted look in his dark eyes veiled the inner visions of the child whom Bergman had killed but who would otherwise have been the instrument of both their deaths. As Roscoe blinked that image away, he saw again the running man that he had killed, forever dying in mid-stride. Wherever Roscoe looked, whatever he saw, the crying child and the running man were superimposed.

He turned to poetry for the first time in five years, unearthing little-read books in the camp library and doing something he had not done in a long time: writing his own poems to try and express the anguish within. In the works of Siegfried Sassoon and Wilfred Owen – and, of course, the Legion's own American war poet, Alan Seeger, who had died in 1916 on the Somme – Roscoe found a solace and a sense of communion that he did not have with the men around him, who went about their daily routines as though Kolwezi was 'just a job' they'd done.

A poem of Wilfred Owen's ran through Roscoe's head, day and night, like the melody of a song that will not go away: 'I am the enemy you killed, my friend'.

The running man fell and heaved himself in unending agony along an eternal gravel path, groaning the words of the poem.

Roscoe's private torment was intensified by his inability to imagine what life had been like for the black man he had killed and thus come to terms with what he regarded as murder and maybe lay the ghost to rest. What scenes had that man called home? Where had he learned to hurdle like an Olympic athlete? Had he lived in a mud hut in the bush or a hovel of flattened oil cans in some shanty town? Had he a wife or maybe children? There were no answers – and never would be.

Comparing the verse of the First World War with his own post-Kolwezi work, Roscoe came to see that Owen and Sassoon and the rest had written to celebrate a noble grief for dead friends and other men's suffering, whereas Jack Roscoe's melancholy – or so he accused himself – was comprised at least in part of that less worthy sentiment, self-pity. He despised himself for it.

His self-imposed isolation from the men around him, including Bergman, brought a new perspective on the soldier's trade.

In return for his lost innocence he had gained, if nothing else that day in the dust and under the sun, with the smell of roasting human flesh in his nostrils, the understanding of one great truth. Soldiers, he now knew, are not responsible for war; they bloody their hands and dirty their souls fighting the battles arranged by cleverer men – soft-spoken civilians with clean hands and big bank accounts and power-hungry politicians seated at conference tables safely distanced from the firing line.

At the age of twenty-four, such thoughts are hard to handle on one's own. Roscoe tried talking things over a couple of times with Bergman, who listened patiently and tried to be helpful but plainly did not understand the turmoil in his friend's mind. Because there was no one else with whom he could ever broach the pent-up complex of feelings and insights, Jack Roscoe took to drink and found in the gentle goddess alcohol a figure of winged mercy who swooped tenderly down each night and shut his inner eyes to the horrors he had seen, so that he could sleep.

In the few days of action under the hot African sun, so often only millimetres or milliseconds from injury or death, Bergman had felt more alive than ever before. He looked forward eagerly to the next chance to measure himself against the challenge of battle. The problem, as he saw it, was that it could be years before the Legion went to war again – and he wanted another taste of action soon.

Roscoe wanted out on the first possible day.

For these diametrically opposite reasons, signing on for an extended tour of duty was out of the question for either man. Sergeant Coetzee, who was also due for demob in the near future, encouraged Bergman to think of Africa, saying that he was the kind of man who could make a good life south of the Equator. He gave Bergman the names of a couple of former Legion officers who were in the business of recruiting mercenaries.

The last day for extending their service contracts with the Legion came and went; by inaction Bergman and Roscoe became civilians at dusk. To re-enlist now would mean starting over again as *engagés volontaires* at Castelnaudary. Next morning, Bergman walked out of the gate of Camp Raffali for the last time without a backward glance or thought.

Paradoxically it was harder for Roscoe to leave the Legion than he had thought it would be. He could not stay, yet found it hard to go, obsessed by the thought that he had failed to fulfil the oath of loyalty sworn to his comrades five years before on the wet, windswept parade-ground at Castelnaudary.

Together with Bergman he put on civilian clothes for the first time in five years and walked out of the gate, past the guard-room, unsaluting and unsaluted. They took a taxi into Calvi town, to kill time until the ferry sailed to Marseille. From there the plan was to head for Antwerp, which Coetzee said was the best place in Europe to sell diamonds. He had divided the stones into three small piles, covered them and then drawn lots with the two younger men, in case one pile were worth more than another. Roscoe and Bergman knew nothing about pre-cious stones and had no idea what their shares were worth, but Coetzee had come up with some names of diamond dealers in Antwerp. Through the Legion's NCO network he seemed able to find answers to the most unlikely questions.

Selling illicit diamonds turned out to be harder than they had thought. The dealers shook their heads disparagingly over the dead Cuban's diamonds, offering to buy a few of the larger ones and inferring that the rest were worthless industrial stones. They knew that there was no way by which two young men of twenty-four with Legion-short haircuts could be the legitimate owners of uncut stones. With Kolwezi still very much in the news, they knew exactly where the stones had come from.

Disappointed at the poor offers, Bergman persuaded Roscoe to wait for Coetzee, in the belief that he could probably get them a better deal. Apart from anything else, the South African sergeant could understand Flemish, which he called Hollands. Bergman thought that might make a difference in Antwerp, although Roscoe said gloomily that Yiddish would be more useful when it came to selling diamonds.

They filled the time until Coetzee's demob date by heading south again and drifting along the Cote d'Azur, spending their savings from five years' soldiering at an alarming rate.

I knew Jack was sick but couldn't diagnose the illness. He soaked up booze like a sponge on legs. I didn't try to match him glass for glass, just kept him out of trouble and carried him back to our hotel room dead drunk some nights, feeling that it was all my fault.

A few times, I tried to talk him out of that black depression. The trouble was that I was no good with words and Jack was verbally very adroit. I'd seen some of those poems he wrote. I didn't like them, but they were clever.

One of them still sticks in my mind:

> A black sandbag is all you are
> And when I dig the steel in deep
> You are not supposed to weep.
> A little sand should trickle maybe
> But you lie crying like a baby . . .

Whenever I thought I was getting close to what bothered him, Jack would slip away out of reach, as though his own destruction was too urgent a priority to let my friendship slow it down. Some days I wished the sorry bastard would end the agony and drink himself to death . . . which is why I'd privately decided to follow up Coetzee's suggestion of finding work in Africa as a soldier of fortune. I was twenty-four with a taste for adventure, my solid build and tough-guy features looked better in uniform than civilian clothes. Also I liked the ring of the words . . .

'Mercenary? Oh no, ma'am, I'm a soldier of fortune.'

Shallow, but there it is. In those days I fancied the image of myself at the wheel of a jeep bouncing over dusty tracks on some African savanna with a .50 calibre machine-gun mounted on the rear, manned by my trusty comrade. Here the vision was unclear, the comrade faceless – but he sure as hell wasn't Jack Roscoe! What was I doing there? Why, rescuing damsels in distress, of course! And they – all beautifully proportioned and sexually generous – showed their gratitude to their heroic rescuer in appropriate ways. The dreams faded out into a shot of the sunset with THE END superimposed. I guess a lot of young men would still buy that kind of fantasy; it's easier than real life.

Anyways I'd planned to sell my share of the diamonds,

tell Jack I was splitting – and head for the great unknown in
Coetzee's vast continent. It didn't turn out like that because
of a dream of Roscoe's which was stronger than mine.

During our four years on Corsica, he had spent a lot of
time drooling over the rich men's toys moored in the harbour
at Calvi. Lying on his bed in the barracks, he used to pore
endlessly over boat magazines when most of the other guys
were studying the female anatomy in close-up and glorious
Technicolor. I couldn't count the number of times I had sat
waiting outside ship-chandlers' while Jack mooned about
inside, happy as a pervert in a porn shop as he fingered
shackles and toyed with compasses and bilge-pumps. Some
men have boating in their blood and he was one of them.

Many a sleepless night we had lain in a storm-lashed
two-man bivvy high in the Corsican mountains, with me
listening to Roscoe rambling on about ploughing a lonely
furrow in the wake of Sir Francis Chichester and Thor
Heyerdahl. Didn't mean a thing to me, but for Jack the
sound of wind and rain buffeting the thin canvas above our
heads was the howling gale filling a mainsail as he battled
his way against the elements, rounding Cape Horn!

I went along with his obsession, as a guy does when his
buddy cares deeply about something. I trudged around
harbours in our spare time, pretending to be interested in
the difference between one boat and another – in fact, they
all looked pretty damn similar to me!

. . . which is what gave me this idea. We'd headed back to
Marseille to meet up with Coetzee who was due to arrive
on the overnight ferry from Corsica. With an hour or so to
kill, Jack an' me went into a bar down by the harbour
called Chez Lars. Now there was a larger-than-life figure
from the Legion! Lars Larsen was a huge Swede who had
been an adjoint-chef in the old second para battalion
during the French war in Vietnam – ten years before the
Yanks arrived. He had dropped at Dien Bien Phu in 1954
and still walked with the limp he got that day. Lars was
what he himself called a strongbody – the only man I ever
saw actually lift two brawlers up off the floor and bang
their heads together in mid-air!

That day Jack was already pretty slewed at 10 a.m. I saw the look Larsen gave him when he passed the third glass of beer across the counter. It wasn't condemnatory. It was just plain sad. From his side of the bar, Larsen had seen more than a few Jack Roscoes in his time. It was like he was serving a dead man.

The chain of thought led me back to the last time Jack and I had been in a bar called Au Son Des Guitares, down by Calvi harbour. We had picked up a couple of gorgeous and very sexy German girls who had come there on holiday looking for sex. (There's a lot of women turned on by athletic guys in uniform and a fair number of them manage to take their vacations near Legion bases!) These two had hot pants all right. It was obvious we were going to score – or more exactly, that they were . . .

Jack's hand was lying on this girl's boobs and she had one leg over his thigh, rubbing herself against him and kinda purring. He didn't seem to be paying attention. I pushed my girl's head down out of the way and followed his eye-line to realise that he was watching a thirty-footer cast off and motor out of the harbour, more interested in that than the girl pleasuring herself on his thigh!

So there I sat in Larsen's that morning, having this flash revelation of what I thought would be Jack's salvation. But how to set it up? I wondered. Subtlety has never been my style and I didn't want this one to go wrong. Jack was always a stubborn s.o.b. and once he said no, that was it.

Hearing a blast of ship's siren as the ferry docked, we left the bar and walked down to the terminal, along a quay lined with fishing boats, colourful with bunting. It was a sunlit morning with the heat already building up. Roscoe had a headache and was wearing very dark wraparound sunglasses.

'Have you ever thought of buying a boat, Jack?' I asked kinda casually.

'Thought about it,' he grunted, far away.

'Thanks to the Cuban's pouchful of marbles,' I said, 'we're rich enough to buy one straight out. At least, we will be as soon as we sell the stones.'

'We?' Roscoe sounded bitter. 'I thought you were planning to try your luck in Africa, as a soldier of fortune with Coetzee?'

I hadn't realised it was so obvious. 'There's no hurry for that,' I said quickly, trying to convince myself as well as Roscoe. 'You know what, Jack? I've got the rest of my life to play soldiers. I could use a break first.'

He wasn't helping me one little bit. I pushed on slowly, as though the idea was breaking surface of its own accord. 'Why don't we buy ourselves a boat and maybe sail it around the Med for a while? Maybe around the world, who knows? It'd be fun.'

Roscoe slipped off the sunglasses. A spark of enthusiasm showed for a second through the gloom in his dark, haunted eyes. It flickered and went out with: 'Except for one thing, Peter. You don't like boats.'

I tried to prolong the moment of eye-contact. It was the first time since Kolwezi that I'd managed to penetrate the shadows among which my buddy spent the sober hours. 'I never fancied crewing for someone else, Jack,' I said. That much was true; I'd had enough of being shouted at by the De Wildes of the world to last me for a lifetime. 'But being master of my own vessel – that'd be something else, wouldn't it? Just you an' me and no one to yell orders at us. Think about it! The freedom of the deep blue sea and all that kinda stuff. How 'bout it, Jack?'

As the ferry drew in to the ramp, Coetzee was on deck, looking uncomfortable in civilian clothes. I gave him a wave. Roscoe wasn't looking at the ferry. He was scanning the yachts and fishing boats bobbing gently on the harbour swell. I could see that the thought of just taking off into the great blue yonder on his own craft was like a shot of some potent drug, straight into a vein, changing his pulse to a rhythm of life.

His eyes opened wide, as if all the colours of brass and paintwork and bunting on the boats and the reflections of the early sunlight dancing on the water had cut through the world of grey in which he was living.

'Are you serious?' he asked.

'Affirmative,' I said.

This was the old Roscoe looking at me now. The black dog ran yelping into the shadows. I had to stop myself grinning at my own cleverness. It seemed the trick had worked.

'Never been more serious in my life, pardner,' I said, sticking out a hand that Jack gripped hard. It was like pulling a drowning man on board the life-raft.

He punched me lightly in the chest and said softly, 'I know exactly the kind of boat to buy. We're going to have a ball, Peter.'

We flew north to Antwerp with Coetzee. Roscoe spent the journey with his head stuck inside yachting magazines. The best offer we received for our diamonds was worth, Coetzee said, not much more than a quarter of their real value. However, as he pointed out, we couldn't cut the stones ourselves and didn't have a lot of options. Roscoe accepted. He would have taken even less than we were offered. All that mattered to him was having enough to buy a boat! Coetzee hung onto his stones, saying that he had a pal in the Illicit Diamond Police in Johannesburg who would help find a buyer.

We found Stella Maris lying in the marina at Cap d'Agde. She was a pretty 8½-metre fibreglass-hulled four-berth cabin cruiser, registered in Bremen, with an aluminium mast, a full set of new sails and a 50-horsepower Perkins marine diesel, plus a rigid inflatable tender with its own outboard motor – rather like the Zodiacs we had used for amphibious training in the deuxième REP. According to the yacht broker who was a Dutchman, the boat was going cheap because her owner needed cash in a hurry.

I tried to interest Coetzee in buying a third share. The Coot thought we were both crazy and said so, limiting his contribution to a name. We used a bottle of Veuve Clicquot, for which he paid, to rechristen our boat REP II. Coetzee said no other name would do for a boat owned by two ex-paras.

As soon as she was ours, we set about painting and

*varnishing the woodwork and overhauling cordage and
sails. I took it easy but Jack worked night and day to get
REP II seaworthy. It was a helluva lot more fun than
polishing boots, that's for sure.*

One week later, Jan Coetzee watched *REP II* motor between the
arms of the harbour mole at Cap d'Agde on a heading of south-
east by south. There was a stiff south-westerly breeze which
made ideal sailing weather. The two skippers had tossed a coin
for the right to choose their first port of call and Roscoe won.
They were heading for Palma de Mallorca on the first leg of the
round-the-world voyage.

Bergman cut the motor as they cleared the mole, the open sea
ahead. He cupped his hands to his mouth and called across the
water, 'Are you sure you don't want to come along for the ride?'

'Negative,' Coetzee waved his hands in pretended horror at
the idea. 'When I die, I want to die dry. And later rather than
sooner, eh?'

REP II wallowed in the swell while the two new skippers
raised a small jib and the mainsail. The wind caught her.
Roscoe scrambled inexpertly back into the cockpit and grabbed
the helm as *REP II* heeled over to port and gathered way. He
and Bergman continued exchanging amiable insults with
Coetzee until out of voice range.

The big South African stayed on the mole until *REP II* was
just one of a score of specks on the sunset sea. His thoughts
were half a world away, seeing African sunsets over the endless
velvety rolling veldt in his home country.

As he drove off in a hired car for Perpignan airport, he was
thinking of his own dream of founding a rather special kind of
airline in which he would have liked Peter Bergman as a partner.
He had a feeling that their paths would cross again, as happened with men who had served together in the Legion.

.7.

Salt water was the best medicine to heal the wounds in Roscoe's soul. Learning the vagaries of wind and current on the open sea was a round-the-clock therapy which left no time for him to dredge gloom from the past. He slept little, using his spare time getting to know every inch of *REP II* above and below the waterline, like a lover obsessed with exploring his mistress's body.

Roscoe was the better skipper by far when they were, as he called it, under canvas. He had a feeling for the poetry of wind and sail while Bergman preferred motor to mainsail and took no pleasure in tacking against the wind when it was his turn at the helm. He allowed Roscoe to instruct him in the age-old skills of sextant and compass but generally preferred to crew and let Cap'n Jack do the driving – or else drop the sails and motor for a while.

They moored in Palma harbour for a few days on a mad spending spree, buying expensive gadgets for the boat, luxury food, a larger fridge to keep it in and a more powerful outboard. They bought windsurfing boards and two sets of scuba gear with which to discover the silent world beneath the waves.

If the days were fun, the nights were a revelation to Bergman. Ashore in the evenings, he would watch Roscoe's smouldering dark-eyed good looks at work, amused that his buddy could – as the Legionese expression had it, *draguer n'importe quelle nana* – pick up any girl. The classier she was, the more potent was the aphrodisiac in the words: 'We were paras in the Foreign Legion.' It was Roscoe who got the pick of the girls; there was something about Bergman's hard-eyed stare and his broken nose that made some women wary of him.

From Mallorca they headed north to the Côte d'Azur where Bergman had always wanted to try his luck at the gaming tables. He was good at cards; in the Legion he had often doubled his pay during a weekend poker session and since Kolwezi he had been feeling extra lucky. The first night in Monaco he lost $1000 at each of three games: *chemin de fer*, roulette and baccarat. Convinced that persistence was the clue to success, he went back next evening with twice as much money in his pocket. On the third night his stake money was everything he had left. Right up to the last minute he was convinced that his luck was about to change.

With Bergman broke, Roscoe advanced his buddy all the money he had left to stake on one glorious evening of gambling madness. Dressed in white tuxedos bought for the occasion, they started with dinner at the Casino, drank champagne and watched incredulously as the last of their money was shovelled away into the croupier's pile on the green baize table.

Bergman awoke next morning feeling gloomy. Roscoe said to look on the bright side: they still had the boat and would earn some more money by plying for hire. Thanks to his looks and persuasive tongue, they found plenty of charterers – always female. Through the summer of '78 *REP II* pursued a zigzag course eastwards along the northern shores of the Med, leaving behind at each port a couple of satisfied girls who promised to tell their friends when they got home.

In between charters Roscoe was writing what he said was a novel entitled *Sun, Sail and Sex* but Bergman began to hunger for action more exciting than the panic of trimming sails in an unforeseen squall or the need to cast off fast to avoid a jealous boyfriend. He complained about the endless chores of looking after the boat. It was *your goddam boat*, not *our boat* any longer. By September the great adventure seemed over, replaced by squabbles over trivial things like whose turn it was to clean the salt water head or do the shopping in the next port.

They moored in the harbour at Kusadasi in Turkey, more or less agreed to sell *REP II* as soon as possible and go their separate ways. It was easier said than done, in a market with more vessels for sale than potential purchasers. Food supplies at a record low, Roscoe went hustling holidaymakers to charter *REP II* for day trips or a cruise along the coast. He came back with two long-legged blonde Swedish girls in tow and showed them over the boat. The girls seemed hesitant and talked in the cockpit for a long while in Swedish while Bergman and Roscoe, clad only in denim shorts, waited on the foredeck for their decision.

'What are they on about?' Bergman asked, unable to follow a word. 'Haven't they got any money?'

'From the way they're sizing us up,' said Roscoe, 'I think they're deciding who gets you and who gets me.'

'Oh God,' yawned Bergman in mock-complaint. 'We're trapped on a treadmill of sex, Jack.'

The treadmill stopped turning in the early hours of the following day. An autumn storm that blew up out of nowhere raped *REP II* on the rocks of Samos and pounded her to death before dawn. Once the fibreglass hull opened up, the only course was to abandon ship.

As he steered the inflatable dinghy through the heavy swell to the shore, just visible in the pre-dawn gloom, Bergman was feeling glum. All their capital had gone to the bottom. He cut the outboard, beached the dinghy and helped ashore the two Swedish girls, Marianne and Eva. They were shivering from cold and fear, and dressed only in their wet underwear. Except for a few clothes and their handbags, all their belongings had gone down in the wreck.

As the men pulled the dinghy higher up the pebble beach to avoid it being damaged in the heavy swell, there was already flotsam from *REP II* littering the water's edge. Roscoe headed up the beach towards where the girls were pulling on wet jeans and sweaters.

'Could have been worse,' said Bergman quietly, so they would not hear. 'You an' me are trained to swim five hundred metres in full combat gear, Jack. We might have swum ashore but they'd never have made it, with that sea running. So we were lucky. If we hadn't been able to launch the dinghy at the last moment, those girls would have drowned, man.'

Roscoe's head was aching from too much Turkish wine the previous evening. He turned and threw himself on Bergman, knocking him back into the waves and trying to force his head under water.

'You smashed our boat up,' he gasped through gritted teeth as they tumbled breathless, locked together in the undertow. 'That's all that remains of our diamonds going to the bottom out there, you stupid bastard. You call that lucky?'

Bergman managed to break the grip and surfaced, gasping for air. He landed a blow on Roscoe's jaw that sobered him up a bit and then fended off the feeble jabs that Roscoe aimed at him to use up his anger.

By the time they staggered back onto the beach the girls had found shelter in a fisherman's cottage on the clifftop. The storm had died as swiftly as it had risen. In any other circumstances, it would have been a beautiful dawn. The two men sat shivering on the rocks as the sun came up in a cloudless sky, waiting to see if anything worth salvaging was washed up. The entire bay into which they had been driven by the wind was littered with broken or shattered reminders of the great plan to circumnavigate the globe.

'It was your fault,' said Roscoe morosely. 'If I'd been at the helm, this would never have happened.'

'Now hold on!' Bergman wanted to avoid an argument. 'I may have been at the helm, Jack, but what the hell were you doing to help? You didn't even come on deck until after we'd hit the rocks and by then it was too late.'

'You could have called me on deck!'

'What do you mean? I yelled my goddam head off. You must have been too pissed to hear. I could hardly leave the helm in a gale and come below to get you, could I?'

Roscoe pulled a life-jacket marked *REP II* out of the shallows and hurled it back again, far beyond the breakers. He drifted away to the far end of the beach. Bergman was gloomily surveying the useless wreckage when the after-storm calm of waves lapping and seabirds calling was completely shattered by a blood-curdling noise. He lifted his eyes to find the source of it and saw Roscoe, stark naked and running along the water's edge, jumping over the flotsam and laughing his head off.

The cliffs echoed the sound back in a weird cacophony. Roscoe fell onto the pebbles and rolled into the waves, laughing helplessly. When he had got back his breath, he crawled back onto the beach, rolled onto one elbow and shouted slowly for clarity: 'It's all gone, Peter. All gone. We're free.'

He ran back, splashing through the shallows, pulled on his wet jeans and stuck out a hand for Bergman to shake.

'Seriously, Jack,' said Bergman, 'what the hell *were* you doing between when I shouted for you to come on deck after the first squall hit and when we actually went onto the rocks?'

Roscoe laughed until tears ran down his face and he collapsed on the pebbles and rolled helplessly down into the spume and the wreckage.

Bergman stood over him. 'Come on, you stupid bastard. What's so funny?'

Roscoe was wheezing, trying to get his breath back. 'I was in the bunk with Marianne. She had her legs clamped so tight on my ears I didn't hear a thing. And when we struck the rocks and everything turned upside-down, I . . .' He began laughing again.

'I thought she was having an orgasm,' he gasped. 'She nearly twisted my head off between those powerful thighs of hers. It wasn't until I felt cold salt water gushing all over us that I realised we were sinking and Marianne was screaming and clinging to me so tightly because she was frightened of drowning.'

Bergman collapsed helpless with mirth at the image Roscoe's words conjured up. He lay on his back, legs in the water, bellowing with laughter. The noise echoed back from the cliffs and set Roscoe off laughing again.

At the top of the cliff, the two Swedish girls were standing by the ancient car which the old fisherman had laboriously hand-cranked back to life, so he could drive them into town. One of them turned to the grizzled old man who could understand very little English. Pointing to the two men fooling about on the beach below, she spoke slowly and clearly: 'We go without them, please. You see, they are mad.'

When the old guy returned from town, we offered to sell him the equipment we had salvaged from the wreck. He knew he had us by the short-and-curlies and haggled prices down to rock bottom, calculated in gasolene for the inflatable's outboard. That shrewd old devil worked it out so that in return for just enough juice to get back to the mainland he could grab everything we had to sell.

We had just concluded the deal when a complication arrived in the shape of the fisherman's oldest son who decided to take us to the cleaners. He sat on his father's upturned boat with a big grin on his face and told us in broken English to go fuck ourselves. Apparently the local police were on the way, alerted by the girls' story and he reckoned on having our gear for nothing once we'd been hauled off to gaol. I'd heard that the Greek authorities made the owner of a shipwrecked boat pay Customs duty on the full value and clapped you in gaol if you couldn't pay, so I didn't want to spend too long arguing.

Before I'd thought of a solution to this new problem, Jack had solved it by calling the son names and jabbing him with a wicked left hand to goad him into a fight. The Greek took a swing at Jack and never knew what hit him. He was just a big-mouth brawler, whereas we were trained in dirty tricks – pros at the game. The old man didn't seem too worried. I had a feeling he was maybe pleased that someone had taught his son a lesson. He helped us fill the petrol tank on the inflatable. The last thing I did was give Jack's expensive 100-metre-proof diving watch to the old guy as a present for his son when he woke up, in the hope that the gift would keep both their mouths shut till we were safely back in Turkish waters.

We motored slowly back to the mainland in the inflatable, economising on fuel and feeling pretty damn low. At Kusadasi, the mainland port opposite Samos, we sold the dinghy and the motor and split the proceeds fifty-fifty. There was enough to buy us each a ticket to somewhere else.

Why didn't we say goodbye there and then? I guess we couldn't really believe we had gotten through all that money so fast and really were flat-broke. The whole riches-to-rags saga of REP II had taken place inside three months.

About midday we were sitting in a bar next to an ancient caravanserai on the waterfront, going over the best moments in our wild odyssey, when a couple of Turkish policemen arrived, together with the two girls we had last seen semi-naked at dawn on the beach of Samos. Marianne and Eva had crossed on the ferry and been hassled by the Turkish immigration for not having exit stamps on their passports, so they were feeling pretty mean when they set eyes on us, apparently living it up in the first bar they walked past!

They accused us of all the crimes in the book, including rape. At first the cops – being Turks – didn't take the girls' accusations too seriously. However, cops are pretty much the same the world over, and when these two found out that we had just sold the motor and the dinghy, they said we had broken some law or other. Our money was confiscated, down to the last cent.

Then they hit us with Catch 22! It is an offence for a foreigner to be broke in Turkey. The only thing that saved us from going to gaol was Jack's sexual technique! Marianne, the girl with whom he had been making love when he should have been helping me on deck, took a pile of soggy traveller's cheques out of her handbag at the police station and literally bailed us out in return for Jack's continued services.

We spent the rest of that unreal week together as a foursome. Jack and I couldn't even buy a beer without asking one of the girls for money, but for some reason it seemed funny. I don't recall much about those few days except a long conversation over little cups of Turkish coffee one drowsy afternoon when the two girls tried to understand why Jack an' me were buddies. We seemed so dissimilar, they said, with him always scribbling poetry and me looking like a soldier out of uniform. I guess women never do understand men's friendships.

Come Friday, we took the girls to Izmir Airport for their flight back to reality. Half an hour later I was at the poste restante counter, picking up a new credit card to replace one that had been lost in the wreck. In the batch of mail was a printed invitation that had travelled from France to my mother's address in Toronto and back to Turkey.

To celebrate what the whole world recognised as a masterly feat of arms at Kolwezi, the new colonel of the deuxième REP had invited all past members of the regiment to a weekend get-together at the base in Calvi. I used my new credit card to buy two air tickets to Paris. I never stopped to think whether Jack would really want to go back and be reminded about Kolwezi.

We sailed into Calvi on an overnight ferry from Marseille packed with returning ex-legionnaires. It was a floating reunion from stem to stern; the bar had not done such good trade in years. Then came two roistering days and nights without sleep back in the all-male atmosphere of the Legion.

Among the familiar faces was Coetzee who had flown all the way from South Africa just to be there. On the Monday, he was flying home, while Jack and I were catching the ferry to Marseille with a vague plan of finding a crewing job somewhere along the Côte d'Azur.

The Coot caught up with us in Au Son Des Guitares, down by the port. He took out a wad of traveller's cheques, tore several off and countersigned them.

'What's this?' I asked.

'Buy an air ticket to Jo'burg,' he said. 'I want you to come and see me about a job just now, Pete. We'll go across to Kruger and look at the big game. South Africa's a good country for a man like you. You'll like it, genuine.'

I looked at the traveller's cheques and along the bar to where Roscoe was sitting alone. He had been high all weekend, but in a frenzied overdone way which made me wonder whether he was running from the black dog again. I didn't feel that I could walk out on him.

'Thanks for the offer, Coot,' I said, 'but Jack's my buddy.'

'Are you two joined at the hip or something?' Coetzee yelled at me.

'Suppose,' I wondered aloud. 'Suppose Jack comes along too?'

He shook his head, his hand poised over the traveller's cheques. 'Make up your mind quick, eh? I've got a plane to catch.'

'I'll come if Jack can.'

'What the hell!' The big South African shrugged. He signed several more cheques and pushed them across the table. 'OK, so Roscoe comes too. See you both next week.'

.8.

At first I didn't recognise Coetzee when he came to meet us at Johannesburg's Jan Smuts Airport. It was Roscoe who nudged me and hissed, 'Jesus! It's the Great White Hunter himself!'

I elbowed Jack in the ribs to shut him up. I'd known all along that I would have to watch the undercurrent of animosity that ebbed and flowed between him and the Coot. Jack did a fair impression of the Coot in a little speech laced with words like genuine, bleddy and bleck. It had raised laughs among the English Mafia in the Legion but I hoped he wasn't going to try it here.

When I saw the Coot, I had to stop myself from smiling too. He was wearing a khaki bush shirt and baggy shorts down to his knees with long socks and canvas boots. Clamped on his head was a sweat-stained wide-brim hat with a leopard-skin band! To Jack's and my European eyes, the effect was way over the top. Most of the people in the International Arrivals area were in business suits and city clothes.

He hustled us across to the private side of the airport

where a Beechcraft Bonanza was parked, which belonged to him. Each side of the fuselage bore the legend FLY COETZEE AIR, painted above an Annamese dragon, our emblem from the deuxième REP. My eyes accustomed to the sleek lines of jet aircraft, I thought the Beech boringly old-fashioned at first sight.

· Coetzee told us that he had bought up a bush airline which had gone bust and also owned a Titan Courier with extra tanks that gave it a range of over two thousand miles. That sounded more like a real aircraft to my ignorant ears.

'So why'd you come to collect us in this one?' I asked.

The Coot just laughed. 'You'll see!'

He clambered onto the wing and into the pilot's seat, motioning me into the right-hand position while Jack used the double doors at the back and sat down in the passenger compartment behind us with the baggage. He had plenty of room back there but Coot and I were jammed shoulder-to-shoulder.

Coot had just gotten his commercial pilot's licence but he had been flying privately since he could drive a car. He said it was no big deal, just a part of living on a remote farm in the Northern Transvaal where he had grown up. I watched him zip through the pre-flight checks without effort, get clearance from the tower, open the throttle – and away we went!

I had been expecting high-G acceleration from that 285-horsepower engine up front. After rolling along the runway for ten or twelve seconds, we were still going slower than a car in the fast lane. When we lifted off at 70 knots, I couldn't believe it. Coot hardly touched the controls so it seemed like the Beech was flying itself.

At 100 knots true airspeed our rate of climb must have been around 1,000 feet per minute but the engine was quiet; we didn't have to raise our voices to talk. Jack was silent in the back. I glanced round and saw him resting a piece of paper on the folding table to scribble one of his goddam poems. Upside-down I read something about soaring above guilt-edged clouds before Jack covered the paper.

The sheer poetry of flight was getting to me in a different

way: I didn't have to put it into words. It always seemed
more important to me to live a good experience rather than
waste time thinking about it — but that was the difference
between Jack and me . . .

Coot levelled out at 3,500 feet. He was giving me a
running commentary on what he was doing, what the
different controls were for, what to do if this or that
happened. He was so talkative, I thought maybe he was
showing off, although that wasn't his style at all. He could
have been talking Swahili for all I understood. I could only
catch a word here and there: 'Now at 3,500 feet the 75 per
cent power setting (2,500 rpm / 24 in. manifold pressure)
gives an indicated 165 knots which computes into a TAS of
173 knots . . .' And: 'If you climb the A 36 Bonanza to
12,000 feet and use a 55 per cent power setting, you can add
11 per cent to the range, genuine!' And: 'There are four
degrees of washout on the wings, Pete. Now, the flaps are a
watered-down Fowler type . . .'

That sort of stuff was exhilarating. The words Coot was
using didn't mean a thing to my brain, but I swear they
connected in my bowels. Maybe that's what poetry does to
people like Jack.

It was just as well I wasn't too bowled-over because,
without any warning, Coot lifted the throw-over control
yoke and swung it across in front of me. 'You've got it!' he
grinned. 'She's all yours, Pete!'

Like I said, I hadn't understood one single word so far.
My eyes had been glued to the dials and controls, the
switches and buttons. The last time I looked out of the
window, the haze-covered sprawl of Pretoria was on our
left. Below us now was an endless expanse of open country,
dotted here and there with farms. Not even on the sea had I
felt so much space around me.

I placed my hands warily on the control yoke and my feet
on the rudder pedals and felt . . . There's no other way to
explain it, but to say that I felt the Beech's control surfaces
talking to me through my fingertips and the soles of my
feet! I could feel the forces bearing on the airframe as
though my own nerves were threaded through the

inanimate alloys of which the craft was made. I felt the airflow pushing against the rudder and the ailerons as if they were made of my skin. Man becomes machine? The hairs stood up on the back of my neck.

Coetzee was a good instructor. I knew that from the way he'd run our platoon in the deuxiéme REP. *His voice fed the information I needed into my left ear just at the moment I needed it: the functions of the various dials, knobs and switches on the instrument panel. Everything he said made immediate sense. Nothing had to be repeated because I already knew it somehow. If I believed in reincarnation, that would be one explanation. Maybe it's like that when a prodigy picks up an instrument for the first time and knows how to play Mozart. It was a moment of revelation as time-stopping as an orgasm.*

In that second I knew that I was born to fly! It was awful to think that I might never have discovered my destiny but for the chance of palling up with Coetzee in the Legion. How else would a poor boy from Toronto have made friends with a Transvaal farmer and been given such a break? How goddam cruel of Fate, I thought, if I'd got my arse shot off at Kolwezi or drowned in the shipwreck on Samos, to die never knowing the thrill of piloting a light aircraft. It was like all my life until then was just preparation for that moment.

When I tried to convey something of this experience to Wu, he said that I was talking about the moment of my spiritual birth, when I began to be Me and not just a lump of clay shaped by where-I-was and what-I'd-done. He said it was then that my spirit came out of the shadows of time and settled into my flesh.

The next hour at the controls passed in seconds for Bergman. They left the haze of Johannesburg and Pretoria behind and pursued a zigzag cross-country course selected by Coetzee to show off something of his country to two Europeans who had thought it was all going to be like the media pictures of mine-tailings and riots in shantytowns. They overflew fertile farmland and unfenced plains where grazing herds of antelope and giraffe scattered at the noise and shadow of the Beechcraft.

'Where are we heading?' shouted Roscoe from the back seat.

Coetzee thrust a map at him and pointed. 'The Waterberg, between Vaalwater and Thabazimbi.'

Roscoe took the map and read the place names. What kind of a country had neighbouring towns with names like Warmbaths, Naboomspruit and Mabula? And what about Bophuthatswana, a homeland over which they were flying at that moment?

'How do you pronounce this place?' he shouted.

Coetzee grinned, 'We shorten it to Bop.'

Roscoe looked down as they circled a few hundred feet above a village of white-painted circular mud huts with thatched roofs. Timeless Africa, he thought, a flush of exhilaration coursing through his veins.

Coetzee was so impressed with his pupil in the right-hand seat that he took the controls back only for the approach to his private airfield.

'Home, sweet home!' he called, pointing an arm through the open window. Roscoe stopped scribbling and looked down to see a landing-strip that looked too short to be real. There was a windsock, a hangar and on a hillock stood a sprawling, single-storey white-walled house with a thatched roof and a huddle of workers' huts behind it. Nearby was a wind-driven water pump slowly turning in the breeze. In the far distance a few dots of white showed where Coetzee's neighbours lived.

It was the beginning of summer. Clouds were building up for the afternoon showers as Roscoe left Coetzee and Bergman clambering over the two other planes in the hangar. His nostrils full of the smells of Africa, he walked up to the house, a couple of black servants carrying the baggage behind him.

There he introduced himself to Coetzee's wife Sophy, a pretty, quiet woman who smiled a lot. Within a quarter of an hour she had told Roscoe the story of her life. She and Jan Coetzee had been childhood sweethearts and it was her decision to marry another man which, so she said with her quiet smile that dared him to disbelieve, had sent Coetzee off to join the Legion ten years before. Now they were together again after a recent divorce had left her with a couple of young children to bring up.

It was raining now. They sat on the covered stoep and Roscoe asked questions about the country. Like her husband, Sophy Coetzee wanted him to like South Africa and its people.

'Please,' she said, 'don't judge us by European standards, Jack. Life here is very different. Not all Vaalies are hymn-singing, bearded folk-heroes with a Bible in one hand and a gun in the other. We're real people. If we have different solutions to problems, maybe the problems are different, eh?'

As happens with some Europeans when they first set foot on the Dark Continent, Roscoe was falling in love – not with Coetzee's wife but with Africa itself. Dinner was in the open air, on a terrace adjoining the house. The rain had left the evening air fragrant and cool. They ate *braaivleis* coriander – ribs barbecued over an open fire – with *bobotie*, a dish of richly flavoured curried mince that was Coetzee's favourite food. But there were also *sosaties* and *pofadder* and a *melktert* to end with, washed down with a large quantity of Castle beer.

While they ate, the radio was reporting the day's news. After the white government of Rhodesia had bowed to the wind of change, a fifty-year-old Methodist bishop had been elected the country's first black prime minister. Joshua Nkomo's supporters had declared war on the bishop's followers with the result that Rhodesian troops had been despatched across the Zambian border to destroy Nkomo's home.

'Our neighbours,' said Coetzee cryptically.

Sophy had left them to read the children a bedtime story. Bergman wanted to talk flying so Roscoe left the table and walked down to the perimeter fence. It was dusk. As the lights came on, he could see the coiled razor wire that ran along the top and the foot of the fence. Beyond lay the vast black expanse of Africa – the Dark Continent, the space on old maps that had been filled with decorations of fanciful legendary beasts and enscrolled warnings like *Hic Sunt Leoni*! The romances of Haggard and Kipling and Edgar Rice Burroughs flitted through Roscoe's memory but also Karen Blixen's evocative prose: 'I had a farm in Africa . . .'

Roscoe recited the opening of the book, spine tingling with subdued excitement as he sniffed the night, inhaling deeply with his eyes closed. He was sure the air smelled different from the way it did in Europe. Here it was perfumed by the scent of rain on warm earth and strange blossoms, certainly. But it was more than that. Blood . . . He sniffed again, certain he could smell blood. It was blood spilled in violence – an infinitesimal one part in a trillion – but also an eternal flow of menstrual blood and warm, nourishing, oxygen-rich blood of the placenta. That was the smell of Africa at night. He thought he could hear drumming faintly in the distance.

Roscoe turned his back on the perimeter lights and let his eyes adjust to the starlight. Above him in the clear sky the constellation of Orion was familiar but in the wrong place and the Southern Cross replaced the Plough, twinkling its warning that nothing – not the sky, not emotions, not moral values – was the same here as north of the Equator. This was the land of the running man and the crying child, yet by coming back to face them he had laid their ghosts to rest at last.

.9.

They spent a week on safari watching Africa's big five – buffalo, leopard, lion, elephant and rhino – plus fifty different kinds of buck in scenery and among birdlife that defied imagination. By the time they returned to Coetzee's farm it was tacitly understood that Bergman was going to stay in South Africa, get his pilot's licence and become Coetzee's partner. He liked the country and the people. His name and blond Germanic looks earned him a friendly reception from the Afrikaners he had met. Another plus was that his knowledge of German enabled him to understand a fair amount of written Afrikaans; he felt that he could swiftly pick up the spoken language.

Roscoe asked a lot of awkward questions, like why Coetzee had chosen a base miles from Johannesburg or Pretoria but near the borders of Zambia, Zimbabwe and Mozambique and who were the phantom partners who were putting up most of the money for Coetzee Air?

When Coetzee hedged, Roscoe said outright, 'I've been reading between the lines in the newspapers, Peter. Something big's going on here, that we're not supposed to know about. I reckon the Coot's so-called partners are politicians, not businessmen. And let's face it, you may be the best flier in the world one day but in a country like this there are thousands of qualified pilots for him to employ, so why drag you halfway across the globe and train you for the job?'

They were sitting after dinner in Coetzee's office on the night before Roscoe was due to fly back to Europe. The office desk was a door over a couple of trestles, littered with spare parts, unpaid bills, radio sets – all the paraphernalia of a small charter airline. The room smelled of grease and oil. On the wall hung a couple of M16 automatic rifles and a double-barrelled twelve-bore that could stop an elephant. There was a large map of the continent of Africa and detailed charts with distances, flying times and charter rates pencilled in. Below them, on a bench sat a VHF transceiver, a single sideband HF set and an impressively large multi-channel communications receiver, all knobs and dials. The up-to-date communications equipment made up for the book-keeping system which was just an old-fashioned spike onto which Coetzee thrust an oil-grubby note after each job.

'You know,' said Roscoe, 'If you two guys are going to spend your time up in the sky, you need a manager with his feet on the ground to keep this place in order.'

'Are you offering?' Coetzee joked.

'Yes.'

I can still see Coot's office as it was that night. We were toasting our partnership in witblitz or white lightning, as they call the local firewater.

I told Jack he was crazy to want to drive a desk but he just smiled that secretive smile of his and said he fancied bringing some sort of order to the chaos. Coetzee was so damned relieved to be shot of the admin side, I think he'd have said yes to the devil taking the job on.

'Only one thing, Jack,' he warned. 'You'll have to keep your mouth shut, eh? I've already told Pete: never discuss with anyone a client, a cargo, a destination or a fee.'

Jack nodded solemnly. I burst out laughing: 'Jesus, Coot! Jack here's so damned secretive, he doesn't tell himself what

*he thinks half the time.' Except in those goddam poems, I
could have added.*

*We were set for success. Instead came disaster. On 3
November 1978 the story broke in the world's Press:
Connie Mulder, the South African Minister of the Interior
was alleged to have appropriated £35 million to set up all
kinds of 'grey enterprises' of which Coetzee Air was one.
Overnight we had no customers and no secret subsidy to
keep us afloat either.*

*I never understood politics. As far as I could work out,
Mulder's only crime was getting caught out. His
misfortune – which blew up into a government-rocking
scandal on the scale of Watergate – was labelled
Muldergate. It broke a lot of people but, to Coetzee's
surprise, we didn't go under. That was thanks to Jack. He
had worked out that although our original sponsors were
out of business, there were plenty of other people who
could use a discreet little airline. He'd disappear to Jo'burg
for a day or two once a month and come back with a new
client, seemingly with no more difficulty than he had
hustled charters for REP II. It seemed that every frontier on
the map of Africa had dozens of customers willing to pay
for the privilege of crossing it without the usual tiresome
formalities. They weren't worried about showing a
passport and having some guy poke through their bags.
The sort of formalities that bothered our new clients varied
from being relieved of all their cash and valuables by armed
border guards to being put up against a wall and shot.*

*We worked for anyone who could pay: black, white and
every other colour you can get to stick on human skin. We
had clients from all over the world. Because we did the job
and kept our mouths shut, it wasn't long before the spooks
sniffed us out and used us for a snatch or a drop or a
clandestine pick-up whenever they wanted what the CIA
used to call plausible denial.*

*Flying for those clients was a hell of a way of getting to
be a good pilot or a dead one! We'd often land on a dirt
road in the middle of the bush at dead of night with only
half a dozen hand-held torches as a flare-path. Sometimes*

we could chance a single pass very low, using the wing
lights as searchlights; sometimes we could only go in
blind – as they say, on a wing and a prayer.

Leading this life, it was only a question of time before I
met and fell in love with a lady called Pilatus Porter . . .

Known unromantically as the Jimmy Durante of
aviation, this ugly, long-nosed, square-sided flying freak
from Switzerland is built by the Oerlikon group to make up
for their ack-ack guns knocking so many other planes out
of the sky.

I first heard about the turbo-prop Porter from a crazy
flier called Brad Mason that I met in a bar in Kinshasa. He
said he had learnt to fly her while working for Air America
in Laos during the Vietnam War. When I got into an
argument with him about the Porter's STOL capability, he
swore that he had landed and taken off in less than a
hundred feet, using inclined landing-strips cut out of near-
vertical mountainsides by Meo hill tribesmen.

Brad's technique apparently involved using the gradient
to stop him incoming and simply dropping off the side of
the mountain to build airspeed outgoing.

Since most of his other hair-raising stories had ended
with: 'There I was, clean outta fuel and two hundred klicks
to go – thought I was gonna die that time for sure . . .' I
didn't altogether believe him. But when he said he had a
Porter in Kenya, used for crop-spraying, and offered me a
demo flight next day, I had to go.

Twenty-four hours later, I was sixteen hundred miles to
the east with Kilimanjaro on the horizon, sitting on a
cushion of cloud. In front of me was an instrument panel
that looked like something out of the 1940s.

Taking off also had been reminiscent of my single trip in
a Spitfire at an air show in Johannesburg. Being just about
the biggest tail-dragger flying, Brad had to swing the Porter
right and left to see ahead over the nose while taxiing. Then
he lined her up on the runway, locked the tail-wheel,
opened up to maximum torque on the brakes and flew her
off without even lifting the tail. We were fifty feet up within
five hundred feet, despite a windsock as limp as the Pope's

erection. Within seconds we were climbing at 2,000 feet per minute. Flaps up and power off, I tried to stall her. There was no G-break, just a gentle nose-sink with 45 knots indicated. Full flaps produced a gentle nod of the nose at 40 knots.

That first landing in the Porter I can still remember. Brad wanted me to understand that STOL really did mean short take-off and landing. He had me approach with full-flap at 60 knots. We held 1500 feet until the boundary fence was directly underneath. I thought we'd overshoot by a mile.

'I've got it!' he yelled.

He yanked the power lever back to the idle stops with, 'Watch this, Canuck! If I lied to you, we die!'

The three-bladed prop turned itself into a drag-producing disc, the nose was lowered to an angle at which I felt like a Stuka pilot on a dive-bombing run and I watched Brad having to add back some power to keep the airspeed up to 60 knots!

Near the ground there was a big change of attitude as he made the round-out and there we were, landed on all three wheels. Brad applied reverse thrust, hit the brakes and we stopped within 50 yards.

'How much?' I asked.

'I'm not selling,' he grinned.

'Oh yes, you are.' I couldn't have walked away from the Porter and said goodbye. Coot yelled blue murder at the price until he saw what she could do.

All in all, he felt pretty much the same about flying as I did. The difference was that, being a married man, he tended to ease back on the stick before the last moment, whereas I'd chance a stall, so to speak, in the expectation of learning a new way out which didn't involve kissing the ground at x hundred mph. Gradually I guess I tended to take the hairier jobs, which made Sophy happy.

Luckily for both Coot and me, Jack took the burden of running the business off our shoulders. It suited us so well that neither of us asked any questions as to what he got out of it.

The Coot himself was a regular upfront guy with no

hidden corners. He couldn't understand Jack at all! One evening when we were alone down at the hangar he came right out with what was on his mind: 'Is your buddy fucking my wife, Pete?'

I laughed, 'No way!'

The Coot so hated desk-work himself that he had come to believe Jack had some underhand reason to be happy back at the farm, hunched over a deskful of paperwork while we were looping the loop and defying the ground all over southern Africa like some superannuated World War One flying circus.

Looking back, I'd say that what Jack liked best about that time was not being alone, yet having time to himself after five years of virtually no privacy in the Legion. I think he wrote quite a bit of poetry during our first months in the Waterberg. He kept some loose-leaf books locked up in the office safe; they got fatter and fatter but I never saw inside them. If he shared his thoughts with anyone, it was Sophy.

Jack never laid a hand on her, I'm sure of that. He liked women and women liked him. The two of them enjoyed being around one another and spent a lot of time talking, but it never went any further than verbal intimacy. I had a feeling that Jack maybe read some of his poems to Sophy, but when I asked her, she just smiled that quiet smile of hers and said nothing.

To give Coetzee some privacy with his family, Jack and I took the bakkie *and went into town most weekends, if we didn't have a job on. Or I'd fly us down to Jo'burg where we could pick up a couple of girls and have a good time. I was a good shot and enjoyed hunting but Jack bought himself a couple of fancy Japanese cameras and used to shoot through a lens. I have to admit he made some pretty good pictures on the dozens of game ranches and nature reserves nearby and when we went camping in the wilderness areas and climbing in the mountains. It was a wonderful life for two young men who loved the great outdoors.*

.*10*.

Ossetin stared fascinated at the elongated neck of the man who had hanged himself from the bars in the cage next to Bergman's, using strips torn from a blanket. The guards had been too drunk to watch the television screens despite the din made by the other prisoners watching the long-drawn-out death agony while the man died from slow strangulation.

Ossetin's nocturnal visits to his zoo had become a routine more pleasurable than sleep. One of the other prisoners was standing at the bars of his cage, gazing at the hanged man. He did not blink even when Ossetin passed a hand in front of his eyes.

In the control room, Ossetin dismissed the guards and sat at the console. He grabbed the camera controls and zoomed in on a pair of anguished eyes staring out of an emaciated face. He thrilled with the knowledge that he alone controlled the dosages of misery for his captives. There was only one way they could escape and even that gave him pleasure. In the morning when the guards were sober enough to cut down the body, he would have it taken to his quarters . . .

He was still alone in the guard-post at 2 a.m. when he heard the open microphone in the bunker pick up, among the chorus of snoring and moans, a loud scream in English: 'Go! Go! Go!'

He turned the camera control to wide-angle and searched for the prisoner who had shouted in his sleep. Bergman was sitting up on his bed, rubbing his eyes and drenched in sweat, pulse racing. The images of the valley beneath Ararat which had made him shout out aloud cross-faded to the reality of his cage, five paces long by three across. The whine of ricochets and the *crump!* of mortar shells in his ears gave way to the night noises of the other prisoners. In the centre of the bunker, the blinking red eye of Ossetin's camera was aimed squarely at him.

Like an inter-tidal creature squirming down into the mud for safety, Bergman lay down again and shut his eyes, pressed his face into the hard mattress and willed himself back into the world of memory where he could forget the present.

Had Van heard his shout? Had she escaped? Where was she now? Alive or dead? If alive, she must have given him up for dead and forgotten him years before. *Van, where are you?*

There were no answers, perhaps never would be. Bergman stretched and twisted on his bed and started going over again everything he knew about the woman who had been with him that night on the border.

'The mantle,' she had told him once, 'fell on my shoulders towards the end of my first term reading Modern Languages at Cambridge. Of course, coming from a family like mine, I had always known it would happen one day.'

November 1979: East-West tension was reaching a new high. In Britain a distinguished member of the Queen's household, Sir Anthony Blunt was named as the 'fourth man', along with Philby, Burgess and Maclean. In Afghanistan, Russian Spetsnaz teams assassinated the native Communist leader Hafizullah Amin and occupied Kabul airport to pave the way for an airborne invasion of the country while four crack divisions of motorised infantry poured over the northern borders of the country.

In Cambridge Van was sitting in the lounge of the Royal Hotel, waiting for her uncle who had left a message at her college porter's lodge to say that he was in town on business, and would she like to join him for dinner?

At precisely one minute to seven she caught sight in the foyer of Neville Hampton's British Warm officer's overcoat, rolled umbrella and bowler hat.

He had been Van's most important male relative since her father died.

She remembered him collecting her from boarding school on *the* day when, aged fourteen, she had been sent for by the headmistress. Her housemistress was also in the Sanctum, as the girls called the head's study, so Van knew something was wrong before she saw her uncle sitting in the visitor's chair.

'I'm so sorry, Vanessa,' he said. 'I'm afraid your dad was on a business trip abroad and had a heart attack last night.'

Van had known the truth even then, long before she was told how her father had died of an overdose of .50 calibre slugs on the Austria/Hungary border. In the head's study that day she had blinked away the tears, tightened her lips and thought, 'I mustn't say anything to give Daddy away!'

It had been Neville Hampton who escorted Van and her mother to Buckingham Palace three months later for the private investiture where the Queen chatted with them for several minutes in a large and frigid drawing-room full of gilt furniture and ormolu clocks. She handed Van the posthumous medal in its velvet-lined case and told her: 'You must be very proud of having such a brave father.'

Only then had Van wanted to cry. She stopped herself by saying under her breath, again and again, 'I mustn't let the side down.'

After she had taken the Cambridge entrance examination it was Neville Hampton who sent her off travelling round Europe for six months and provided the funds from his own pocket. Without a word being said between them, Van had known it was all preparation. She could even put a date on the day she had first worked out that she was destined to follow in the family tradition. It was long before Cambridge – on the afternoon of Boxing Day 1970.

In the grey slate Victorian rectory near Keswick where her grandparents lived, the family was preparing to break up and go its several ways after spending Christmas together. Van had placed her hand on the door handle to go into her grandfather's study when her mother called her back, 'You can't go in, darling. The men are talking.'

'Why not?' Van pleaded. 'I want to ask Daddy something.'

It was a lie; intrigued by the conspiratorial nod that had passed between the men when Cook was clearing away the remains of the sherry trifle, she wanted to see what she was missing. From the other side of the door came the rumble of men's voices: her grandfather's deep bass, her father's and Uncle Neville's tenor tones and the nasal, sarcastic drawl of Uncle John.

'I said, you can't go in.'

'Oh, Mummy. They're only talking.'

'They're not *only* talking, Vanessa,' said her grandmother sharply. 'They're talking shop.'

'Shops?'

'No, darling. They're talking about work.'

Van turned to her mother. 'But Daddy never ever talks about work. He says it's not allowed.'

A look passed between the two older women. 'It's different inside the family, darling,' said her mother. 'Here the men can talk to each other.'

Van was bored, as only a twelve-year-old in a house full of grown-ups can be. 'Aren't you and Mummy allowed to go in, either?' she asked, being deliberately difficult.

'Not really, Vanessa.'

'Well,' said the small girl defiantly. 'I tell you one thing. When I'm grown up, I'll jolly well be allowed to go in with the men and talk shop too.'

Her mother smiled tolerantly. 'Now why don't you take Grandma's dogs outside and give them a run in the garden?'

Van put on a coat and called the dogs, the picture of a dutiful daughter, doing as she was told. The two spaniels were both old and did not need exercise. She slipped their leads on and led them into the garden. It was a dry and sunny day, the Lake District at its best. At the bottom of the garden, a hedge of *leylandii* screened the near view so that Skiddaw's bleak flanks seemed to rise straight out of the greenery.

Crouched double, she pulled the dogs with her and sat down against the warm brick wall beneath the open window of the study. Her hands petting the dogs to keep them quiet, she listened to the voices inside discussing an event which was the beginning of the break-up of the USSR: the rioting in the Polish port of Gdansk.

The names were hard for a ten-year-old to memorise: Gomulka, Gierek, Poznan . . . Van worked out phonetic spellings as a way of remembering them and later used a simple cypher to record them in her diary.

Her father was saying, 'We have a man in there. The militia opened fire on the crowd. Before the town was sealed off, he got off a signal that three hundred at least had been killed. Now there's no news in or out.'

Van heard her Uncle John snorting with his inhaler. And Uncle Neville said, 'This could be the start of something big.'

The memories flitted through Van's mind as her uncle greeted her and made small talk over a glass of Tio Pepe. He asked about her studies and chatted vaguely about his own days as a young man at Oxford.

Van relaxed, drank her sherry and ordered a three-course meal that would be her largest intake of calories that week.

'Fine, Uncle Neville,' she kept replying to his questions about lectures, tutors, digs and friends. 'Everything's wonderful.'

They discussed her preference for Russian over German literature and agreed that she should aim at finding a job when she came down which used her linguistic gifts. Neville Hampton came to the point over his second helping of dessert. It was sherry trifle, on the menu that night thanks to Van. She had telephoned the hotel especially, knowing how much he enjoyed it.

'Politics, Vanessa,' he said.

Her mind was blank.

'You haven't joined any political organisations since you came up to university.'

'They're all crap,' she said, wondering whether it had been a statement or a question.

He raised an eyebrow.

'Sorry,' she apologised. 'It's quite a current expression among students nowadays.'

He had a vague half-smile. 'I was querying your cynicism,

rather than your vocabulary. In my day undergraduates tended to be more involved, one way or the other.'

'Well, I don't fancy going off to dances with the Young Farmers, because I resent being looked over like a prize heifer. And I don't like the idea of marching around on wet Sundays, waving a soggy banner in the rain, so that's the two main parties out of the way.'

'Go on,' he prompted.

Puzzled, she continued. 'Well, there are the Liberals, of course. But any party whose leader goes on trial for conspiracy to murder his boyfriend does rather lack credibility – don't you think?'

'Go on,' he repeated.

'What's left?'

'The CP.'

'You've got to be joking!' Van laughed outright.

After the coffee had been served, Neville Hampton ordered brandy for both of them. He leaned across the table and lowered his voice. 'There's a little job I want you to do for me, Vanessa. I'd like you to join the CP. Nothing ambitious. Just go to meetings and make mental notes of who talks to whom, who organises meetings or brings instructions, who handles the money . . . That sort of thing. Particularly, I'd like to know of anyone who seems very convinced and suddenly leaves the Party for no apparent reason.'

Van burst out laughing, making heads turn at nearby tables. She pulled her chair closer to her uncle's. They had had a good bottle of St Estèphe with the meal, the effects of which, plus the sherry to start and the brandy afterwards, made it all seem even funnier.

'You want me to catch the Cambridge spies, Uncle Neville?' she asked in a hushed voice. 'Surely they've all been caught now?'

The sarcasm was lost. 'Not all of them,' he said.

Across the table, her blue Bowles-Haddon eyes were watching him from a face framed by long blonde hair. He saw his niece for the first time as a very beautiful young woman, but one with duties to fulfil that others did not have.

'Will you do this for me, Vanessa?'

'Well . . .' Van finished her brandy. 'Yes, I suppose so, Uncle Neville.'

'Good.' He reached over the table and patted her arm. 'I knew I could rely on you.'

'Just one thing,' she said. 'What's the pay?' It was the first question to come into any student's mind.

He laughed quietly. 'Very droll. I'm afraid this sort of work's unpaid. One does it because one is asked.'

She cycled back to college that evening recalling his words: *This could be the start of something big.*

The CP meetings were boring. Van wondered how the other regular attendants kept awake without her secret reason for being there. She relayed the gist of the endless discussions to Neville Hampton when they met from time to time. He was interested in everything and asked questions which showed how much he remembered of her previous reports.

It seemed to Van impossible that any real purpose could be served by keeping watch on people as transparently 'revolutionary' as the other members of her cell. They were in the forefront at demonstrations, waving banners, shouting slogans and signing petitions. Once she had mastered the dialectic double-talk, she could predict almost word by word what each one of them would say on a given subject. It was towards the end of her second year that her hunting instinct was aroused by the Treasurer's sudden announcement that he was leaving the Party.

'Ah,' said Neville Hampton when she reported this at their next meeting. 'And you've been thinking that all this was a waste of time, haven't you?'

'Well,' she grinned. 'I don't think Guy Mainwaring is going to blow up the Houses of Parliament.'

'He's a chemist, isn't he? So he'd know how.'

'It was a joke, Uncle.'

'Maybe,' he said.

'Do I have to go on attending these boring meetings?'

There was a twinkle in his eye. 'Look on it,' he said, 'as winning your spurs.'

.11.

Roscoe had tuned into the BBC World Service on shortwave, to listen to the midnight GMT news bulletin. Over the two and a half years of their sometimes turbulent three-way partnership, Coetzee Air had prospered. The communications equipment reflected that, as did what Coetzee fondly referred to as 'the fleet'. In addition to the long-range Cessna Courier and the Beechcraft Bonanza, the hangars below the farmhouse had been enlarged to shelter Bergman's darling Pilatus Porter and a Brazilian-manufactured AS 350 Squirrel helicopter which Coetzee had acquired – like many things in South Africa – in contravention of the UN embargo. It was in the Cessna that Bergman was overdue that night from a clandestine pick-up just outside Bulawayo.

After the chimes of Big Ben, the lead story on the night of 30 March 1981 was of the fighting in Zimbabwe where Robert Mugabe, the former rebel leader who had become Prime Minister, was using the country's security forces to crush a rebellion led by his one-time friend and ally, Joshua Nkomo. In that day's fighting in and near Bulawayo several hundred people had died and no one knew how many were wounded.

The BBC signal faded with a report of the attempted assassination in Washington of newly-elected President Reagan. A Bible station from somewhere in Alabama cut in with an attack on the morality of popular songs: 'What kind of world wants to sing that love is lovelier the second time around, my friends? Where in the Bible does Jesus say that changing partners is permitted?'

Roscoe turned the sound down. He was keeping a listening watch for Bergman on a VHF frequency and trying to catch up on some of the paperwork that kept the planes in the air. The night was hot and sticky, despite the large ceiling fan and an oscillating fan on Roscoe's desk. There had been no cooling showers that day. He knew from the met report that there were storms along Bergman's route, which probably accounted for the poor radio reception.

Hearing footsteps outside on the stoep, he opened the desk drawer where he kept a loaded Walther Police Special. After two years of living on Coetzee's remote farm, that sort of precaution had become second nature, even though the only strangers inside the perimeter wire that night were a couple of clients waiting to collect Bergman's passenger from Bulawayo, a member of the now outlawed Selous Scouts.

'Mind if I come in, Jack?' The door opened to reveal a crumple-suited Englishman. Behind him stood his armed driver, a tall black man who looked to Roscoe like a Zulu.

'Running late tonight, aren't we?' George Dawson closed the door, leaving the black outside.

Roscoe pushed a glass and a half-empty bottle of whisky towards the visitor. 'Peter'll be OK,' he said. 'Help yourself to a drink.'

Dawson poured himself a generous measure of Johnnie Walker and raised it in a toast: 'Here's to the daring young men in their flying machines.'

Roscoe lifted his own glass.

'Mind if I talk,' asked Dawson, 'to pass the time while we wait?'

'Go ahead.'

'Or am I interrupting something?'

Roscoe pushed away a pile of invoices. 'Nothing interesting.'

Dawson's sleepy eyes took in the scene. 'That just about sums up your life, doesn't it, Jack? The way I see it, you're a bit of a spare prick at a wedding here. Or have I got it wrong?'

'It's a partnership,' said Roscoe defensively. 'Each man does what he's best at.'

Dawson put down his glass and accepted a refill. 'Just so long as you're happy pushing the paper while Biggles and Algy are out there having all the fun . . .'

'I've got no complaints.'

'I see you,' persisted Dawson, 'like little Jack Horner, forever stuck in the corner with a duff pie while the other chaps get the plums.'

'Well, that's not the way I see it.'

'Then forget I spoke.'

Ksssh, ksssh, ksssh! The VHF communications receiver on the bench squawked three times as Bergman, inbound, broke squelch by keying his microphone switch but not talking. It was safer than speech, because less traceable.

Roscoe looked at the large brass ship's chronometer on the wall; the call had been his cue to switch on the landing lights in three minutes' time.

'If you change your mind,' said Dawson, preparing to leave, 'remember that my people could use someone like you, Jack. We like the way you run this outfit – and you have connections we should value.' He named half a dozen white and black politicians for whom Coetzee Air had worked.

'Never heard of them.'

Dawson chuckled, 'That's another thing we like about you, Jack.'

'I'm just the office manager,' said Roscoe.

Dawson gestured at the pile of work on the desk. 'As long as you're happy, may Allah be with you and your tribe increase. On the other hand . . .' He scribbled something on the top sheet of the radio log beside the mike '. . . if you feel like a change of scenery, this number can always reach me.'

'You've got it all wrong,' said Roscoe. 'I'm not looking for a job.'

Dawson tapped the side of his nose. 'Let's say I know all about your problem with your mother, Jack. She's ill and you'd like to visit her but you're still posted as a deserter from the paras, aren't you? Well, don't worry, if you want to come home to the UK, we can fix a little detail like that.'

'How?'

'By having you posted to us retroactively,' Dawson winked mock-salaciously. 'Think about it.'

The door closed behind him. With one minute to go, Roscoe's hand hovered over the landing-light circuit breaker. He had a sour taste in his mouth that was not Johnnie Walker's fault. Dawson had stirred up the guilt about the unanswered letters stuffed into a drawer of his desk. He peeled off the message sheet on which Dawson had written a Pretoria telephone number. For a moment he was about to drop the paper into the wastebin, then he changed his mind and pushed it to the back of the drawer with his mother's letters.

For once Van was reluctant to spend time meeting her uncle. With finals only two weeks away, she felt it was a waste of time.

She had nothing to report, having dropped the CP meetings at the beginning of term to concentrate on her revision, but something in Neville Hampton's voice when he telephoned her that morning had intrigued her. That she had won her spurs, in his words, was obvious the previous Boxing Day when the whole family was foregathered by tradition at her grandmother's house and he had invited Van to join him in the study after lunch. There they had spent thirty minutes poring over photographs taken at a unilateral disarmament rally in Grosvenor Square, to see how many faces she could put names to.

She wondered afterwards whether identifying those faces had really been so urgent that he had to bring the photographs with him to a family Xmas party. Or had it just been a way of signalling to the other members of the clan that Van was now one of those who might talk shop in the study? No one had said anything as they came out; only her other uncle, Sir John Bowles-Haddon, had looked at her thoughtfully.

Checking her watch to make sure she was on time, Van entered the second-hand bookshop near the Corn Exchange where Neville Hampton liked to meet her, and literally bumped into him leafing through a book of Edward Lear watercolours of exotic animals.

'Have you time for a spot of tea?' he asked, as though their meeting was by chance.

They ate scones with cream and strawberry jam, chatting about the recent shooting of the Pope by a Turkish gunman and Mrs Thatcher's problems with the miners. When her uncle announced his intention of walking to the railway station in order to catch the train back to London, Van offered to accompany him. It was a pleasant, sunny afternoon as they strolled along to the rhythm of his umbrella tapping the pavement lightly at every other step.

They were nearly at the station when he murmured, 'You haven't been to any meetings recently, I suppose?'

'I want a decent two-one,' she said. 'So I've cut down on the social whirl for the last few weeks.'

A few minutes later he asked, 'Any plans of what you'll do after coming down?'

Van felt a twinge of excitement. It was the kind of oblique remark that usually led somewhere with her uncle. She shook her head.

'You've done the backpacking bit,' he said. 'We got that out of your system before you came up.'

'I still want to travel.'

'But now you can travel in style and comfort – if we find you an employer who'll pay the expenses. And then, there are your languages . . .'

'Obviously I want to use them,' she said. 'I mean, what's the point of reading Russian and German at Cambridge and then taking a job where one's languages slip away like O-level Chemistry and Economics?'

When they were saying goodbye on the platform, he murmured, 'You're rather young. Usually we look for people a little older and with more experience.'

She was used to his bare-bones approach when he was talking business. 'Did you just offer me a job, Uncle Neville?'

'You've been a great help,' he said. 'It's a jigsaw, Vanessa. The bits and pieces you've found out for me were useful.'

'I haven't done much.'

He stood in the carriage doorway and gave her one of his rare, thin smiles. 'The whole art of life, my dear niece, is to do not much but the right things well.'

'Sometimes, dear Nunky,' she said, 'your laid-back style is really infuriating. Are you telling me there's a job for me with your department?'

He sighed, 'There is, but I'm afraid you'd be very bored with us. We can't offer glamour and foreign travel.'

'Then what about Uncle John's people?'

'Not a good idea,' he said shortly. 'But there's one job that might suit you down to the ground, with an old chum of mine who's putting together a team of new faces.'

He took from his waistcoat pocket a card inscribed in copperplate *Neville Hampton, c/o The Guards Club, Piccadilly, London W1.* Turning it over, he wrote a name and telephone number on the back.

'Give this chap a ring when you're next in town,' he said. 'He's expecting your call.'

They chatted until the guard's whistle blew. Walking back along the platform, Van took the card from her pocket. She had always wondered how her formal recruitment would happen. On the reverse side of the visiting card was a telephone number and the name: George Dawson.

. . . which is how Van met up with Jack.

It was only after Roscoe had gone back to the UK that me an' Coot understood how much he had contributed to the success of our little airline. Up till then we had just taken him for granted because he did all the things we didn't want to.

We soon realised that he'd done a helluva lot more than just look after the paperwork, chase up missing spares, keep the bank account straight and arrange refuelling facilities for us in some very strange places. Whilst we had been reaching for the stars, Jack had very quietly done a triage of all our clients and potential clients, dividing them into three groups: the safe-and-sure, the risky-but-rich and what he called the no-way-José brigade. The safe ones he cultivated, the risky rich he charged more and the others he quietly got rid of, without us ever knowing about it.

He also developed a 'freight' side to our operation, which handled anything from diamonds to medicines. If we made a pile of loot on one job, we'd often be flying life-saving supplies free of charge to some remote mission hospital the next day. Our two golden rules were never to annoy the authorities of the country we lived in and never to touch drugs or arms. Within those limits we must, at some time or other, have moved everything that was moveable in a light aircraft.

I don't know about Coot but I realised how different life was going to be without Jack one moonless night when I had a last-moment gut feeling about a clandestine pick-up for some guys that Jack had always refused to deal with. It was on the wrong side of the border, in Angola. The flight from Windhoek had been uneventful. The landing arrangements looked fine: a double line of hand-held torches serving for a flare-path. I touched down and cut the throttle. Then I saw that the guys holding the torches were standing still, keeping well away from the aircraft. Normally blacks would crowd around the plane out of curiosity as soon as we landed.

Instinct told me to open the throttle and get the hell out of there. Thank God I was in the Porter. I gunned that beautiful Pratt and Witney engine just as some cute bastard switched on a searchlight, blinding me. I shielded my eyes and hoped to God there was nothing solid for the next hundred or so feet ahead. There were a coupla bumps as I hit what felt like people, probably decapitating them with the prop. Then I was airborne, wondering what was making that pft-pft-pft noise in the cabin behind me.

Luckily the guy with the searchlight was too clever. He aimed for where just about any other plane in the world would have been but the Porter was climbing at 1,300 feet per minute and his beam was way below my arse. One stray bullet made it through the floor and removed a piece of left arm, ruining my old Legion tattoo.

I turned hard right and levelled out one-handed. There was a wild pattern of tracers spraying the sky through which I had just flown. Judging by the muzzle-flashes there were two .50 calibre machine-guns down there firing at me as well as half a dozen other automatic weapons. That would never have happened on a job planned by Jack.

I got home with a dozen holes in the fuselage and a tail-plane resembling a pepper-pot. Sophy looked unhappy as she sprinkled antibiotic powder in the hole on my arm and bandaged it up. A month later Coetzee came home one night with a piece of his right thigh missing and the Cessna's cockpit full of blood, courtesy of another of Jack's rejects. That time, Sophy got hysterical and grounded him after nightfall!

I could understand it. She was pregnant. They started rowing about her kid becoming an orphan in the womb. I tried not to get involved but to help things out I did more and more of the flying, leaving Coetzee at base to look after the office, which he hated.

A few months after that, Jack resurfaced. He wouldn't say exactly what he was doing – just that he was now working for our old client Dawson in London. Being a spook suited his secretive nature. He seemed to know that Coetzee Air was having financial trouble – or maybe he guessed. Either way, when he offered me a one-off job in Europe for cash, I was doubtful about taking it on, largely because I didn't know the terrain. Jack's briefing was so detailed and precise that I agreed to do it. The fee was generous and I was happy to be working with him again, even if he did laughingly say I was what was known in the trade as 'a disposable asset'. I guess it flattered my ego to feel that I was valued by Jack's people, who had the cream of the world's freelance operators to choose from.

After that, he contacted me once or twice a year. I'd fly to Europe, bring somebody or something across a frontier for him – sometimes by air, sometimes on the ground – and come away cash in hand. And so the years drifted past.

.12.

Five years behind a desk in London had aged George Dawson a lot. He had put on weight and gravity had won a succession of battles with the skin of his face, which made him look like a sad spaniel. His crumpled off-the-peg suit and badly laundered shirt with frayed collar and cuffs would have been more appropriate on an underpaid book-keeper than a middle-rank spook.

He was out of pipe tobacco and had cadged a cigarette from Roscoe to keep him going until lunchtime. On his desk was a copy of that day's *Daily Mail*. The headlines were about the murder of three British hostages in Beirut as alleged retaliation for UK involvement in the American bombing of Libya. Dawson scribbled another line in the crossword, then angrily crossed out what he had written. Properly spelled, it was one letter too many. To get his revenge, he threw the newspaper into the shredder beside his desk and pressed the button.

'Hold it, George,' Roscoe was straining to hear the ringing tone at the other end of the line against the noise of the shredder.

He clamped a hand over his free ear. 'I think I've got through this time. Hallo? Is that Jan Coetzee? *Hoe gaan et het, Jan?*'

'*Goed dankie*. What the hell you want, Roscoe?'

'How're Sophy and the kids?'

'The kids are fine, genuine. Sophy I don't know. She don't talk to me any more, you know how it is.'

'Can I talk to Peter?'

'You could if he was here.'

'When's his ETA?'

'Hold on. You must be psychic . . . Hear that noise?' Coetzee opened the window and thrust the phone outside. 'That's your old buddy coming in right now.'

Bergman cleared the thatched ridge of the house by inches, spun the Squirrel through 180 degrees, flared her and landed outside the office in a cloud of dust and blown paper. As the rotor blades slowed to stop he heard Coetzee's bellow from inside. 'Pete! How often have I told you to land that noisy toy of yours down by the hangar?'

Bergman strolled into the control room, peeling off gloves and wraparound Ray-Ban sunglasses. 'What is the point of rotor blades,' he asked, 'if I have to land on the strip just the same?'

'The point . . .' Coetzee was on his hands and knees, rescuing paper from the floor, '. . . is that every damn time you do that, you blow away half a week's book-keeping.'

'Why don't you keep the door closed?'

'It was closed,' Coetzee glared at him. 'Your down-draught opened it.'

'This'll make you feel better.' Bergman tossed the client's payment – a wad of notes in several currencies – onto the desk below the radio console.

'Phone call for you,' said Coetzee, indicating the handset lying on the paper-strewn desk.

'Anyone important?'

Coetzee laughed. 'Just that *soutpiel* Roscoe, calling from London. Take your time, the British tax-payer can afford it.'

Bergman grabbed a cool beer from the office fridge and picked up the telephone. There was a repeated clicking on the line as some electronic device at Roscoe's end shunted numbers to make the call untraceable.

'I thought you were dead, Jack.' Bergman swallowed beer

and wiped sweat off his brow. He shrugged off his safari jacket
and chucked it one-handed over a hook on the wall. 'Long time,
no hear.'

'How're things with you?' asked Roscoe. 'I heard you getting
on the Coot's nerves.'

Bergman sat in Coetzee's chair, tilted it back and put his feet
on the desk. 'I do my best to. Stops him getting old and set in
his ways. What can I do for you, Jack?'

Roscoe sounded casual. 'Time we had a few drinks together,
old buddy.'

Coetzee was looking angry. He knew what a call from Roscoe
meant. Bergman swivelled the chair to avoid his partner's glare.
'We've a pretty tight schedule for the next couple of weeks down
here, Jack. Can it wait?'

A continent away, Roscoe said, 'No.'

'Tell him the money,' said Dawson, hand clamped over the
mouthpiece.

'I think . . .' Roscoe cleared his throat '. . . that you'll find my
conversation – to borrow an expression from that old Air
America hand who sold you the Porter – really fascinating. And
the fee's twenty G.'

'Izzit sterling, Jack?'

'Affirmative.'

For nearly a minute the line carried only strange electronic
noises-off and the harmonics of other conversations, then
Bergman said, 'I'll catch this evening's flight from Jo'burg and
see you at Heathrow tomorrow morning.'

Van's Hampstead flat was bigger and more comfortable than
Roscoe's pad in Brixton. Since they had begun their affair they
spent two or three nights a week together at her place. There
were books and LPs of his on the shelves; half the clothes hanging in her wardrobe were Roscoe's.

At thirty-two he was four years older than her, a good lover
and a better companion than any outsider would have guessed.
At work he projected a strong-and-silent image that had
tempted Van to make the first move, only to discover that there
were two sides to Jack Roscoe. He read poetry aloud to her,
revealing nuances she had never understood in her own

favourite poems. He knew the names of wild flowers and the Brontës' characters and who played what part in all her favourite films.

But, thought Van – and it was a big but – there was some giant problem buried deep inside Jack Roscoe and her name was not Florence Nightingale. If he had been content to leave emotion out of their relationship and just have fun together, the affair might have lasted a long time. But Jack was complicated: he wanted more and Van wasn't giving. She had been planning for some days to tell him that it was all over but, after her briefing by Dawson, it seemed underhand metaphorically to kick her lover in the balls at the start of his first operation as controlling officer.

Listening to Roscoe splashing in the bath like some aquatic animal, she blinked away the image of him packing up his things and looking hurt. Later . . .

'I've set the alarm,' she called.

'Thanks.' Roscoe was climbing out of the bath. 'I'm meeting someone at Heathrow tomorrow morning.' He came into the bedroom with a large towel wrapped around him, sarong- style. Rubbing his hair dry with a hand-towel he looked at her for a long moment, sensing something in the look she was giving him.

'What's up?' Van asked.

'Nothing,' he smiled uneasily. 'But you look tense. Had a bad day?'

She turned away and felt him come close. His arms slipped around her: strong, well-muscled arms pulling her back against him.

She shut her eyes and turned in his embrace, pulling his mouth down to her lips in order to stop him talking, wishing that he could have been just the macho stud she had thought he was. To speed things up, she loosened the towel around his waist and touched him lightly with her fingertips.

'There's no hurry,' Roscoe murmured.

He touched her shoulders and ran down her spine strong fingers that knew where to go. Briefly his large hands girdled her waist and held her for one breathless moment, then one hand went lower to hold her buttocks while the other brushed against her breast, setting the skin afire through three layers of material as he slipped off her jacket and started to undo the buttons of her blouse.

The fingers that knew her body, knew her clothes. They slipped the blouse free of the waistband and undid the zip of her skirt with slow caresses. Slip, bra and pants dropped to the floor one by one as Roscoe buried his face in the silkiness of her hair, the softness of her breasts and belly. When he was ready, he picked her up and laid her gently down on the bed, stroking her long smooth legs from ankle to crotch.

After the first time they made love he had written a poem about the hockey games on wet playing fields, the horse-riding and long walks with elderly relatives on grouse moors – all the activities which, he believed, had made her legs the way they were for his pleasure.

Van lay with one hand half-hiding her face and eyes closed, soaking up the sensations; it was never the same twice with Roscoe. She shuddered as his fingers found her swollen lips and tugged them gently open.

'You bastard,' she moaned softly and pushed his hands away.

Slowly and gently Roscoe picked up her rhythms, responding to them and leading her further and further into passion. He touched and stroked and probed and sucked, whispering the words that stopped her thinking. When Van came, shuddering on top, her face above him was contorted in ecstasy with a pre-echo of the lines that age would one day use to paint her as an old woman.

Roscoe let her collapse on top of him and stroked her back and shoulders until she calmed. In an instant of clarity he knew that they would never lie together again.

Van lay unsleeping in the dark. From his breathing she could tell that Roscoe was awake. She wanted to scream, 'Go away, Jack! Leave me alone.'

'Who is Peter Bergman?' she asked at last, desperate to talk about anything except Roscoe and herself.

He switched on the reading light and put both pillows over the phone on the bedside table. 'Where d'you get that name?' he asked.

'Dawson, of course. He said not to tell you yet.'

'You should have said.'

'I just did.' She let the impatience show. 'Who is he, this Bergman?'

'If you've been briefed, you'll know.'

'Oh don't be infuriating, Jack.' It was such a relief for her to snap at him. 'I know he's a personal friend of yours – and that's all.'

Roscoe lit a cigarette. She shook her head when he offered it to her. 'We shouldn't be talking about this here,' he said.

'Stupid,' she said. 'If Big Brother is listening, he can also see you at the airport, meeting the man tomorrow morning, can't he?'

'You would think that, being in Movements Analysis.' Roscoe sat up and looked at her body, lying so innocently beside him. Steel beneath silk, he thought.

'Well?' she prompted.

'Bergman,' he said solemnly, 'is the best friend I ever had. He's also the bravest man I know.'

'That's some tribute.'

'He's some man.'

She was guessing now. 'He saved your life – or something dramatic like that – when you were in the Foreign Legion together, am I right?'

Roscoe started. 'Did Dawson tell you that?'

'Not exactly,' she admitted. 'I just put together things he said and little bits I've gleaned from you.'

Roscoe was silent, remembering how it had been at Kolwezi.

'So I'm right,' said Van, watching the shadow pass behind his eyes.

He nodded. 'Peter saved my life twice.'

'And sometimes he works for us as a freelance?'

'Now and again.'

'Always with you as his control?'

'He wouldn't work for anyone else. We were partners, running a small bush airline in South Africa for a couple of years.'

'Sounds exciting.'

'It had its moments.'

'If you're such great pals, why did you two split up?'

Roscoe shrugged. 'I wanted to come back to Europe when my mother got ill. Peter liked it out there. So when Dawson offered me a job, I came back and he stayed. Anyway, Bergman's not a British subject, so we couldn't employ him on staff.'

There's more to it than that, she thought, closing her eyes. 'From what Dawson said, it's my guess that whenever we want a plausibly deniable frontier-crosser, we give your old pal the shitty end of the stick.'

Roscoe laughed softly. 'You don't know Peter Bergman. He loves the whole adrenalin-pumping, ball-breaking scene. He'd do it for free, that guy! Just for the kicks.'

'I can't wait to meet him,' Van purred with pretended passion.

A couple of minutes later she felt Roscoe's weight shift on the mattress and opened her eyes to see him leaning over her with the question, 'Why exactly did Dawson brief you on this, Van? And why didn't he tell me that he had?'

It's all over, she thought, looking up. That was goodbye, Jack Roscoe. I wanted to be sure that what I felt for you was only lust – and now I am.

'Why?' he repeated.

Van wriggled out from under him and sat up, pulling the sheet over her breasts. 'You know Bergman's taking someone in with him on this run in Turkey, to identify the client?'

'Craziest thing I ever heard,' said Roscoe angrily. 'I told Dawson so. He says it's an order from the top – from our revered new Director-General herself.'

'Well, I'm the officer going in with Bergman,' said Van. She saw the shock on Roscoe's face as he went pale. 'Didn't Dawson tell you?'

.13.

It was a mild, drizzling April morning. Neither Roscoe nor Bergman wore a raincoat. They were getting steadily wetter as they walked briskly along the Bayswater Road, past some artists' paintings hung on the railings, protected from the weather by sheets of plastic.

Bergman was angry. 'I'm a solo operator, Jack,' he growled. 'You know that.'

Over the years of working with Coetzee his accent had become more South African than Canadian: 'When the sewage impacts against my rotor blades, I take evading action fast. The last thing I want in a crisis is to have to waste time looking after some woman who's come along for the ride.'

He seemed bigger and wider than Roscoe remembered, and took up more space on the pavement than other people. Pedestrians instinctively got out the way of the broad shouldered man from the open spaces who did not look as though he made a habit of stepping aside.

Bergman was thinking the reverse: that six years of living and working in London had shrunk Jack Roscoe and made him . . . He searched for the right word and found it in Afrikaans: *verkrampt*.

'Shut up and listen,' said Roscoe. He had spent two hours that morning arguing with Dawson before being given an ultimatum: 'Do it or you'll be taken off the operation!'

'She's not some woman,' Roscoe parroted Dawson's arguments. 'You'll see when you meet her, Peter. We're talking of a trained officer of the Service whose presence at the border is an integral part of the plan.'

Bergman snorted disbelief. 'For Christ's sake, Jack! I don't even live on this continent but I can think of a thousand easier places to bring someone over to the West than across the Turkish/Armenian frontier. There, if the Reds don't get you, the Turks will. They're shit-hot, those guys, genuine. I'm telling you, Turks don't mess around. With Bulgars, Greeks, Russians, Armenians, Iraqis and Syrians for neighbours, they're surrounded by people who hate their guts, so they shoot first and think afterwards. So why pick . . .'

A middle-aged Japanese businessman, accompanied by two of his younger executives, all in identical company T-shirts and shorts with red sweat bands round their heads, jogged out of the park and across the road to their hotel. Bergman took advantage of the lull in the conversation whilst the Japanese were within earshot to have a good look at the man walking beside him. It looked to him as though Roscoe had been on the bottle all night and not slept a wink.

'It has to be Turkey, Peter.'

'Give me one good reason,' Bergman insisted.

Roscoe pulled a face. The Service's very specific guidelines for use of freelancers did not include discussing the whys and wherefores of an operation.

'Because . . .' He gave way. 'Because the guy who's setting it all up on the other side is an Armenian officer in the KGB. He has a cousin in the border guards on that sector who's making the on-the-ground arrangements. That's why.'

Bergman grunted cynically. 'Then there's the fee you're offering me, Jack. Twenty grand is a suspiciously generous amount for people as mean as your employers to fork out for a job where I just have to slip across a border with everything already set up for me. And what do I do there? I ask you. Collect bodies, one, alive and willing, you reply. OK, that's my business, Jack. So why the pile of loot? What's the catch?'

'Peter, will you slow down?' Roscoe remonstrated. 'If it's the size of the fee that's worrying you, blame me. I decided what seemed like fair money for the risk.' And I still feel guilty for walking out on you and Coetzee . . .

'That's my point,' snapped Bergman. 'The fee reflects the risk.'

They walked a few more paces before he asked, 'And who the hell's in charge, this time? That slob in the dandruff-covered suits we used to work with in Africa, George Dawson?'

'I am.'

Bergman looked at Roscoe. Surprise showed in his voice. 'You're in overall charge of the op, Jack?'

'Yes.'

'You've had promotion, eh? So show it by getting rid of the girl. Let me go in alone. You know it makes sense.'

Waiting at a pedestrian crossing for the green light, Roscoe tried to make eye contact. It was not easy. Bergman's ugly face had always been difficult to read. From years of looking long distances in bright light, he had deeply cut crow's-feet at the corner of his eyes which seemed to have sunk back in their sockets to escape the African sun. Narrowed to slits, they were always roaming, checking out people and buildings in the background.

'Do me a favour, Peter,' begged Roscoe. 'Just listen to me. If I could get Van out of this operation, I would.'

'Who?'

'The officer who's coming with you to the border is called Van. It's short for Vanessa. I shouldn't be telling you this, but we're lovers. Do you think I'd send her on an operation with you, if I had any choice?'

'Jack, old buddy . . .' Bergman did not believe his ears. 'You're telling me that I'm supposed to shepherd your girlfriend through a minefield?'

He shook his head incredulously; these Britishers were unreal. Or . . . 'There's something you're hiding from me, Jack.'

Roscoe looked at his watch. They were already late at the safe house in the mews opposite, but instead of heading across the main road towards it, he turned right into the park.

'I'm going to bend all the rules, Peter,' he said. 'But for God's sake keep your mouth shut.'

'Did I ever not?' Bergman protested. 'I could have been a priest, the secrets I've heard . . .'

'Her full name is Vanessa Bowles-Haddon.'

Bergman laughed. 'Sounds like one of the Prince of Wales's classy girlfriends,' he joked, hoping to loosen things up.

'Try again.'

'Captain of the Roedean hockey team, maybe?'

'Getting warmer. Try again.'

'You ain't kidding?' Bergman muttered thoughtfully. 'Well, the name's a distinct improvement on – what was your last girl called, Brenda?'

'Glenda,' Roscoe corrected him. 'Come on, even you illiterate bush pilots read newspapers, don't you? Think back two years, Peter. A knight of the realm who . . .'

It took Bergman half a dozen strides to put it all together.

'Shee-it,' he clicked his fingers. 'Sir John Bowles-Haddon, the most embarrassing defector since Burgess and Maclean? That guy? She's related to him?'

Roscoe's expulsion of breath was audible. 'I've done it now, Peter. If you say a word, they'll castrate me.'

He monitored his own classic polygraph reaction: pulse racing as though he had been running and the palms of his hands moist with sweat. He rubbed them on his trousers to get them dry. Against all his training he had given real names to an outsider.

I trust Bergman with my life, he told himself. You just have, his other self replied.

It was past five o'clock when they left the house in Bayswater Mews. Bergman had spoken during the briefing only to query accuracy of maps and interpretation of satellite photographs, times and distances and the phases of the moon – digesting all the relevant information in order to come up with his own private flight plan.

Slamming the front door, Roscoe offered, 'I'll walk you to the Underground.'

Bergman waited until they had exited the cobbled mews and

were walking along the main road before he spoke. 'If I put together your official briefing and our little chat in the park, Jack, my trip to Turkey is the last stage in one of the big operations of all time.'

'Keep talking,' said Roscoe. He desperately wanted a drink in the pub at the end of the mews but that was too close to the safe house for privacy.

'One,' said Bergman, 'the Intelligence Secretary to the Cabinet Office defects to the Russians. Two: a couple of years later he wants to come back home.'

'Three, you go and get him.'

'No,' Bergman disagreed. 'My Number Three is: did he fall or was he pushed?'

'What?'

'Exactly, Jack, old boy. Did Sir John Bowles-Haddon really defect two years ago? Or did he go across to spread some disinformation – in which case, job done, he now wants to come home and enjoy his reward?'

'I don't know.'

Bergman grabbed Roscoe's sleeve and stopped him dead in his tracks. They stood in the middle of the pavement, glaring at each other. Other pedestrians gave them a wide margin.

'Well, I suggest you find out, old buddy,' Bergman hissed. 'If he's been screwing the Russkies, they just might be angry, don't you think? And one thing's certain: either he's screwing them or he's screwing you. So tell me which.'

'I don't know,' Roscoe repeated. 'And that's the truth.'

'Fuck it,' said Bergman angrily. 'I've had enough of this. Include me out.'

He started to walk away. It was Roscoe's turn to grab his friend's arm. 'You can't back out now, Peter,' he pleaded.

'Don't tell me what I can do, Jack.' Bergman grinned, showing his teeth and jutting out his chin, Cagney-style. 'If I want out, I get out. Bergman's rules, OK? That's why I'm still alive in this wicked world, Jack Roscoe. And what are you people gonna do to stop me? Have me locked up for the duration?'

Roscoe was sweating again. The DG would have his balls if Bergman turned the job down now; the countdown clock was already running. And as for Peter himself, the least they would do was to lock him away in a safe house in the country for weeks or maybe months, until everything was over.

Turning onto Bayswater Road, he deliberately slowed down to prolong the conversation.

'I'll tell you what I know,' he offered. 'You remember back in April '86 when a policewoman was shot dead outside the Libyan Embassy in St James's Square?'

'I read about it.'

'Her death resulted in the expulsion of Gadaffi's mission from Britain, right? Two weeks later, several pieces of charred paper from the incinerator in the basement of the embassy revealed to our side the extent, and the high level, of the Libyans' work for the KGB in Britain.'

'I'm still listening.'

'A number of those pieces of paper could only have come from the Cabinet Office. There are ways of checking these things. Sir John was on a courtesy visit to Australia and New Zealand at the time. It was during the parliamentary recess. He could not have been arrested there without embarrassment. On the way back to Britain he went missing in Delhi Airport and resurfaced two days later in Moscow. It obviously hasn't worked out for him over there because now he wants to come home. There, you know as much as I do.'

Bergman's busy eyes scanned the street. Nobody seemed to be taking any special interest in them. 'Why did you get me involved in this can o' worms, Jack?' he muttered.

'Because you're the best.'

'*Dankie*,' Bergman said sourly. 'I abdicate.'

'You can't,' Roscoe pleaded urgently. 'Please, Peter. Not now. Apart from anything else, I need you to look after Van. How do you think I feel about her going in?'

They were walking slowly.

'The business of the girl,' said Bergman, thinking aloud, 'is the craziest detail of your crazy plan. You think I can't recognise this Bowles-Haddon guy from a mug shot without having someone finger him for me?'

'In the darkness of a moonless night?' Dawson had made it sound such a telling argument.

Bergman laughed. 'Come on, Jack! I earn a good living pick-

ing up customers who are mostly blacks, and usually on moonless nights. I never collected the wrong guy yet.'

Roscoe released another item: 'He's apparently had plastic
surgery. Only a close relative could recognise his voice and ask
him intimate questions to establish identity with one hundred
per cent certainty.'

'Crap!' was Bergman's reaction. 'If necessary, I can memorise
a dozen questions that only the right guy can answer. Whose
idea was it that your girlfriend has to come all the way across a
border just to identify her uncle?'

'I don't know, Peter. But I'll tell you what I think.'

'You do that, Jack.'

Roscoe picked up the innuendo. 'I'm not concealing anything.'

'I hope not.' There was an edge of menace in Bergman's
voice.

'Van should have been sacked when her uncle defected . . .'

'That thought had occurred to me too.'

'. . . because there's no way someone connected – never mind
related – to such a dangerous security risk can pass positive
vetting nowadays.'

'Check.'

'Yet all that happened was, she was shunted sideways into
Movements Analysis.'

'And how did she account for this remarkable good fortune?'
Bergman's tone of voice was biting.

'She couldn't. Until Dawson briefed her for this job. Now she
thinks she was kept on for the purpose.'

Bergman took a deep breath. '. . . which means that your
people knew all the time he'd be coming back.'

'Maybe.'

Bergman stopped in the middle of the pavement. He threw
his head back, filled his lungs with the moist London air and
roared with laughter in a way that Roscoe recognised from the
old days. It was the what-the-hell belly-laugh he had heard on
Samos, the morning after *REP II* had gone to the bottom. It was
pure Henry Morgan at Port-of-Spain, Sir Walter Raleigh at the
scaffold . . .

Roscoe relaxed; Buccaneer Bergman would pick up the

gauntlet. Anyone else would have backed out at that moment, but not Peter. So he had handled it right, after all . . .

Bergman stopped laughing. His shrewd eyes took in Roscoe's relief. 'This girlfriend of yours, Jack . . . What was her reaction when she heard that she was supposed to come along for the ride?'

'She said that sort of thing came with the job.'

'Then either she's stupid or she's pretty cool.'

'Oh, she's cool, Peter.'

'Sounds like my kind of girl, Jack,' Bergman grinned. 'You know, I can't wait to meet her. Why don't we all get together for a drink tonight?'

'You're crazy,' sighed Roscoe. He felt warm and peaceful now. Bergman's security-defying suggestion was just like old times.

'Come on, Jack.' The good-humoured, bear-like clout across Roscoe's shoulders nearly knocked him off balance. 'Gimme her address. Just say it and I'll meet the two of you there. I brought a bottle of the Coot's *witblitz* with me. We'll drink it together, the three of us.'

Roscoe laughed openly. 'No way.'

'You mean, I'm being watched?'

'I should think so,' Roscoe shrugged.

Bergman looked up into the rain and felt it trickling down his face. He sounded sad. 'Tell you something, Jack. You're getting like your employers, deskbound. Europe shrinks a man some-how, you know that?'

I ate a steak and French fries in the restaurant of the airport hotel Jack had booked me into. Then I went upstairs to my room and counted the contents of the brown envelope he had given me: £10,000 in crisp new £50-notes – with as much to come again at the end of the job. It was a worryingly large fee.

On the way back to the airport I'd bought a six-pack of Carlsberg lagers . . . Oh, what I could do with just one can right now! Anyway, I turned on the television and started drinking lager and witblitz *chasers. It wasn't the evening I'd planned. My previous jobs for Jack had been much lower-level and we'd had some fun together before and after* work. I never much liked his girlfriends – he picked 'em too clever for my taste – but it was more fun than sitting alone in my room with the television and Mr Carlsberg for company.

I paced up and down that bedroom like a caged lion. Each time I came to Europe I had the same feeling of being physically stifled, hemmed in by walls and conventions and sets of values that reduced men to less than what they might be – my old buddy Jack was a case in point.

I paced my way through an Australian soap and a quiz game without hearing a single line of dialogue. I was thinking of Roscoe all those years ago when we were polishing boots in Castelnaudary. Trouble was, Jack had never changed from the guy who stuck his neck out for Corporal De Wilde to give him hell. He was still the same romantic innocent that he had been at nineteen, which made him potentially a dangerous man to work for.

Through the acoustic double-glazed window I could see the lights of jumbos coming silently in to land at Heathrow. I envied those pilots up there on the flight-deck. They made me wish that I was back in Africa, flying quick-in and quick-out on a job where I was at the controls. That was my style; I wasn't made for sitting around waiting in hotel rooms while other guys called the shots. I turned off the television and lay thinking on the bed, with the last can of Carlsberg in one hand and the envelope of money clenched in the other.

The set-up was all wrong . . .

I knew damn-all about how the Brits worked, but what I did know made it hard to credit someone of Jack's seniority being put in overall charge of an operation as big as this one was turning out to be. It was no routine cross-border safari, but part of a much larger scenario and Roscoe just was not senior enough to be entrusted with it. Unless . . .

I shook the empty bottle of witblitz. No wonder I was feeling a bit slewed . . . I dunked my head in the washbasin and leaned my brow against the cool glass of the window as everything came clear.

Oh Jack, I thought, either you're not telling me

everything, or they're screwing you, in which case they're
screwing me too.

It seemed to me that the whole scenario was some kind
of double blind, with a remote puppet-master planning for
Roscoe to carry the can after it all blew up in my face. And
then, just when I thought I had it cracked wide open, the
picture slipped away in the witblitz fumes because of Van. I
hadn't met her in the flesh but I had a pretty good image in
my mind. On the way to the subway Roscoe had dragged
me into a pub and shown me a photograph of her that he
carried in his wallet.

I have a good memory for faces. Looking out at the
night, I saw that wide, intelligent brow, the clear blue eyes,
her strong nose and good mouth. It was an oh-so-English
face. A posh school, Roscoe had said. A titled family, a
double-barrelled name and a dead hero for a father . . .

That's what put me off the scent. I reasoned that if a girl
like that was being sent in with me, to the sharp end where
people get hurt, the operation must be kosher. Miss Vanessa
Bowles-Haddon did not look like the kind of person who
gets fed into a hamburger machine . . . Jack, yes. And Peter
Bergman, freelance aerial clown – him too, maybe. But not
that kind of long-legged, blue-blooded thoroughbred. She
was no loser.

So what the hell was the score? I drained the last can of
Carlsberg, flipped a coin and decided to go along with the
plan that Roscoe had elaborated in that pretty little cottage
in Bayswater Mews. I would take the job for the pure hell
of it – but keep a very, very tight watch on my arse.

.*14*.

The spit of land south of the Turkish port of Kusadasi was called Barbarossa's Point. Within its crook lay a natural harbour, on the sandy bottom of which were visible the remains of a Roman mole and medieval jetties where pirate galleys had moored.

Bergman was wearing just a pair of shorts, with Jesus sandals on his feet. Save for the puckered bullet-scar that showed white on his left arm, his skin was tanned all over by the African sun to a leathery shade of brown. To escape from the moist heat of the beach he clambered up to the top of the headland where stunted trees were swaying in the onshore breeze. There he stood on the ruins of the pirate castle looking out across the Aegean. Squinting against the glare of sun and haze, he saw the mountainous outlines of the Greek islands looming through the humidity like a school of giant hump-backed whales resting on the surface of the sea.

'It's beautiful,' said Van. 'Is that what you're thinking?'

Bergman had not heard her approach barefoot, carrying her sandals. She was wearing a light, sleeveless cotton frock, belted at the waist. From the way her nipples showed through the cloth, he thought she was naked underneath. The sexual tension of pretending to be on honeymoon with Vanessa Bowles-Haddon was getting harder for him to handle each day.

'Yeah,' he agreed, dragging his eyes away from her and back to the horizon.

'What are you looking for?'

Bergman pointed to the nearest island. 'That's Samos. Jack and I wrecked a boat over there, way back.'

When Van did not pick up the cue, Bergman took a quick look-round. There was no one in sight.

'What's the news?' he asked.

Van grimaced. 'I called my cut-out and got instructions to hold for another three, maybe four days.'

'Why not talk to Jack direct?' Bergman snapped.

'I can't reach him without breaking security,' she explained. 'We pass coded messages to each other via the travel agency that hired us the Land-Rover.'

'What the fuck are your colleagues playing at?' Bergman let the anger out. 'At this rate, we're going to end up doing the job on the night of the full moon. It's crazy, Van. Every night those bastards in London keep us waiting, it'll get lighter. You'd think even they would know what that means.'

'I suppose there's some hold-up on the other side,' Van tried to justify the delay.

Bergman looked as angry as he felt. Instinctively she stepped back a pace, then stood her ground, reminding herself that she was the ranking officer and Bergman just a hired freelance.

'You listen to me,' he growled. 'Tomorrow you're going to get Jack on the line for me to talk to. To hell with security. Any more delays and I'll call the whole thing off, genuine.'

Van remembered Dawson's warning: 'Bergman is a man who resents discipline.' He had added ambiguously, 'You may have to use your feminine wiles to pacify him while you wait for the Go signal.' Had Dawson known there would be a delay?

'There are problems, Peter,' she said. 'Communications from the other side can't be easy, to put it mildly.'

'Fuck their problems! What about mine?' Bergman balled a fist and punched a tree hard to get rid of his anger.

Van saw blood on his knuckles. Very macho, she thought. In fact 'macho' is a one-word description of Mr Peter Bergman . . .

He was slipping and sliding down a cliff-path to the sandy beach below. There he dropped his shorts and angrily kicked off his sandals before running into the waves naked and swimming fast straight out to sea, fighting his way through the dangerous offshore currents with a powerful crawl stroke, burning up energy to release inner tension.

'It's all right for you to talk, George Dawson.' Van spoke to the seagulls. 'Keeping a man like that under discipline is easier said than done.'

They had already been in Turkey for three days, slowly driving in a hired Land-Rover down the Aegean coast. For cover they were acting the part of a misty-eyed honeymoon couple, in no hurry to sample the more spartan delights of eastern Turkey, for which the rear of the vehicle was equipped as a camping van.

They had stayed in tourist hotels on the coast, lingering over candlelit *mezeler* meals of hummus, falafel, tahina, *tsadzik* and kebabs. They drank too much wine, went to discos and did not get up early in the morning. But every night Bergman had slept on the floor, leaving the bed for Van.

The sexual tension had been building between them ever since they got off the plane on arrival in Turkey. It was one thing to be briefed to act like a honeymoon couple in public and quite another to spend night after night with a stranger in the intimacy which their cover story imposed. Van wondered how her colleagues who worked together as couples managed that side of things. On the first night Bergman had stared at her see-through nightie that revealed proud nipples and the triangle of pubic hair.

'Do you mind?' she said. She could feel his eyes following her hungrily as she moved around the room, doing her hair and putting clothes away in the wardrobe.

'You could have packed something less transparent,' he suggested harshly.

She looked at him lying on the floor, wrapped in a sheet taken from the bed.

'On a honeymoon?' she said scathingly. 'I'm sorry if it

bothers you, but I could hardly pack a flannelette nightdress in my trousseau, could I? And it's too damn hot to go to bed in a bra and pants just to spare your sensibilities.'

Bergman had pulled the corner of the sheet over his head and turned to face the wall. With each delay he had grown angrier – until now, Van felt, he was likely to do something reckless, like pulling out of the whole operation. That was always a risk when using a freelance, so tonight she planned to release the coiled spring inside him and herself. The idea was enticing.

From what she had seen of him, Peter Bergman was the Action Man that Jack Roscoe sometimes pretended to be. He had not the same smouldering good looks but was attractive in a bluff, outdoor way. The coldly arrogant gaze and weather-beaten face both frightened her and turned her on. Bergman had a powerful, well-muscled body and moved with a kind of controlled violence that made Van want to know what he was like in bed.

She started following in his tracks down to the beach, uneasy with the suspicion that the delay was going to be longer than Bergman would accept. In her indoctrination on the Russian desk, she had learnt that there were two nights when most Soviet border guards were drunk: at New Year and after the May Day parades. It was her guess that May Day was when they would do the job – but she was not going to tell Bergman that.

May first was still two weeks away and there was only one way she could think of to keep him docile until then. Remembering Roscoe's face when she had told him that she was breaking off their relationship, Van reflected that the great advantage of a short affair with his old buddy was that it was unlikely to get complicated by emotion. The man swimming so far out that his head was just a dot visible from time to time on the crest of a wave was not the sort who fell in love – and that suited her fine.

She picked her way down the cliff-path. There was no one else on the beach. After waiting until the distant dot turned and headed for the shore, she slipped off her dress and walked naked into the water, swimming slowly out to meet him and deliberately not showing what a strong swimmer she was. She planned to let herself get into trouble with the currents, so that Bergman could help her back to the beach. A man like that should really get a kick from rescuing a maiden in distress, she thought. If it didn't turn him on, swimming naked beside her in the clear blue water, what would?

'Are you gay?'

Bergman closed the bedroom door and locked it. 'Is that a joke or a challenge?'

Van came close to him. She licked her lips and waited for him to make a move.

When he did, it was to take hold of both her arms painfully hard and say, 'Look, Miss Vanessa Bowles-Haddon, I'm not a eunuch!'

'I never said you were.' She ignored the pain and met his gaze as Bergman brought his face close to hers. She was tall. Wearing heels, her eyes were level with his.

In them he saw just a hint of mockery. He could smell her perfume. They were both still perspiring from dancing in the stuffy basement discotheque and had walked up five flights of stairs because the lift did not run after midnight. Van was breathing deeply, her breasts brushing against his chest with each inhalation.

Bergman was acutely aware of her long, shapely legs, revealed by her skirt when they were dancing. He was aware of her feet planted close to his, of her belly only inches from his groin. 'In case you're wondering,' he said angrily, 'I've picked up the signals you've been putting out all evening over dinner and down in the disco – but I'm not interested.'

'I'm sorry about that.' Van searched his eyes, as blue as her own, but harder to see into.

'It just happens,' said Bergman, spitting out the words, 'that I don't fuck around with my buddy's girl.'

'You what?' She stepped back, half-amused and half-angry.

'You're Roscoe's girl.'

She broke free of his grasp. 'I am nobody's property,' she said quietly but with vehemence.

He groaned. 'I put it badly. What I meant . . .'

'Now you get this straight,' said Van levelly. 'Jack and I had an affair which is now over. There is nothing, repeat nothing, between us.'

'Is that the truth?' Bergman was trying to recall exactly what Roscoe had said to him in London.

'It is the truth, Peter.'

'Then so's this.' He placed her hand on his groin.

With an intake of breath Van thought, Oh God, I really want you, Peter Bergman. There was a pain deep in her belly that only he could take away.

He pulled her into an embrace. She felt his lips on hers, his strong arms holding her, his hands feeling her spine, kneading her buttocks. Her arms rested on his, briefly pressing him away and then yielding as a strong finger pressed against her coccyx and made her arch her belly towards him. Her arms went around his neck. The pressure of his leg parted hers and a hand – how many did he have, for God's sake? – sneaked inside her dress, found her bra strap, unhooked it and enveloped her left breast.

After all the waiting, Van was breathing fast with excitement. She kicked off her shoes to make Bergman taller than her. She slipped Bergman's shirt down over his shoulders and ran her fingers over the rippling cords of muscle on his back. The bunches of muscle on his chest were hard against her breasts.

Bergman lifted her skirt. With a series of electric shocks his hand moved up her thigh and inside the elastic at the top of her leg.

She heard herself say, 'Yes. Oh, yes.'

Then, to Van's surprise, Bergman broke away and walked outside onto the balcony, leaving her clutching the wardrobe door for support and feeling sick. In the mirror she saw her hair was dishevelled, her eyes wide and her cheeks flushed.

Amber lights were twinkling on Samos and a cluster of steadier white points showed where some fishing boats were working with acetylene flares closer to the mainland. A thin sliver of crescent moon was already in the sky. It was the moon that worried Bergman; a full moon was a hunter's moon and he was likely to be the prey of this one.

He heard Van come after him. There was a flash of light as she opened the curtains and he felt her slip both arms tentatively round his waist, standing behind him.

'What's the trouble?' she whispered in his ear.

'I want you,' he said. His voice was even lower than usual.

Her hand dropped from his belt buckle and across his hard, flat belly, touching him. He was still hard.

'If it's any consolation,' she said softly, 'I've found it more than a little frustrating to sleep alone in the same room as a hunk of man like you.'

Still girdled by her arms, Bergman turned slowly and saw that she was naked. He broke her grip and stepped back to look at her breasts, her belly, her legs. Gently he placed his large hands under her breasts, lifted their weight of soft flesh and bent his head to kiss her nipples.

'You're beautiful,' he said, straightening up.

Van's hands were busy with his belt, loosening his trousers and pulling the shirt off so that they stood, both naked in the faint sliver of light that escaped between the curtains.

Bergman took Van's face in his hands and turned her so that the light from the room spilled onto it. 'Do you swear to me that there's nothing between you and Jack?' he asked huskily.

A man of honour, she thought: he really is! Injecting an appropriately solemn note into her voice, she whispered, 'I swear.'

'I'll kill you if you're lying,' murmured Bergman, his mouth close to hers. From the tone of voice, Van did not think the threat was entirely a joke.

He pulled her inside the room and elbowed the balcony doors shut. She was unprepared for his violence: he seemed to want to eat her and explore her and use her, without waiting for her to catch up – and yet her body responded to him as it had to no other man.

He held her trapped in front of the mirror while he caressed her breasts and slipped his strong right hand down her belly to part her legs and lift her off the ground one-fingered, a prisoner at his mercy.

Van tried to slow him down. She had planned to make love a

couple of times to get rid of the tension, with herself in control – as she had been in control of her other lovers.

This man, she now realised, was different. He was in control of her. For one flash second she recalled Roscoe's technique of gentle persuasion – the endless caresses of fingers and tongue before he entered her. Then thinking was impossible as Bergman bent her over the dressing-table and took her from behind so hard that she thought she would suffocate.

'No, Peter!' she gasped.

In the mirror she saw his eyes fixed on her body, teeth white in the half-light, his powerful muscles thrusting, thrusting, thrusting into her until she thought she would stop breathing.

She ordered her hands to tear away his powerful grip on her breasts. Instead, she saw them in the mirror clasping his hands and squeezing harder still. Her body would not obey the brain's commands; it wanted to yield and grab and suck this powerful man further and further inside her, like a mindless female creature intent on devouring the male.

From a long way away she heard herself calling again, 'No, Peter. No!' as the room went black and she was aware only of pulsing waves of pleasure that washed through her whole body and brain, melting them into a great ocean of moist, dark sensuality. Dimly she recalled a Victorian novel that had passed from hand to hand in the fourth form at boarding school. One phrase had excited her inexplicably: *He had his way with her*. Bergman, she thought, is the first man to do that with me.

She opened her eyes at last to see his face over hers, looking puzzled more than concerned.

'You OK?' he asked. 'I've been talking to you. You didn't answer.'

Van wanted to reply but her tongue was too heavy. All her body was throbbing, her skin screaming to be stroked. She felt him kissing her nipples and wanted that to go on for a long, long time like it had with Roscoe. But this was not gentle Jack . . .

Bergman knelt above her and buried his face in her belly, slipping lower with each kiss.

'This one's for you,' she heard him murmur.

Even then he was in control, pinioning her hands that sought to stop him as he led her far beyond any pleasure she had known before. Each climax incited a new and deeper wave of lust until Van found herself matching Bergman's violence: tearing from his body her pleasure, as he tore his from her flesh.

In one brief lucid interval while they lay perspiring side by side she thought: I should resent the way he never asks what I want or what I'm feeling . . . For there were none of Roscoe's gentle questions, no music, no reading of poetry in the early hours. Bergman just took her, each time in a different way. She had never known such mindless ecstasy with any other lover.

As he picked her up off the bed yet again, she felt alarmed at the storm of sexual violence he had unleashed within her. In the space of one night's lovemaking he had erased every memory of her previous lovers.

Van awoke to find that it was past 9 a.m. Beside her Bergman lay naked with an arm sprawled across the pillows, fast asleep.

'Greedy bastard,' she said. 'It's the same every night. You steal all the bed and leave no room for me.'

He grunted in his sleep. She sat up wondering what she had got herself into. They had been lovers for only a week and yet she had told this man things about herself that she had never told to Roscoe in all the time she had known him. For the first time ever she had broken security with an outsider by telling Bergman about herself, wanting him to know the person she really was – not the role she was playing – wanting him to feel for her what she felt for him.

She looked at the bedside clock. There was a telephone check to make in less than two hours' time. Van padded to the bathroom, showered, woke her lover and together they made their way lethargically down to breakfast.

There were never any endearments from Bergman in the morning. The only reference he made to the past night was a sleepy grin and: 'Did we have fun?'

At least I got that right, thought Van, following him along the hotel corridor. She felt remote and disconnected – floating. The long-held-back flood of her own emotions had taken her by surprise. They were way out of control.

'I'm so hungry, I could eat a horse!' The Canadian–South African accent floated back to her ears.

Breakfast was served on the terrace by the hotel swimming-pool. Sitting there, waiting at their table, was Jack Roscoe. He stood up with a grin, took off his sunglasses and thrust out a hand.

'Hi, Peter,' he said. 'To hell with security. I owe you an apology for the way we've kept you hanging about.'

Bergman stole a quick look at Van beside him. Her face was puffy, her lips bruised.

The grin froze on Roscoe's face. His hand dropped.

'You bastard,' he hissed at Bergman. 'You're fucking Van, aren't you?'

Bergman raised both hands in surrender. 'Back off, Jack. We're supposed to be a honeymoon couple. That's our cover, remember?'

'Don't lie to me.'

Roscoe was talking to Van now. He hated himself for saying the words: 'I know your face after you've been making love.'

A waiter was approaching the table, to take the order.

'Stop it, Jack,' said Van huskily. 'I told you back in London it was all over between us. This is nothing to do with you.'

Roscoe closed his eyes, not wanting to look at her. There was a crackle of snapping frames and lenses as he crushed the sunglasses into a useless ball of plastic and threw it down on the table like a challenge.

He turned to Bergman and said through gritted teeth. 'You cheating bastard! By God, you'll pay for this.'

I remember the look you gave me that morning, Jack. Those crazy dark eyes of yours were burning coals of pure hatred for stealing your girl, as you saw it. Without letting me or Van explain anything, you just upped and went, with those as your last words.

I didn't know what you meant until the world blew up in my face at the border. You hoped I'd be killed, didn't you? And maybe Van too. But I'm still alive so far, old buddy. And if that fat little pervert Ossetin lets me live long enough, one day I'll get out of this cage and come looking for you.

And when I find you, Jack Roscoe, you die!

PART 4

INTERLUDE
Summer 1992

.1.

For his first visit to Marseille in fourteen years, Jack Roscoe had chosen the Monday after the *Fête de Camerone*, the most famous date in the Legion's calendar. Former legionnaires who had spent the weekend on Corsica celebrating with the *deuxième REP* would be stepping off the overnight ferry in an hour or so and dropping into Larsen's bar for a few beers before heading back across the world to wherever their other homes were.

After a night spent in a crowded couchette compartment on the train from Paris, Roscoe felt like stretching his legs and walked from the station to the Vieux Port area. Finding the bar not yet open, he dumped his backpack and guitar case on the pavement outside the Maison de la Presse next door and killed time by glancing at the headlines of the previous Friday's *Daily Telegraph*. There was a war going on in what had been Yugoslavia. On the other side of the Atlantic, a stunned Los Angeles was looking at the damage caused by four days of rioting, looting and killing, following the acquittal of four white policemen on trial for beating up a black motorist.

The date at the head of each page reminded Roscoe that it

was also the sixth anniversary of the incident on the Turkish border. He put the newspaper back on its rack wondering whether that was the real reason why he was here, re-visiting scenes of his past on the off-chance of meeting an old comrade or two.

The sound of bolts being pulled announced the opening of the bar. Larsen had aged; he was now completely bald and had a large paunch hanging over his belt. He stood yawning and stretching in the doorway before grunting, '*Salut!*' and limping back to the counter. Without recognising Roscoe, he knew at a glance that his first customer of the day was an *ancien légion-naire*. A second look at the well-worn back-pack and guitar case which Roscoe was carrying made the huge Swede think them strange luggage for a man who looked nearer forty than thirty.

Roscoe bought a beer and sat listening to the Legion gossip flowing across the old-fashioned zinc-topped counter.

Larsen was a one-man poste restante service where old comrades from all over the world left messages for each other. 'Bergman?' he scratched his bald scalp. 'Peter Bergman, Canadian flier? He's dead. He got shredded in Turkey, a few years back as I recall.'

Roscoe grunted ambiguously. It was a chance in a million, but he still tried every possible lead.

'*Tu permets?*' Larsen leaned over the counter and removed Roscoe's dark glasses to study his face, deducting the wear and tear of years, like a police artist with an eraser in his hand.

'I remember you,' he said triumphantly. '*C'est toi qui as fait naufrage* – you and Bergman wrecked a boat on some Greek island.'

Roscoe nodded.

'Name and unit?'

'Jack Roscoe, but I went under the name of Raven in the *deuxième REP*.'

That name tagged another file in Larsen's computer. He snapped his fingers. 'Have I got a surprise for you, Jack Raven! Stay there and don't move!'

He made a brief phone call from behind the bar and came back beaming. 'Old friend of yours hit town last night. He flew over from Corsica because he was in a hurry to get home for some reason but he missed his plane because him an' me got talking, so he had to spend the night here.'

'Who?' asked Roscoe.

Larsen grinned mysteriously. 'I fixed him a room for the night with a pal who runs a small hotel along the street. He was just checking out when I called, so that's twice you're lucky. He'll be here in a minute.'

A group of first-engagement men in uniform from the barracks at Aubagne came in and started playing the machines. Roscoe watched them fooling around together; it made him feel old.

Jan Coetzee's voice jerked him out of the reverie, hitting him with a thump between the shoulder blades: 'Jack Roscoe! *C'est pas possible!* How are you, *soutpiel?*'

When old comrades from all over the world met friends they had not seen for years, the Swede who had taken root in France thought that all the hassle of running a bar in Marseille was worthwhile. His grin of pleasure wider than his face, he pulled three beers and thrust two across the counter with a gruff, 'These are on me.'

Coetzee was genuinely pleased to see Roscoe again. His shrewd, sun-bleached eyes took in the younger man's worn denim suit and scuffed trainers. The years, he thought, seemed to have rubbed off some of Roscoe's sharp edges; the too-handsome face had a few lines where life had written its message and erased the smart-arse smirk that had got on his nerves when Roscoe was younger.

Clinking glasses, Roscoe's first reaction was disappointment. The happy-go-lucky red-haired sergeant who had brawled his way through the carnage of Kolwezi now looked like a middle-aged businessman. He had put on weight, his hair was thinning and bleached a pale sand colour. The Italian tie, cream coloured silk shirt and expensive grey suit which Coetzee was wearing made Roscoe conscious of his own travel-stained clothes and two-day growth of stubble.

'What are you doing in these parts, Jack?' asked Coetzee, smacking his lips. Larsen always served good beer; this was Tuborg Export on draught.

'It's a long story, Coot,' said Roscoe. 'Must be ten – no, eleven – years since we last met.'

'Are you still working for those spooks in London?'

'Does it look like it?' Roscoe retorted. A punch in the solar plexus made him gasp, 'Hey, back off! That hurt, Coot.'

The young legionnaires in uniform were staring at them curiously.

'I tell you this,' said Coetzee angrily. His accent was pronounced. 'One thing I never liked was that bleddy Brit habit of yours, not answering my questions.'

He raised his fist again. Roscoe grinned and pushed it away with an apology. 'The answer is no. I was sacked years ago.'

Coetzee laughed. 'Can't say I'm sorry, Jack. Your spook pals were good payers but they gave me the creeps, genuine. That fat slob who drank too much, with the dandruff on his lapels – what was his name, Dobson?'

'Something like that.' Roscoe shifted on his bar stool.

'What they sack you for?' Coetzee pried.

To hell with all the bits of paper I signed, thought Roscoe. If Coetzee's a Russian spy, I'm Jane Fonda's toyboy, so here goes: 'They kicked me out because I didn't buy the official line that Bergman was dead. You know Peter – like a rubber ball, always bouncing back from hell . . .'

Roscoe's eyes met Coetzee's level gaze. He continued, 'I thought that maybe he had survived that snafu in Turkey somehow and vanished into the Gulag. So I tried to hustle the Service into making an offer to trade him back – or at least to put out feelers through the normal channels.'

'You say, you *thought* he was still alive.' Coetzee's voice was gentle. 'And now?'

Roscoe shrugged.

'I saw a magazine article in *Time* or *Newsweek*,' said Coetzee. 'It was all about how the Gulag has been shut down. There were photographs of empty camps and the final prisoner walking out, free at last. So if Pete was still alive, he'd have resurfaced by now, *né?*'

Roscoe laughed sourly. 'You believe that crap in the media, next you'll be seeing fairies. Of course some camps have been closed down but others are still there, take it from me. The

Gulag wasn't invented by Sovcom, it existed under the Tsars. It's as much a part of Russia as the Kremlin and the Bolshoi Ballet. Believe me, Coot, there are still a few thousand prisoners here and there that Moscow wants to hang on to for some convoluted reason or other.'

'How d'you know?'

'I talk to old friends in the business.'

'So you think Pete . . .?'

'No,' said Roscoe, tight-mouthed. 'The way things worked over there, a tough operator like Bergman would have been shoved into a hard-discipline, low-rations camp. People didn't survive six years of that and stay sane, so let's hope he's dead by now, one way or the other.'

Coetzee poured some of Roscoe's beer into his glass and raised it in a toast. 'Well, here's to Bergman on Cloud Seven. Best flier I ever saw touch down on a dirt strip.'

They clinked glasses.

'So the Brits screwed you?' Coetzee's voice had changed; there was a trace of I-told-you-so.

'My own fault,' shrugged Roscoe. 'When I realised that my bosses in London were writing Peter off because he was a colonial, a freelance – or maybe just because he didn't go to school with any of them, I started making enquiries on my own. I was warned a couple of times about what they call "unauthorised activities". I knew what would happen if I carried on, but I couldn't just sit on my arse and do nothing.'

'So what did you find out, eh?'

'Sweet fuck all,' said Roscoe. 'I kept slamming into a brick wall because somebody very high-up in Moscow or London didn't want me to cause waves.'

'Brit bastards,' said Coetzee softly.

'What do you know about them?' Roscoe asked. In the Transvaal he had made a game of baiting Coetzee. 'You've never even been to Britain.'

'I don't need to. They been in my country.' Coetzee poked Roscoe in the chest. 'Nobody knows the Brits like my people, Jack – unless it's maybe the Irish. My grandmother died in one of Queen Victoria's concentration camps, along with thirty thousand other Boer women and children, genuine. I bet you never learned about that episode of the Hope-and-Glory days in your school history lessons, eh? Luckily for me it was after grandma had given birth to my mother and not before! My great aunt was in the same camp. When her own baby died, she gave my ma the titty instead. Brits? You should have asked my great aunt, she'd have told you!'

Roscoe changed the subject. 'What's the walking-stick in aid of? Are you and Larsen running a Limping Man's Convention?'

Coetzee grimaced and tapped the stick against his stiff left leg. 'I thought I was Pete Bergman. One dicey landing too many in that Porter of his and I lost a knee-cap and wrote off a good airplane. End of flying career. Damn nearly end of Jan Gropius Coetzee, genuine. I spent three months in hospital, getting stitched, pinned and welded together but I've still got some problems with busted vertebrae.'

Roscoe winced, knowing how much the other man must hate being grounded. He changed the subject: 'So how's Sophy and the kids?'

Coetzee finished his beer before answering, 'I don't know, Jack. She left and took the brats with her the day I had the crash.'

'She walked out on you?' Roscoe was surprised.

Coetzee grinned wryly. 'There's your Afrikaner woman, Jack. She don't say much, but when she's made up her mind, that's it, eh? We'd argued about my flying for a long time – you know that. To be fair, Sophy had warned me she couldn't take much more. That day I piled up the Porter, she got a message I was lying on the veldt, ready for recycling by the worms. So she packed her bags and went.'

Roscoe looked away. He was not good at sharing pain. 'And how's Coetzee Air? Making money, I hope?'

The Transvaaler drained his glass and spoke into it. 'It hurts me to admit this, Jack, but my outfit was never the same after you bowed out. When Pete walked into the golden bullet, I should have sold up but, like most *voortrekkers*, I'm too stubborn to take the easy way out.'

Coetzee laughed at himself. 'I ended by selling up for peanuts. What's left of my little airline now has some fancy Swahili name and specialises in flying rich tourists to places where they can still have the old-fashioned fun of shooting the planet's endangered species.'

'So where do you live now?' Roscoe asked.

'Here in France. I got citizenship before I left the Legion and when everything went wrong back home I came over to Europe to start over again before it was too late.'

Despite everything, thought Roscoe, Coetzee did not look as though he had let life wear him down too much.

After a few minutes the conversation was fading out. Coetzee looked at his watch. 'Well, I got a plane to catch, Jack. It was nice talking with you, eh?'

Roscoe slapped him on the shoulder. 'It was good to see you too, Coot.'

Bending down to pick up his overnight bag, Coetzee accidentally knocked over Roscoe's guitar case. 'Sorry,' he apologised. 'Is this yours?'

'That,' said Roscoe, 'is how I earn my living.'

Coetzee looked interested. 'I recall now that Pete told me once that you were good. He heard you playing an organ in a church that made his hair stand on end.'

'Oh, not classical music,' Roscoe hastened to straighten the record. 'I left it far too late ever to get back into that scene. But when I'd stopped drinking my severance pay from the Service, I thought it was time to try my luck in the music business. My mother just died and I sold up her house to buy myself some good instruments.'

'So what kind of music do you play, Jack?'

As Larsen was busy looking after the other customers, Roscoe stepped behind the bar to fix two more beers.

'Everything,' he said. 'You name it, I've done it, Coot. I've played in studded leather pants and body make-up in a rock-and-laser show that toured the mid-West, I've given piano lessons in a Mexican convent, done a Country Music act with a pretty girl singer all over Australia . . .'

'What's she like?' Coetzee interrupted. He seemed to have forgotten that he was in a hurry to catch a plane.

'Marlene?' Roscoe smiled. 'She is six foot of peroxide blonde Californian womanhood with an excellent voice and a body to match. Wearing white Stetsons and rhinestone suits we toured the Pacific Islands, Hong Kong, Thailand . . . Made enough money to have a lot of fun – and spent it all without a thought of the morrow.'

'And what's Marlene doing for the next couple of weeks?'

'She found what she was looking for in life,' sighed Roscoe.

'Which is?'

'A millionaire in Hawaii. I left her there, drinking highballs at the poolside and hanging *loas* round the visitors' necks.'

'. . . which leaves you looking for a new partner?'

'That's why I'm here, Coot. I reckoned there must be a lot of cabaret jobs along the Côte d'Azur in the summer. Maybe Larsen can help me find some work.'

Coetzee limped to a table with his drink and sat, the injured leg stuck out stiffly in front of him.

'Join me,' he said. 'Standing gets painful.'

Roscoe sat.

'How do you fancy working with me again, Jack? I've got the ideal singer for you to work with.'

'You have?' Roscoe was intrigued.

'With some help from Lars I bought a night-club when I came back to France – down by the waterfront in Bordeaux. And right now I gotta problem: I need an MD, fast.'

'Why me?'

Coetzee grinned. 'Do me a favour, Jack. I want you to back this girl who's appearing in my club. She has a voice and a face like an angel, genuine.'

He studied the man sitting opposite him for a moment, seeing the slightly ravaged dark good looks and thinking that Roscoe was probably having even more success with women now than when he was younger. 'The two of you would look pretty good on stage together,' he decided.

'What's the catch?'

'No catch.'

'So why does this great singer need a partner in a hurry?'

'Can you write music, play keyboards, take a band-call?'

'No problem,' Roscoe nodded warily. 'But level with me, Coot. What happened to her previous MD?'

'They had a row after Maria found him in bed with the bass-player's wife. She attacked him physically and caused some damage to the parts he was using at the time,' Coetzee grimaced. 'So he came to the club next day and tore up all her music in revenge.'

'Oh no!' Roscoe held his head in both hands and groaned. 'I've had that scene, Coot. A lot of singers enjoy dressing-room dramas but they are not, repeat not, for me.'

Coetzee took a publicity photograph from his wallet and placed it on the table. 'This is Maria.'

'A stage name?'

'It's real. She's Greek, named after Callas.'

Roscoe whistled as he picked up the picture.

Coetzee lit a thin black cheroot. 'D'you ever come across a really evil sergeant in the first infantry regiment called Costas Grivas?' he asked through the smoke.

'An eagle-and-snake man?' Roscoe thought about it. 'No, I don't recall the name.'

'Before your time. He was a legend – him and a one-eyed captain by name of Koenig. They made a two-man team that tried to win the Algerian War all by themselves – and they damn near did, except the politicians got in the way. Well, Grivas left the Legion during that OAS business in 1962. Then he went back to Cyprus to set up a restaurant in some tourist resort and father five daughters. Maria is the eldest.'

Roscoe nodded. 'So that's why you're taking an interest in the girl? I thought . . .'

Coetzee shook his head. 'There's a queue of men twenty years younger than me and a lot better looking. But I don't hire Maria just to do a favour to an ex-legionnaire's daughter, Jack. No way. This girl has real star quality: the voice, the personality, the looks. One day she's going to make it to the top, genuine.'

Roscoe laughed. 'What the hell do you know about the music business?'

Coetzee poked him with his stick, hard. 'You are a condescending British bastard, you know that, Jack Roscoe? About music I don't know the difference between a portamento and a portmanteau. But about business, I know what pleases an audience – and that girl has what they used to call *It*.'

Roscoe tilted his chair back on two legs and looked away. It had always been easier for him to walk into an argument with Coetzee than to avoid one and he wasn't looking for trouble. He pushed the publicity photograph back to its owner.

Coetzee puffed at his cheroot in silence before trying another tack. '*A moi, la Légion!*' he said softly.

He knew no former legionnaire could ignore that call for help. 'I need you, Jack. Maria's fans are voting with their wallets. Every night she doesn't sing in my club, I'm three-quarters empty. When she does, I'm three-quarters full, genuine. Now, I've got a mortgage to pay off – and a very unsympathetic bank manager. I don't keep up with the payments, I lose my club. It's that simple.'

'I'll think about it, Coot.'

'I need an answer now.'

In the picture lying on the table between them, the girl's eyes accused Roscoe. Of what? he asked himself. Of owing Coetzee a good turn. He could spare a few days to go to Bordeaux and help him out of a problem, so . . .

Roscoe looked up to see Larsen's eyes on him. Reading his thoughts, the big Swede gave a theatrical wink and grunted, '*Démerde-toi! Vas-y!* Go for it.'

'Well?' Coetzee looked anxious.

Roscoe took a deep breath. 'I guess this is why I came here today, Coot. Sure, I'll come and help you out for a couple of weeks. After that, we'll see.'

.2.

With the air-conditioning switched off, the basement club smelled of stale cigarette smoke, food and drink. Without cloths to conceal them, the plywood tops of the tables were a mess of cigarette burns and the contents of upended ash-trays. The gilded chairs stacked on the tables could have done with a coat of paint. By the daylight which filtered through the grimy pavement-level windows, the carpet and furnishings had the tatty look of clubs all over the world whose owners cannot see the point of wasting money on furnishings which the customers will never appreciate in the dim lighting used during business hours.

A young North African girl in jeans and a Michael Jackson T-shirt was using an industrial Hoover on the fitted carpet and singing along with some Arabic pop music on her portable radio.

'What do you think?' asked Coetzee.

'Smells just like home . . .' Roscoe wrinkled his nose.

The interior of Le Girondin was the same as all the other night-clubs where he had worked: a fantasy palace by night and a dump by day. Exploring backstage, he found that the dressing-rooms were tiny – more like cupboards than rooms. They smelled of stale sandwiches, sweat and shattered dreams. Only Coetzee's office seemed to have had any money spent on it in the last decade. The oak-panelled walls were lined with signed photographs of stars and would-be stars who had worked there. In one corner stood an expensive modern desk and executive chair. There was a refrigerated drinks cabinet, television, tape-deck and . . .

'The casting couch,' said Roscoe, subsiding onto it. 'Is this where you auditioned what's-her-name, Maria?'

Coetzee smiled at the thought. 'She's not the sort who'll take off her pants to get a job.'

'So where is she?' asked Roscoe, accepting a beer from the fridge.

Coetzee looked uneasy. 'She's late,' he admitted.

'That's a good beginning, Coot.'

'Yeah.' There was a pause, then: 'Say, why don't you come upstairs and leave your bags in my apartment? I can put you up for a few nights, if you want.'

'OK.' Roscoe was half-regretting the impulse that had brought him to Bordeaux. He had only just got over the break-up with Marlene, so what the hell was he doing getting involved with a temperamental Greek woman singer who didn't even turn up on time for rehearsal?

He followed Coetzee upstairs past two floors of the building which were let out to a software retailing company. On the top floor was Coetzee's small bachelor apartment. It was neat and comfortable but not luxurious. Roscoe dumped his backpack in the guest room, an overgrown broom cupboard with a built-in bunk, and then joined Coetzee on the roof terrace which over-looked the wide river Garonne. A strong floodtide was pushing back inland the brown run-off from a million vineyards. Seagulls were wheeling overhead crying. A Royal Navy frigate on a courtesy visit was mooring at the quay below Coetzee's terrace.

Coetzee showed Roscoe some old prints of the scene in front of them as it had been in the days of sail. Then ocean-going ships had moored at the quays of Bordeaux ten abreast, waiting to be loaded with casks of claret that had been shipped down the river on sailing barges. The port owed its prosperity to the Romans importing from Turkey some grapevines, which were not indigenous to France. They had first planted them near St Emilion, Coetzee explained, in trenches that could still be seen, hacked out of the limestone bedrock. In the Middle Ages when Aquitaine belonged to the English Crown, the wine trade had made Bordeaux an English town on French soil.

'Fascinating stuff,' murmured Roscoe. He knew Coetzee was just talking to distract him.

'Where's this singer of yours?' he asked at last. 'That's what I'd really like to know.'

An hour later Coetzee had gone downstairs to the club to deal with some staff problem and Roscoe was dozing on the terrace, stretched out on a sunlounger, when he became aware of a dark-haired girl in her mid-twenties looking down at him. The face was the face in the publicity photograph but, as Coetzee had said, it looked ten times better in three dimensions.

'You are Roscoe?' Her voice had a singer's huskiness and a strong Greek accent.

'You are late,' he replied.

It was like a child's game, neither wanting to look away or blink first. The advantage was with Maria who had the sun behind her, while Roscoe was nearly blinded by the light in his eyes.

'What kind of musician are you?' she asked. 'Jan tells me you were in the Foreign Legion.'

'I was a bugler. I play really great fanfares.'

Maria turned away. Arms folded in front of her, she looked tense and angry.

'It was a joke,' Roscoe called after her. 'Coetzee and I met in the Legion – but that was a lifetime ago.'

He stood up, noticing how tightly Maria's lips were pursed as she took rapid puffs on her cigarette. From her eyes, he deduced that she did not like what she saw: his dark two-day stubble, old jeans and a shirt that was grubby from sleeping on trains.

Roscoe did like what he saw. Maria was several inches shorter than him. She was not slim but had a classical hour-glass shape with tiny waist, good breasts and generous hips. The figure of a Cretan priestess, he thought.

She moved like a cat, looked older than her age – Coetzee had said she was only twenty-four – and was wearing a simple sleeveless cotton dress with matching fabric sandals of a screaming canary yellow that made her olive skin seem dark. Despite the colour of the dress, as Roscoe's eyes adjusted to the light it was her olive-skinned face that drew all his attention.

It was a face from a two-thousand-year-old Greek vase: wide-eyed, bold and full of feminine challenge, framed in a mane of black curly hair that moved in the gentle breeze like seaweed in the water. Helen of Troy must have looked like that, he thought.

He held out a hand. 'Let's start again – da capo. My name's Jack.'

Her grip was surprisingly firm. 'I'm sorry,' she said. 'Is not personal but I don't think this idea going to work. Already I told Jan, is waste of time. 'E don't believe me. Very stubborn, that man.'

Roscoe took his guitar out of its case. Her voice intrigued him; he had to hear her sing. 'Suppose we give it a try?' he said calmly. 'Let's work through a couple of numbers and see how things come together.'

'All right.' Maria crushed out her cigarette and immediately lit another, then sat on one of the plastic chairs by the table with a take-it-or-leave-it gesture.

Roscoe knew several of the songs she named and busked an accompaniment in a key to suit her voice, taking it easy, not try-ing to be clever but just getting to know her musically. The more he heard, the more Maria's voice intrigued him. It was lower than that of any woman singer he had previously worked with, but had a richness and control that was extraordinary. Although she was singing quietly just for the two of them, he could sense that at full power in front of an audience she must be a very moving performer.

Also, her range of material was unusual – not just the usual female standards, but some arias that would have given her namesake Callas a moment's thought. And there were some unusual songs she had found for herself on a tour of South America.

After a few songs he felt her relax and let her real voice come through as she grew more confident in him. To work with Maria Grivas, Roscoe sensed, would be a musical challenge greater than any he had known before.

He stopped in mid-song. 'You know,' he said. 'Your repertoire is lousy.'

'Oh, thank you,' she said.

'Who the hell chose it for you?'

She stayed silent, her lips pressed tightly together.

'Did I say something wrong?'

'Oh no,' she said. 'I am Greek girl. When a man is talking I stay respectfully silent.'

'Shit,' said Roscoe. 'I didn't mean it like that.'

'What did you mean?'

He put the guitar down. 'You have a voice that's as distinctive as Streisand or Nana Mouskouri or Ella Fitzgerald. You need your own material. I'd like to write it for you.'

'Time for a break,' announced Coetzee three hours later.

The white plastic table on the roof terrace was covered in manuscript paper on which Roscoe had been working. Coetzee cleared a space and put down a tray of coffee. In a frilled dress-shirt and black evening suit, he looked like every other suave night-club owner.

'How's it?' he asked.

'Fine,' said Roscoe. He put down the guitar and stood up to ease his cramped back muscles, surprised to see that it was dusk. Neither he nor Maria had moved for hours, they had been so intent on each other musically.

Maria took a large cup of steaming coffee from Coetzee and held it in both hands, looking at Roscoe across its rim. 'He is good, Jan,' she said.

'As good as Jean-Luc?'

'Better,' she said firmly, her eyes fixed on Roscoe. 'Jean-Luc – I work with him for two years, you know. Always he play for himself. Now Jack, he play for me. I been waiting long time to meet musician like him.'

Her voice was hoarse from all the cigarettes she had smoked during the workout.

'Thank you,' said Roscoe. He was wary of admitting just yet

the kick he had got from working with her throughout the long session.

'Is like . . .' Maria turned away and looked over the river where the British frigate was floodlit, with guests walking up the gangway and being ceremonially piped aboard. 'When Jack play for me, is like I put my foot to cross the water and he place each note like a step-stone, just in right place.'

'Stepping-stone,' said Roscoe.

She turned and moved towards him with a movement that reminded him of a sensuous cat coming to be stroked. She stood close, staring up at Roscoe with a look that sent shivers along his spine. 'What's that word in English?' she asked. 'Scary? That's what it is.'

'I know what you mean.' Roscoe could not take his eyes off the woman with whom he had been working. 'Somehow I know just how you're going to phrase a line – when you're going to breathe and when you'll hold a note.'

He stopped; it was hard to explain their musical rapport for Coetzee's benefit. Between him and Maria, nothing needed to be put into words.

Coetzee's eyes flicked from Roscoe's face to Maria's and back. 'Well,' he said cautiously. 'It seems like we're going to work together, eh?'

'Is right,' Maria broke the spell by bobbing quickly up to plant a kiss on Roscoe's cheek and move away. '*A bientôt, Jacques!* I go home to fetch my stage dresses. I didn't think I be needing them tonight.'

The clatter of Maria's heels was halfway down the stairs before Roscoe picked up her meaning. 'What did she say about working tonight?'

Coetzee was looking impressed at the stack of manuscript paper. 'You have about three hours to tidy up all this scribble, Jack. Well, just enough of it to do a set or two. Maria usually goes on at midnight and again at two a.m. I'll lend you one of my dress-shirts to wear and a pair of DJ trousers. They'll be baggy on you but I'll tell the spot operator not to light you below the waist.'

'Now hold on, Coot,' Roscoe took the armful of paper covered with his scrawled notation and chord symbols. 'It'll take me a couple of days to put this stuff together and write out the bass and percussion parts, rehearse the other musicians and . . .'

'Sure, I know.' Coetzee put an arm around Roscoe's shoulders. 'But just tonight I want you and Maria to busk a couple of sets to get me out of trouble.'

'Come on, Coot. It's not on, and you know it.'

Coetzee hugged Roscoe., 'Jack, *mijn beste vriend*, did you ever hear the saying "The show must go on"? I can't close the club and I can't find a top-of-the-bill act at zero notice to replace Maria, so it has to be this way.'

'It's not possible, Coot!'

'I tell you something,' said Coetzee. 'I was sitting on the stairs down there quietly listening for part of the time you and Maria were rehearsing. I was stunned, genuine. I think the customers will love you.'

'You Vaalie bastard,' Roscoe swore. 'You were planning this the whole time, weren't you?'

'Let's say I was keeping my fingers crossed.'

'That's why Maria was so difficult to begin with? Because she knew what you had in mind. No wonder the poor girl was scared stiff.'

'I'm sorry I had to play a trick on you.' The grin on Coetzee's face gave the lie to his words.

Roscoe looked from one piece of paper to another. There would be no time for any more rehearsal, nor would that have done Maria's voice much good. A reformed smoker himself, he thought, she smokes too much . . .

'OK,' he said. He felt a flow of adrenalin course through his veins. 'We'll do it. By God we'll give the bastards a show for their money, Coot!'

At that moment he wanted more than anything else to find out whether he and the woman with whom he had been working could fool an audience with hardly any rehearsal, no backing and only their talent, professionalism and sheer nerve to see them through.

'Put us on as late as you can,' he shouted after Coetzee who was disappearing downstairs. 'And give me a thirty-minute call so I can shave and take a shower first. I'll be up here to the last minute, working on the dots.'

Roscoe sat down at the table on the deserted terrace and took a pencil and eraser to clean up the accompaniment to the first song. After a couple of minutes he stopped. It was no good, he couldn't concentrate on the dots. His thoughts elsewhere, he found himself picking out a tune on the guitar from memory. It was 'Maria' from *West Side Story*.

He stopped playing and stared for too long at the twin flood-lights lighting up the reception on board the Royal Navy frigate. When he turned his head away the image on his retinas became two eyes accusing him in the night. Two dark eyes staring. . .

Words clamoured to fit the pictures in his head. He took a clean piece of manuscript paper and found himself scribbling a long poem which began:

> Your face, when first I saw it on a vase
> Accused me with its wide-eyed stare
> Caught by a Phrygian potter's brush
> Framed in wind-blown, wild black hair . . .

.3.

The summer of '92 was unseasonally cold and wet in south-west France, but for Roscoe it was the model of what all summers should be – a succession of days each of which was better than the previous one.

Musically, Maria was his ideal partner. He spent the days writing music for her and rehearsing with her and the other musicians. Each night the club was open he found in accompanying her voice on keyboards and guitar a thrill and satisfaction that he had known with no other singer. Each time they went on stage the act got better, to judge by the audience reaction. Coetzee was soon talking of bringing a record producer he knew down from Paris to listen to them.

For the first time in his life Roscoe found the confidence to set his own words to music, writing songs for Maria to sing. One after another, they slipped into the act until Coetzee stepped in, as the owner of the club, and insisted that the paying customers wanted to hear familiar material as well. There was no argument, just an easy give and take – a kind of unspoken partnership in which Coetzee ran the business while Roscoe and Maria brought in the paying customers. Before the first week was out, Roscoe agreed to stay for the whole summer; to walk away from working with Maria had become unthinkable.

One afternoon Coetzee took the two of them up the Dordogne to see a small riverside cottage that he had won in a card game. Its isolation, yet nearness to Bordeaux, made it ideal as a place for Roscoe to practise and compose without being disturbed by any neighbours.

Next weekend when the club was closed, Coetzee drove his Chrysler Voyager to London and back, in order to collect Roscoe's belongings. They turned out to be a couple of thousand books and a huge collection of records, cassettes and CDs, all carefully crated and catalogued, plus Roscoe's music computer and hi-tech portable recording studio. Driving away from the cottage after unloading, Coetzee heaved a private sigh of relief that Roscoe looked like settling in the south-west of France for a while.

A few weeks after that, it came as no surprise to Coetzee when Maria kissed him goodnight at 4 a.m. on Sunday morning, just as he was shutting up the club. He had known for a while that Roscoe and she were lovers. She put her arms around his neck and said in her husky, post-singing voice, 'Oh, Coot, if you want to reach me, these next days – you call Jack's house, yes?'

Coetzee felt a twinge of jealousy, instantly suppressed. 'I call Jack's house,' he agreed. 'And I call Jack a lucky guy.'

She kissed him again – on the lips this time – and hugged him for a moment, unaware of the physical effect she was having. The closeness of her warm body in the skin-tight satin dress ignited a fire in Coetzee's loins that hurt. He pushed her gently away with a fatherly kiss on the cheek.

'Is all your fault, Jan,' she smiled, too bound up in her own happiness to be aware of what he was feeling. 'It was you brought Jack and me together. *Kali nikhta!*'

Outside the club, Roscoe was putting his guitar and a case of music into the boot of his new Peugeot sports convertible. Like Maria, he was still dressed in his stage clothes: black DJ trousers and a loose shirt of the same material as her emerald green dress.

Coetzee stood on the deserted pavement as they drove away

into the early morning, along the cobbled quayside and across the elegant Pont de Pierre that linked Bordeaux to the right bank of the Garonne.

Going up the stairs to his lonely apartment, Coetzee stuffed his pride into his pocket – something he found difficult – and sat down to write the first letter in a long while to Sophy and the kids.

Les Trois Moulins was a typical Dordonnais riverside village where a few dozen low-roofed limestone houses clustered between the escarpment and the river itself so tightly that, seen from the opposite bank, the roofs merged into one expanse of tiles. There was a bar, a baker's shop, a small general store, a *mairie* and a war memorial in front of the twelfth-century church. The riverbank was taken up by an immense cobbled ramp. In the days of Les Trois Moulins' prosperity it had been covered by casks of claret, stacked there for transportation by barge to Bordeaux and Libourne, the last navigable point on the Dordogne for ocean-going ships. Now half the village houses were unlived-in and the quay was moss-grown and empty, as obsolete as the three ruined windmills on the limestone spur above the village, from which the place took its name. The sleepy charm of the place was that of a hundred other villages up and down the river.

As Roscoe drove back from the club that Sunday morning, some people were already up and about. The baker was at work, scenting the air as they drove through the village with the perfume of his fresh bread and croissants. A small group of men and boys were fishing from the bridge, beneath which flowed the river swollen by the summer rains.

A mile downstream, where a bend in the course of the Dordogne hid the village from view, the scene had not changed much in two centuries. On the bank the rotten hulk of an old wine-barge waited to be washed down to the sea during a winter flood. Fish jumped and left neat circles in the slow-moving water. There had been a towpath here in the days when horses pulled the barges upriver. Now the stretch that remained served as an unmade road, linking the few riverside cottages with the village.

Roscoe bumped along its rutted surface in low gear, waking Maria. At the cottage, she walked inside with half-closed eyes and fell against Roscoe with that exhaustion of body and soul that only athletes and performers know.

'I'm so tired that I could cry,' she said. 'This not how I planned to come to you, Jack. I wanted it to be . . . so special for you.'

Roscoe scooped Maria up like a sleepy child and carried her into the bedroom where he laid her on the bed and pulled the covers up. Then he walked outside to stand in the morning chill, drinking in the freshness and the silence for a few minutes. It was like a benediction after the noise and the crowded atmosphere of the night-club. Stripping off his stage clothes, he plunged into the river and swam upstream against the current then let himself float back to the cottage, his mind a blank.

He did not believe in any specific image of God, yet in that moment of wordless communion with the ever-flowing river Roscoe felt the presence of something eternal, of which Maria and he were a part. It made sense that immersion was used to symbolise the remission of sins . . .

He climbed back onto the bank and sat soaking up the scene, gazing over the river and listening to the sounds of water and trees. A movement in the bushes twenty paces away caught his eye. He stayed as still as a rock while a doe put her velvety head out from cover and sniffed the air. Roscoe was downwind. Avoiding any abrupt movement he rolled slowly behind a bush and watched as the doe moved cautiously towards the bank and bent her head to drink. A fawn trotted warily out of the bushes after her, followed by a second one. Roscoe slid behind a fallen tree-trunk and lizard-crawled into the cottage to find his camera case and the long 400 mm. lens he used for nature photography.

The deer were still drinking when he inched his way silently back to the hide. It was as though they were posing for their portraits. Roscoe shot most of a roll of colour film, including wide angles of the peaceful, primeval scene. Twice the doe looked up in Roscoe's direction, hearing a shutter noise. Each time he took her portrait full-face and full-frame. The second time she bent and licked the upturned face of one of her fawns.

Roscoe captured the moment of intimacy on the last frame of film and stayed motionless until the deer disappeared as silently as they had come.

He sat on the riverbank for a long time before going into the kitchen. The walls were covered with poster-size prints of his wildlife photographs from the Transvaal but none was better than the shots he had just made of the doe and her fawns. He sat down at the table with pencil and paper and stared into space for a long while. For once it was impossible to put into words what he was feeling because there were no words big enough.

It was nearly midday when Roscoe threw open the bedroom window with a squeal of unoiled hinges. He looked out at the idyllic scenery around the cottage, of which he could never get enough. The sun's heat caressed his naked body with the firmness of a strong but gentle hand. He closed his eyes and remembered the very first time Coetzee had driven him and Maria out to the cottage for the inspection visit. Then he had sat on that same window ledge, naked to the waist and with the sun on his bare chest, feeling that he had come home for the first time in his life.

Behind him, he heard Maria make a little waking-up noise, like a cat purring as she stretched luxuriously between the sheets.

'Jacques?' she called softly.

After two months of working with her, Roscoe still enjoyed the way she pronounced his name, drawing out the long, soft French J and caressing the unvoiced second syllable with a click of her tongue against the palate: 'Jacques!'

He padded back to the bed, barefoot. 'Are you awake?'

'No.' She squinted at him against the light pouring through the window. 'Close the shutters, please.'

'It's a beautiful day and it's time to get up,' Roscoe insisted softly.

'Later,' Maria pleaded, eyes closed. 'Later it will be more beautiful still, you'll see.'

He pulled her out of bed, protesting and still wearing her stage dress.

'Come and see it now,' he insisted. 'The light is different in the afternoon.'

At the window, Roscoe stood behind Maria, arms loosely around her waist. 'Look out there,' he whispered. 'Isn't that the most beautiful view in the world to wake up to?'

'If you say so.'

He buried his face in the mass of dark curls that came down to her shoulders.

'Oh my God!' Suddenly awake, Maria turned in his arms and looked up at Roscoe's face, so close to hers. 'I forgot, today is your birthday, Jack. I wanted to give you a present and all I did was fall asleep.'

He chuckled. 'And what's this mysterious present?'

'Me.'

'But I've already had you,' he teased. 'Many times. A present has to be something new.'

'Oh, this is new.' Maria nodded seriously. 'This present is all of me. Only my body you had until now. Today I give you my soul, Jack. Now all is yours.'

Gazing down into her wide, serious eyes, Roscoe wanted to drown in their dark pools. 'I feel the same,' he said huskily.

'Do you?' she asked. 'For a man is different, I think. You have secrets from me, I know. Like the river outside the cottage, some parts of you are so deep, no one ever see them.'

She planted a kiss on his chest, ran her fingers through the hairs and said, 'You say nothing because I am right. No matter, Jack. The important thing when you love someone is to give – don't matter what you get back.'

She pushed Roscoe gently down on the edge of the bed. In the pool of sunlight she danced for his pleasure, the silhouette of her body showing clearly through the back-lit green satin of her dress. With the first steps Roscoe picked up the rhythm of her movements, clicked his fingers in time and sang the words with her. He knew the dance; it was a part of their stage routine – a finger-snapping Greek *hora* in which Maria's charisma made the audience see the non-existent partners who passed her from one to the other around the circle of dancers as she smiled at each one in turn, now flirtatiously, now demurely.

This time she danced with no faked smiles for phantom

partners, but seriously, like a temple virgin dedicating herself to
Roscoe, waiting for her on the bed. At the end of the dance, he
applauded softly as, with one of her cat-like gestures, she wriggled out of the dress and threw it away from her. It fell to the
floor, like a pool of green foam from which she stepped to
stand, legs apart and hands outstretched to him.

In the back-lighting, the fuzz of her pubic hair glowed like a
soft beacon between her legs. She came to him and knelt on the
bare tiles, looking up into his eyes. 'You are so beautiful,' she
whispered.

'I'm supposed to say that to you.' His voice was hoarse with
desire.

'I am Greek woman. We do things different.' Her face was
coming closer and closer to his.

'Differently,' he corrected.

'Ssh!' Her lips brushed his. She closed her eyes and touched
his face with her fingertips, like a blind woman feeling a statue,
exploring his eyebrows and nose and the stubble on his chin.
Then her fingers slipped lower to his collar bone and the muscles of his chest and arms.

Roscoe reached for her breasts and framed them in his hands.
He watched the dark nipples erect themselves. Then her curly
head dipped and cut off his view as she bent to caress and kiss
his flesh.

Making love with Maria was like nothing Roscoe had known
before. It was both more sensual and yet purer than what he
had felt with any other woman. He had no sense of himself and
her as being separate bodies, no awareness of making love to
another person. It was as though they really were one flesh, as
though in caressing her body he was himself caressed, as
though in feeding her hunger for his body he slaked his thirst
for hers.

She raised her face to him, licking moist lips. 'Happy birthday!' she said.

The caresses ended in a drowsy entanglement of legs and
arms. His last thought was: this beloved flesh . . .

He awoke to find Maria supporting her head on one arm
and studying his face in close-up. She ran her fingers through
his straight, thick dark hair, so different from her own fine

curls. Then she traced the line of his profile, moving her index finger down the brow, the nose, the lips, the chin.

'So strong you are,' she murmured, liking what she saw.

Roscoe pulled her close in the embrace of one powerful arm. 'Like Samson,' he said, 'I was strong until I met Delilah. Now look what you've done to me.'

'I like what I've done to you.' Maria's voice was husky from singing and cigarettes. She reached for the packet of Gauloises beside the bed but Roscoe knocked them to the floor, out of reach.

She laid her head on his chest, taking pleasure in the well-muscled body beneath her. 'When we first met, you were not happy, Jack. Sometimes you looked so angry, I was thinking you could kill people.'

Her free hand stroked the skin of his arm. She lowered her head and planted a kiss on one nipple, inhaling deeply. 'I love the smell of you,' she said.

Roscoe raised Maria's head from his chest and turned it sideways so that he could admire her profile, framed by the tumbling mass of dark curly hair. His hand slipped slowly down her neck, then lower still and brushed against her breast.

Her sharp intake of breath was followed by: 'On a man's birthday, a woman can deny him nothing.'

'Another of your old Greek sayings?' he joked.

'No, I just made it up.'

'Well, I've got a new English saying for you: on a man's birthday, he should give pleasure to others.'

Maria watched Roscoe's face as he stroked her belly and slipped his hand between her legs, opening her lips and touching her gently as she moved rhythmically against him. The first time they had made love, she had stopped him touching her because she had never been able to let any previous lover bring her to orgasm that way. Her other men had wanted to conquer her and take their pleasure from her. But with Jack it was different; everything was different with him . . . She closed her eyes, trusting him.

Watching her unhurriedly pleasuring herself, Roscoe studied the soft olive skin of her face, her breasts, her belly and her smooth, lightly tanned legs as she rubbed them languorously together. He bent his head and kissed the closed eyelids, then her mouth, then first one nipple and the other, sucking gently, caressing with his tongue.

Maria lay, cradled in his strong arms, floating through shifting warm colours that became sequences of notes so pure that they would never be sung. In the background, through the open window, she could hear the breeze faintly sighing in the poplar trees along the riverbank.

Between half-closed lids, she watched her lover tenderly watching her pleasure that was not secret but his to share. She ached to give to him. Give, give, give, she thought dreamily. I give you even my pleasure, Jack . . .

When he heard Maria's moan, Roscoe held her tightly and watched her face. As her eyelids opened in that wide-eyed stare that he had recognised the first day, she clutched him with both hands, digging her long nails into the flesh of his arms. He winced, not with pain but with the intensity of her pleasure, which hit him in the belly.

Maria gasped for air, then all her tensed muscles went limp. She shuddered and buried her face in the hairs on his chest, murmuring, 'Oh, Jack. My Jack.'

As he entered her a gust of wind from nowhere erupted into the room with a swishing of willow leaves and went banging its way though the house, slamming doors and windows. It was, thought Roscoe, as though the river god had sent his blessing on their union.

.4.

It was afternoon when Maria went round the cottage, throwing open shutters and exclaiming with pleasure at the different view from each window.

Roscoe sat up in bed, listening to her. The light flooding into the room was filtered through the foliage of the willow tree just outside the window. It bounced off the old, cracked terracotta tiles on the floor and tinted the lime-washed walls a pale green. The only furniture apart from the bed on which he lay was an old straw-bottom chair, a dressing-table and a wardrobe, all of which had been in the house when he moved in. Inside the doorless wardrobe hung his stage clothes and the few casual garments he had bothered to bring from England. All his formal clothing like suits and ties, he had dumped in an Oxfam shop, wishing that one could get rid of memories as easily.

The scene in front of him could have been a still-life painted by Van Gogh at Arles, until Maria returned to get dressed in the pool of sunlight by the window and turned it into a composition by Degas or Renoir which Roscoe amused himself by titling silently: *The Greek Woman At Her Toilet*.

He lay on one elbow watching Maria brush her hair, enjoying the intimacy of the situation and the way she moved like a wild animal, with the combination of vigour and femininity that had turned him on the first moment they met.

Maria went into the kitchen to make some coffee. Roscoe heard a burst of a chat show on France Inter, then silence broken by her swearing in Greek at the electric kettle.

'I should have told you,' he called from the bed. 'There's a fault in the wiring. The kettle always blows the fuse. You'll have to heat the water on the gas stove.'

A loud plop sounded from the surface of the river that ran only a few metres from the open window of the bedroom. Fish for supper, thought Roscoe drowsily.

Maria returned with a large bowl of coffee in one hand and a heated-up croissant in the other. Roscoe reached out for her but she dodged away, placing his brunch out of reach on the windowsill with a smile and: 'Now you must get up for it, you lazy man.'

Still naked, Roscoe carried croissant and coffee outside, stepping out of the window and taking a half-dozen paces to the edge of the bank. He dunked the croissant French-style and munched it all soggy, then drank the strong black coffee, feeling good, naked in the open air.

Upstream a couple of ancient wooden boats were moored to yellow plastic buoys. In each an elderly man sat fishing. They were both looking skywards. Roscoe followed their eye-line to find a black kite circling lazily in a thermal. It plummeted down to the river and swooped upwards again, clutching a large trout in its talons.

Jerked wide-awake by the caffeine, Roscoe dived into the river and swam against the current up to the boats. He chatted to the old men about the weather and how the grape-harvest was going to be the worst for a century, due to the rain and the lack of sun. Floating back with the current, he saw a flash of kingfisher blue at one of the cottage windows as Maria moved about inside. Most of her clothes were of vivid primary colours, like her moods and thoughts – always clear-cut and passionate.

He heaved himself out of the water and lay on the bank, letting the warm air dry his body and trying to work out which of the deep pools was the one to fish that day. In less than an hour he was putting away his rod, with six large river trout gutted and ready for cooking. He placed his catch in a sealed plastic bag and weighted it down with a stone in the shallows to keep cool. Beside it went a bottle of a neighbour's homemade white wine for which he had bartered some fish a few days before.

The sultry afternoon drifted by with Roscoe working on some musical arrangements and Maria dozing beneath the canopy of the willow tree. Like most Mediterraneans, she preferred not to expose her skin to direct sunlight for long; the pleasure of a warm day for her was in lying in the shade. In order to keep cool they swam naked repeatedly in the now deserted Dordogne and made leisurely love on the grassy riverbank to the sound of music by Satie drifting through the windows of the cottage.

Since the two old fishermen had packed up and gone home, Roscoe and Maria had seen no one on their stretch of the river. For such a vivacious person, Maria spoke little that afternoon. Responding to the silence, she communicated mostly with smiles and touches. When she did speak, it was in a whisper that just reached from her deckchair to Roscoe's as they sat sipping *pastis* in long glasses and waiting for the evening cool which did not come that day.

The smoke from Roscoe's barbecue fire rose in a thin vertical column through the motionless air. From the south where the Pyrenees lay, came rumblings of distant thunder. Wearing just a pair of shorts, Roscoe grilled the fish over the embers while Maria set the outdoor table, coming and going in the blue dress that made her look like some exotic bird, fluttering back and forth between the house and the river.

They ate avgolemono soup which she had made, with bread smothered in terrine de rillettes and pâté de campagne, followed by the fish with boiled new potatoes dripping in local butter. To drink, there was the cooled bottle of wine. The simple meal had that magic of an unhurried feast in the open air. All around the horizon, dry lightning flickered and the clouds grew heavier and heavier.

After dinner, Roscoe strolled along the riverbank, hand in

hand with Maria, watching Nature's fireworks. Thinking aloud, he murmured, 'I think I'll make Coot an offer for this place. He wants to get rid of it. It needs rewiring and plumbing, but otherwise I wouldn't change it much.'

A little later, Maria said, 'Flowers. You need a garden, Jack – with flowers and herps . . .'

'Herps?'

'Like basil and thyme and sage –'

'You mean herbs.'

'– and rosemary,' she finished. 'The fish would have tasted even better cooked with rosemary.'

'That's for remembrance,' Roscoe mused.

She didn't get the reference.

'Shakespeare's *Hamlet*,' he explained. 'When Ophelia goes mad.'

It was the little lacunae in her education or his which reminded Roscoe that they had grown up in different cultures – he in Britain and she in Cyprus – speaking different languages, learning different versions of history.

'Why did Ophelia go mad?' Maria wanted to know.

Roscoe did not remember exactly. 'For love,' he guessed.

'And what happened to her?' There was something of a child's eagerness-to-know in Maria's voice.

'She drowned herself.'

The heavy clouds had made it prematurely dark. Maria looked away from Roscoe's face and across the Dordogne's untroubled surface, covered in cotton-wool pollen from the poplar trees.

'I could do that,' she said. 'Drown myself for love.'

Roscoe caught her arm. 'You are an over-passionate Greek woman,' he said softly.

'And you,' she whispered back, her dark, wide-open eyes fixed on his, 'are a cold-blooded English man.'

The exchange of tender insults was saluted by the first crash of thunder nearby. Roscoe's inner camera captured Maria's face, lit by the lightning flash. In that second he would have traded his gifts for words and music, to be able to draw and freeze a moment of beauty – or better still, to paint her face on a vase for another man to enjoy in twenty centuries' time.

'What's the matter?' she asked, seeing the shadow pass behind his eyes.

'Nothing,' he lied.

Roscoe wished that he had Maria's innocence which enabled her to accept the happiness they shared without thinking of past or future. At each pass in their journey of mutual exploration, he felt a need to turn and scan the landscape of their emotions as though on the lookout for pursuers from the past who would one day call him to account.

The next day dawned hot and stifling. The old men fishing talked to Roscoe during his morning swim of *la canicule*: the dog days with the heat that kills the very young and the very old. It was the hot dry wind blowing from the mountains that made tempers snap, cars crash and men back up an argument with a blow – or so they said.

The fish were not biting that day but the flies were. Myriad small black insects, borne on the thunderous air, got in the eyes and the mouth. Leaving Maria asleep in bed, Roscoe pulled on a pair of cut-off denim shorts and trainers. He jogged along the towpath, warming up for a run that took him along the river to the village then uphill through the vineyards and into and out of the small wooded re-entrants that broke the line of the escarpment. It was a tough ten-mile circuit. Since moving into the cottage he had taken up running again and did this circuit several times a week.

Maria was still asleep when he returned, so he swam to cool down and then tackled the bramble-infested garden with a borrowed scythe, getting a kick from fighting the heat. In late afternoon there were sudden gusts of wind that set dust-devils whirling. They scorched Roscoe's chest and back like the sand-loaded scirocco from the desert. The air was thick with pollen from the poplar and willow trees that lined the riverbanks. Heavy black clouds started building up again and the thunder was getting nearer.

The storm broke before suppertime, sending them running indoors through a cloudburst in which the rain turned to sleet and coated the ground for a few seconds with a false snow. Maria stuck her hand out of a window and collected a handful of hailstones which she ate, swearing they had a special taste, unlike that of earthly ice: '. . . a hint of ambrosia – which was the food and drink of the gods, Jack.'

She collected some more and rubbed them into Roscoe's face. When he asked why, she whispered into his ear something in Greek that sounded midway between a prayer and a wish.

He caught one word. 'What's that mean: *ambrotos?*'

'Immortal.'

'And?'

Maria pulled Roscoe's head down and buried her face in his rain-slicked hair briefly bejewelled by the hailstones. She held him there, unable to account for the premonitory surge of protective instinct she was feeling.

'In my grandmother's village in the Tróodos Mountains on Cyprus . . .' She spoke slowly, her mind a long way away. '. . . they rub hail onto a baby's face to give it long life. She used to do that for me, Jack. Those people in that village say she was a witch.'

'And was she?'

'I think so,' Maria nodded seriously.

After the torrid heat of the day, it was a relief that the air had cooled down by fifteen degrees or more. The house had no gutters, so water poured off the roof and ran down the outside walls, soaking the ground and oozing in through the doors to make puddles on the floor. There was no point in trying to do anything about it. In the middle of the storm a lightning strike on the overhead power line took out the electricity supply.

As Coetzee's club did not open on Mondays during the summer, they took the power cut as a hint to eat out and drove through the downpour to Bergerac where Roscoe knew a small restaurant in the medieval quarter overlooking the river. The workmen's menu was simple but generous: potage, hors d'oeuvres, *lapin à la moutarde*, followed by cheeses and a *gateau basque* with as much local red wine as they could drink included in the price.

The rain had stopped while they were eating. Since Maria did not know the old town, Roscoe took her on a gentle stroll arm in arm through the deserted, glistening streets while, above them, storm clouds raced across the face of the moon.

In the small cobbled square of restored medieval timber-frame houses where the statue of Cyrano stood, Maria asked, 'Who is that man with such a long nose?'

'Cyrano de Bergerac,' Roscoe answered. 'He was a poet and a soldier.'

'Like you?'

Roscoe shook his head. 'He did both things well. I write poems but I was never a good soldier.'

'I am so glad.' Maria stared up at the statue, glistening in the moonlight. A cloud plunged them into darkness. She turned to Roscoe. 'I could not love a man who had killed someone.'

Roscoe thought of the running man he had killed at Kolwezi. He had been black as the night around them . . .

'What did he do?' she asked.

Startled by the question, he asked, 'Who?'

'This Cyrano,' she said. 'Why is he so famous they make a statue from him?'

For Roscoe, the magic of the evening had gone. 'He wrote love poems,' he said slowly, 'for another man to claim as his own.'

'How sad!' Maria cried. 'Why ever should he do that, Jack?'

Between a gap in the clouds the moon flooded the square with light again. Roscoe looked up at the statue so that she could not see his eyes. 'Because Cyrano believed his nose made him ugly. And the girl was very beautiful, so he thought she would not love him.'

He tried to pull Maria away from the statue, with: 'It's going to rain again. Come on. We're miles from the car.'

She slipped through his arms and walked away from him across the silvered cobbles: a black-haired woman in a red dress turned black by the moonlight, trailing blue Gauloise smoke after her.

'I think you are a little like this man Cyrano,' she said.

'No.'

'Yes.' Maria paused. 'You have two sides, like him. There is the man I love, the man I make music with. And there is another Jack Roscoe hidden inside you, am I right?'

Roscoe felt very sober.

'Sometimes at night, Jack, you are talking when you dream,' whispered Maria. 'Of Birmingham maybe? Or Burma?'

'Bergman,' he said.

'Yes. Who was that person, Bergman?'

A cloud blacked out the square. Maria came close to feel Roscoe shaking.

'Are you crying?' she wondered aloud. She put her arms around him. 'Oh Jack, what is it? You can tell me.'

The first drops of rain came on a gust of wind that hit them like a slap in the face. Roscoe let Maria hold him and pull his head down to her breast. They clung together in the empty square and let the cloudburst drench them from head to foot in seconds.

During the applause, Maria stepped into the spotlight and unclipped the mike from its stand. Her head was haloed with smoke from the cigarette in her right hand. Sometimes she sang for the pure pleasure of making music. That night – the first performance since her decision to live with Roscoe – she was singing for him.

Coetzee had said nothing to them about the man sitting at his personal table. By the third verse of Lena Horne's old standard 'My Man', conversation in the club had stilled completely. The words of the song could have been written for Maria, to express what she felt about Jack Roscoe. Nobody moved or talked as she put an extra edge of feeling into the words that night. The eyes of Coetzee's guest were fixed on the woman in the glittering red sequin sheath dress that fitted her body as closely as the song suited her voice.

Roscoe's fingers hit the notes before he thought about them. The twin sounds of voice and piano melted into one to make a moment of musical perfection, delicately framed by Roscoe's arrangement for the bass and drums. On the stage a musical miracle was happening that occurs only a few times in a musician's lifetime. For Roscoe and Maria it was like making love without touching – the essence of their souls entwined upon a bed of harmony.

At the end of the number, there was that momentary hush which tells a performer that he or she has transported the audience somewhere else. Maria stood immobile, holding everyone in suspense, and then with perfect timing lowered the mike to cue the applause. She made the musicians stand and take a bow, pulled Roscoe close to her and hugged him in the spotlight.

'Was perfect, Jack.' She had forgotten to breathe at the end of the song and had to drag in a huge lungful of air, like a runner at the end of a race. She exhaled and leaned against him, enjoying the feel of his strong arm around her waist, supporting her.

There were twin spots of high colour in Maria's olive-complexioned cheeks and her eyes were shining. 'You played like an angel,' she said.

Roscoe was equally high on the drug of a successful performance. He laughed, 'You sing like one.'

She purred with the pleasure of the moment. 'It was your playing made it possible. Jack, you're the most wonderful man in the world.'

The applause had died, so that the mike picked up her last sentence loud enough for people to hear. There was a chorus of ironic shouts and whistles from the audience – and a rhythmic clapping for more. The drummer, who was always clowning around, started crooning into the hi-hat mike the words of 'The Most Wonderful Man In The World'.

Coetzee turned to the American sitting beside him and asked, 'So man, was I wasting your time, eh?'

His guest was a record producer, based in Paris. He had not moved a muscle since Maria came on stage and took his eyes off her now to smile ruefully at Coetzee. 'Damn you, Jan,' he said. 'You know what I'm thinking.'

'Maria is some singer, eh?'

'Some duo,' the producer corrected Coetzee. 'That Jack Roscoe is a fine musician, y'know. Without his accompaniment, she wouldn't come across one half so well.'

Coetzee poured some more champagne into both glasses. 'About the material you've been listening to,' he said apologetically. 'I let them do quite a few of Roscoe's songs here because my clientèle like them, but don't worry; for a record they have plenty of well-known songs to choose from.'

'Worry about it?' The record producer shook his head. 'You

gotta be joking. That Jack Roscoe is one helluva songwriter, Jan. It's his output I want to record, not the other stuff.'

Coetzee blinked. Jack's scribbling? Oh well . . .

The producer pulled out a note book and extracted a Harley Davidson brute of a fountain pen from another pocket. 'Who's their agent, Jan?'

'Me.'

'Well, keep it that way, fella. If you're on even ten per cent of those two beautiful people, you'll end up a millionaire. I can see Maria and Jack topping the bill at The Palms in Las Vegas one day.'

PART 5

THE MESH
Autumn 1992

. 1 .

The Piskaryovskoye Memorial Park outside St Petersburg was the largest cemetery in the world, with the remains of half a million people who died in World War Two during the siege of what was then called Leningrad. Some were soldiers who met death from fire and steel but most were civilians – women and children whose end came from starvation and hypothermia. They made thin corpses, but even so it was necessary to lay them three deep in order to accommodate all the mass graves within the forty-acre site. During the siege there were probably another half-million corpses that had never made it to the cemetery, being lost in the snows, eaten by animals or humans – or simply blown to pieces too small to identify and bury.

From concealed loudspeakers the sound of the St Petersburg Symphony Orchestra wafted over the huge slabs of wet granite that led from the memorial statue at one end to the eternal flame which flickered and roared in the wind at the other. Not a sweet wrapping, a drink can or an untidy blade of grass marred the geometric precision of the site.

On the last Monday of November 1992 the weather in St Petersburg was cold and squally under a grey sky. In the harbour the cruise ship *Anton Chekhov* was inching in to its moorings. Madeleine Wharton looked out of the window of her luxury cabin on main deck and thought it a fitting day to visit a graveyard. Piskaryovskoye was the first call on the printed excursion itinerary in her hand.

The four-day round-trip from Helsinki was cheap as cruises go. The catch, if there was one, was that the shore excursions had to be paid for on board in hard currency, which made the *Anton Chekhov* a small but useful money-spinner for Boris Yeltsin's hard-pressed Treasury. It was also a loophole for people who wished to enter Russia without applying for a visa in the usual way; passengers who paid for an excursion were, by a quirk of Russian bureaucracy, entered on the ship's group visa and allowed to go ashore on their own afterwards simply by showing their passports at the bottom of the gangway. That suited Madeleine Wharton very well. At an airport she would have been recognised by someone in the business of watching faces, who would have wondered what the Director-General of Britain's SIS was doing, making an unaccompanied visit to Russia.

A thin, elegant and lonely woman of fifty-eight, Madeleine had not left her cabin since joining the ship at Helsinki. A hefty bribe in dollars to a steward before the ship left Helsinki harbour ensured that all her meals were brought to her, avoiding the need to meet or speak to any other passenger. She had spent the voyage immersed in a well-thumbed copy of *The Herries' Chronicle.* Although ostensibly on holiday, she was dressed in one of her habitual dark grey two-piece business suits, the only concession to femininity being a Victorian floral brooch pinned on her lapel.

An announcement over the ship's loudspeaker system warned that the day's excursion was about to depart. Madeleine used a single discreet dab of almost invisible mauve lipstick and turned away from the dressing-table mirror as though it were no friend. She knotted a Paisley headscarf under her chin, put on a pair of dark glasses and a fawn raglan raincoat, checked her appearance in the mirror, picked up her umbrella and was ready for work.

Anastas Lirian was proud of his new black Mercedes limousine with the curtained rear compartment. It was the sort of rolling status symbol once reserved for Politburo members and now favoured by Russian Mafia bosses and the new breed of post-USSR tycoon. At fifty-five Lirian was living very well for a man who had been declared redundant just over a year earlier when the KGB was first abolished and then resurrected, only to be slimmed down by several hundred thousand employees in the Yeltsin administration's cutbacks.

Lirian sat playing chess in the rear seat of the Mercedes as it drove in through the VIP gates of the cemetery and crunched twin tracks through the freshly raked gravel to park near the main memorial. His driver was a stunningly beautiful young woman in her early twenties who called Lirian by his first name.

'We're early, Anastas,' she said, passing him a cup of thermos coffee.

He took the cup absently and sipped from it, his mind on the board in front of him. The drama being played out there was the last ten minutes of the final game in the Fischer-Spassky confrontation at Reykjavik, Spassky to move. If only, Lirian thought for the thousandth time, they had sent me and not Spassky to Iceland . . .

Twenty years before, Lirian had been the most brilliant up-and-coming player in the Soviet Union, on track to become all-Union and then World Grand Master. His swarthy Armenian complexion had been to blame when he was taken quietly aside by the Chairman of the Russian Chess Federation and told that his chess-playing days were over because the Politburo had decided that too many Jews, Armenians and other foreigners were winning Soviet chess titles.

As consolation, Lirian was promoted to play the game of Intelligence. He had protested, and continued arguing even in Yuri Andropov's office on Dzherdzhinsky Square. In a rare moment of tolerance, Andropov had told his brilliant new recruit, 'The rewards at our game are far greater than even for a state chess-player, Anastas Romanovich. You already have wealth, privileges, foreign travel. To those we can add power. And the game we play is Real Chess where good players are not limited to sixty-four squares. The whole world is our game board. What more could a player of your skills want?'

'Fame,' had been Lirian's succinct reply.

His sights had been set on a niche of his own in the pantheon of chess grand masters alongside Botvinnik and Kasparov and the rest. Instead his star had risen in the misty constellations of Intelligence where only a handful of colleagues and enemies knew his name and achievements.

'Anastas!'

Lirian lifted his eyes from the board. It was time to get back to the present.

'The coaches are just arriving in the tourist car-park,' said the girl in the front seat of the Mercedes.

He folded the board away. There was no question in his mind: Fischer would not have stood a chance against him. And then things would have been so different.

'. . . but, Nadochka,' he finished the thought aloud, 'I'd never have found you, would I?'

Unlikely as it would have seemed to anyone who knew him, Lirian had fallen in love for the first time in his life.

Nadya did not reply. She was busy watching Madeleine Wharton step down from the first coach.

'You remember the drill?' Lirian prompted.

'I wait for her to walk behind the car, then slip out and put on her coat, glasses and headscarf. I join the tour group and stay with it until we do the same thing in reverse in the women's toilets at the Hermitage Museum.'

Lirian passed the empty cup back to her. 'Don't forget,' he cautioned, 'to walk like a woman of nearly sixty.'

Nadya's hazel eyes teased him in the rear-view mirror. 'Why do you think I'm wearing these awful old flat-heeled shoes, Anastas?' she asked. 'Don't worry, I'll have plenty of time to study her walk as she approaches.'

Madeleine stood in the drizzle with a few other tourists. The guide, who did not want to get wet, was telling them that they were free to wander where they wished in the park, so long as they were back at the coach in fifteen minutes. On account of the weather, most people were staying in the coaches.

Madeleine strolled away from the other hardy souls with umbrellas and coats. Tidy ranks of single red roses lay on the wet grass – the previous day's offering from relatives and survivors of the siege. One of the things Madeleine liked about the Russians was the way they continued honouring their war dead instead of forgetting them as soon as possible, which seemed to be the fashion in the West. She still felt angry over the poor turnout at the Cenotaph in Whitehall on Remembrance Sunday earlier that month. It was forty years since her older brother Second Lieutenant Julian Wharton had gone to glory with the Gloucesters on the banks of the Imjin River. Now nobody but her seemed to remember his sacrifice. If there had been a grave in Korea or a spot of earth anywhere she could associate with her brother's memory, she would have crossed the world to lay a red rose on it.

The drizzle slid horizontally beneath the umbrella to speckle her sunglasses as she strolled towards the waiting black Mercedes, wishing that she had brought a flower to lay that morning at Piskaryovskoye *in memoriam*.

The music from the loudspeakers grew louder and faded as the wind whipped the sound first towards and then away from Madeleine's ears. The effect was eerie in the rainswept cemetery. She recognised the music as Shostakovich's Seventh Symphony. It had been written in Leningrad itself during the siege when the people now lying beneath her feet were dying. Enfolded in the music she found the thunder of the German guns and the scream of shells and bombs that had beaten on the composer's ears as he laboured on the score by candlelight.

Shielded by the car, the exchange of coat, glasses, umbrella and headscarf went smoothly.

'Where are you sitting?' asked Nadya in perfect English.

'Fourth seat on your left as you enter the coach.'

'Did you speak to anyone?'

'They're all German,' said Madeleine, as though that answered the question. 'Hence my choice of the first coach. I froze off one lonely widower who tried to chat me up. I don't think he'll bother you.'

For a moment she thought that Lirian had chosen an inappropriately young and attractive girl as her stand-in. Then the quick transformation of clothing, umbrella and glasses was complemented by a long-legged stride that imitated her own as Nadya moved away in the direction of the group re-assembling near the coaches.

'Welcome to St Petersburg,' said Lirian's smooth voice. He had slipped into the driving seat, leaving the curtained rear compartment for his guest. Madeleine took in his spectacles with wire rims and metal arms that hooked round his ears. He had put on some weight, she noticed, and had a pot-belly. The once hawkish face was now almost avuncular; only the dark eyes behind the pink-tinted lenses still had the same reptilian glitter.

Lirian started the engine and pulled out of the cemetery and onto the main highway leading into the city.

'We want to deal,' said Madeleine. She found small talk boring and went straight to the point. 'But the price is too high, Anastas Romanovich.'

Lirian took a packet of Marlboro off the dashboard and shook out a cigarette one-handed.

'Kindly don't,' she said.

He shrugged and threw the cigarette out of the window. 'It's a seller's market,' he countered. 'Probably the only one in Russia right now. Medvedev wants two million dollars, won't take a penny less.'

The haggling over money lasted until well into the city and was still unresolved as they crossed the Kirovsky Bridge over the Neva with the Hermitage well in sight.

'There are other complications too,' said Madeleine. 'Identification is one.'

Lirian shrugged, 'You're still worried this is not the real Sir John Bowles-Haddon we're offering you?'

'We have reason.'

'Don't worry, the incident in Turkey was a set-up to provide Sir John with a cast-iron alibi. There was never any danger of him being hurt.'

'Why did he need an alibi?' she asked. 'He was safe in Moscow. We couldn't touch him there.'

'To visit his mother,' said Lirian. He watched his passenger's face in the mirror for some reaction but was disappointed. 'The old lady was too ill to travel. Despite his plastic surgery and the changed voice, Sir John didn't feel safe passing through British immigration. So we set up the fake run for home via Turkey as a way of him dying for the record, literally under observation by your people.'

'And did he visit her?'

'Every six months until her death last year. He was very upset at being unable to get to the funeral in time. That may account for his changed behaviour.'

Lirian parked the car near the museum and turned to her. 'It's time you went inside the Hermitage.'

Oh my God! Madeleine looked away and clutched her throat. She had just worked something out.

Looking out of the window she said distantly, 'Back in '86 you told London that he insisted on his niece being present on the Turkish border to identify him. It wasn't an accident that she nearly died, was it?'

Lirian's snake eyes glittered. 'Sir John said to me at the time, "Nobody will suspect me of killing my own niece to provide myself with an alibi." Clever, wasn't it?'

Clever? Yes, Madeleine had to admit it was clever. 'One million sterling,' she said, her mind made up. 'That's our final offer. You can tell your boss General Medvedev that in my opinion Sir John Bowles-Haddon is not worth buying back at half that price. Frankly, I wouldn't choose to have the old queen back for free. Most of the beans he spills will turn out to be marbles. They'll give a lot of people indigestion to no purpose.'

'Two million US dollars,' said Lirian. 'Or no deal.'

Madeleine cut in on him. 'I'm known to my staff by several sobriquets, Anastas Romanovich. None of them is very complimentary, which I take as a tribute to the tight ship that I run. One of the nicknames is The Iron Virgin. Can you guess why?'

He waited.

'Because I've never been screwed,' she said. 'Not physically,

politically or financially. When I do lie down and open my legs –
and I'm speaking professionally of course – it will be in aid of
something far more important than this pathetic old traitor. Is
that clear?'

Lirian knew when he had met his match. 'The message,' he
said, 'is couched in exactly the kind of language General
Medvedev understands. I'll deliver it to him verbatim.'

.2.

George Dawson was waiting next morning as arranged outside the dock gates. His car was a dented old black Volga with plates bought for cash from a man in the black market behind the Baltic station. The genuine plates included a 'foreign driver' code which ensured that the GAI traffic police would log the car's every movement.

Dawson leaned back and opened the rear door as Madeleine Wharton walked through the gate in a group of tourists.

She slipped into the back seat of the Volga, opened the window to let out some of the stale tobacco fug from Dawson's pipe and ordered him, 'Drive.'

'Where to?' he asked.

'Oh just drive, George,' she snapped. 'It doesn't matter where.' The enforced wait in St Petersburg was getting on her nerves. The *Anton Chekhov* did not return to Helsinki until the following day and there was nothing she could do about it but stay in her cabin, reading.

Dawson was handling the car very cautiously, always giving way to other traffic.

'Is this vehicle clean?' she asked.

'Check it myself every morning,' he confirmed.

'There's a car following us.'

'It's Lirian's bird, riding shotgun as a courtesy to you, just in case.'

'That man is a crafty dago.'

'And so say all of us, including his master. Medvedev hates Anastas's guts.'

The dead pipe was clamped between his teeth, making it hard to hear what Dawson said. 'Medvedev took advantage of Yeltsin's cutbacks two years ago to get rid of Lirian but Anastas finagled his way back. He's a survivor.'

'And the girl?'

Dawson concentrated on his driving. 'You met the delectable Nadya? She was a swallow. Got the push at the same time as Anastas.'

'Do they sleep together, George?'

'I've visited his apartment in Moscow a few times. She's always there.'

'What is his game exactly?'

'Lirian's on the make, like everyone else in Russia.'

'Be specific.'

'When they started selling off the old KGB archives to the highest bidder, Anastas had the angles all worked out like the good chess-player he is. He managed to convince his old boss, Medvedev, that the best man to fix the deals was A.R. Lirian. You know what Medvedev calls him? *Nash yerevánski zhílik* – our Armenian hustler.'

'He took Lirian back on the staff?'

'Anastas is cleverer than that,' Dawson chuckled. 'The first deal he made was to stay freelance. He gets no salary but takes five per cent of each sale, payable in hard currency.'

'What's he do with the money?' Madeleine Wharton was not particularly interested in the answer but had an ability to conduct one stream of thought in her head and carry on an entirely different conversation at the same time – which often confused her subordinates.

Dawson laughed. 'Invests in expensive carpets. By paying in dollars, he gets them for virtually nothing. Then he ships them to Istanbul where a cousin of his owns a carpet warehouse. I bought a couple from him last month and sent them home via the bag.'

'We pay him five per cent as well,' she said.

'For services rendered,' Dawson agreed. 'Anastas tags the disinformation in each package for us so that we can sort the fools' gold from the real stuff.'

'And who puts the disinformation in, in the first place?' Madeleine had worked out the answer; she wanted confirmation of the system.

'Lirian does. That's the way things work in Russia.'

'We should complain to General Medvedev, George. After all, we pay good money without Lirian's fiddle.'

Dawson glanced at her in the driving mirror. Was she serious? Complain about corruption in Russia? As well complain about the winter or the queues . . .

Unable to read what was in Madeleine Wharton's mind, he continued answering her questions as they cruised through back streets devoid of traffic with the black Mercedes following a hundred metres behind.

'Damn, damn, damn,' said Madeleine apropos of nothing. 'I resent doing purely political jobs for Number Ten.'

She disliked everything about the deal that had brought her to St Petersburg. Nobody in London's Intelligence community wanted Sir John back; the only reason for the deal was that the Prime Minister wanted to humiliate his predecessor who had employed the old traitor for years as Intelligence Secretary in the Cabinet Office.

'Fill me in on the chronology,' she ordered.

'It's simple,' said Dawson. 'For whatever reason, Sir John apparently took to cruising the Moscow meat market. It's a little park by the Bolshoi Theatre. Gay-bashing is a traditional Russian sport so no one was surprised when he got rather badly beaten up a few weeks ago. If a militia patrol hadn't happened along by chance and scared away the two heavies who were laying into him, he'd have died. It was that incident which brought him to Medvedev's attention after all these years – hence the offer to trade him back.'

'And now he's locked up in a safe house?'

Dawson laughed. 'For casual violence Russian cities are

worse than Chicago in the thirties: every day there are machine-gun assassinations, usually because someone isn't paying protection money to the right people. Lirian says they've put Sir John under lock and key because Yeltsin doesn't want some street hoodlum blowing away an asset worth a couple of million dollars.'

How wrong can you be? Madeleine thought. Medvedev's original offer to sell Sir John back had been made before the nearly fatal mugging. It was her belief that there had been a leak in London and that one or more of Sir John's former colleagues had decided to avoid the embarrassment of his homecoming by hiring a contract killer to bump the old man off in Moscow – ostensibly just another victim of the wave of violence sweeping the former USSR.

If her analysis was correct, it explained the current Russian insistence on payment up front. Moscow was worried that Sir John might have another accident on the way home and wanted to be paid before delivery, just in case . . .

'According to your report, George, he's unrecognisable due to plastic surgery.'

'. . . and he's had his voice altered surgically.'

'So the problem is twofold,' said Madeleine. 'A: we don't want to pay until we're sure he's the real McCoy. B: they won't hand him over until we pay.'

'We have to pay first.'

Madeleine disagreed. 'I got my fingers burnt with that cock-up in Turkey just after I'd taken over as DG. The Service lost some cash and a lot of credibility on that one, George. If I were paranoid, I'd say that my predecessor smelt a rat when he pleaded ill health to retire early, in the hope that I would fall flat on my face during my first month in office.'

'The thought had occurred to me.'

'Well, this time I shall certainly not hand over the money before I'm sure we're getting what we've paid for. I'm also deter-mined to get the goods home intact.'

Madeleine sat watching a succession of eighteenth-century vistas of churches, palaces and bridges across rivers and canals. They opened and closed again, one after another, as the car passed the end of each wide avenue. All the major buildings still wore the coats of yellow, blue and pink paint that Peter the Great's Italian architects had decreed as an antidote to the dull grey Baltic sky. Venice of the North? she thought. What a facile nickname for such a magnificent capital! It was more like driving through a gaudily repainted Paris without the traffic and with half the streets flooded.

She switched track: 'Eyes and ears, George.'

He glanced at her in the driving mirror. 'Mm?'

'Rumours,' she said. 'Gossip, call it what you will.'

'St P. is full of rumours,' he hedged. 'The problem is not picking them up, it's sorting wheat from chaff.'

'You know what I mean,' she said impatiently. 'I'm not talking about *babushki* gossiping in the bread queue.'

He took the pipe from his mouth. 'There is one thing,' he said. 'Anastas is trying to sell me a Romanoff restoration plot.'

'A what?' Madeleine leaned forward.

'Exactly.'

She sat back. It was at moments like this that she missed a cigarette. How much to tell Dawson? One had to sow seed to reap a crop, so: 'I was in Washington last week, George. There were whispers at dinner parties in Georgetown that a lot of hot American money has been moved into roubles through a network of Boston banks during the last couple of weeks. Cash from drugs, from Mafia protection rackets, gambling in Las Vegas – even money from the Vatican Bank. You name it, hundreds of millions of dollars are apparently being funnelled through a consortium of banks in Boston to St Petersburg. Could there be a connection? Every revolution needs cash.'

Dinner parties in Georgetown, dear God! Dawson chuckled to himself. How the rich lived! Aloud, he said, 'I didn't bother to report it to London because it's so far-fetched. According to Anastas, our old pal General Medvedev is involved with a group of nutters . . .'

'Like whom?'

'Nobody you'll have heard of.'

'Try me.'

'Lirian mentioned a Spetsnaz colonel by the name of Plotnik

and some crazy priest called Archbishop Alexei who's active in the right-wing Pamyat movement.'

'And you didn't report this?' she rapped.

'I was waiting for some corroboration. If I sent to London everything I hear, you'd need a new department just to handle the signal traffic.'

'Tell me more about this restoration plot.'

'Lirian says that Medvedev, Plotnik and the others want to set a Romanoff on the long-vacant Throne of All The Russias and declare St P. the capital of a federation of the old Baltic port-cities.'

'A sort of modern Hanseatic League?'

'PanBaltia, Anastas called it. By dumping the unproductive hinterland they hope to qualify for admission to the Common Market.'

'You should have put this in your reports,' Madeleine scolded. 'Economically it's a sound idea.'

'Politically, it stinks,' he said scornfully.

'Your job is to report, not analyse.'

'The Balts hate the Russians,' Dawson said with the air of a schoolteacher explaining some oft-repeated lesson to a retarded pupil. 'During the War, Estonia, Latvia and Lithuania all marched to the German drum the moment the *Wehrmacht* arrived. Having just kicked out the Russian armies of occupation, the last thing they'll do now is pal up again with either Moscow or St P. – with or without a Tsar on the throne.'

Madeleine disagreed. 'With the present rate of inflation of the rouble, George, all this buying into Russia that I learned about in the States can only mean one thing: a *coup d'état* in the very near future.'

'What are the cousins doing about it?'

'Some lobbyists on Capitol Hill have persuaded the White House to declare a hands-off attitude to the movement of money until they see which way the wind is blowing off the steppes,' she said grimly. 'Thus nobody's doing a damned thing.'

'Ah!' Dawson thought he understood where she was leading. 'That's why you want Sir John back fast. You think all hell's about to break loose here – a revolution or something – and we'll lose him in the cafuffle . . .'

'I,' Madeleine said stuffily, 'don't want him back, period, George. But the PM does and I am his servant – as are you. So let's do our job and get him back home a.s.a.p.'

A militiaman on the junction of the Nevskiy Prospect and Sadovaya Ulitsa held up an arm to stop them. It was pure officiousness; there was no other traffic in sight but Dawson obediently waited until the man waved them on.

'Correction,' said Madeleine. 'I've got a better idea. Tell Lirian you're going to London for a few days' leave – as though we'd gone cool on the deal.'

'And really?'

'There is someone who can identify Sir John for us: the same person we planned to use last time – his niece, Vanessa. What's she doing these days?'

'No idea.'

'But you knew her.'

'Not really.'

'You debriefed her. I read the report in the file. Now I'm stuck on that damned ship for another two days and nights, George. I don't want anyone else involved, so get on the next plane to London and track the girl down wherever she is. Remind her she's still bound by the Act but tell her no more than that we want her to do one more job. I'll indoctrinate her myself when I get back. And no waves in Century House, George. Indeed, no waves anywhere. Understood?'

'And supposing Miss Vanessa Bowles-Haddon doesn't agree to help us?'

'Offer her money. Use your discretion as to how much.'

'She might still say no. As I remember, Van's got a mind of her own.'

Madeleine let her impatience show. She had to use Dawson because she did not want to widen the circle and risk another leak which might lead to a second and probably fatal accident. Also he was one of the few senior officers in the Service with no allegiance to either of the two warring deputies who caused her more problems than the opposition. But sometimes he was so slow on the uptake that she felt like screaming at him.

'Then dangle in front of the girl, my dear George,' she said tightly, 'the bait of being privy once again to the secrets behind the headlines. It's a drug that always works. People who have been in this business can never say no to doing one more job.'

.3.

Vanessa Bowles-Haddon awoke at her usual hour of six o'clock. She lay in bed for several minutes running through the details of the busy day that lay ahead, then rose and dressed in a white polo-neck sweater and jodhpurs. In the stables, she saddled her horse, a beautiful white Arab gelding with a coat like silk and the movements of a four-legged aristocrat. She rode him at a walk to the end of the drive and along the road to the lake shore. There she gave him a hard gallop, enjoying the sun on her face, the wind in her hair, the rhythmic movement of the horse's powerful muscles beneath her. The regular morning ride was an important moment of peace in her busy schedule.

At that early hour Lake Geneva was beautiful: the water was like a sheet of polished metal, the city on the other shore lay still slumbering. In the distance, the 130-metre-high water-spout caught the low-angle sunlight and glowed like a pillar of flame. A chauffeur-driven car heading for the city passed close without slowing down and made the Arab shy. She calmed him with a firm hand and a steady voice, her thoughts elsewhere. The businessman in the rear seat turned round to look back and wonder who was the blonde-haired, blue-eyed woman in the saddle, so obviously in control of the horse and everything else in her life.

A couple of miles along the shore, Van turned and galloped back, slowing the gelding to a walk for the last quarter-mile, in order to cool him down. Back at the white-columned house on the lake shore which had been her home for the past two years, his hooves clip-clopped on the cobbles of the yard past the garage which housed a Rolls Corniche, her own yellow Nissan 300 ZX convertible and a four-wheel drive jeep used for skiing weekends.

Van rubbed the gelding down in his loose box and mixed his feed. She enjoyed these morning chores. Later the gardener would turn the horse loose in the paddock.

On her way into the house, Van stopped for a moment to enjoy her beautiful home. The garden in which she stood was immaculate and the large house contained more art treasures than many museums. At the end of the garden a motor-boat used for water-skiing bobbed at its mooring beside a ten-metre sail-boat.

In the sun-filled breakfast room she drank a cup of strong black Brazilian coffee and ate a dish of muesli. On the walls hung a small Mary Cassatt watercolour and a larger Berthe Morisot oil painting of mother and child which had been her birthday present from her lover and the owner of the house, Roberto Perreira. Through the serving hatch she gave the cook the day's orders for the staff. Roberto would be returning from Rio that evening, expecting to find his household running perfectly – and there were half a dozen guests for dinner. She scribbled a menu and thrust it through the hatch, with orders for a couple of guest rooms to be made ready in case any guests wished to stay over.

Her duties taken care of, Van ran up the elegant marble and gilt staircase. There were two dressing-rooms adjoining the master bedroom. Hers was as tidy and organised as the rest of her life. Glass-doored built-in wardrobes covered three walls: one for business wear, one for evening dresses and one for casual clothes. From the business side, Van chose a dark grey suit and a plain red silk blouse to wear underneath. The effect with her pale skin, clear blue eyes and straight blonde hair was severe. She accentuated it deliberately by the choice of plain black shoes and a black handbag.

A glance in the full-length mirror and a quick decision: she rejected the too-sober accessories for a red handbag in Thai silk with matching shoes and gloves.

The clients at her discreet little antique shop in the Grand' Rue were mainly rich Third World diplomats who found Vanessa Bowles-Haddon the epitome of the English lady aristocrat. They were fascinated by her cool reserve and classy clothes. The way she dressed and talked – equally at home in English, French, Russian or German – had contributed much to her success in selling objects of virtu to the members of Geneva's international stratum.

There was a small combination safe let into the wall beside the dressing-table, from which Van took a slim diamond necklace, earrings and bracelet. Like the Berthe Morisot, they were a present from the man who owned the house.

She wrapped the jewellery carefully in tissue paper and put it in her handbag; it was too valuable to wear all day but there might be no time in her busy schedule to come home and change before she drove out to the airport at Cointrin that evening to meet her lover, whose face watched her from a photograph on the dressing-table. At forty-two, Roberto Perreira was her elder by ten years. He was handsome, charming, intelligent, generous and considerate. Unfortunately, like many Latins, he believed that a woman's function was to get married and bear children, while Van was in no hurry to lose her waistline and change him from an attentive lover to a philandering husband.

She picked up the photograph, studying the arrogant dark eyes, the strong nose and sensual mouth. During his absences she missed Roberto's ability to charm away her business cares, about which she never talked to anyone else. She missed too his amusing conversation and extravagant spur-of-the-moment ideas for having fun, but her feelings about him coming home were mixed.

In Rio his mother would have been nagging him to settle down and have children. So Roberto would alternately charm and bully her once again to get married and pregnant. After a few days he would turn sulky, seemingly unable to understand that she enjoyed the sense of achievement which came from running the business which she had founded and built up from nothing.

Relationships had foundered on less, Van sighed. She put down the photograph and slipped onto her wrist a diamond-encrusted watch from which she saw that she was five minutes behind schedule. She scolded herself for daydreaming, kissed Roberto's photograph, grabbed handbag and gloves and ran down the stairs to start another day in her life as a rich and beautiful woman at the top.

'The answer's no.'

Van spoke with her back turned to Dawson. 'I have to tell you that when I looked across Christie's saleroom this morning and saw your face from the past, I shut my eyes. I failed to bid for the next lot because I kept them shut and counted to ten, hoping that when I opened them again, you'd be gone like a bad dream in the morning.'

She looked out across the parkland, the lake shore and the lake itself. Apart from birdsong and distant traffic noises, the garden had that quiet that only the rich can enjoy near a big city. The white Arab gelding grazed peacefully in his paddock at the side of the house. The boats danced on the glittering wavelets at the moorings. The sun was shining, the house and garden were beautiful but there was a shadow over everything that had not been there that morning. It was a Dawson-shaped shadow. She turned around and studied him, contrasting his crumpled appearance with the way she was dressed.

Catching her eye, Dawson read the thought. He remembered her during the years she had been with the Service, when she dressed, walked, talked and behaved like the other young female officers in Century House. That, he now realised, had all been an act. This elegant, poised, beautifully dressed and made-up woman standing in a millionaire's garden beside Lake Geneva was the real Vanessa Bowles-Haddon. She looked like a model from *Vogue*.

Dawson had tracked her down that morning at Christie's Geneva saleroom, bidding for small enamelled snuffboxes against a small handful of top dealers and collectors. The prices had made him blink; the involuntary gesture had almost been taken as a bid. Later, in her shop in the heart of the Old Town, he had felt equally out of place while she talked fluently in three languages on the telephone with the clients for whom she had been bidding.

During the breathtaking drive in her yellow convertible through the traffic in downtown Geneva and along the open road to her luxury lakeside home, Van had done nothing to put Dawson at ease. He had worked out for himself that the decision to bring him home for lunch was not for friendship but for privacy.

A buffet lunch for two had been laid on a marble table on the lakeside terrace. Van motioned at the bottle of Mumm champagne in the ice bucket. 'Help yourself and pour one for me while you tell me what brings you back into my life, Mr Dawson.'

'A job we'd like you to take on for old times' sake.'

'What kind of a job?'

'I can't say yet.'

'Oh really?' She crowded into two words all the contempt she felt for the clandestine world with its Boy Scout codes of behaviour: be-prepared, need-to-know, don't-ask-me and all the other pat little phrases.

Dawson spread butter on a slice of pumpernickel and helped himself to slices of *getrocknetes Büntnerfleisch* to make an open sandwich. 'I'm sorry to intrude in your life like this,' he said. 'I really am.'

Van sat down on the other side of the table and served herself. 'When I left the Service, Mr Dawson,' she said, 'I told you that I wished to have nothing more to do with the so-called Intelligence community, ever. I thought that had been understood.'

'I know how you feel.'

'Do you?' she said sharply.

Dawson's arrival had opened up old wounds. Van faced him angrily across the table. 'But that wasn't good enough for you people, was it? It's as though anyone signing the Official Secrets Act has renounced their privacy and freedom of action for life, so far as you're concerned. I'd only been in Switzerland a few months when Madeleine Wharton, of all people, just happened to brush against me at an Embassy reception in Bern and suggest that I might like to help out with an operation in Beijing which had gone wrong. She talked as though she were doing me a favour!'

'A lot of people fall for it,' said Dawson warily.

'Well, I don't happen to need the money.'

So far Dawson had not achieved a moment's contact. 'I don't think it's the money that hooks people,' he began cautiously.

'I can't think of any other reason, unless they're certifiable masochists.'

Dawson swallowed champagne and disagreed mildly: 'Usually, what gets them is the drug of being privy to secrets once again – of knowing what's behind the news and being a part of it.'

Van stood up, her appetite spoiled. 'There's an old saying that you can't con an honest man, Mr Dawson. I may not be the world's most honest woman but I have no illusions about the sordid world you inhabit, so the answer's still no.'

He nodded, his sad, saggy face accepting the insult as merited.

'Enjoy your lunch,' said Van. 'Then you can get on the next plane back to London with the message to whoever's the current top dog that Vanessa Bowles-Haddon is the one member of her family who does not beg Santa every Xmas for a new cloak-and-dagger outfit.'

Dawson stood up and watched her walk to the house without a backward glance. All in all, he was not disappointed with the conversation. On the face of it, Van had said no, no and no. But against that, she had brought him back here to talk when she could have told him to piss off at Christie's. And she had asked what the job was, which contradicted her apparent refusal to want anything more to do with the Service. If he read the signs right, Vanessa Bowles-Haddon *could* be hookable like everyone else. As always, it was a question of finding the right fisherman and giving him the necessary bait.

.4.

On the tiny stage of Le Girondin, blinded by the follow-spot, Maria could see nothing outside the pool of light in which she stood. The audience applauded as she ended the second set of the night with an old Billie Holiday number that Roscoe had re-arranged especially for her.

Jan Coetzee signed for the house lights to be brought up. A glass of beer was thrust into Roscoe's hand and Dawson's voice said, 'That was great playing, Jack. I didn't know you could. During that Errol Garner medley I shut my eyes and thought it was the man himself playing.'

Seated at the piano, with his back to the audience, Roscoe was staring up at Maria's shadowed face, framed by the halo of back-lit hair from the spotlight. He took the glass and swallowed a deep draught of beer. Without looking round, he said, 'I wondered when you'd walk back into my life, George.'

Backstage he introduced Dawson to Maria who was instantly suspicious of this man from the past of which Roscoe never talked. After they had changed from their stage clothes, she chatted to regulars at several tables, watching Roscoe and Dawson drinking at the bar.

When she joined them, Roscoe took her hand and announced, 'George wants a bed for the night. I invited him to stay. Is that OK?'

'Why not?' she shrugged. 'If he is friend of yours, Jack, why not?'

On the way home she sat in the rear of the Peugeot so that Dawson could sit in front. By feigning tiredness she avoided having to talk. Roscoe did not seem to notice. Back at the cottage, he threw a couple of logs on the embers of the open fire in the huge old hearth and asked, 'So what are you doing these days, George?'

There was a snap and hiss as Dawson opened a can of beer from a twelve-pack out of Coetzee's fridge. He shrugged. 'Nothing exciting. I'm Madeleine's gofer. She says gofe and I gofeth.'

'Big deal,' Roscoe whistled mockingly.

There was the sound of a zip-fastener clearly audible through the half-open door of the bedroom and a clatter as Maria kicked off her high-heeled shoes onto the tiled floor. Dawson's sleepy gaze took in the bookshelves full of Roscoe's novels and books of poetry, the large wildlife photographs on the wall, the collection of old LPs and new CDs, the expensive hi-fi, the musical instruments and recording gear.

He also noted the woman's touch in the décor. The kitchen equipment was primitive but there were fresh flowers on the table in front of him and an arrangement of dried herbs on the sideboard. Several watercolours of Dordogne scenes hanging on the walls were signed *Maria*. On the chimneybreast hung a large and beautifully executed framed charcoal sketch which she had done of Roscoe fishing. There was a hint of Roscoe's knowing smile about the lips but the eyes were as Dawson had never seen them. It was the face of a man who has just said, 'I love you.'

Roscoe was on his knees with a set of bellows, puffing the embers into life. Dawson's eyes kept going back to the charcoal sketch. It made him wonder whether his confident boast to Madeleine Wharton was going to be justified.

At first she had said, 'Not Roscoe. I'll never use him again, George. An insubordinate, undisciplined drunk . . .'

But then Dawson had explained his plan, persuading his boss that Jack Roscoe was the only person liable to persuade Vanessa Bowles-Haddon to be co-operative.

As the flames licked up the chimney Roscoe and he settled down to a beer session, chatting about old times. The pitch was typically Dawson when it came, out of a cloud of pipe smoke: 'I'm not here to put any pressure on, Jack. I appreciate how you feel about the Service giving you the sack. In fact, I envy you the life you've got now. You seem to have things all sorted out . . .'

He waved the pipe around. 'A beautiful place to live, a lovely woman to keep you warm at night. So why the hell would you want to come back and do a one-off job? I wouldn't, that's for sure.'

He finished the last beer and opened a bottle of duty-free whisky he had bought on the flight from London. 'I feel like rat shit, coming down here to disturb your happy home life, Jack. When the boss called me in this morning – that is, yesterday morning – I told her you wouldn't ever do another job for us, no matter what the money. But then I thought I owed you the chance of deciding about this one for yourself.'

'Come on, you crafty old sod,' said Roscoe. 'What's so special about this one?'

Dawson poured a tumbler of whisky each and raised his. 'Here's to old times, Jack.'

They drank.

Dawson blew out his cheeks. 'It's a job in Russia.'

The surprise was evident in Roscoe's voice. 'Me, of all people, cleared for a job in Russia, George?'

Dawson ignored the question. 'I thought you'd want to take it on – for Pete Bergman's sake.'

A cold hand touched the back of Roscoe's neck and raised goose-pimples. He swallowed all the whisky in the glass and poured some more. 'You said it was Madeleine Wharton's idea to send you here, George. Now you say you thought of me for the job.'

'Dear Maddy just wants the job done, Jack. Doesn't care by whom. I thought it might give you one more chance of turning something up.'

'No!' Roscoe's voice was harsh. 'Peter was killed. We saw the bodies next morning.'

'We saw some bodies being carried away,' Dawson agreed. His eyes were narrowed to slits, either against the smoke or to stop Roscoe reading his thoughts. 'It now appears the whole snafu on the border was an elaborate pantomime – and those bodies were just props laid on beforehand. So Bergman could have survived.'

Roscoe did not want to hear this. He shook his head. 'Van said . . .'

'. . . more or less the same thing I did: that she *thought* he must be dead.'

'If Peter didn't die . . .' Roscoe's voice tailed away. 'If he didn't die that night, he must be dead by now. And if I couldn't get a lead then – just after it all happened – how the hell will I find out anything useful six years later?'

'Because . . .' Dawson put down his glass and pipe. He held the pause with a sense of timing that would have won awards on the West End stage. 'Because your contact in Russia for this job is Anastas Romanovich Lirian, that's why. Remember the name?'

Roscoe nodded.

'Lirian masterminded the double-cross in Turkey, Jack. He's the only man in the world who can tell you what really happened to Bergman. Can you pass up a chance of talking to him?' He met Roscoe's agonised gaze. 'Well, can you?'

Roscoe could not sleep. Cold sober despite all the beer he and Dawson had put away, he prowled around the cottage listening to the snores coming from the spare room.

A half-finished arrangement of a song Roscoe had written for Maria lay on his workstation. He slipped the headphones on and tried to work out what was wrong with it by playing each part on the keyboard, one after the other. Staring at the score on the monitor screen, he found the harmonies he had written for violin and viola trite and old-fashioned.

Maria and he were due to record a trial album for the record company in Paris in less than two weeks' time. If that went well, the contract was for three albums spread over the next two years, launched with a big publicity budget and a European tour complete with television appearances. Apart from rehearsing the new material, Roscoe knew he had a lot of work still to put in on the arrangements of songs already in Maria's repertoire: extra instrumental parts were needed for the recording session which were not required in a live show. If he went with Dawson now, he would be betraying her and letting Coetzee down. But if he did not go . . .

He switched off the computer and removed the headphones. Dawson's snores were an ugly counterpoint to the drumming of the rain pouring down outside. A puddle had seeped under the kitchen door where the stone threshold and tiles had been worn down by generations of peasant feet. The fire in the hearth had gone out and the kitchen was chilly.

Roscoe padded through into the bedroom where Maria half-woke and turned towards him as he slipped into the bed.

'You're cold,' she murmured.

Roscoe lay still, feeling her warmth beside him. 'I have to talk to you,' he said quietly.

'In the morning, Jack.' Maria snuggled closer.

'No,' said Roscoe. 'It has to be now.' After Dawson's coaching, the words came out pat. 'George has offered me a job worth ten thousand pounds. In the morning I'm going away. I'll be back in three days.'

She was suddenly awake, switching the light on and staring at him, wide-eyed. 'You can't be serious, Jack! To go away for three days now, with all the work we have to do . . .'

'We can use the money to buy the cottage from Coetzee – like we planned.'

'Such a crazy idea, Jack,' she said. 'Soon we shall have money from the recording contract, you'll see. This man Dawson has got you drunk!'

'I've never been more sober in my life.' Roscoe put out the light and reached for Maria. Dawson was wrong: he owed her a proper explanation, not just a few lies. He groped for the words that would make her understand. 'There are a lot of things I have to tell you – about my past, before we met.'

'I don't want to listen.' Maria tried to get out of the bed and to reach the light.

Roscoe held her. 'I want you to listen to me. Please. I need you to understand why I have to do this.'

'You are hurting me, Jack.'

'I'm sorry.' He released her and wondered where to begin. 'You say I sometimes talk of Peter Bergman in my sleep . . .'

'And when I ask what is wrong, you say nothing.'

'Well, now I'm going to tell you everything.'

As Roscoe drew word-pictures for her in the darkness Maria saw young men in uniform and a toddler blown to pieces at Kolwezi. She saw the running man whom Roscoe shot – and always beside Roscoe was Bergman, Bergman, Bergman.

'He is the man,' she whispered, 'that made you do all these evil things. I hate him.'

'No,' Roscoe said softly. 'He's the guy who twice saved my life. I owe him a debt of honour.'

'Is all the past,' she pleaded. 'It was a long time ago, these things you tell me, Jack. The present is us and what we have together. Don't throw it all away, just for a guilt from the past.'

'Three days,' he said, 'that's all.'

Somehow she knew he was lying, even though he did not yet know it himself.

Roscoe told her of standing on a rainswept parade-ground, chanting in unison the legionnaire's oath: '. . . and never to abandon a wounded, or even a dead, comrade – I swore that, Maria.'

'I don't care,' she said, blocking her ears.

Yet when he told her about Van and their affair, Roscoe felt Maria listening again, wanting to know about this other woman in his life. 'Was she more beautiful than me?'

'Nobody is more beautiful than you,' he said.

'And did you love her?'

'I thought so at the time.'

'What is she to do with this Bergman?'

'She . . . fell in love with him.'

'And he?'

'. . . felt the same, I guess.'

'He stole her from you,' said Maria triumphantly.

'That's what I thought, but listen . .'

Roscoe gave her the outline of the operation in Turkey and

how he had gone to the hotel in Kusadasi where Bergman and Van were staying to deliver a warning. 'It was nothing definite – just a whisper that MIL had picked up, of a scam being played on the British.'

'MIL? What is that?'

'Turkish Intelligence.'

'Ah, the Turks,' she said, as though they were to blame. 'So you went to the hotel – and what happened there?'

'It was mid-morning. Van and Peter were still in bed. They were supposed to be honeymooners – it was their cover – so I didn't think too much of it. I just drank a coffee by the pool and waited for them to come down to breakfast. The moment I saw Van's face I knew they'd just been making love.'

'But she had told you that your affair with her was over.'

'I hadn't believed her. I was sure I could talk her round when we all got back to London.'

Maria's hand found his face in the darkness. 'Poor Jack!'

'If it had been anyone else, I would have killed the guy with my bare hands.' Roscoe had played the scene over so many times in his own mind. 'I couldn't speak, Maria. I just left the hotel – I think, without saying a word. It was more than jealousy. I saw Van and Peter exchange a smile before they saw me. And I knew in that second that the two people I was closest to in the whole world had come together in a way that would exclude me for ever.'

Now Maria thought she understood it all. 'You were so jealous or so hurt,' she said wonderingly, 'that you let this friend Peter walk into an ambush to get your revenge?'

'No,' Roscoe said. 'I drove away – not back to the Nato base at Izmir but to a headland overlooking the sea and sat there trying to get control of my feelings.' He paused. 'It took quite a while before I was ready to face the two of them again. When I got back to the hotel, they'd checked out.'

'And you left it at that?'

No, he said again. Driving after them too fast on a bad road, he had missed a bend and wrapped his car around an olive tree.

As the first light of dawn came through the shutters, Maria read on Roscoe's face the anguish he had felt that day, sitting impotently in the wrecked car, waiting for a breakdown truck.

'I understand.' She pulled his face to her breasts and held him tightly. 'But there is nothing you can do now, Jack. Your friend is dead and you grieve for him, I know. But there is nothing to be done.'

Roscoe disengaged himself and sat up. 'Bergman had more lives than a cat. Could be, he's still alive. I have to find out and this is the only chance I'll ever get.'

He walked to the window and threw open the shutters. Outside the clouds had broken up and sunlight was sparkling on a million drops of moisture clinging to the leafless branches of the trees along the riverbank. He looked at the trees and the sky and the river which he had come to love but the magic had gone.

Against the background of her dark hair spread on the pillow, Maria's age-old Greek eyes watched him.

'Don't go,' she pleaded.

Only in Greek could she have found the words to express what she was feeling. For her Roscoe's past had acquired a geographical reality. It was a land of menace, ruled by a phantom Dark Lady whose servants were Dawson and Bergman. If Jack went back there – wherever *there* was – Maria was sure he would be in danger. There the Dark Lady was waiting to clasp him to her cold bosom for ever. It was said in the Tróodos Mountains that no man who had been her lover could ever truly escape. But none of these things could she say in words which Roscoe would understand.

As he came back to the bed, she could only plead, 'Don't go, Jack. Please.'

A shutter came down behind Roscoe's eyes. 'I'll be back in three days.'

Maria hit him hard on the left cheekbone.

He blinked 'What was that for?'

She burrowed into him so that he could not see her face, clinging to his body. Gently Roscoe uncoiled Maria's drowning-man grip and lifted her face up. She opened her eyes to search him from face to feet as though she were seeing him for the first time – or the last.

She sniffed the skin of his neck and chest and snuggled lower in the bed, curled foetus-like, pressing her face into his belly and inhaling, eyes closed. She gripped him hard, feeling the power of his flesh in her hand and loving him for it.

'I need you,' she whispered, aching and lonely already. 'I need this flesh in mine, Jack. I have no pride, no shame with you. I am naked before you, as never with another man, I swear. And now you go away.'

'You're crazy,' he said tenderly. 'I'll be back soon.'

She wriggled on top of him and stared into his eyes, willing him to change his mind.

'I love you,' he breathed.

She inhaled, filling her lungs with the air he had exhaled in saying the words.

'You are so beautiful,' she said. For just one moment, his face wore the look she had managed to capture in charcoal. Wanting him was a pain.

'Make love to me,' she whispered. 'I don't care about her.'

'About whom?'

Maria knew that even to utter the Dark Lady's name gave her power. If only there were a way without words to make Roscoe understand the danger he ran . . .

She was crying now. 'Life is so cruel. I only just find you – and now you go away.'

She felt his fingers probing her softness, caressing and loving her the way she had never wanted any other man to touch her. The ache inside grew stronger. 'Oh, Jack, what will I do without you?'

'Only three days,' he whispered. 'I promise.'

As he entered her, Maria gasped and arched her back, then stilled her own passion. She let him make love to her, feeling the muscles of his powerful shoulders and sliding her hands down his back to hold his buttocks, then up to caress his ribs and stroke his sweat-covered chest. She touched him and watched him and smelled him. She licked the salt sweat from his face and held him to her trembling afterwards.

When he lay beside her half-asleep, Maria lit a cigarette and blew the smoke out, savouring the moment and prolonging it within herself, hoping that somehow his flesh had understood what his brain did not want to.

'You didn't come,' he said drowsily.

'I wanted to remember everything.' She lay quietly watching images in the smoke while he slept.

They took Dawson to lunch in a little riverside restaurant in the village, where they were served by an open window overlooking the Dordogne. There were only a few customers; the meal was simple family cooking with nothing to entice tourists on the hunt for gourmet cuisine.

The set menu cost fifty francs for five courses including as much local red wine as they wanted. They ate potage, followed by a huge plateful of charcuterie and another of crudités, then lamb chops, a dozen cheeses and dessert. Dawson marvelled at the cheapness of the food, the quality of the cooking and the beauty of the setting. Watching him charm Maria during the meal, Roscoe thought: what a two-faced old devil you are, George.

Maria seemed more relaxed. She laughed at Dawson's jokes. Between the courses, her hand sought Roscoe's and held it tight. They strolled back to the cottage along the old towpath in that primitive communion of people who are digesting a good meal they have just shared.

Maria fell silent as they neared the cottage, listening to the chit-chat between the two men with an icy knot of cramp in her belly as though she had spent the morning making love to a ghost. She wanted more than anything in her life to hear Roscoe say to Dawson, 'I'm sorry, George. I'm not coming.'

Their bags were in Roscoe's car. As he slipped behind the wheel to drive to the airport, Maria said, 'You are a clever man, Mr Dawson. I wish you hadn't come here.'

Dawson turned his sad-spaniel face to her and did something very out-of-character: he leaned out of the car window, took Maria's hand and raised it to his lips. 'You're a very beautiful woman,' he said solemnly. 'Don't worry about Jack. He can take care of himself.'

Roscoe gunned the motor, let in the clutch too fast and fish-tailed away on the wet grass, driving dangerously fast along the narrow and slippery tow-path, within inches of the bank itself. It gave him an excuse to keep his eyes on the track ahead and not look in the rear-view mirror to see the woman he was leaving, her face framed in windblown, wild black hair . . .

At the first bend he did glance back. Maria was still there, standing with one hand raised in farewell, her eyes accusing him even at that distance, making him want to stop the car and say to Dawson, 'Sorry, George.'

But he could not do that because of the debt of honour that was so long overdue.

. 5 .

It was the so-called Happy Hour. The steak-and-salad pub just off Oxford Circus was noisy with conversation, a bass-boosted sound system and a television set turned up loud. The staff were all Australian: tall, suntanned refugees from Bondi Beach.

The pub was a far cry from Madeleine Wharton's usual haunts. Hating noise, she was annoyed that Dawson had suggested such an unsuitable place for her meeting with Roscoe. They made an incongruous pair. He was wearing an open-neck shirt, windcheater and lightweight trousers and had an empty beer glass in front of him. Madeleine was dressed in one of her habitual dark grey suits which she had worn to a meeting at Number Ten that afternoon, immediately after her return from Helsinki. In lieu of a handbag she had a slim black leather attaché-case which she placed on the floor between her feet when they sat down.

She toyed with a glass of amontillado sherry, uncharacteristically talking chateaux and vintages to break the ice. 'I gather from George Dawson that things have turned out quite well for you, Jack. Nice place you've got in the Dordogne, so he tells me.'

Roscoe used sign-language to crack the sound barrier and get another pint of hand-pulled draught from a tall denim-clad waitress. Beside it on her tray was a bottle of Castle beer for another customer. Roscoe looked at the familiar label. It was the brand that he and Bergman had drunk on their weekend booze-ups in South Africa. That seemed a good omen.

His pint was slopped onto the table with a cheerful shout of, 'There you go.'

He raised the glass in a mock toast. 'To what do I owe Dawson's approach, may I ask? I can't have been your first choice, Miss Wharton.'

She took a minuscule sip of sherry. 'Things have changed since you were with us, Jack. The Treasury wants more staff cutbacks. They talk about using freelance effort quote whenever appropriate unquote. Whatever the bureaucrats think, that is something not easily arranged in our line of business. A man like you who's been on staff, vetted inside and out, could profit from the situation – if this job goes well.'

She passed to Roscoe a brown manilla envelope. 'Dawson said you've agreed the fee.'

'Ten thousand pounds for a three-day job.'

She nodded. 'It's way over scale for your last substantive grade, as you know. So we're calling it five thousand pounds a week for two weeks – to confuse the auditors. I've got half for you now. You get the rest on completion.'

Roscoe signed the receipt and his millionth copy of the Official Secrets Act. He shunted the two pieces of paper back to Madeleine, whose hand stayed outstretched until her gold Parker ball-pen was also returned.

'Now I'm yours, body and soul.' Roscoe lifted his glass and drank. 'What's involved? George was vague. A trip to Russia, he said.'

'That's all he told you?'

'Yes.'

'It's an escort job.' Between half-closed lids Madeleine watched Roscoe counting the money under the table. 'Bringing back to Britain someone rather important.'

'A defector with a change of heart?' Roscoe guessed.

'You could say that.'

'And why am I suddenly *persona grata* again?' There were a hundred fifties in the envelope. Roscoe slipped it into an inside pocket where it felt good and thick.

Madeleine pulled her chair closer to him. She had eaten only an apple and two cream crackers on the plane for lunch and was finding the dessert counter at the end of the bar too mouth-watering. She turned her back on it to put temptation out of mind.

'Because we need the help of Vanessa Bowles-Haddon. The returning defector is her uncle. We need her there to identify him. I'll be straight with you: she's already refused to do it. Dawson assures me that you are the only person who can per-suade her to co-operate.'

Roscoe was speechless.

Madeleine closed the attaché-case with a loud click. 'It's a remake,' she said, 'of the operation in Turkey but with a different ending. This time Sir John Bowles-Haddon is really coming home because Moscow isn't giving him any choice in the matter.'

'Oh Christ!'

'My feelings exactly,' she said.

Roscoe regretted his sleepless night. Even on the plane from Bordeaux to Gatwick he had been unable to doze. Now his head was spinning: Sir John, Lirian, Dawson, Van and himself. It was a remake with the same cast; only Bergman's name was missing from the credits.

Madeleine leaned closer and put a firm, well-manicured hand on Roscoe's arm to add emphasis to the order: 'On this oper-ation there must be no – I repeat no – unauthorised activities, Jack. Step out of line once and . . .'

'And what?' he challenged.

She looked away. '. . . and we shan't ever use you again. Just remember that you're being very well paid. Do the job and nothing else. Is that understood?'

Roscoe said nothing; inside he felt ice-cold.

Madeleine met his angry glare without flinching. 'Once we get Johnny Boy back to London, we'll sweat everything out of him, Jack. I have my personal reasons for disliking that man very much indeed so I promise you that he'll be put on the rack and grilled until all the fat has run out.'

Roscoe grunted.

'Whatever people say about me, Jack,' she finished, 'I want you to know that I do understand and sympathise with your feelings about what happened in Turkey. Play straight with me and I give you my personal word that I'll fill you in on what happened to your chum that night as soon as we know.'

Perhaps Madeleine Wharton did have a soul after all? Roscoe wondered. 'It's a deal,' he said.

Like a dog stunned in an accident, Roscoe headed instinctively for familiar places but there were none. In Adelaide, Johannesburg or Los Angeles he could have found a place to sit and think – a place where he had put down roots for a while. In London he was simply an expat who did not belong any more. He called a couple of old girlfriends and listened to their voices on answering machines. There was no point in leaving a message.

He stood for a long time in a call-booth in Oxford Circus Underground station, listening to the phone ringing at the cottage on the banks of the Dordogne. Maria did not answer. Coetzee's reaction to the news of Roscoe's departure at such an inopportune moment had been an explosion of anger so he did not want to ring the club on the off-chance she was there.

The RV with Dawson was in a pub by the Hammersmith flyover. Roscoe arrived early and sat over a pint of Guinness, watching a drag artiste dressed as Shirley Temple trying to raise laughs with jokes about knickers and boobs. It was a relief when Dawson arrived, also early. Their destination – revealed to Roscoe in the car – was not the airport but Devonport dockyard where they arrived just after 3 a.m.

Three hours later they were in a Westland Super Lynx with Royal Navy markings that bucked and bounced above Exmoor in a force ten gale blowing in from the Atlantic. The twin up-rated Gem 41-2 engines screamed a protest as they put out 1,315 horsepower of lift and forward movement to keep the yo-yoing helicopter close to but just above the rugged contours of the moor.

In the stripped-out rear compartment, large enough for ten infantrymen with full equipment, Roscoe struggled into thermal underwear and camouflage parka and trousers. He had to clutch at stanchions to avoid being bounced around like a rubber ball in a box. His own clothes went into a Royal Navy kit-bag whose handles were held by Dawson, sitting with his seat belt tightly fastened, looking grey-faced and miserable.

'What the hell's this in aid of?' Roscoe shouted at him.

Dawson was feeling ill from all the motion. Roscoe thrust a paper bag at him as the helicopter lurched sideways and tilted to make a tight turn around a granite tor which loomed out of the mist closer than seemed safe to either passenger. He waited until Dawson had finished using the bag before shouting, 'Why are we flying so low?'

Dawson fought to control his stomach which wanted to be somewhere else. 'We're looking for a small bivouac, to rendezvous with a Royal Marines detachment which is training on the moor. They're expecting you for a three-day familiarisation course.'

'The entire job is only supposed to take three days!'

'Sorry, chum!'

Roscoe's spirits sank. 'Familiarisation with what?'

Dawson grimaced and braced himself against the floor as the machine screwed itself into a narrow corridor with grey-green rock walls on either side. The acoustic backlash from the ground was appalling.

He had to shout louder to make himself heard. 'Unarmed combat, cross-country endurance, weapons and explosives.'

'Jesus!' Roscoe shouted back. 'Your boss told me this was an escort job, George. So what the fuck's going on?'

Dawson clutched the bag more tightly. 'Don't ask me, chum,' he moaned and was sick into the paper bag.

Clinging to a stanchion, Roscoe realised that he had been conned. Madeleine Wharton had known all along that the job would take more than three days. Probably Dawson had too. That's why the money was so good. They had screwed him. But he could not back out now because he would never get another chance of picking up Bergman's trail.

Since going to live at Les Trois Moulins, Roscoe had cut down on his drinking and had been taking regular exercise. He had lost twenty pounds of flab and was fit, compared with most men in their late thirties. The three other men on the so-called familiarisation course were in their mid-twenties and a lot fitter than he was. After a couple of hours' keeping up with them on the moor Roscoe was ready to drop.

The other trainees were called Able, Baker and Charlie.

'Great,' said Roscoe. 'That makes me Dog, I suppose.'

The instructor – a hard-bitten Falklands vet of Roscoe's age with a Welsh accent – chuckled. 'You got it in one, sir. No real names on this exercise, if you don't mind.'

'What do I call you?'

'I expect you'll call me some rude names before we're off the moor, sir. To my face, just call me Drill Leader.'

Drill Leader was the kind of overgrown schoolboy who relished sleeping in the rain without a tent and eating chemically heated food that had been cooled and diluted by rainwater before it could be swallowed. He knew the moor backwards and led the four trainees unerringly from one unpleasant experience to another: crawling on bleeding hands and knees along stony stream-beds to leave no scent trail, hiding under near-freezing waterfalls until ordered to come out, then warming up by running cross-country and jumping three-metre gaps with 70 lb Bergens on their backs. When they climbed the hand-picked slippery vertical rock faces their rain-soaked canvas packs grew heavier with each painful inch advanced.

Drill Leader's idea of a team-game was making a human ladder in which the lowest man's shoulders had to bear the weight of two other men and their packs whilst the fourth man clambered up the pile to the top.

In pouches each man carried a hundred rounds of live ammunition for the Heckler & Koch SA 80 assault rifles which Roscoe had not handled before. The only time Drill Leader smiled in the entire three days was when pointing out the differences between the SA 80 and the old SLR with which Roscoe was familiar.

'Beautiful weapon, this is,' he said sibilantly, caressing the barrel of what he called the Hockler as another man might stroke a stockinged leg. He made it clear to Roscoe that an SA 80 was far too exquisite a work of art ever to be laid down on the ground. Rifles were carried at all times – even when eating – and never slung, even when the going was so rough that it required at least three hands per man. At night the SA 80s went into the sleeping bags before the men did.

On Day Two, they exchanged these weapons for Kalashnikov AK 74s which Drill Leader produced from a padlocked cache in a dry sheep cave. Roscoe found the Russian weapon a great improvement over its predecessor, the more famous AK 47. It was lighter, more accurate and had a higher rate of fire than the old model. Drill Leader spoke of Mikhail T. Kalashnikov and Carl Stoner as other men might mention Alexander Fleming or Louis Pasteur.

The explosives course would have raised eyebrows among most armourers, whose motto is Safety First. It laid emphasis principally on working in foul weather with numbed fingers and a near-total lack of equipment. The trainees learned to do some surprising things with Semtex plastic explosive and a detonator, relandscaping a small granite tor in the process.

Roscoe had the feeling that Able, Baker and Charlie had done it all before. From a few clues they let drop talking among themselves, he guessed they were from the Mountain Warfare Cadre of the SBS. They had all the jargon pat, talking of 'brammer' and 'the ish' and the end of the course as their 'run ashore'. They were hard-eyed young men who spoke little even among themselves. Roscoe had met the same type twenty years before with the SAS at Hereford.

To him they spoke exclusively Russian, of which they had a far more colloquial grasp than he did. He found it hard to drag the right expression out of his memory when tired, wet and hungry but when he spoke to them in English, they ignored him until his memory returned.

The third day of Drill Leader's yomp dawned fine and clear. The trainees had already been up and moving for three hours when Roscoe groaned with relief at the sight of the Sea Lynx heading across country straight at them. The relief was short-lived. The helicopter picked up Drill Leader with his training equipment and spare weapons but left the four trainees behind.

With full packs they were expected to cover the twenty-five miles to a map reference where: '. . . transport will await you until 18.00 hours, my lovely boys. Miss that and you can expect to spend another night on the moor. Got it?'

In case that seemed too easy, Drill Leader complicated things by dividing the men into two teams. Not only were they to race each other but, as he put it, '. . . take the odd moment to slow the other lads up with a few dirty tricks. Know what I mean, boys?'

Roscoe and Charlie arrived late at the rendezvous because Able and Baker had blown up a footbridge over a swollen river with some Semtex which they had filched from the stores while loading them aboard the helicopter. There was no transport waiting – just a track leading across the empty moor. They had no food left and it was getting dark.

Roscoe slumped to the ground and fell asleep instantly. After ten minutes he woke up shivering from the cold and the wet. He stood up, blinked his wind-sore eyes and rubbed a muddy hand across his three-day beard. 'I've had enough of this shit. I'm off.'

Charlie pulled his belt tighter. '*Kudá idyósh?*'

'*Yob tvoyú mat!*' muttered Roscoe: motherfucker! He had had enough of playing Boy Scouts. He dumped his filthy, muddy pack and the rifle in the ditch and squelched downhill in wet boots, not caring whether Charlie followed. Downhill was where people lived, thought Roscoe. Downhill was food and warmth.

He plodded numbly on for five more miles until he saw the lights of the farmhouse, guessing what he would find inside. In front of a roaring log fire sat Dawson, Drill Leader and the other two trainees. There was hot food and beer on the table. Along one wall was a row of bunks with dry bedding.

Roscoe reached for a can of Pils, only to have it knocked out of his grasp by Drill Leader. He was red in the face with anger. 'Where's your pack and rifle, boyo?'

'Sod off,' snarled Roscoe. 'I've had enough of your stupid games.'

The face-off was interrupted by Charlie pushing open the door. He was carrying Roscoe's rifle and pack in addition to his own. When Roscoe muttered thanks, he shrugged, '*Nichevó.*' Forget it.

Roscoe filled his mouth with baked beans and buttered toast. He closed his tired eyes, stinging from the wood smoke. The taste of the food was straight from childhood, blissful with memories of campfires in the rain.

Dawson prodded him awake with: 'Have a quick shower and get changed. You've got a plane to catch.'

Before Roscoe fell asleep in the car, he asked the question that had been bothering him. 'Those three other trainees, George. Russian-speakers. What's their part in this operation?'

'They're the back-up,' said Dawson.

'Back-up?' Roscoe was almost knocked out with the after-effects of the hot shower and warm food. 'You mean, they're the snatch squad in case Sir John won't come of his own free will and we have to grab him – is that it?'

It was hard for him to stay awake. In Les Trois Moulins Dawson had made the job sound like money for jam: £10,000 for a three-day jaunt. The way it was building up now gave Roscoe the feeling that he would be earning every penny of the fee. If there was a back-up squad of hard men like Able, Baker and Charlie, then somebody at the top of the pile was preparing for a messy ending.

.6.

Dawson drove fast along the M4 motorway; he had tickets for the Swissair breakfast flight from Gatwick to Geneva. Roscoe woke up as they passed the Swindon turn-off and listened to the briefing. The plan of action did not impress him. He had spent the wet, sleepless night hours on the moor working out his own priorities and knew that he had to swing the operation his way from the start because he would never get another chance.

'Load of crap, George,' he said. 'Forget every detail of your plan. I know Van. If we arrive out of the blue and I come up with: "The Service needs you . . ." or "What fun it will be to play secrets with us once again!", we've lost the game. Once Ms Vanessa Bowles-Haddon has turned me down, that's it for keeps. She doesn't change her mind easily.'

'So what's your bright idea, Jack?'

Dawson was thinking of Madeleine Wharton's instructions: 'I don't care what you have to do, George. Watch Roscoe like a hawk but get Sir John back here p.d.q. Nothing else matters.'

'Scrub the flight to Geneva,' said Roscoe. 'We'll start by going to St Petersburg.'

'Now listen, Jack.'

'No, you listen to me!' shouted Roscoe. 'I'm fucking tired, bruised from head to toe and every muscle in my body aches. I could sleep for about three weeks solid but until the end of this op I don't think anyone's going to get much zizz. Either you and Madeleine Wharton agree to do things my way or you can kiss goodbye to me talking Van into this scenario for you.'

Dawson felt the first twinges of his ulcer playing him up. With nothing in writing from the DG, he had no insurance policy. 'OK, OK,' he said placatingly. 'So what's the plan when we get to St P.?'

'Lirian wants the deal to go through, right?'

'He wants his money: five per cent from them and five from us.'

'That's what I figured. So if we tell him that Van is the key to his deal going through, he'll move heaven and earth to get the one thing which will persuade her to co-operate.'

'Which is what?'

'Confirmation that Bergman's still alive. And if he is, his release as a small deal on the side in payment for Van's co-operation in the main transaction.'

'And how do we get Bergman home?'

'The same way we get Sir John out, whatever that is.'

'You make it all sound simple, Jack. But supposing Bergman is dead?'

Roscoe was so tired that his eyes kept closing. 'At least, then we'll know for sure,' he mumbled half-asleep. 'Have you got a better plan?'

'No.' And that's the truth, thought Dawson.

Roscoe dozed uneasily on the flight. For some reason his over-tired brain fantasised that the recent changes in Russia had turned it back to the land of gentle romance depicted in Turgenev's novels, for which he had had a passion in his teens. As the Tupolev jumbo touched down at Pulkovo Two, St Petersburg's international airport, he was almost expecting to see Chekhovian ladies in crinolines walking little dogs past gentlemen in frock coats and top hats.

The reality was very different. Pulkovo Two looked more like a temporary warehouse on an industrial estate than the international airport of Russia's second city. There were no glossy shops, no smart hotels and none of the glamorous ambiance normally associated with international air travel. Standing behind the immigration officer, Anastas Lirian beckoned to Roscoe and Dawson to pass straight through without waiting in the queue. There was an argument between him and the immigration man which was solved by a couple of dollar bills changing hands.

Roscoe had forgotten that to get through a Russian crowd, one had literally to elbow and shove people out of the way. As he pushed his way to the Arrivals exit after Lirian, the odour of sweat and garlic hit him, overlaid with cheap eau-de-Cologne. Touts tried to manoeuvre the Westerners towards unlicensed taxis and shouted the names of hotels, promising special rates. A heavily made-up, buxom blonde girl thrust her card into Roscoe's hand. He read: . . . *personal services with discounts for really hard currencies!* and threw it away. A large man in a leather jacket and leather peaked cap who looked like an out-of-work KGB heavy was openly offering black market rates for sterling, Deutschmarks, Swiss francs and yen. A small, dowdily dressed woman of indeterminate age clung briefly to Roscoe's arm, holding in front of his face a piece of paper torn from a child's exercise book on which was written in English: *My baby dying. Please give me antibiotic you have. Any kind. I pay dollars.* Roscoe shrugged her off and followed Lirian towards a black Mercedes parked in the No Waiting area with its engine running.

It was, Roscoe reflected, a different scene from his last visit. Then St Petersburg had been Leningrad. He had been travelling on an Irish passport and spent a lot of time looking over his shoulder. He recalled the bowel-emptying fear he had felt, walking through Customs with a package of dollars in a raincoat pocket which he was to deposit in a dead drop by the Peter and Paul Fortress. Every step of the walk along the banks of the icebound Neva to the fortress was etched on his memory, as well as the return journey with a roll of film in his pocket. How different to be ushered through the airport by the KGB or whatever it was called this week, in the person of Anastas Lirian . . .

Once clear of the crowd, Dawson murmured, 'Don't forget this is my territory, Jack. So whatever happens, keep in touch, OK? You can always leave a message for me at the hard currency bar of the Bolshoi Hotel.'

In the car-park ten dollars went into the hands of the racketeer who had stopped his pals from stealing the wheels of Dawson's car. It was drizzling and someone had stolen the windscreen wipers. For another dollar Dawson bought a pair of wipers from someone else's car and drove out of the car-park to find Roscoe, Lirian and Lirian's Mercedes gone.

Roscoe had opened the door and caught a whiff of expensive perfume.

'Hallo,' said Nadya Gutman. Her voice was low and friendly with none of the hard vowels that many Russian-speakers seem unable to lose when they talk English. And her physically perfect face was only inches from his, eyes wide and inviting.

Roscoe shook her hand. 'Nice to meet you,' he said. There was a half-played game of chess on the pull-down table in front of his seat. Lirian got in the car from the other side and folded table and board away to make more room. In a voice devoid of intonation, he said, 'Do we have a deal or not, Jack?'

Roscoe would have liked to haul him out of the car, thump his beaky nose flat and keep hitting until Lirian told him what had happened that night in Turkey. He disciplined himself to control his temper.

'The money's been agreed,' he said. 'The problem lies in identification and for that we need . . .'

Roscoe made mental notes during the journey. All the old habits came back: checking distances by the car's milometer, counting the turn-offs, noting where the GAI traffic police had their checkpoints. On the St Petersburg–Helsinki road the passage of the Mercedes was logged three times. *Plus ça change*, he thought, *plus c'est la même Russie.*

Shortly after passing through the town of Vyborg – the last built-up area before the Finnish frontier – they turned off the main highway, ignoring a No Entry sign. Here they were stopped by men in GAI uniforms at a red-and-white boom across the road. Lirian used their telephone to have a long argument with whoever was at the other end of the line. Meanwhile the GAI men gathered around the car, admiring both the vehicle and the driver.

To frustrate them Nadya came and sat in the curtained rear compartment, chatting to Roscoe. She was a girl who exuded sexuality; he found it hard to keep his eyes on her face as she sat, one stockinged leg curled under her, toying with a necklace and asking him questions about being a musician. Beneath her low-cut silk blouse she was not wearing a bra, he noticed.

When the Mercedes was allowed to proceed, it was with Lirian at the wheel. At the next bend a concrete blockhouse was manned by troops whom Roscoe identified as Special Forces from their blue airborne berets and the hooped blue-and-white T-shirts visible at the open necks of their fatigue jackets. They had the same alert eyes and coiled-spring fitness as the three SBS men on Exmoor. Most were armed with AK 74s and carried at least one additional weapon. They waved the Mercedes onwards without stopping it.

As Lirian drove further into Colonel Plotnik's empire, there were tank tracks in the sandy soil at the side of the road and the sound of automatic small arms fire and light artillery was clearly audible above the noise of the car's engine, coming from firing ranges deep in the forest on both sides of the road. Each guard post was expecting them, alerted by the previous one.

At the Villa Orlova itself they were kept waiting at the double gate, the only break in the twin perimeter fences. Between the wires were free-running Alsatians. On the fence posts were video cameras and proximity detectors. The wire was fixed to insulators and the dogs kept well away from it, which probably meant that it was electrified.

The huge, sprawling rococo house standing on a knoll overlooking the Gulf of Finland was big enough to be a five-star hotel. If the elaborate architectural style was pure Disneyland, Roscoe thought that the sophisticated security screen around the property was straight from Silicon Valley. Should Madeleine Wharton be planning for Able, Baker and Charlie to slip across the Gulf and snatch Sir John from the villa one dark night, she had better think again.

With Nadya chattering beside him for the last few kilometres it had been hard to concentrate on distances and turn-offs but Roscoe had a reasonable idea of where they were on the map he was carrying in his head. His estimate was confirmed by the sight of blue water through the trees as they drove up the mound towards the villa itself.

'This is where you're keeping him?' asked Roscoe.

'There he is!' Nadya pointed to a grove of birch trees whose silver trunks and bare branches were dappled by the late afternoon sun. A tall grey-haired man in a knee-length fur coat was strolling through them, his back to the car.

Sir John Bowles-Haddon was consumed by a sense that life had been very unfair to him. Few would ever know what he had achieved. His name would figure in no history books, unless he rated a mention in *The Guinness Book of Records* as the only person simultaneously to be both a Knight of the Realm and a Hero of the Soviet Union. And now he was just a worn-out asset being sold for cash, despite his years of loyal service to Moscow . . .

He slumped on a bench in a wooden belvedere overlooking the Gulf and reflected how Peter the Great had stood not far away on the banks of the Neva, sniffing the winds of knowledge blowing from seventeenth-century Europe and deciding to build his new capital there. The site had been chosen for strategic reasons which were out of date before the city was half-built, but by then it had cost the lives of tens of thousands of Swedish prisoners of war and even more Russians.

Yet Yeltsin's protégé Anatoly Sobchak had been elected Mayor of Leningrad in 1991 on condition that he change the name back to *Sankt Peterborg*. That was the Russian mind, reflected Sir John bitterly: the more you made them suffer, the more they loved you for it. God knows, Lenin had caused enough misery in Russia but even he could not equal Peter the Great's record of human suffering, so Lenin's Town had become St Peter's Fortress once again.

This far north, November was already mid-winter. To keep warm in the crisp breeze blowing off the Baltic, Sir John stood up and continued walking through the birch trees at a brisk pace. In front of him, the ground sloped away to the bleak shore where there was a boathouse, guarded by sentries. Across the water to the west, the Finnish mainland was visible as a hazy smudge on the horizon.

A flash of naked skin between the trunks of the trees drew Sir John's eye to where a young Spetsnaz conscript on fatigue duty was chopping logs, stripped to the waist despite the cold. Eyeing his naked torso appreciatively, Sir John thought that in the West the boy would have won titles, like Mr California or Big Bulge . . .

At the sight of the rippling muscles and tanned skin gleaming with sweat, the Englishman felt a quickening of his pulse. The boy raised the heavy axe above his head and brought it down on another birch log, splitting it neatly into two equal halves. He grunted with the exertion. Grunt, lift and chop. Grunt, lift and chop. The pile of split logs grew steadily

Suddenly aware that he was being watched, he turned and wiped sweat off his brow. Sir John offered a cigarette and chatted. He made jokes about big choppers and how dangerous they could be if not properly held by a man who knew how to handle tools. The boy – a peasant's son from Siberia – was puzzled, uncertain what the foreigner wanted.

'Lovely bunch you've got there, darling,' murmured Sir John. He licked his lips at the thought of getting his hands on the boy's thick leather belt, undoing the heavy buckle, slipping the coarse trousers down over his tight little buttocks and grabbing a mouthful of the elixir of youth. There was no one in sight. If the boy had given even a hint that he understood . . .

Sir John sighed. It was a pity. After all the years of repressing his true sexual identity, even thinking about such an alfresco encounter was delicious.

'Flowers at this time of year?' the boy queried, thinking he had misunderstood the foreigner's accent. 'You want me to pick you a bunch of flowers, Excellence?'

'Never mind,' Sir John sighed. He patted the sweaty shoulder. 'Never mind, dear. You just carry on chopping the logs to keep us warm in the long winter of discontent that lies ahead.'

On the far side of the villa, masked from Sir John's view by the house itself, Roscoe had just stepped out of Lirian's car. Nadya appeared to twist her ankle as she followed him out and clung to Roscoe's arm, nestling it between her breasts and holding on tight for balance while she examined one of her two-inch heels.

'It seems all right,' she said, slipping the shoe back on.

She was smiling at him, her face provocatively close to his. Over her head Roscoe saw Lirian watching them. He disengaged himself from the girl and ran to catch up before Lirian went into the house. When they were alone on the steps leading up to the porticoed front door he put the question he had waited six years to ask: 'Anastas, you were there at the border, that night in Turkey. Did Bergman die?'

'Not exactly.' The snake eyes glittered. Lirian was thinking of his commission on the deal which now appeared unlikely to be concluded. It would affect all his plans, so carefully laid.

A sledgehammer started battering inside Roscoe's ribcage. There was a huge lump in his throat. He caught Lirian's sleeve. 'What's that mean: not exactly?'

Lirian was looking at the Mercedes where Nadya was delicately hitching her tight skirt a few inches higher above her knees in order to manoeuvre her shapely legs behind the steering wheel.

'He was injured,' he said. 'Injured and taken to a military hospital near Yerevan, that's all I remember.'

'After that?'

'I don't know, Jack.' Lirian turned to Roscoe a face devoid of expression. 'I don't know what happened to him after that. I'm only a freelance now, so you'll have to ask General Medvedev himself. He's the big boss around here, you know.'

.7.

In the large dining-room of the villa General Grigori
Sergeyevich Medvedev poured two glasses of near-boiling tea
from the antique samovar on the sideboard and passed one to
Roscoe.

The general's surname in Russian meant *bear*. In his ill-
fitting suit he shambled round the room blowing on his tea to
cool it: a large, unkempt man with eyes invisible beneath the
thick, beetling brows, the hair on his head as thick as a door-
mat. Medvedev's resemblance to the Russian bear was not just
in name and physique; in temperament he was just as ursine –
deceptively slow-moving, violent, dangerous and unpre-
dictable.

'Long time, no see,' he growled in English with a throaty
Russian accent.

'Long time, Grigori,' Roscoe agreed.

They had met at diplomatic receptions when Medvedev had
been working in London, attached to the Russian Trade
Mission on Highgate Hill. The first detail which surfaced in
Roscoe's memory was that two of Medvedev's informants had
been found strangled on Hampstead Heath shortly before their

handler was thrown out of Britain by the Iron Lady. The hands that had poured out his tea were peasant's hands, hairy, broad and powerful like the rest of Medvedev's body – good hands for throttling a potentially embarrassing asset.

Roscoe raised his glass, placed a lump of sugar between his teeth in the Russian manner and swallowed some of the scalding black fluid. He noticed that the general was blinking rapidly and had a tic under one eye, presumably a sign of stress.

'Lirian tells me we have a small problem,' Medvedev growled.

'It could be a big one,' said Roscoe. 'The magnitude depends on you, Grigori. If I don't persuade Sir John's niece to identify him, London won't pay you one penny.'

'And you think that digging some poor *zak* out of the Gulag – which no longer exists, of course – will change this girl's mind?'

'I'm certain of it.' Roscoe's throat was tight from tension. 'This poor *zak* saved her life. She'll do this job to get him out. Otherwise you lose the deal, Grigori.'

Medvedev slumped in a chair and sat mulling over the news. The deal was only for one million pounds sterling but at this juncture in his plans every payment counted. If London wanted some unimportant agent thrown in as make-weight for Sir John's exchange, he had no objections.

'Wait here.' He lumbered out of the room to use one of the secure modems upstairs.

Roscoe helped himself to another glass of tea and wandered around the room. It had once been a library but the books and bookshelves had been destroyed in a bombardment by Finnish guns during the brief winter war of 1940 and never replaced. The pine-panelled walls were covered by an extraordinary collection of firearms on three sides of the room. On the fourth side tall French windows gave a view over the shore, the boathouse and across the Gulf of Finland looking westwards. In the growing dusk visibility was closing down rapidly, making Roscoe regret that he had not had time to make an effective recce outside in daylight.

All the weapons in the room had been purchased over the years for Spetsnaz training purposes and had ended in Plotnik's personal collection when superseded by more advanced technology of death. One wall held assault rifles and their kin: a Garand M1 and an M16 from America, a Sten gun and a Bren from Britain, a FAMAS assault rifle from France, an Uzi from Israel, a Swiss Sturmgewehr 57, an HK11A1 from Germany, a Beretta model 12 . . .

Roscoe's eye ranged over them, identifying most but not all. He took a couple of guns down from their hooks, cocked them and tried the actions. Like every other weapon in the border zone they were regularly cleaned and oiled by Plotnik's armourers and were in perfect working order.

He turned to the second wall on which hung pistols and revolvers from all over the world ranging from the Browning 9 mm., Walther PPK and Smith and Wesson 38s and 44 Magnums with which he was familiar to more exotic Makarovs, Berettas and a Steyr GB80 from Austria. The third wall was covered with a display of military and civilian shotguns and hunting rifles. In one corner of the room a locked, glass-fronted cupboard held boxes of ammunition in various calibres.

Roscoe stuck his head out of the door leading into the hallway. A Spetsnaz girl soldier who looked part-Chinese was covering him with a loaded AK74M, the butt folded back to make it a machine-pistol, of convenient length inside a house.

'*Gdye ubórnaya?*'he asked: where's the toilet?

She jerked her head at a door halfway along the hall without speaking, followed him six paces behind and kicked the toilet door open when he tried to close it.

Roscoe was wondering why there were two more armed sentries on the first-floor landing. What could be so valuable it needed guarding like that, given that the house stood inside the ultra-secure perimeter through which he had just been driven?

He stood peeing with his back to the sentry. 'Get a kick out of watching men holding their pissers, do you?' he asked over his shoulder.

'Fuck you too, wack!' she said in a perfect Liverpool accent. Roscoe grinned; all Spetsnaz troops spoke one or more foreign languages well enough to pass as natives.

He was just finishing when he heard her heels click together as Plotnik crashed through the front door.

'*Gdyé chort generál?*' he shouted at the startled girl. She nodded upstairs without making the mistake of taking her eyes off Roscoe. The assault rifle in her hands stayed pointing firmly at his kidneys.

Plotnik stopped short when he saw Roscoe emerging from the toilet, zipping up his flies.

'What the hell's that civilian doing here?' he asked the girl in Russian.

'I don't know, Colonel.'

'You don't know? What is this place, a hotel?'

'Relax, Ivan Ivanovich!' It was Medvedev's throaty growl coming from the head of the stairs. He pushed one of the sentries out of his way and lumbered down to the ground floor, the staircase shaking under his weight. 'Jack Roscoe is an old pal of mine from London, eh Jack?'

From Dawson's description, Roscoe had already identified the crew-cut colonel before hearing his first name and patronymic. There was a brief exchange, fast and slangy, between Plotnik and Medvedev, of which Roscoe could follow hardly a word although he thought the gist of it was to do with *sínniy*, meaning the gay Sir John and *dyéneg*, meaning money.

. . . and then the word that stood out like a crash of thunder: Bergman!

'What's the news?' Roscoe asked.

Plotnik glanced at the girl sentry. Remembering her language specialisation, he snapped, 'Dismiss!'

She threw a parade-ground salute and left on the double.

'What's the news?' Roscoe's pulse was racing. Coming in through the front door he saw the tall Englishman who had been walking among the trees when they arrived.

'We're making enquiries,' said Medvedev. 'It's not easy to trace people, Jack.'

'Don't give me that, Grigori.' Roscoe was not having any flannel. 'At the peak of the Gulag you had every one of five million prisoners documented. You never lost one of the poor bastards, no matter how hard they tried!'

'That was then,' growled Medvedev. 'Now nothing in Russia works, you must know that. The archivists are sacked, the records all dumped. It'll take time to trace this man Bergman.'

'Bergman?' said Plotnik. 'First name?'

Roscoe spun round to face the colonel who was leaning against the newel post of the staircase, cleaning his nails with the tip of a narrow stiletto.

'Peter,' he said. 'Peter Bergman, a Canadian flier.'

'The man's dead!' Roscoe heard Sir John's oh-so-English voice behind him. 'The poor fellow died of his injuries shortly after the incident on the Turkish frontier. I did what I could for him but it was no good. He passed away without recovering consciousness.'

Roscoe turned to stare. A wan smile flitted over Sir John's face. 'Was he a friend of yours? I'm so sorry.'

The words echoed in Roscoe's head like a gunshot in a cellar: *died of his injuries . . . died of his injuries . . . died of his injuries*. He felt cold from head to foot. He had come so far and this was the end of the trail: Bergman was dead after all – and had been dead all the time.

Plotnik startled him with one word: 'Wrong!'

Everyone turned to look at the lean, crew-cut colonel toying with his stiletto.

'The Englishman is lying,' said Plotnik in his hard American accent. 'I happen to know that Peter Bergman was still alive this time last year.'

Roscoe could read nothing in the impassive, high-cheek-boned Slav features. He controlled the flush of hope which the words had given him and asked, 'How do you know, Colonel?'

Plotnik did not reply. He was not in the habit of giving infor-mation to foreigners.

'And is he still alive, this Bergman?' Medvedev growled.

Plotnik thought of the emaciated, handcuffed and hobbled prisoner being hauled about the helicopter which was to take him back to Perm 39B a year ago. To his mind, Bergman was probably tough enough to have recovered and survived. Then he remembered Ossetin and shook his head. That sadistic little eunuch of a camp commandant would not have forgiven a pris-oner who had caused him so much trouble.

He spun the razor-sharp knife in the air, caught it by the flat of the blade and slipped it back into his ankle-sheath.

'It's extremely unlikely,' he said.

Nadya drove Roscoe back into the city in Lirian's car. Her conversation was full of innuendoes. If Roscoe wanted to see the town, she would take him to some interesting places that tourists never saw. If he wanted company, she was free tonight, with Lirian tied up in some meeting back at the villa, so . . .

'Thanks,' he said. 'I've had a long day. I need some sleep.'

She leaned across the passenger seat to hold his door open and managed to brush her breasts against his arm, wafting her perfume up into his nostrils. 'If you change your mind and want some company, Jack – just call me on this number.'

Roscoe slipped the card into his pocket and watched the Mercedes accelerate away. With a squeal of tyres it wove a passage through the build-up of evening traffic, crossed a red light and disappeared from view.

In the basement of the Bolshoi Hotel the atmosphere of the hard currency bar was like a Prohibition speakeasy. Drinks prices were even higher than in a smart hotel in London or Paris. Most of the customers were Russian, into some racket or other. They paid in dollars, sterling or Deutschmarks as though frightened that the money in their pockets might become roubles when their new Mercedes changed back into pumpkins on the last stroke of midnight. At the end of the bar near the entrance a group of heavyweight bodyguards stood waiting to drive their employers home.

On the small stage a Muscovite rock group with the English name of Gorby's Go-Go Girls was kicking to death Mick Jagger's 'Can't Get No Satisfaction'. The lead singer, with Mongolian features and the same thick lips as his idol, was barefoot and naked to the waist, wearing only a pair of peasant trousers in some thick homespun material, tied up with string. He was either prodigiously well-hung or had a length of hosepipe stuffed inside them. With his sweat-shiny torso and dayglo-green Mohican haircut he looked like a mutant spawned by Genghis Khan out of Ol' Blubberlips.

The PA was a typically Russian compromise: brand-new Bose speakers fed by an ancient home-made amp that kept breaking up with each overload from the bass drum. The noise level and distortion hurt Roscoe's sensitive musician's ears but no one else appeared to mind.

The tables in the centre of the bar were dimly lit but in the gloom of the curtained booths at the sides he could make out nothing at all. In the first two booths he peered into couples were copulating to the rhythm of the band. A hand grabbed Roscoe's shoulder and he found himself spun round and being shouted at by one of the heavies from the bar, who was mouthing not threats but helpful advice.

Roscoe grinned thanks. In the booth indicated, Dawson was sitting alone with a bottle of Johnnie Walker Black Label. By the glimmer of the booth's single low-wattage bulb both bottle and drinker looked the worse for wear.

Roscoe recounted his visit to the villa, shouting into Dawson's ear. The level of the PA made it unnecessary to worry about security.

'Time's running out,' was Dawson's comment. 'When is Medvedev going to get back to you?'

'Tomorrow morning, first thing,' Roscoe yawned. 'Right now, I'm going to hit the hay.'

Dawson passed over a room key and drained his glass. 'Who brought you back here?' he asked. 'Lirian?'

Roscoe stood up, yawning. 'No. He stayed on for some meeting with Medvedev, back at the villa. His girl drove me back.'

'Oh, the delicious little Nadya.' There was a knowing leer on Dawson's face.

'What's that lecherous look supposed to mean?'

Dawson poured the last of the whisky into two glasses. 'A really high-class hooker,' he said. '*Oná byla lástochka.*'

'Jesus!' Roscoe whistled. 'A KGB-trained swallow? I thought they were just a rumour.'

'Nope. Nadya really was a sexpionage agent, as I think the cousins still call them.'

'So what's she doing, working for Lirian? He doesn't strike me as the type who uses women.' Roscoe looked at the card on which Nadya had written her telephone number and wondered aloud, 'What does a beautiful piece of horseflesh like her see in that pot-bellied little creep?'

'It's a mystery to me, Jack,' Dawson chuckled. 'Nadya apparently got the push at the same time as dear Anastas, during Yeltsin's big clear-out two years ago. Since then, she surfaces from time to time, always with her keeper.' He licked his lips. 'With her face and body, she could make a fortune working the smart hotels.'

Roscoe tore the card into small pieces and dumped them in the ash-tray. With what Dawson had just told him, Nadya's offers made sense. Like Russian dolls, each twist of a Lirian scenario concealed another and another. Life, he thought, was complicated enough without getting entangled in some sub-plot the little Armenian had thought up. To drive away the lingering traces of Nadya's scent, he decided to try once more to call Maria.

.8.

Roscoe struggled to wake up. It was like climbing a riverbank slippery with mud; each time he was nearly at the top
he slid back to the bottom. There was someone shaking him,
trying to drag him out of the stream of subconscious images
and back onto the dry land of everyday.

In the dream Nadya and he had been making love on the
riverbank outside the cottage when Maria drove up with
Dawson in her old Renault 4. They stood over the couple on the
ground, Maria's eyes accusing Roscoe who tried to explain that
what he was doing was a physical act with no emotional sig-
nificance. Each time he opened his mouth to speak, Nadya
pulled his face back to hers and kissed him on the lips, whispering that she had important news about Bergman.

While Roscoe was straining to hear the news, Maria ran into
the river to drown herself. Roscoe wanted to dive after her, to
save her and tell her that it was a misunderstanding, but could
not disentangle himself from Nadya's body. Like a Hindu goddess she had grown a multiplicity of arms and legs that caressed
and held her prey so that he could not break free until it was too
late. Despairingly Roscoe saw Maria's head vanish in a

whirlpool. He wanted to howl with anguish at his loss but still the sex goddess was repeating again and again: 'Wake up, Mr Roscoe! Wake up, please!'

Her voice was not Nadya's. The Liverpool accent belonged to the half-Chinese girl soldier who was leaning over the bed and shaking Roscoe's shoulder to wake him up. Behind her in the doorway stood the *dezhúrnaya* – the floor concierge – looking curious.

'Come,' said the girl. She was speaking English so that the woman standing in the doorway would not understand. 'You gorra gerra move on, like. We got news.'

Roscoe sat up. The girl was wearing civilian clothes. Her dark hair was dragged back from her forehead into a tight bun at the back. Her teeth were not perfect and her breath smelled slightly of garlic. She was a real person; this was no dream.

They were halfway to the lift when a phone started to ring in one of the bedrooms along the corridor. Roscoe was convinced it was the call he had booked to Maria before going to sleep but by the time the surly *dezhúrnaya* had taken her time finding the right key on her desk and re-opened the door, there was no one on the line.

They were sitting at the large oval table in the dining-room of the Villa Orlova: Roscoe, Medvedev, Plotnik and a girl photographer from the Spetsnaz infiltration and recce unit who was wearing a white coat over her uniform. It was she who passed the sheaf of black-and-white photographs across the table to Roscoe.

The face was that of a stranger. Roscoe's morale hit a new low. He shook his head. 'This isn't Bergman.'

Plotnik spread the other photographs fan-wise across the polished walnut surface. 'Look again,' he said.

Roscoe examined one picture after another: full face, right and left profiles. Gradually a feature in one photograph fleshed out a detail in another. It was possible by glancing fast from one picture to another to put together a composite that could be Bergman. The clincher was one shot in which Bergman's left forearm was visible. What looked like a burn-mark was, Roscoe realised, the old bullet-scar that had ruined Bergman's Legion tattoo.

'Remember,' said Plotnik, 'that this man has been starved for a long time, Mr Roscoe.'

The face in the pictures was thinner than seemed possible and the deep-sunk eyes were the eyes of a man who had spent years looking into hell.

Roscoe's hand was trembling. He rested it on the table to make the shaking less obvious. There was in these grainy available-light photographs something of Bergman's indomitable spirit. This was a man who had been living on the rim of Dante's inferno, but he had not fallen into the pit. The face on the table did not belong to a madman or someone whose will had been broken.

But the pictures could still be fakes . . .

Roscoe lifted one 10 x 8 black and white print to his nostrils. It had the sour smell of hypo – photographic fixer. That proved the print was fresh from the developing dish but it did not prove anything about the negative.

'I had to use a fast film,' explained the photographer in Russian. 'That's why the pictures are so grainy.'

Roscoe grunted. In front of him, Bergman's sunken eyes had a faraway, unfocused look. In one picture he was holding a copy of the *New York Times*. Plotnik pushed across the table to Roscoe a front page bearing the same headlines. It was dated the previous day.

Roscoe turned the photograph round to face the girl photographer opposite him. 'If this picture was rigged,' he promised, 'I'll personally kill you.'

'Kill me,' offered Plotnik with an evil grin. His American accent was strong. 'I was there, Roscoe. I talked to your old buddy while she was taking the pictures with this.'

He took a Pentax 35 mm. camera with a 1.2 lens from the girl beside him and held it up.

Roscoe put out a hand for the negatives. Plotnik's photographer handed him a roll of film and a magnifying glass. 'Frame sixteen is the one you want,' she said. 'That's Bergman holding the *New York Times*.'

Roscoe checked the frame number. It was hard to compare the neg with the positive enlargement, but so far as he could tell, it was the same picture. He sniffed the film. It too smelled of hypo – but it could have been a copy of a faked shot. With modern darkroom technology there was no easy way of telling.

Plotnik was reading his thoughts. 'I talked with Bergman quite a while,' he said. 'For the best part of a year he hasn't spoken to anyone, so at first it was hard for him to concentrate on what I was saying. I asked him for a recognition signal that only he could have sent and only you would understand.'

Roscoe was wary. 'And?'

There was a flash of curiosity on Plotnik's lean face. 'Bergman said, quote, I'll bet Roscoe still blames me for breaking reptile on Sammy's, unquote, end of message. It sounded like nonsense, so I asked him to repeat it.'

The hair on the back of Roscoe's neck stood erect as he recalled a rocky beach at dawn, strewn with wreckage. Two naked young men were laughing in the surf, trying to drown each other. Only Bergman could have sent that message. Not reptile, but *REP II*. Roscoe had blamed Bergman for *breaking REP II on Samos*.

'Satisfied?' asked Plotnik.

Roscoe nodded slowly to cover his racing pulse and the furious conflict of emotions raging within him.

Back to basics, he thought. Only fifteen hours had passed since he left the villa, the previous evening. In that time Plotnik's people had tracked Bergman down and the colonel himself had gone to whatever prison he was in. To get there, take the photograph, have a conversation and return to the villa within such a short space of time meant that Peter Bergman was not far away. And if he could fashion a recognition signal like that on the spur of the moment, he must be in remarkable mental shape for a man who had spent six years in the Gulag.

Roscoe felt drained by the incontrovertible evidence that Bergman was alive. It was almost an anticlimax after the six years of wondering. He licked his lips that were dry from tension. What next? His mind was blank. Until that moment, he had always half-assumed that the trail would end at some unmarked grave.

Medvedev's black Volga stopped outside the door marked Departures at Pulkovo Two.

In the curtained-off rear passenger compartment he put a restraining hand on Roscoe's arm. 'No hurry,' he said.

'My flight is about to close.'

'The plane leaves,' growled Medvedev, 'when I say so. Do you see anyone out there you recognise?'

Roscoe looked through the curtains. 'Surprisingly, yes,' he said.

'No surprise,' said Medvedev. 'Show me.'

Roscoe pointed at Charlie, the SBS man who had carried his pack at the end of the yomp on Exmoor. Dressed in nondescript anorak and old jeans, he looked quite at ease, leaning against the wall, smoking a *papirós* as though waiting for someone. There was a rapid exchange in Russian between Medvedev and the half-Chinese Spetsnaz girl, who was sitting beside the driver. She was in civilian clothes, wearing a fur hat and a smart raincoat.

Unable to hear where one slang expression ended and the next began, Roscoe could not follow a word of Medvedev's instructions. The girl got out of the car and strolled casually towards the terminal building.

From his wallet Medvedev took out a torn piece of a creased and faded photograph. 'Give that to the Bowles-Haddon girl,' he ordered.

Roscoe looked. It was an old picture of Van. 'What's this?'

'Just do it, Roscoe,' ordered Medvedev.

Through the curtains, the two men in the rear seat saw the girl walk casually up to the man smoking and apparently ask the time.

Off-guard, he pulled back his cuff to check his watch. She kneed him savagely in the groin. As his head came forward, she butted him in the face. Two militiamen closed in on the scene of violence before any passers-by could intervene. Between them they carried Charlie away, doubled up and retching as he clutched a broken nose and his groin.

'That was stupid,' said Roscoe. 'There must have been other ways of . . .'

Medvedev moved with a speed that seemed impossible for so large and heavy a man. He sat forward, turned and grabbed Roscoe's lapels with his arms crossed, yanking them tight around the neck and effectively cutting off the oxygen supply to his victim's brain. Roscoe felt a roaring black emptiness rush up inside his skull, the veins stood out on his temples and his face turned purple.

'Don't ever question my authority,' growled the general. 'Ever.' Like a huge bear he shook Roscoe viciously to make the point who was master, then dropped him coughing and gagging back into the cushioned seat.

The girl opened the front passenger door and slipped back into her seat, not even out of breath. 'Showed that focker a thing or two, d'i'n I, eh?' she said for Roscoe's benefit, adding in Russian, '*Vypolnila zadáchu, továrish generál!*'

From the glove pocket she took a make-up compact and began touching up her smudged lipstick in the vanity mirror.

'On your way, Jack,' growled Medvedev.

.9.

Sweat ran down Bergman's spine. He had done several hours of karate practice and t'ai chi exercises in order to regain control of his trembling muscles and calm the feverish sweating, the irregular breathing and the pulse hammering inside his skull in reaction to the unaccustomed shot of adrenalin caused by Plotnik's visit.

The cage was both his prison and personal space. No one had entered it since the day Ossetin locked him in, eleven months before. Plotnik had sensed the problem and asked permission before entering, repeating the message several times: 'Do you remember me, Bergman? I'm Ivan Ivanovich Plotnik.' He had been uncertain which of the bearded, filthy men in Ossetin's zoo was the one he sought until Bergman answered in a whisper, 'I remember you, Colonel.'

Bergman had thought he was hallucinating, that the voice and the lean figure in camouflage fatigues on the other side of the bars were just fabrications of his imagination, at last gone out of control.

And afterwards, in memory, the visit had the disjointed feeling of a dream. Plotnik's first act had been to hand the prisoner a rechargeable razor. Someone else had cut his tangled, lice-infested hair while Plotnik plied him with questions about Jack Roscoe and Vanessa Bowles-Haddon. He had given Bergman a newspaper with English writing on it. Then a woman photographer had asked about using a flashgun and Plotnik's medical officer had said quickly, 'No flash. It could damage his retina permanently.'

She had examined Bergman before they left, listening to his heart and lungs, taking his blood pressure and drawing a couple of blood samples. Bergman had been too excited to give a sample of urine, so she had made two of the guards carry away the full toilet can instead.

It was a dream with a bad ending: Plotnik's entourage left without taking the prisoner with them. Stunned by the whole performance, Bergman had not even argued when the colonel said, 'Get yourself into shape. I'll be back – and that's a promise!'

The only proof that it was not a dream were Bergman's clean-shaven chin which he kept touching and the camouflage canvas ration-pack of concentrated food supplies that the Spetsnaz team had left behind – with a threat to emasculate Ossetin if any guard laid hands on it.

When Wu's exercises had calmed him down sufficiently, Bergman sat on the bed and munched a muesli bar. That was real enough. He pulled the tab on a self-heating can of stew and ate it with more pleasure than from a meal at the Ritz, trying to recall all the other news Plotnik had brought. There was a pile of newspapers on the bed to read but the events and names of public figures meant nothing to a prisoner who had spent six years in the Gulag, cut off from the world. After so long in the dreamtime, reality was hard to absorb.

'You've got a bloody nerve, you know.' Van settled in the executive chair behind her desk and studied Roscoe across the small office above her shop in Geneva's Grand' Rue. 'That old dogsbody Dawson was here a few days ago. The message I sent via him ought to have been crystal clear to a cretin. I'll tell you the same as I told him . . .'

'I'm not here on behalf of the Service,' Roscoe interrupted her gently. 'They sacked me years ago.'

'May one ask why?'

He shrugged, 'I asked too many questions about you-know-what. You warned me what they would do. In the end you were right.'

Van looked at Roscoe more closely. His clothes were inexpensive but clean and reasonably new. She shifted in her chair, uneasily wondering for a moment if he were down on his luck and about to ask her for a handout.

'Then what do you want?' she asked frigidly, coming to the point.

'A beer,' said Roscoe. 'I flew in on a Russian plane with no bar and do I need a drink!'

She opened the small fridge built into her desk. 'There's champagne or champagne,' she said. 'Take your pick. My clients are all diplomats, aristocrats or mere millionaires. That's all they drink.'

While she took a phone call in German from a client for whom she had been bidding at auction that day, Roscoe opened the bottle and poured two glasses. He drained his own and refilled it, watching Van handle the cut-and-thrust of an intricate verbal battle about attribution of the silver doll's-house toys sitting on her desk, their value and her commission.

She looked so poised and in command of herself, he thought. Her black silk suit must have cost a fortune without the matching accessories – and the jewellery she was wearing looked genuine to his unpractised eye. Roscoe decided that he had been right not to come here straight from London. Whatever her past links with him, Vanessa Bowles-Haddon was not someone who could be conned into doing what she did not want to.

One wall of her expensively decorated office was lined with reference books and auction catalogues. Roscoe pulled a few out and found them covered with notes in the uncrackable code of Van's hasty scrawl. Sensing that his oblique scrutiny was irritating her, he put them back and studied the shop below through the one-way glass window. A middle-aged roly-poly West African in a robe and an embroidered cap was buying miniature portraits in enamels for which he was paying with a pile of crisp new banknotes. They were being counted by one of the assistants, an elderly man dressed as soberly as an under-taker.

Van put down the phone.

'That customer,' said Roscoe, pointing through the glass. 'What does he want those baubles for? He doesn't look to me like a collector.'

She glanced through the one-way glass.

'His brother's a Head of State.' She named the country. 'The whole family may have to run for the airport in the middle of the night. For them, miniatures are a safer investment than stocks and shares. They appreciate well, they're easily portable and convertible anywhere in the world.'

'You know most of your clients so well?'

'All of them,' she said. 'The sort of prices at which I sell, we're not dealing in trinkets that a tourist takes home for a souvenir.'

Roscoe picked up a couple of the doll's-house toys. There was a tiny table and matching dinner chairs. The sideboard had each plate separately crafted and invisibly soldered in position. 'What's this lot worth?'

A hint of a smile touched the corners of Van's mouth. 'A bit less than my client is paying.' She did a quick sum on a small calculator. 'In US money, they're worth around two hundred thousand dollars at today's prices.'

Roscoe whistled, 'A handful of toys? You're kidding?'

'I never joke about money,' she said.

Roscoe looked down into the shop, wondering what the con-tents of the elegant little display cases were worth.

'Every item in the shop is small,' he remarked.

Van laughed briefly. 'That's the idea. I deal in objects of virtu – small, beautiful and portable things that people can col-lect discreetly or use as investments which don't need to be declared.'

'Here's to the rich!' Roscoe turned back to face her, his glass raised in a toast to which Van did not respond.

'What do you want, Jack?' she repeated her question.

'Help.'

'Why should I help you?' She sat and waited, her blue eyes cold and noncommittal.

Roscoe removed from his wallet the torn and yellowed half-photograph that Medvedev had given him at Pulkovo Two Airport. He laid it on the table in front of Van and watched her face freeze.

Van looked from the photograph to Roscoe and back again. She touched the picture with one elegantly manicured finger and withdrew her hand without picking it up. In the margin at the bottom of the picture, the bleached-out words *AND ME* were just discernible, but only because she knew they were there. She had written them.

Van's voice sounded strange in her own ears as she asked, 'Where did you get this, Jack?'

'What is it?' he asked.

'You don't know?'

'No idea.'

'Tell me where you got it!' she ordered.

'Tell me what it is and I'll tell you where I got it,' he bargained.

She picked the yellowed piece of paper off the table and turned her back on him. It was habit, so that a client sitting in Roscoe's chair could not follow the numbers she was dialling on the combination lock of the wall-safe. But this time it was also a way of hiding her face in case it betrayed her emotions to this man from her past. She felt weak at the knees and pulled the chair nearer to the safe so that she could sit down to reach inside, pushing aside the small boxes and envelopes of precious objects to reach what she was seeking.

In the faded photograph clenched in her left hand she saw the girl she had been . . . was it only five or six years ago? Could it possibly be only that long since the businesswoman in the black silk suit had been the laughing girl in jeans and T-shirt?

For a moment she forgot Roscoe sitting behind her. Hanging above the safe was an antique Tibetan silk scroll that Roberto had brought back from a business trip to Beijing. He had had the inscription translated for her. It was a saying of the thirteenth Dalai Lama: *Lo, the serpent gods and demons lurk behind me, stern and mighty!*

The girl in the photograph, Van thought, had been an innocent child, unaware of the demons lurking behind her until it was too late. It was a long time since she had cried about anything. She let the tears flow now, but silently as she had learned to do in her dormitory cubicle at school.

From the back of the safe she took a book of poems that had been a school prize. Pressed between the pages were flowers and other things that evoked memories of happy days and beautiful places: the brass baseplate of a cleat from a dinghy she had sailed with her father one golden summer at Salcombe, a ribbon from a gondolier's hat, a rosette won at a gymkhana when she was fourteen, Roberto's first love-letter to her . . .

Between two pages at the back of the book was the other half of the photograph. It too was yellow from incomplete fixing. The creases were the result of spending a whole year in a plastic bag, rammed into a hole in the ground in eastern Turkey.

In control once again, Van closed the safe. She wiped her eyes on a tissue and took from her handbag a pair of sunglasses, slipping them on before turning to place the two halves of the photograph on the desk between her and Roscoe. They fitted to make an informal two-shot of a couple with their arms around each other, laughing for the street photographer who had been so mean with his chemicals. *PETER AND ME*, the complete legend read.

She turned it round to face Roscoe. 'You can work that one out for yourself,' she said.

The picture had been taken two days before the border-crossing. Van remembered tearing it in half before they set out that night under the full moon hanging above Ararat. When she had given one half to Bergman and kept the other for herself, he had laughed at her premonition.

Beside the telephone, Roberto Perreira's framed portrait asked whether she cared more about the laughing man in the old photograph than she did for the millionaire who had shared his home and his wealth with her through two whole years.

'It's true,' she said.

'What is?' asked Roscoe.

She shook her head – it was nothing to do with him – and pointed at the old photograph. 'Now tell me where you got this, Jack.'

By way of answer, Roscoe spread fan-wise across her desk

the pictures of Bergman which Plotnik had given him.

'These were taken yesterday,' he said. 'As of twenty-four hours ago, Peter was still alive!'

He watched Van's face for a reaction. Her eyes were hidden behind the dark glasses. Only the mascara-streaked tissue in the wastebin beside the desk told Roscoe that she had been crying.

'I felt the same,' he said – and realised how stupid the remark was when she half-snapped and half-sobbed, 'Did you? Did you really, Jack?'

He stood up abruptly as though she had hit him and walked to the one-way window, staring down into the shop and leaving her in privacy.

'If Peter's alive, he's a rich man.' Van's voice startled Roscoe but he did not look round.

'He never saved a penny,' he grunted.

In a detached monotone, her thoughts elsewhere, Van told Roscoe about the letter of credit that she had used to start her business – and of her private promise to Bergman's memory that half of it was his, if he should ever come back from the dead.

'What's it worth now?' asked Roscoe.

'Well, I don't own everything in the shop; some things I sell on commission. I suppose Peter's half must be the best part of a million dollars.'

Van sat at the desk where she had negotiated deals in six figures without feeling the remotest twinge of emotion. Now all the old confusion churned inside her. She could hardly breathe, let alone think. One hand touched the yellowed photograph of the man she remembered. The other lay on a picture of an emaciated prisoner. Oh God, she thought, how Peter must have suffered!

She looked at Roscoe's back. 'You've got some kind of rescue plan,' she said. 'And you want me to help?'

He turned to face her. 'Will you?'

Van clamped down on the whirl of emotions inside herself. First she had to get things straight, so: 'I asked you a question, that evening at Kenwood, Jack. Remember?'

Roscoe did not reply. She had caught him off balance. He had not allowed in his mind for Van having any reservations.

'You know what I'm getting at?' She held his eyes. 'I'm going to ask you again. Why did you come that day to the hotel in Kusadasi?'

'I told you.'

'I didn't believe your answer then and I don't believe you now.' It was her bluff against his.

The inner distress showed on Roscoe's face.

'I'm waiting.'

He sat and swallowed another glass of champagne, trying to wash the guilt down but it stuck in his throat. In a half-strangled voice he began the confession.

'I came to give you . . . a warning,' he said.

'Oh Christ,' Van spun the chair angrily, not trusting herself to look at him.

'I knew it,' she said, talking to the wall. 'I knew you wouldn't have broken security and jeopardised the whole mission just because you were jealous.'

There were beads of sweat on Roscoe's forehead as he told her of the whisper from Turkish Intelligence.

'So you should have called everything off?'

'If it was up to me, I would have done.' He desperately wanted her to believe him. 'But London was categorical that the op was to continue. The only concession I won was that I might deliver a warning to you and Peter to be extra careful at the border – to arrive early and recce the RV, that sort of thing.'

She spun back to face him. 'And instead of warning us, you were so damn jealous that you let Peter walk into an ambush!'

'You have to believe me!' Roscoe's eyes pleaded with her. 'I couldn't help my feelings when I saw you with him beside that swimming-pool.'

The scene was fresh in his mind: the blue of the pool and the deeper blue of the sea below the hotel terrace: the white concrete of the hotel: the crisp linen on the breakfast table: the waiter hovering attentively – and the single look like a kiss without touching that Van gave Bergman before she saw Roscoe sitting there.

The confession was the easier because he had already told Maria. Roscoe looked up to find Van watching him, unblinking. 'By the time I got back to the hotel,' he said, 'it was too late. You'd checked out.'

'And you left it at that?' Maria's question had been full of sympathy; Van's was like a lash.

'No!' Desperate for her to believe him, Roscoe reached for Van's hand across the desk but she sat back out of the way, waiting for him to continue. She felt as cold and remote as a judge listening to a defendant in court.

Roscoe poured another glass of champagne for himself. 'I drove after you along the main road heading east. At first I wasn't too worried about catching up because you were in that lumbering Land-Rover – remember? – and I was doing 120 to 150 kilometres an hour with my foot flat on the floor. Avoiding a mule-cart on a bend, with a bus coming the other way, I went clean off the road, across a ditch and into a field.'

'What kind of a field?' she rapped.

'Huh?'

'You heard. What was the crop?'

Roscoe shook his head. 'It was an olive grove. The car wrapped itself around one of the trees – a write-off. By the time I had some more wheels, there was no way I could catch you up.' He remembered shedding tears of impotence as he sat in the wreck, realising the price that Bergman and Van might have to pay for his momentary rage.

The long silence in Van's office was broken only by the background hum of conversation from the shop below.

'I believe you,' she said softly. Knowing Roscoe, she knew also that he had paid a thousand times over for what he had done, or not done. If now he was trying to right the old wrong, of course she would help him get Bergman back from whatever hell-hole he was in . . .

The pictures on her desk floated before her eyes. What did she truly feel about Peter Bergman? It was something she had never been able to clarify for herself. Had he really been the lover whose memory still haunted her, whose touch she ached for in the night? Or had she built a fantasy out of the two exotic, danger-filled weeks they had spent together, living on the razor's edge – and out of his single act of incredible heroism, throwing away his life to save hers?

There was only one way to find out: by helping Jack Roscoe get him back.

'Right, Jack,' said Van. Her voice was level and under control. 'Tell me what I have to do.'

She listened intently to his plan and sat back in her chair two hours later, summing up the odds in one sentence: 'It's you and me taking on one hundred and fifty million Russians . . .'

'If you put it like that.'

'. . . and British Intelligence.'

He looked puzzled. 'The Service is neutral in this.'

'Do you have that in writing from that super-bitch Madeleine Wharton?' she asked. 'No? You surprise me! Do you even have it oral from that two-faced lush George Dawson?'

Roscoe grinned; Van had never liked Dawson. 'George is OK. He knows what I'm up to. He won't do anything to . . .'

'Oh, Jack!' Some people, Van thought, never do see the demons all their lives. How could Roscoe be so innocent? 'I grew up among these people, remember? I know how their minds work. Madeleine Wharton won't want Peter walking around, shooting off his mouth after all these years about our costly failure in Turkey. She lost a lot of face in that snafu – and that's what her kind hate more than anything else. So get this! There are only two people in the world we can trust to get Peter out of Russia: you and me!'

.10.

'*Bózhe moy!*'
  '*Chort vozmí!*'
'*Yob tvóyu mat!*'

The escalation of oaths punctuated Colonel Plotnik's reading.

In the Intelligence section of the camouflaged Spetsnaz base concealed beneath the thick conifers that surrounded the Villa Orlova, Staff Sergeant Ekaterina Borisovna Antonova was watching the colonel seated at her desk. His crew-cut head bobbed up and down in alarmed reaction to the folder of press cuttings she had assembled for him.

He finished reading, looked up and barked, 'Why didn't you show me these earlier?'

'It was only when I saw the last cutting that I remembered some of the others,' she said. 'It took me several days' work to backtrack and find them all. Did I do right, comrade Colonel?'

'*Tebyá lyublyú!*' said Plotnik softly by way of answer, repeating in English, 'Ekaterina Borisovna, I love you!'

Her uniform suited Ekaterina's short, chubby figure about as well as a pair of Doc Marten's would have looked on the Queen Mother. The plump little legs that emerged from her unflattering straight skirt were unable to reach the floor as the crew-cut colonel in battle fatigues stood up and lifted her in one-armed embrace, her face level with his own. Ekaterina's boots dangled just below Plotnik's knees. He gazed into her startled eyes, kissed her on the lips and put her down. Her colleagues in the Intelligence section, used to their colonel's extravagant behaviour, took no notice.

Ekaterina polished her steamed-up glasses while he reread the file of press cuttings she had assembled for him. She was the best linguist in Plotnik's Intelligence section – and probably the best in all the *Voiská Spetsiálnovo Naznachéniya*. As the colonel read, she occasionally helped him out with a translation, fast and accurate as the .50 calibre machine-gun which was her designated weapon.

The cuttings were accident reports, obit notices and other non-events which, as Plotnik marvelled: '. . . only you in all the world would have spotted for me, Ekaterina Borisovna.'

Vanguardia reported from Barcelona the death by heart attack of Señor Alexei Romanov, a car salesman, aged forty-seven. His vehicle had plunged off a mountain road while he was visiting clients in the Pyrenees. His body had been found in the wreckage with a broken neck. From America, The *Atlanta Independent* reported the death of a petrol-pump attendant on night duty: Franklin Delano Romanoff, twenty-nine years old and a native of Decatur, had been beaten to death with a truck spanner in the small hours by robbers who got away with less than two hundred dollars in cash. In Paris, *Le Figaro* had a small item about a car crash with no witnesses at 2 a.m. on the Boulevard Périphérique in which the completely carbonised body of a taxi driver had been identified by dental records as Sergei Romanov, aged fifty-one. A small clipping from London's *Guardian* was the obituary notice for Professor Anatoly Romanoff, aged sixty-two, a musicologist and beekeeper who had died in Oxford, apparently of anaphylactic shock after being stung by his own bees.

There were a dozen other cuttings in the file with dates spread over the last two weeks.

'What are the odds, Sergeant,' Plotnik mused, 'against this being chance?'

'I asked the numerates.' Ekaterina pointed through the glass to where half a dozen of her colleagues were busy pirating Sonic the Hedgehog. They were not moonlighting; the games were sold on the black market in Scandinavia on Plotnik's orders, to make good the recent massive cuts in his budget, decreed by Moscow.

'And what did they say?' he asked.

'The odds are about four million to one. Or was it four trillion? I forget. I'm no good at sums, Colonel.'

As Plotnik jumped into his jeep and headed for the Villa Orlova with her folder of cuttings on the seat beside him, Ekaterina went back to scanning the world's Press. She was damaging her eyesight, reading newsprint for fifteen, sixteen hours a day in twelve different languages but she didn't care; like most of his troops she would have given her life for her colonel.

Plotnik was an *afgányetz* – a survivor of the hopeless Soviet invasion of Afghanistan. The *afgántsy* were the élite of the Russian armed forces and had become a sort of freemasonry in the military. It was through this network that he had become embroiled with General Grigori Sergeyevich Medvedev, who had come to him appealing as one patriot to another.

'Our country is falling to pieces,' Medvedev had said. 'One hundred and fifty million Russians are sliding into anarchy, Ivan Ivanovich. The last time that happened, twenty million of our people died in the Civil War, remember? And whatever Russian history books say, it wasn't Winston Churchill's interventionist forces who killed them! We did it ourselves and we'll do it again very soon if the current trend isn't swiftly reversed.

'We must act and act fast to save what is savable. A few men of courage are all we need to found a new Russia on the Baltic. True, it'll be a small state compared with the old one but the Principality of Muscovy was also tiny to begin with. There are advantages in being small: by getting rid of the unproductive hinterland where every factory is obsolete if not downright dangerous and financing a massive investment and modernisation programme, we'll make our new Russia a viable state within ten years at most. Then we'll invite the rest of our Godforsaken people to join us – on our terms. Whilst Yeltsin and the Old

Guard in Moscow carry on dancing the Kremlin kolo – all so busy watching their backs that they can't see the disaster in front of them – we'll save the Russian nation from extinction.'

The day after Medvedev's proposal, Plotnik had learned that a general with whom he had been a cadet at Frunze Military Academy, had sold thirty T-74 main-battle tanks to the Georgian insurgents. Paid in gold bullion he had flown out of the country in a stolen Air Force jet with his booty. To the south of St Petersburg Red Army units kicked out of the Baltic States were selling everything from Kalashnikov assault rifles to heavy artillery, trading them to black marketeers in return for enough gasolene with which to drive home.

There were civil wars raging in twenty countries of what had been the USSR, where only a strong government in Moscow had maintained the *pax sovietica* between hereditary enemies. As Plotnik saw it, if there was one thing more dangerous than a modern weapon in the hands of a trained soldier, it was the same weapon in the hands of a civilian who wanted to cleanse the world of his neighbours because they had a different colour, language or religion.

In Azerbaijan, Plotnik knew that the chaos might have global consequences. A discrepancy in the tally of nuclear weapons based there had revealed that at least three warheads had been smuggled across the border into Iraq, together with the missiles that could deliver them to New York or London.

As a patriot, Plotnik had listened to Medvedev and seen his duty clearly.

In the vast attic of the Villa Orlova six Spetsnaz girl clerks sat facing a line of secure modems, occasionally referring a problem to their supervisor, a haggard American in his early thirties by the name of Leonid Blok.

Speaking geographically, they and he were at the villa. Electronically they were a department of the Blok Banking Corporation; with headquarters in Boston, Massachusetts, it was a financial octopus founded by Leonid's grandfather. Old Man Blok, as he was known in financial circles, had been born in St Petersburg and dreamed all his adult life of coming back to live there one day. Although his bank owed its initial growth to being set up as a CIA proprietary and channel for illicit funding of covert operations, it was Old Man Blok's astute feel for wheeling and dealing in currencies without asking too many questions that had lifted the organisation to a plateau of wealth and influence of which the general public was completely unaware.

Legally the girls and their machines were neither in the Villa Orlova nor in the headquarters of BBC in Boston, Mass. They and their supervisor were the entire staff of the PanBaltia National Bank whose legal address was only a stone's-throw from the Moscow Kremlin, a fact of which even Leonid himself was unaware. From the roof of the villa a parabolic satellite antenna bounced scrambled signals to and fro across the Atlantic. All over the world major investors funnelling funds to Boston would have been horrified to know that their deposits were immediately transferred to Russian soil. In the convoluted world of international merchant banking it was a far from unique situation.

There was a large LED display on a screen at the end of the attic, constantly updating the flow of investments in dollars, yen and most other major currencies. The totals were already larger than the national debt of many Third World countries, with the symbols K and M used to cut down the number of zeros.

Leonid finished tapping something on a keyboard, stood up and rubbed the bridge of his nose. His red-rimmed eyes were blinking rapidly from lack of sleep. 'Hi there, Ivan,' he said with a tired grin when he saw Plotnik enter with Medvedev. 'Come to see where the real work of your Romanoff restoration is being done?'

The colonel grunted. In his book a returnee like Leonid was still an *émigré* – a greedy little opportunist seeking to profit from Russia's problems as his ancestors had for centuries before they were killed off and driven out during the October Revolution.

Plotnik was sickened that it should be necessary to involve such parasitical money-grabbers in what he would have preferred to be a glorious feat of arms against all the odds, but Medvedev had persuaded him at their first meeting that no modern revolution, however successful militarily, could sustain itself more than a few days without financing on a global scale. The Spetsnaz colonel had allowed himself to be convinced because Medvedev's speciality for the past thirty years had been the financing of destabilisation operations around the world, including Operation Chicapa which had led to the Kolwezi raid. Unlikely as it might seem, the bear-like Russian general and Leonid's bird-like grandfather had been players on opposing sides of the same game.

'It's going well, Leonid,' said Medvedev. He gestured at the screen approvingly. 'Another week at the most should see us home and dry.'

'Except for this.' A grim-faced Plotnik waved the folder of press cuttings.

'Ah yes,' said Medvedev. 'That is a problem.' He had only brought Plotnik up to the attic to give himself a few minutes' thinking time.

'Anything I can help with, General?' asked the American.

'No, Leonid,' Medvedev smiled grimly. 'We have a minor hitch. Nothing important, you can leave it to us.'

The general led Plotnik away from the tapping of keys, the flashing lights and the beeps of electronic connections. Plotnik slapped the folder of press clippings on a trestle-table littered with standby computer modules, where Medvedev sat and read the clippings or Ekaterina's translations one by one with irritating slowness. His only reaction was a rhythmic scratching of one thick fingernail against the grey stubble on his heavy jowls.

When he had finished, he growled, 'Ten little Romanoffs. Soon there'll be none, Ivan Ivanovich.' He glanced at the screen which had just recorded another huge deposit in Japanese yen.

'This,' said Plotnik, slapping the folder of cuttings, 'means that someone has leaked our plans to Moscow. There's no other explanation.'

'This is no time for a witch hunt,' growled Medvedev. 'What we have to do now, is grab the next in line before he too meets with an accident, *právda ili nyét*? Then we'll bring things to a conclusion so fast here that Moscow has no reaction time. That way, it won't matter what they know or don't know.'

'You're right,' agreed Plotnik. 'I'll despatch a snatch team that . . .'

'No!' Medvedev grabbed Plotnik's arm. 'This is too important to delegate, Colonel. You must go yourself and get this Prince Anton.'

'No way,' Plotnik disagreed. 'I can't leave here now, with the preparations for the coup in their final stages.'

'Come now, Ivan Ivanovich,' Medvedev chided. 'Your staff work's all done. The speed with which our *Voiská Spetsiálnovo Naznachéniya* move is legendary. I'm sure you can grab the Prince and have him back here within twenty-four hours. For the best Special Forces commander in the whole of Russia, the job should be a push-over. Isn't this exactly the kind of mission your people train for all the time: a hijack or an assassination?'

'What do we tell the target?'

'Tell him?' Medvedev chuckled. 'Nothing at all. Just grab him, Ivan Ivanovich. Bring him back here and I'll tell him how lucky he is to be our new Tsar. What's his name?'

The lights on the display board changed again, in the sterling column this time.

Plotnik consulted the file. 'Prince Anton Romanoff, French citizen, playboy and professional gambler. Just the sort of scum we got rid of seventy years ago, Grigori Sergeyevich.'

'Remember what Lenin said at a similar moment?' Medvedev growled. 'Forget the man's morals. Like Old Man Blok's grandson over there, this shabby little princeling exists to serve our country's needs. And when you've grabbed him, I think you must arrange a fake accident to put Moscow off the scent for these last few crucial days.'

'That'll take even longer.'

'Someone is trying to pre-empt our restoration of the Romanoffs, Ivan Ivanovich. I need these last few days to maximise our funding. So that's an order, Colonel: grab the Prince and arrange an accident to account for his disappearance.'

The two men glared at each other until Plotnik stepped back with a grimace, 'Aye, aye, General.'

Now that he had won, Medvedev felt expansive: there was nothing like killing two birds with one stone.

'Take the girl, Nadya.' He was smiling at the thought. 'Use

Lirian's girlfriend to seduce the Prince. She'll know what to do. This sort of operation is what she was trained for, after all.'

'I wouldn't work with that slimy turd Lirian if you paid me a million roubles.'

Medvedev's eyes had disappeared again beneath the beetling brows. 'I'm not asking you to,' he said softly. 'For all we know it could be our Armenian hustler who leaked the information to Moscow. Think about it – he's a prime suspect. So I'm keeping Lirian himself right here with me.' He jabbed one thick and hairy thumb on the table as though crushing a bug.

Plotnik shook his head. 'It couldn't be Lirian. He doesn't know anything of what goes on up here – or in my base.'

'Maybe,' said Medvedev mysteriously. 'But let me tell you, Anastas Romanovich Lirian sniffs out secrets like some other men smell pussy. So take the girl with you, Ivan Ivanovich. She'll perform perfectly, you'll see. They trained them very well at Verkhonoye.'

.11.

Verkhonoye! Nadya was never sure whether she had been born there or whether her true self had died within the grim walls of the high-security KGB training school. The only certain thing was that the young woman who emerged at the end of the course through the iron-barred gates of the school, guarded day and night by armed sentries, was a different person from the innocent girl who had first walked through them.

Nadya's memories of early childhood were vague. She could recall a few unrelated incidents before the orphanage – some conversations with her mother in the camp, both of them huddled under one blanket on the bare boards of a three-tier bunk. But her mother's face was less clear in memory than that of the woman who had adopted the half-starved, bewildered little girl of six and looked after her until she was sent to the orphanage two years later.

Nadya's first memories of the *Oktyábrskiy* orphanage in Kazan were of being frightened that she would be sent back to the camp if she did not behave herself. The discipline was draconian; she accepted it because she knew there was something worse. She was clean, polite and always volunteered to help the house-mothers with extra duties, despite the other girls calling her a creep. There were many nights when she cried herself to sleep to a chorus of taunting and blows from the other girls in the dormitory. It was an all-female establishment; the boys were in a separate building, half a kilometre distant.

The face which Nadya remembered most clearly from this time was that of an English teacher at the local secondary school. Nearing retirement, he had sensed in the over-serious, waif-like girl in orphanage clothes a hidden talent for languages and gave her extra coaching, to find that he had a prodigy on his hands – the dream pupil that made up for a lifetime of academic drudgery. By the age of fourteen Nadya spoke, read and wrote fluently in English and was showing equal promise in German. It was her misfortune that, in addition to her burgeoning linguistic prowess, she developed at puberty a face and body of such outstanding beauty as to bring her to the attention of one of Lydia Furtseva's talent-spotters.

At midnight on 9 December 1989, the steel-and-concrete membrane that divided East Berlin from West Berlin ruptured and tens of thousands of young people poured across in both directions.

Nadya learned of the event during Marxist Theory class at Verkhonoye the following afternoon. Her instructor was Helmut Krenz, a pale-faced, earnest East Berliner in his early thirties who had studied under Professor Raïssa Gorbachev at Moscow University. He replayed the recorded television coverage of the crowds dancing and singing in front of the Brandenburger Tor and invited the class to answer the question: how can this happening be explained in terms of Marxist Theory?

Usually Krenz's period was a boring but easy lesson; by turning around his text, the students automatically got the right answers. It was a trick they had learned early in their school careers – like reciting the catechism, on which the methods of teaching were based.

This time their instructor was no help at all, but sat, shaking his head at the screen as though he could not believe his eyes. Nervous of making a wrong guess in the absence of the usual clues, the girls were embarrassed and confused.

At nineteen, Nadya was one of the younger ones. Their ages ranged from eighteen to twenty-one. They were all attractive, exceptionally well-dressed and made-up by Soviet standards. At Verkhonoye Western fashions and make-up were classes taken as seriously as Marxist Theory.

Nadya's best friend and room-mate Valentina suggested to Krenz that the television pictures must have been faked. Another girl asked if the smashing down of the Wall was a CIA plot. Others, groping for the Party line, hazarded guesses that the Wall was no longer needed because living standards in the GDR were now higher than in the West and *Flucht aus der Republik* had become a crime that only lunatics would commit.

Nadya had grown to like Krenz, despite the over-zealous way he berated her during German conversation classes in front of the whole class for her smallest errors in pronunciation or usage. She knew that he only did this because she was the best German-speaker on the course and he was secretly proud of her progress. Sometimes she wondered, in the privacy of her bed at night whether Krenz was in love with her and whether she was falling in love with him. For a girl of nineteen who had come from a single-sex orphanage to study at the girls-only college, they were harmless fantasies.

She watched Krenz sweating with embarrassment in front of the class when he finally admitted to the girls that there was no Marxist explanation for what had happened. A stunned silence followed, as though their confessor had told a group of novices that God's telephone line had been disconnected for non-payment. As the bell rang for the next session, Krenz took off his glasses and stared into space, avoiding the girls' eyes as they collected their books and hurried away to the daily workout in the gym.

Discipline was strict at Verkhonoye. Arriving late at a lesson meant an interview with the Principal, Lydia Ivanovna Furtseva. For more serious misdemeanours such as failure to do homework or exceptionally poor marks in a test, the punishment was a hundred timed press-ups in the open air, whatever the weather. For persistent failure to keep up with required academic standards, a student was given one warning and then expelled in disgrace – a stigma that would be difficult to expiate in the Soviet Union. Linguistic standards were high; every student could speak at least one European language idiomatically before she was admitted.

Nadya's intake of students had been at Verkhonoye exactly eight weeks when their elegant Principal walked in at the end of the afternoon gym session and dismissed the PE instructor. In her late forties, Lydia Furtseva was dressed impeccably; she could have been the wife of a diplomat or a Politburo member, in her silk blouse and mid-length skirt from Paris, her calf-length Italian boots and fashionable coiffure. By her side stood the Director of the training school, a middle-aged KGB colonel in a well-cut Western suit.

'You were brought here for a very special purpose,' he told them. 'You are all intelligent, attractive and good Socialists, eager to serve your country – and doubtless eager to find out why you are here.'

There was a murmur of assent. For two full months the students had worked hard with no idea of the purpose of their studies. The guesses ranged from a dormitory rumour that Verkhonoye was a training establishment for high-level diplomats to the theory that they were to become top-secret cypher clerks working in embassies abroad.

For twenty minutes the Director's speech droned on, full of references to duty to the State and Socialism. When he had finished speaking, Lydia Furtseva clapped her hands and ordered the girls to assemble in a half-circle round a vaulting horse in the centre of the gym.

'During the time you have been here,' she said, 'you have all been evaluated by myself and the staff. Some students have failed tests and been sent away, for various reasons.'

One of the reasons was sexual experience; any girl who was not a virgin had been rejected at the initial medical examination. Repeated disobedience or even a tendency to question the authority of the instructors was another disqualifier. The in-depth psychological profile of each student which had been drawn up had also eliminated any girl who had been in contact with religious or other moral values or had an instinctive idea of right and wrong.

'Those of you who are left,' Furtseva continued, 'have had plenty of time to wonder what you are being trained for here. Today you can be told.'

The Director smoothed his curly grey hair with a well-manicured hand and looked at them, one after another, standing round him in their gym singlets and shorts. 'In the same way that a young man, called to serve his country as a soldier, must learn to do things which are unpleasant – even repugnant to his conscience – so you girls will have to overcome many scruples before the end of your training.'

'What can he mean?' Valentina whispered to Nadya. 'Are we going to be trained as assassins?' Nadya had an urge to giggle, swiftly suppressed.

The Director clapped his hands and called, 'Lights!'

The gym, which doubled as a cinema, was plunged into darkness, leaving the girls staring at the screen on which flicked *VERKHONOYE TRAINING FILM No. 1 (restricted).*

There was at that time no sex education in Russian schools, so that the students at Verkhonoye were far more ignorant than Western girls of the same age. The scenes of explicit sexual activities which followed shocked them all. They watched the colour film of copulation, oral and anal sex with a mixture of emotions ranging from curiosity to disgust. As the lights went up, the girls avoided looking at each other. Several were blushing furiously and looked distressed.

Lydia Furtseva and the Director smiled at each other. They had seen the same reactions so many times.

'Your bodies,' the Director told the girls, 'are weapons in the fight for world Socialism. Here at Verkhonoye you will be trained how to use them as young men are trained to use weapons and kill for the same cause.'

He beckoned to Valentina. 'Strip!'

Valentina looked to Lydia Furtseva for guidance. 'Do what you are told, girl,' she commanded.

Slowly, with her eyes closed, Valentina pulled off her vest and slipped down her shorts.

'And your bra and pants,' said Lydia Furtseva.

Huge tears coursed down Valentina's cheeks. 'I can't, comrade Principal,' she stammered. 'I'm having a period!'

'Ah,' said the Director. 'We'll deal with that little problem later.'

He pointed at Nadya. 'You take her place.'

Nadya walked out and stood beside him. She felt her cheeks blush scarlet and tried not to meet the eyes of the other girls.

'Take off your clothes!' ordered Lydia Furtseva. 'Come on, hurry. We've all got the same equipment, there's no need for bourgeois modesty.'

It's a medical examination, Nadya told herself. She pulled her gym vest over her head, unhooked her bra and laid it on the vaulting horse beside her vest.

He's a doctor and I'm the patient, she told herself. I must do what he says.

She tried to gain time by folding her shorts and panties, placing them beside the other clothes, hoping for she did not know what.

'Now,' the implacable voice of the Director ordered, 'lie on your back on the horse. No, not like that, girl! Spread your legs apart so that everyone can see what you've got there.'

Nadya felt the smoothed, cool leather of the horse under her back which was moist with perspiration. She looked sideways to find the Principal eyeing her with her usual cool disdain. Desperately Nadya tried to put a name on the perfume Lydia Furtseva was wearing as a way of concentrating on something – anything other than what was happening to her. It wasn't Chanel No. 5 . . . No, Ma Griffe, that was it!

She felt the Director's hands part her legs and pull them down to hang either side of the horse. 'That's better,' he said.

He's a doctor, she kept repeating to herself. He's a doctor examining me. I have to do what he says . . .

The Director was talking to the other girls now, his back to Nadya spread-eagled on the horse. '. . . your bodies are not private property . . . like a soldier's weapons . . . you are here to be trained how to use them . . .'

Oh God, thought Nadya, I must be dreaming this.

The illusion vanished as she felt his hands pull her thighs further apart. 'This,' he said, patting her vulva, 'is nothing special. You've all played with it yourselves, so why shouldn't I?'

Nadya kept her eyes fixed on a rope hanging from the ceiling as he took her labia between finger and thumb and tugged the folds of flesh gently, teasing her pubic hair, then his other hand took hold of her left nipple and stretched it up from her breast, letting go as a boy might ping an elastic band.

'Vstavái!' he ordered, patting her pubic mound like an owner patting the flank of a racehorse in the paddock.

Nadya slid off the horse and stood up. The other girls were staring at her, wide-eyed. They all seemed as dazed by the experience as she was. In a corner of the gym, Valentina was huddled, her back to everyone, sobbing. Nadya tried to cover her breasts and pubic hair, saw the frown on Lydia Furtseva's face and let her hands hang down at her sides.

The Director patted Nadya approvingly on her bare bottom. 'You'll be a good student, I think.'

He smiled at Lydia Furtseva, 'Over to you, comrade Principal.'

Lydia Furtseva motioned at Nadya to put on her clothes and addressed the other girls in her usual well-articulated voice: 'Now that that's out of the way, I've got some good news for you all.'

She smiled at them in an almost conspiratorial way. 'You've all been working very hard since the beginning of term. As a reward, tonight you'll be excused private study because we're holding a dance. You will all wear your best dresses. No trousers. Shampoo your hair and wear make-up. Be in the gym at eight p.m. to welcome your guests. We've invited a party of cadets from Kazan Military Academy – the future leaders of the armed forces. I expect you all to make sure they have a really good time.'

The evening began awkwardly. The cadets, delivered by two covered trucks, stood together at one end of the room in their best uniforms, eyeing the girls at the other end. The numbers matched exactly. A few couples started to dance but they were mainly girls dancing together.

A bar had been installed along one wall of the gym with soft drinks and alcohol dispensed by one of the serving women from the canteen. The boys started drinking beer with vodka chasers; most of the girls chose soft drinks. After half an hour, the Principal came into the gym and ordered the girls to stop dancing with each other. Each, she decreed, must pick one of the cadets as her partner for the evening and dance with him. The lights were turned down low and the PA turned up.

Nadya headed for a tall, fresh-faced boy with freckles. From his accent she knew him for a Muscovite, despite the country-boy looks. He made a lewd joke about her breasts to the pal he was drinking with, which made Nadya blush. Then he led her into the centre of the floor. The music was very loud. Shouting in her ear, he told her his name was Kolya and that he was in his second year at Kazan. He was quite a good dancer but held her tightly and thrust his left leg rather often between hers.

Nadya was embarrassed that he had an erection and tried to pull away from him without success. His hands found excuses to touch her breasts and twice she pulled his right arm higher to stop him fingering the cleft between her buttocks. At the end of the first dance, flushed with embarrassment, she left him only to be intercepted by Lydia Furtseva and ordered to go back for another dance.

Bewildered, Nadya obeyed without question. In the dim lighting she could see that she was not the only girl who was unhappy with what was going on. Some of the boys were undoing their high uniform collars to cool off. They were all drinking heavily and making dirty jokes.

'So, you're back,' smirked Kolya. 'Tell you off, did she, the boss?'

Nadya did not know what to do or say. He handed her a glass of vodka which she swallowed. It was the first time she had tasted neat spirit. He laughed when it made her cough, put down his own drink and pulled her towards him, kissing her hard on the lips. She tried to resist but he was very strong and held her tightly, thrusting his tongue into her mouth. Above the music Nadya heard a girl scream.

Kolya began undoing her dress, trying to get his fingers inside her bra. Several of the other girls were having the same problems, she saw. She looked around the dimly lit gym for the Principal or an instructor but there were no staff present. On the floor, the dancers were thinning out as the cadets started leading their partners outside.

'Come on,' urged Kolya. 'I'm feeling real horny tonight. I gotta get my rocks off, baby. Which is your room?'

'It's not allowed,' said Nadya sharply.

He fell about laughing. 'You're kidding! I've been here before.'

She followed him along the corridors where he seemed to know his way. Thinking that the matron who supervised private study and lights-out would refuse to allow the cadets upstairs, Nadya pushed past Kolya and ran ahead to find her. For once she was absent, her desk unattended. From the bedrooms along the corridor came confusing noises: male laughter, girls crying, and a rhythmic thumping which sounded to Nadya like people fighting.

Following her up the stairs, Kolya had been reaching under her skirt while she tried to push his hands away. In her room he slammed the door and threw her on the bed, kneeling over her and snapping the buttons off the front of her dress in his hurry to pull it down over her shoulders.

'No, please,' she said. 'Please don't.'

'Are you a virgin?' he panted.

'Yes,' she said, hoping it would calm him down. 'Please don't, Kolya.'

He laughed, pulling her breasts free of her bra and slapping them hard. 'Hey, they're really good. You've got a great pair of knockers there, baby. Really bouncy.'

She whimpered because he was hurting her. Freeing one hand, she slapped him in the face, thinking that if she could sober him up, he'd apologise.

At that moment the door burst open. 'Oh Valentina,' Nadya sobbed, 'please help me!'

She stopped when she saw the streaks of mascara running down her room-mate's face. Valentina was bent over nearly double, her skirt thrown up over her head from the back. A pair of tattooed and hairy forearms clamped her to the cadet who shuffled barefoot into the room behind her, his trousers round his ankles. As Valentina collapsed onto her bed under his weight, the cadet's buttocks spasmed, causing Kolya to cheer him on. '*Davai!* Bullseye, man! Give 'er the full magazine!'

He laughed, enjoying the pleasure of using his weight and strength to hold down Nadya's squirming body. Unable to struggle free, her head pinned to the bed by his shoulder, she saw herself in the full-length wall mirror wide-eyed with shock, her dress torn and Kolya lying over her at an angle. His trousers were down round his knees, prevented from falling down further by his high boots which he had not taken off. Above them his hairy legs were tanned brown, contrasting with the white skin of his buttocks.

On the other bed, the second cadet was turning Valentina over onto her back. Her thighs and his still-erect penis were red with blood. She reached out one bloodied hand to grasp Nadya's fingers as the boy pulled her legs apart again. Nadya held tight and closed her eyes but there was no way she could block out the filth the boys were talking.

She felt Kolya's teeth on her nipples and his hand forcing her legs apart, ripping her panties away. 'No, please!' she whispered as his finger entered her.

'Get your legs open,' he ordered through gritted teeth, 'or I'll really hurt you.'

'Oh, please, please, please.'

He was big and in a hurry. Nadya's whimpers became sobs and the sobs became groans until she shrieked with the pain.

The conversation at breakfast was subdued. Some of the girls had bruises on their faces and all were bewildered by what had happened at the dance. There were whispers that the cadets would be court-martialled.

The rumours were corrected at 8 a.m. when Lydia Furtseva announced that the morning's timetable had been revised. All the girls were ordered to go immediately to the gym for another film show.

The 'films' were video recordings of what had happened in the bedrooms upstairs the previous evening. Nadya was horrified to see the first pictures, obviously shot through the wall mirror of another girl's room. She felt herself blushing for the girl as she was stripped by her partner and lay down on the bed with him. Not enthusiastic but obliging, she took hold of the boy's erect penis and placed it between her breasts. Nadya glanced at the girl in question who was sitting behind her, face scarlet with embarrassment.

Valentina had covered her face in order not to see the screen. Lydia Furtseva stopped the tape and ordered all the girls to watch and concentrate so that they could criticise each other's performance afterwards. The events in every bedroom had been video-recorded.

The tape was restarted. One by one, each of the girls saw her deflowering replayed for everyone to watch in colour and full sound. The commentary was provided live by the Principal, who strolled around the room in a powder-blue angora sweater and midi-length skirt, as calm and self-possessed as always. Twice she praised a girl for actively encouraging her partner. More often her comments were devoted to how a girl could have prolonged or heightened her partner's pleasure. She criticised her students' performance in the same dispassionate tones a sports coach uses when talking about last week's match.

'You all have a lot to learn,' was her stern conclusion.

None of the girls had the remotest idea that their selection and the abruptness and timing of their group introduction to sex had been worked out by a team of KGB psychologists. Even the matter-of-fact language used by the Principal to describe what amounted to organised rape was a script she had learned and used many times to confuse and disorientate her students.

The bewildered girls were so intent on the screen that they had not seen the Director enter. He walked to the front of the class looking displeased.

'None of you,' he said severely, 'performed very well last night. You were ordered to make sure those cadets enjoyed themselves – and what happened?' His voice rose to a scream: 'They had to do most of the fucking work themselves! Obviously all you prim little cows require a lot of practical instruction in how to pleasure a man. Perhaps why you were so bloody useless is because you think that your precious little cunts are private property, to be used only on special occasions?

'Well, I have news for you, there is no such thing as private property in the USSR! You belong to the State and your desirable young bodies are weapons in the fight for world Socialism. Here at Verkhonoye you will be taught how to use them for every conceivable variation on the sexual act. Last night was just the first lesson in this new subject on your curriculum. By the time you've finished being trained here, you girls will be the best fucks in the whole world!'

PART 6

ROMANOFF ROULETTE

.1.

The corpse was frozen stiff, thirty metres down a crevasse on the Sassières Glacier near the French-Swiss border. The mask of the downhill racing helmet had been crushed concave into the bones of the face by the impact of the fall. With the plastic ski-boots and the shiny dayglo green-and-purple suit the result was more like a robot whose battery had gone flat than the body of a real, flesh-and-blood man.

'*Il était dingue, le prince.*' The guide who had volunteered to go down the narrow gap between the grinding, crunching cliffs of ice in order to recover the body said what the rest of the team was thinking: only a crazy Russian would have been skiing high up on the glacier above Val d'Isère. If a tourist had not been watching through a telescope and sounded the alarm, no one would have known what happened until the body was washed out of the base of the glacier decades later.

Slowly and cautiously the guide was hoisted the last few feet with the corpse still lashed to his back. He gave an exclamation of relief as a hand was stretched out to pull him and his burden over the crumbling edge of ice and snow that was trying to hurl him back to quick-frozen death in the blue depths below.

The medic with the mountain rescue team that day was not the regular *médecin-capitaine* but a doctor who said he was from Paris and had volunteered to replace the regular man, ill with sudden food poisoning. Before anyone could stop him, he prised up the ski-mask and pulled hard. There was a soggy tearing noise as the skin of the face, frozen to the mask, tore away from the raw flesh beneath. He grunted with disgust at the gory result. One of the team made a joke about a quick face-lift and another man passed the doctor a wide crêpe bandage, which he wound several times around the head to keep the face from falling off completely.

The chief guide used his two-way radio to call the mountain rescue base in Val d'Isère and stand down the helicopter. 'No medical facilities required,' he said. 'We'll bring the body down on foot.'

'Identity?' queried the laconic voice at the other end of the link. There was a pause filled by crackling static from a storm that was building over Mont Blanc.

'His *carte d'identité* was in a pocket,' said the man standing over the corpse. 'I've got it here. Surname is Romanoff. First names, Anton Nikolaevich. Date of birth: the twenty-fourth of August, 1950.'

The team started cautiously on the long trek back to the valley below. The first stage was dangerous; if one bridge of fresh snow over a crevasse had opened up beneath the weight of a lone skier, another could easily collapse beneath the combined weight of the team and sledge. They stayed well spaced, using ropes front and back to ease the sledge over the hummocks of snow. If the doctor did not talk much to the guides on the way down, they assumed that he was tired from the climb up. It was a race against dusk.

On the way down the guides swapped anecdotes about the dead Prince. He had been a permanent fixture in the chic cafés and hotel lounges from Val d'Isère to Chamonix. They had often seen him returning from a night at the Casino in his open sports car when they were clomping back to bed at dawn after an all-night search. Many a time they had seen *le fou du hors-piste*, as he was known, high on the mountain above them in his dayglo ski-suit when they had been bringing down other bodies.

Prince Anton had lived for the snow – a world-class downhill skier who could have won an Olympic medal if he had not been such a dilettante. They agreed on that and on one other thing: like all Russians, he had been crazy. Crazy was the only word for a man like Romanoff who insisted on skiing on a glacier that had claimed so many lives.

At the foot of the glacier, they carried the stretcher to the four-wheel-drive truck and bumped their way down the track to the little town below. They came into Val d'Isère as the light was going. From a hotel room across the street from the mountain rescue centre, Plotnik watched the people milling around the rescue truck. He was angry, as always after losing a man. The corpse lying in the ambulance had been one of his ski troops, drugged to slow down his reactions as he plunged to his death in the glacier wearing Prince Anton's clothes. The fact that he had had only a few months at most to live, due to inoperable breast cancer, did not lessen Plotnik's hurt.

Dressed in roll-neck pullover and jeans, the lean and angry Spetsnaz colonel passed for just one more ghoul as he joined the small crowd in the street. A couple of gendarmes were watching the guides transfer the shape in the body-bag to an ambulance whose driver was talking to the doctor. Plotnik was not worried; his medic spoke French like a Parisian.

He stayed on the fringes of the crowd until the medic gave a small signal – a tug on an earlobe which told the colonel that the corpse was faceless – before going back to his room to wrap up the snatch operation. With a towel hanging out of the open window to tell the rest of the Spetsnaz team to make their own way back to Geneva Airport, Plotnik dialled the number of another room in the hotel.

He heard Nadya's voice answer and said, 'Hallo, I'm trying to trace a friend from Orlando.'

'You have the wrong number,' she replied, and hung up.

The pick-up had been easy, a simple matter of Nadya walking out of the hotel doorway ahead of Prince Anton Romanoff and pretending to slip on the icy steps. He helped her up and found himself holding the most attractive girl he had touched in a lifetime of womanising.

Nadya's story was equally simple: she had had a row with her boyfriend, a medical student from Munich. He had driven off, leaving her stranded in the ski resort of Val d'Isère on the wrong side of the frontier with no money, no credit card – and now a sprained ankle. It was all too much. She dissolved into tears.

The Prince was dressed casually but expensively: handmade shoes, Daks trousers and a cardigan from Pierre Cardin. His well-tanned face, which had been handsome when younger, was a picture of self-indulgent boredom to begin with. By the time Nadya had finished pouring out her hard-luck story for his sympathetic ears, Prince Anton had a glint in his eyes. A sexual connoisseur, he was working out the best way to seduce this innocent little German student with her Berliner accent, cheap chainstore clothes and no make-up.

He began with an expensive seafood lunch in a little restaurant he frequented near his hotel. Nadya looked suitably impressed at the prices on the menu and the way he ordered the waiters about. She drank several glasses of Alsatian wine during the meal and became very talkative. The few discrepancies in her story Prince Anton took as proof that Nature had over-endowed Nadya physically and skimped a little in the upstairs department. She seemed a little tipsy as he helped her back to her hotel room, unaware that his own room had been expertly burgled during the meal.

'I shouldn't have drunk that wine, you know,' Nadya giggled, flopping onto the bed as he locked the door. 'It's made me feel all muzzy.'

She checked the Timex watch on her wrist. Her job now was to keep Prince Anton occupied for the rest of the afternoon; she did not think it was going to be difficult. He lifted her head and kissed her lips. Sliding his hand inside the cheap pullover, he marvelled at the two firm breasts whose proud nipples matched Nadya's slightly pouting lips. She tried to pull the garment back over herself but giggled and gave way when he insisted, letting him pull it right over her head to leave her clad only in a pair of Levi's and her trainers.

'I don't believe this is happening,' she yawned cutely. 'You're a real prince and I'm . . .'

'. . . a very beautiful girl,' he murmured, undoing her left shoe. 'That boyfriend of yours must be insane to walk out on you.'

Her right shoe dropped to the floor beside the other. Somehow Nadya's jeans had come undone. She wriggled out of them and watched through half-closed eyes as Prince Anton stripped naked, already excited. At least, she thought, this one's not old, ugly or impotent . . .

'What are you thinking?' he asked.

'You're so strong,' she said drowsily. 'You look really fit.'

The Prince was thinking that Nadya was a living work of art. Her creamy skin was without blemish that he could see. With a half-smile she watched him examining her pert breasts, her flat belly and the triangle of fair, silky pubic hair like a faintly drawn arrow signalling the way to go. Her left hand was caressing her breasts. With her right hand she parted her legs and slid her middle finger inside the folds of her vulva.

Prince Anton prided himself on being able to read every woman like a book; it crossed his mind that this was not the behaviour he would have expected from the distraught girl who had fallen literally into his arms in the hotel entrance a couple of hours before. Then he ascribed Nadya's lack of self-consciousness to the alcohol she had consumed.

'Oh God, this is so sexy,' she said. 'I don't know what's happening to me!'

The Prince moved towards her but she rolled away and lay on the far side of the bed, eyes closed, stroking herself. Each time he touched her Nadya shrugged him off. Fascinated, he watched the fingers of her free hand flutter from one erect nipple to the other. Her full breasts heaving as she gulped air, she moaned once, arched her back and shuddered repeatedly, teeth clenched in a silent grimace.

Nadya opened her eyes to find the Prince lowering himself on to her. He smelled of vanilla-perfumed tobacco and Paco Rabanne aftershave. She licked her lips and held his gaze, challenging him wordlessly to transport her further than she could manage for herself.

Each time he climaxed her clear hazel eyes challenged him: *Again! Again!* As the afternoon passed in a haze of sex and

Thai Gold, the Prince expected that with each orgasm his lust would end. Somehow Nadya's eyes, her voice, her perfect body and her seeming insatiability incited him to continue. When he tired, she knelt astride him and offered her breasts to his lips and fingers, impaling herself and thrusting for his pleasure. She used her hands and her breasts, her legs and her arms to heighten his pleasure in ways he had never experienced before.

He smothered himself in her smooth flesh, losing himself in her again and again and then ordering her to caress him with her lips and hands until lust once more blocked all thoughts other than the urgent need to drown in her. The successive ejaculations burned in his prostate; he could not remember a sexual encounter that came anywhere near the ecstasy of that afternoon.

When the bedside telephone rang, he murmured drowsily, 'Leave it.'

Nadya leaned across him and picked it up. Prince Anton heard a voice with an American accent say, 'I'm trying to trace a friend from Orlando.'

'You have the wrong number,' she replied, and hung up.

'Come here,' Prince Anton stretched out an arm.

Nadya slipped away from him with: 'I must go to the bathroom first.'

The Prince lit another of her cigarettes. They were so good that he wondered with what aphrodisiac her medical student boyfriend had spiked them, in addition to the hash. He heard water running in the bidet and the toilet flushing. Nadya was taking a long time, he thought. When she came back to the bed he was smiling, with his eyes closed. He could feel his erection returning. The mattress moved under her weight, then a stiff finger jabbed him on a nerve centre by the spine, causing a shaft of pain that made him wince.

'Jesus!' he exclaimed, eyes wide open. 'That hurt.'

'Sorry,' murmured Nadya. She dropped the syringe to the floor. He had not even felt it going in.

.2.

Roscoe was taken aback by Coetzee's reaction when he rang from a call-box in Bordeaux-Merignac Airport. He had forgotten swearing Maria to secrecy when he left with Dawson the previous week. On the flight from Geneva he had been so involved in the planning of Bergman's rescue that he had taken it for granted that Coetzee knew what was going on.

The familiar voice with the Transvaal accent put him straight: 'You've got a nerve, turning up here just a week before the recording, you bastard.'

'I haven't come back for that, Coot.'

'Then what the hell do you want, man?'

'I need your help.'

'You don't need my help,' snarled Coetzee. 'You need a psychiatrist, genuine!'

He collected Roscoe from the airport and drove him without a word through the lunchtime traffic of Bordeaux. Parking outside the club, he jerked his head upstairs. 'We better talk in my apartment. Maria is working downstairs with Jean-Luc.'

'Who?'

'The guy who was her lover before you came on the scene.'
Roscoe winced.

'That girl of yours has got guts.' Coetzee spat the words out and released some of his anger by punching Roscoe in the chest. 'She swallowed her pride and asked Jean-Luc to help her knock your material into shape for the recording.'

Roscoe stood in the rain at the head of the basement steps. Through the open door of the club he could hear Maria's voice singing 'The First Time Ever I Saw Your Face'. The accompanist was playing a competent if uninspired harmony on Roscoe's Fender Rhodes piano.

From even just a few notes a musician can always tell how another performer is feeling. Within two bars, Roscoe felt sick with the measure of Maria's unhappiness. He wanted to run down the stairs and take her in his arms, but that was not why he had come back to Bordeaux.

He turned to find Coetzee glaring at him murderously. 'Either you get back down there, Jack – where you ought to be – or get the hell out of here.'

Roscoe put a hand on Coetzee's arm. 'Look, Coot! I didn't plan to let Maria and you down like this.'

'You're letting yourself down, man.' Coetzee shook him off. 'This is the big chance of your life you've thrown away, Jack Roscoe.' He turned away and limped upstairs.

In the tiny kitchen of his apartment, Coetzee pressed the button marked *Stage Sound* on the wall intercom. Maria was arguing about the musical key of one of Roscoe's arrangements. The man's voice threatened to walk out if she did not do things his way.

Coetzee hit the *Silence* button in a gesture of disgust. 'You are a shit, Jack Roscoe.'

Roscoe helped himself to a beer from the fridge and let Coetzee vent his anger. Outside the window, he saw the rain slanting down on the cobbled quay and the wide Garonne beyond, swollen and brown with floodwater. It was raining inside him too: cold and empty at the thought of Maria working downstairs with another man. Perhaps he should not have come back? But he needed Coetzee's help. '*A moi, la Légion*,' he said.

'I hear you, man,' grunted Coetzee. 'What you want?'

'I want you to fly one last mission, Coot.'

'You're crazy.' Coetzee tapped his stiff leg. 'Even if I wasn't grounded, why should I do you a favour?'

'It's not for me, Coot. Peter Bergman is still alive in Russia. I may need your help to get him out.'

'Jesus, Mary and Joseph,' said Coetzee. 'So that's why you ran out on us? Why didn't you say?'

It took an hour to put Coetzee in the picture. He stared at Roscoe's sketch map of the area surrounding the Villa Orlova and shook his head gloomily.

'You want my professional opinion, Jack? You haven't a chance in a million of getting Pete out of there by a clandestine airlift, if your British pals drop you in the shit.'

Roscoe's dark eyes challenged Coetzee. 'Remember the legionnaire's code we learned to chant when we were raw recruits on the parade-ground at Castelnaudary? We swore on our honour that we would never abandon a comrade, wounded or dead, on the field of battle. Jesus Christ, Coot! We swore not even to abandon our weapons! There has to be a way . . .'

'Grow up,' Coetzee snorted. 'You and I have both used up a lifetime's luck since we learned the legionnaire's code, Jack. I'm fifty years old and you're nearing forty.'

'We're neither of us in wheelchairs!'

'Don't get me wrong, man. If we were in combat, I'd crawl out of cover to pull Pete to safety. But this is different. To get him out of Russia if your big deal goes wrong, you'll need a small army and the luck of the devil.'

'I'm going to do this thing if it costs my life, Coot.'

'Custer's last words.'

'If Custer had had a contract with Coetzee Air, we'd have got him out of Little Big Horn, wouldn't we?'

Coetzee shifted uneasily. 'With Bergman at the controls, maybe,' he admitted. 'Unfortunately Pete's not going to be the pilot on this trip, Jack. He's the passenger and probably a sick one at that.'

'If it was you or me stuck there, Coot, Pete would move heaven and earth to get us out,' argued Roscoe. 'You know he would.'

Coetzee scratched his bald scalp reflectively. The daylight had gone; they had been talking in circles for hours.

'Pete was never stupid. Like all fliers, he told some crazy stories but on the job he calculated each risk down to the last bleddy gallon of fuel – before take-off, not afterwards.'

His finger stabbed at Roscoe. 'And remember this, Jack – most of the time in Africa me and Pete were flying over bush country where the biggest risk was some goddam terrorist loosing off a SAM-7. Air-snatching Bergman from the Villa Orlova is a different ball-game. It means flying right through one of the most intensive radar screens in the world. Those guys have an air defence system backed up by jet fighters, batteries of surface-to-air rockets and God knows what. Not even Pete himself would think of hedge-hopping across the Russian border and back.'

'There was that German kid who piloted his light aircraft right to Moscow and landed it on Red Square a few years back, remember?'

'A fluke!'

'Was it? Or was he just too small, too quiet, too low and too slow to show up on their screens?'

'Could be,' Coetzee admitted grudgingly.

'So what would it cost us to buy a light aircraft in which to nip across the border, land on a piece of roadway and snatch Bergman to safety?'

Coetzee sat down on the window seat, his bad leg stuck out stiffly in front of him. With the bad weather, it was giving him pain. He wished he was twenty years younger and able to echo Roscoe's words: 'I'll do it, if it costs my life.' But Time was the enemy who won every battle . . .

'OK,' he said. 'On the return journey we've got a pilot, plus three passengers and one of them is maybe a stretcher case. So we need a twin-engine job. You're talking something like a Piper Aztec.'

'How much?'

'I can lay hands on one second-hand just now for . . . In sterling, it would be thirty-five thousand pounds cash.'

'Can you drive it, Coot – just this once?'

Coetzee tapped his stiff leg with the walking-stick. 'I can't even get this leg into a pilot's seat, never mind operate the rudder pedals. Do you think I didn't try?'

'But with your old-pal network, you must know a hundred other fliers who would do it for money, Coot.'

'Be realistic, Jack. Even if we had the cash to buy a plane and find a pilot crazy enough, where would he land? To take off fully loaded, an Aztec needs a run of over one thousand feet of unobstructed, hard, level ground. One of Plotnik's tanks on the road – or even a kid's bicycle – and you don't take off. Oh, and while I think about it, how do you get Bergman and the girl from the villa to this stretch of road, wherever it is, at exactly the moment when . . .'

'OK, think STOL.'

'Short take-off and landing? Well, the ideal aircraft for a job like this would be a Pilatus Porter like Pete used to fly out in Africa. But forget quietness. Being a turbo-prop, she's noisy. I've seen Bergman touch down in that long-nosed tail-dragger with an air speed of sixty knots – and stop her within a ground roll of one hundred and fifty feet, using reverse thrust. Genuine!

'Going up, even Pete would need a bit more room than that – say five hundred feet. Better than that don't exist, Jack. But where do we lay our hands on one of those birds in a hurry? They cost money. There's another snag: the Porter has a wingspan of fifty feet. You got roads that wide in the middle of this Russian forest, Jack?'

Roscoe was silent for a moment, then: 'There's a helicopter pad at the villa itself, Coot . . .'

'Rotors?' said Coetzee. 'Well, for a start you're talking double the cost of fixed-wing. Pal of mine in Toulouse has a three-seater Engstrom Shark for sale. Nice machine. It's the 280 C model. I guess he'd take around sixty-five thousand pounds in cash if we're still talking sterling. Have you got that kind of money? Oh, and the cabin would be a mite crowded on the return journey. There's also a minor problem about speed. The Engstrom's max is around one hundred and twenty knots so we'd have to hope nobody notices us going in or tries to stop us coming out. Of course, we could be lucky if all Colonel Plotnik's élite troops are drunk or asleep . . .'

'Knock it off, Coot.'

Coetzee stood up to ease the pain in his leg. He walked up and down the room and ended facing the window. In the dusk a waterscape of rain and river met his eye.

'Water!' He spun round to face Roscoe. 'You said those guys you trained with on Exmoor were not SAS?'

'I'm ninety-nine per cent certain they were Royal Marines from the Special Boat Squadron.'

'Could it be that your old pal Dawson and this dragon lady boss of his are planning to snatch Sir John by water if the deal with Lirian doesn't go through – maybe using a rigid inflatable – same as we trained in, back in the *deuxième REP* on Corsica?'

'Not a chance. Plotnik's men would blow them out of the water. Except . . .' Roscoe felt ice-cold. Coetzee had put his finger right on it.

There was no way he was going to tell the other man about Dawson's rumour of a *coup d'état* in Russia. But if a coup did take place, there would be a window of opportunity: for just a few hours everyone at the Villa Orlova would be looking the other way. Then two or three men in a fast RIB could do the impossible. That must be the Service's fail-safe plan. Why else the three SBS men?

'I've got to catch the return flight back to Geneva,' he told Coetzee. 'The plane leaves in less than an hour. Will you do something for me? Ring your Swedish pal in Marseille . . .'

'Lars Larsen?'

'. . . and ask him to recommend a couple of ex-Legion men in Finland who have a lot of balls. Second requirement is that they know how to handle a fast powerboat.'

'How much can I tell him?'

'No more than that.'

At pavement level Roscoe and Coetzee met Maria coming up from the club with a swarthy, Italian-looking man carrying a guitar case. From their faces it looked as though the on-stage argument was unresolved.

'How's it?' asked Coetzee.

Catching sight of Roscoe standing behind him, Maria's face lit up as though a halogen spotlight had been turned on in the yellow lamplit street. She threw herself into his arms.

With a nod to Coetzee, the guitarist hurried along the street to open a car door and thrust his guitar inside, out of the rain.

'Oh, Jack!' Maria's arms were round Roscoe's neck and she clung to him, filling his nostrils with the smell of her, warm and womanly. 'My Jack! You've come back. I feel wonderful now. I was so worried for you, my love.'

Roscoe found his arms around her. He buried his head in her hair.

'Everything is going to be wonderful,' she said. 'We got through a lot of work while you were away, you'll see. There's still time . . .'

She kissed his rain-damp neck, her hands clutching at his shirt through the open anorak, struggling to hold him to her. Roscoe felt her body against his, enjoyed the familiar feeling of her soft, full breasts against his chest, her belly against his, her legs parting for him from habit.

'I haven't come back to stay,' he said. 'The job's taking longer than I thought. I have a plane to catch.'

She pulled away, to see on his face the truth that hit her like a blow in the belly. Coetzee had the door of his pick-up open and was shouting at Roscoe to hurry up or miss the flight to Geneva.

'You're a beautiful woman,' said Roscoe, voice husky with desire. 'I love you very much, Maria. Believe me, I would give everything I have to stay here with you. But I must go away again.'

He pushed her gently away. Maria placed both hands over her mouth to stop herself screaming with disbelief. Then she forgot her own anguish and clutched Roscoe's arm to hold him back as he tried to get in the door Coetzee was holding open.

Roscoe wanted to tell her he would soon be back – not because it was true but because she wanted to hear it. An icy premonition stopped him saying the words. He slammed the door and slid the window down to say one last goodbye.

As the car moved off, he heard her heels running along the pavement and saw once again in the light of a street lamp the face he had imagined on a Greek vase – with wide, accusing eyes and wind-tousled hair. It was not possible to tell whether the drops running down her cheeks were rain or tears.

'I am looking after the cottage for you,' she called after him. 'When you come home you will see that I planted those herbs we talked about, Jack. There is thyme and sage, lavender and basil, mint and dill. And there too I planted one rosemary bush. You said that's for remembrance, Jack.'

.3.

To avoid the complications of having to transport an unconscious man, Plotnik's medic was using a technique of heavy
sedation developed for prolonged dental surgery without general anaesthetic. Intravenous injections of a drug from the
benzodiazepine family, whose best known member was Valium,
were administered to Prince Anton at thirty-minute intervals.
They left him conscious, able to walk and talk normally but in
a state of total calm and suspended will. The Prince could
answer simple questions but not exercise any initiative. The
only after-effects would be a complete blank in his memory
from the time when the telephone rang in Nadya's bedroom
until he found himself sitting at 35,000 feet, heading for St
Petersburg in the first-class cabin of an Ilyushin jumbo with
Plotnik giving him the choice of being a live Tsar or a dead
commoner.

The descent into Pulkovo Two was bumpy, as they came
down through a thunderstorm. On the ground, the Ilyushin
bounced three times and shuddered as reverse thrust was
applied the moment the wheels hit the runway. Plotnik heaved a
sigh of relief to be back on terra firma, mission accomplished.

Then the runway lights were suddenly switched off, leaving the jumbo rushing at 100 m.p.h. through darkness broken only by its own landing-lights.

'A power cut?' asked the Prince who was sitting in the window seat.

Plotnik knew the airport's electricity supply was independent of the public network. He did not reply.

Prince Anton knew he ought to be worried; instead he found himself laughing, 'And these are the people who want me to be their Tsar?'

'Some of us do, your Highness. Others obviously don't.'

Through the window Plotnik saw the Follow Me truck veer away from the lights of the terminal buildings. The Ilyushin stopped by a set of mobile steps in the middle of nowhere. The flashing lights on the plane and the truck revealed a small convoy of black limousines parked on the taxiway with their lights off. A farm tractor nudged a set of steps up to the door nearest the first-class compartment and a couple of heavily built men lumbered up them and into the plane, shouldering aside the stewardess who had opened the door.

Both heavies had KGB Men's Outfitting stamped all over their badly fitting suits. Plotnik waited in his seat for them to identify themselves. In the tourist-class cabin he had three of his men, plus the medic, but to initiate a fire-fight in a crowded civilian airliner would cause unacceptable casualties. With huge relief he saw Medvedev's bulk loom in the doorway behind the two stooges.

The colonel stood and shouted an order to disembark fast. As the four Spetsnaz men ran into the first-class cabin, Prince Anton stood up and languidly handed his case and overcoat to them. Plotnik admired the princely style, drug-assisted as it was. Two of his men grabbed the Prince's arms and hustled him off the plane and down the steps as the runway lights came back on.

A dozen or more vehicles with flashing lights and sirens wailing swarmed from cover behind the airport buildings and headed across the airport towards the Ilyushin and the line of cars.

The steps were pulled away from the aircraft which taxied

slowly towards the arrivals terminal, the first-class door still open. On the ground, Plotnik took Prince Anton's arm to keep him moving through the drizzle and into the curtained rear compartment of General Medvedev's stretched Volga limousine. Climbing in last, he was amused to see the general in the rear seat, in the act of kissing the Prince's hand. One of the heavies slammed the car door behind Plotnik's back and the line of vehicles accelerated away bumper-to-bumper.

'Forgive me, Highness,' Medvedev was doing his best to be courtly; the normal bear-like growl had been replaced by a breathy falsetto. 'We should have liked to mark your arrival in Russia with a more stately reception but this method of getting you into the country seemed more prudent in present conditions.'

The Prince withdrew his hand. 'I feel like a visitor from outer space,' he joked, still floating; the medic had been overdosing him, to be on the safe side. 'My next line is: take me to your leader.'

'You're sitting beside him,' said Plotnik dryly. He pulled down one of the collapsible seats. 'This is your Chief of Staff, General Medvedev. I'm Colonel Ivan Ivanovich Plotnik.'

Prince Anton laughed at the unreality of it all; the amount of Midazolam floating around his brain was the equivalent of enough Valium to keep a wardful of wrist-slashers partying from Christmas Eve to New Year's Day.

A noise like the end of the world startled everyone except him, and made the driver swerve. There was a jolt that had them all sprawling on the rear seat as the car behind accelerated and ran into the back of Medvedev's limousine. With his left hand, Plotnik grabbed the door handle a split second ahead of one of the heavies who had the same reaction: to get out fast.

The noise receded, dopplering down to the sound of four large turbo-prop engines. Medvedev's convoy had just driven across the runway, narrowly missing an incoming Antonov cargo plane. Everyone took a deep breath and sorted themselves out. Prince Anton laughed and lit one of Nadya's cigarettes. As the Thai Gold did its work on top of the drugs already in his system, a huge smile spread over his face. He winked at Plotnik and said, 'That girl, Nadya. I'd like to meet her again, Colonel. See if you can fix it for me, there's a good fellow.'

Medvedev took a full bottle of vodka from the built-in drinks cabinet and poured three glasses. Prince Anton swallowed his in one gulp as the general and Plotnik raised theirs in a silent toast.

They drove out of the airport with a double file of Plotnik's men on motor-cycles taking station ahead and behind the convoy. Using headlights – forbidden to ordinary motorists – and with flashing green lights clamped on the roofs, the cars and their escort raced through the dark countryside on the crown of the road, scaring other vehicles out of the way and onto the verges in a reflex reaction that came naturally to Russian drivers.

Prince Anton felt a delightful drowsiness creeping over him. One of the heavies took the lighted cigarette from his fingers and extinguished it for him. With a yawn, he said to Medvedev, 'Colonel Plotnik did a smooth job, getting me here in one piece. We must think of a suitable way of rewarding him.'

'It's been thought of,' growled Medvedev in a return to the bear-voice. 'In the Coronation Honours I've drawn up for your approval, Highness, Colonel Plotnik is promoted to General.'

'And what's General Medvedev promoting himself to?' asked the Prince mildly.

Medvedev blinked and took note that, although Anton Nikolaevich Romanoff might appear a dilettante playboy, he was not stupid and would have to be carefully watched.

Plotnik prided himself on being able to go without sleep for three days and nights with no medication. It looked as though he was going to test himself to the limit, he thought grimly. Whilst he was in Switzerland collecting the Prince, Medvedev had moved the whole schedule forward and decided with Archbishop Alexei that the coronation must for constitutional reasons be performed in one of St Petersburg's several cathedrals.

Within an hour of his return to the Villa Orlova, Plotnik was heading back into St Petersburg at the wheel of a beaten-up old Zhiguli saloon which attracted no attention in the sparse pre-dawn traffic. He was wearing a leather jacket and a matching cap to conceal his military crew-cut. There was an unlit taxi sign on the roof of the car. The two men sitting in the back seat were armed with concealed PM-63 machine-pistols which measured just thirteen inches long with the butt folded, and weighed little more than a kilo. Keeping station a hundred metres behind was another nondescript taxi with four identically armed men inside.

The front-seat passenger sitting beside Plotnik was a fat little man in the black robes of an Orthodox monk, whose flourishing beard hid an obstinate chin. He kept touching the sensitive skin of his shaven scalp with a hand on which gleamed a large ruby set in a gold ring. A priest's black stovepipe hat was held on his lap.

Archbishop Alexei had majored in Marxist Theory under Professor Raïssa Gorbachev before changing faiths. At thirty-seven years old, he was the youngest and most ambitious of Russian Orthodox patriarchs and an active figure in the Pamyat movement. Plotnik did not like him but had to admit his brain was first class.

Once in the city, the Zhiguli headed west along Nevskiy Prospekt and turned right to follow the Griboyedov Canal northwards to the Cathedral of the Resurrection.

'St Petersburg,' the archbishop reflected, 'is almost as rich in cathedrals as waterways, Colonel. We have plenty to choose from.'

'*Nyet*,' decided Plotnik, after a brief look at the building. 'Useless.'

They continued to the cathedrals of St Isaac and St Nicholas. '*Nyet*,' he said each time.

The Kazan Cathedral was where the colonel would have liked to hold the coronation. Used since 1932 as a Museum of Religion and Atheism, it had been built in 1801 – a direct copy of St Peter's in Rome. The sublime colonnade of the sandstone façade glowed in the moonlight reflected off the surface of the Griboyedov Canal. Plotnik had no eyes for the architecture; for him the church symbolised Russia's finest hour, for in the crypt lay entombed the body of his great hero, Marshal Kutuzov – the one-eyed strategic genius who had in 1812 destroyed the Grand

Army with which Napoleon had conquered the entire continent of Europe.

Sadly Plotnik had to admit that the Kazan Cathedral was not defensible even for the brief time it would take the archbishop to crown and annoint the new Tsar. It was getting late and would soon be dawn as they headed back along the Nevskiy Prospekt towards the east of the city and the last cathedral on the archbishop's list.

'Ah,' said Plotnik, getting out at the Cathedral of the Trinity. 'This is the one.'

Archbishop Alexei lifted the long skirts of his robe and hurried to keep up, his shorter legs trying to match Plotnik's long strides. 'It was built,' he puffed, 'by Peter the Great himself in honour of his thirteenth-century hero, Alexander Nevskiy.'

'It's not the history of the place,' said Plotnik shortly. 'It's the geography that interests me.'

Taking only a bodyguard of two men, he followed the priest around the cathedral, which lay in the heart of the *Nevskiy lavra*. To the archbishop the *lavra* was a monastery but Plotnik saw in the complex of medieval buildings a mini-fortress, easily defensible for a limited period by a small, determined force. On one side flowed the Neva, on another the smaller Chórnaya Reká, or Black River. A dozen helicopters could land in the monastery's central courtyard where they would be invisible to anyone outside. The *lavra* also had the worst-case advantage of adjoining the Nevskiy Bridge leading out of the city for a rapid getaway by land in case of need.

'History counts too,' insisted the archbishop, catching up. 'When I crown the new Tsar, the appearance of legitimate succession is important for the masses – as with the Pope and St Peter's. Here, beside the high altar we have the casket containing the remains of Alexander Nevskiy himself. After I have annointed the Tsar's brow with holy oil, he can kiss the casket. The millions watching on television will be impressed.'

For different reasons the place suited them both equally. Plotnik squinted at the lightening sky to the east. The countdown was already running; his place was back at base. He shouted to his men in the second car to take the archbishop home but found the priest a difficult man to get rid of.

'I'd like to ask a favour.' Archbishop Alexei led Plotnik out of earshot of the escort. 'For the coronation we shall need some of the Romanoff Crown Jewels – enough to look good on television.'

'Where are they?'

'In the Hermitage Museum.'

'What do you want me to do, rob it?'

'That's the general idea,' said the archbishop smoothly. 'Medvedev says you have people who can do that sort of thing.'

'A priest asking a soldier to rob the State?'

'The State stole the jewels in the first place,' argued the archbishop. 'They are the property of the Tsar. You're simply recovering them for their legitimate owner.'

'We'll do a reconnaissance,' said Plotnik.

'It's done,' said the archbishop. He took a map from a pocket in his robes. 'You go in through the sewers. The manholes to use are all marked.'

Plotnik shone his shielded torch on the plan. This was a complication he did not need, but at least it was one he could delegate. 'I'll get my people onto it,' he said.

'Today?' asked the archbishop.

'It'll be done.'

The archbishop reached beneath his robes again and this time brought out a jewelled crucifix. 'Kiss it,' he commanded.

'You're joking!'

'Kiss it!'

'What the hell for?'

'As a sign of your submission to God's holy will,' said the archbishop. 'He has chosen you as His instrument to hurl back the tide of ungodliness and bring once-Holy Russia back to the Church. You may believe that you are acting for other reasons but that is because you do not understand His ways. Now kiss the cross.'

In the moonlight their eyes met: Plotnik's steely grey and the Archbishop's dark brown eyes that glittered with a burning fervour. After a glance at his bodyguards, Plotnik raised the cross to his lips and kissed it.

'By that act,' intoned the priest, 'and by my sacred office, I absolve you from all previous oaths of loyalty. Now don't deny that your conscience has been troubled, Ivan Ivanovich. You are not a man who changes sides easily, whatever the justification.'

Plotnik grimaced. He mentally damned the man in black for reading his soul! Despite all Medvedev's clever arguments and appeals to his patriotism, he had not been 100 per cent convinced of the rightness of this operation in which he was taking up arms against the government in Moscow.

'You're a clever priest,' he said gruffly.

'Would you have a fool as chaplain in such a desperate endeavour, Colonel?' Archbishop Alexei held the crucifix briefly over Plotnik's crew-cut head. 'You are now God's soldier. Serve Him well!'

It was all mumbo-jumbo, Plotnik told himself. Yet there might be something in it. For whatever reason, his conscience was more at peace than it had been for weeks. Was it just that the priest had voiced his repressed doubts?

The archbishop stood back with a smile. 'Go with God, Ivan Ivanovich!'

.4.

A s the daily Aeroflot flight from Frankfurt to St Petersburg
headed north Roscoe admired what he took to be Van's
cool. She had had her eyes closed ever since take-off. He tried to
doze but kept going over in his mind the telephone conversation
with Dawson from a call-box in Geneva-Cointrin Airport.
There had been odd vibes – as though Dawson were worried
about something that could not be mentioned on an open line.

Roscoe's passport bore a multiple-entry businessman's visa
and Van was travelling on a Brazilian diplomatic visa, so what
could Dawson have meant? He had said, 'If there's any trouble
at the airport, ask for the Bear. The carpetbagger has dropped
right out of sight.'

According to Roscoe's watch there was less than an hour to
go to touch-down at Pulkovo Two when he realised that the
aircraft was heading the wrong way. The afternoon sun, instead
of shining in through the port-side windows of the cabin, was
dead astern – which meant that they were not heading towards
St Petersburg but roughly eastwards.

He looked out of the window. They were flying way below
cruising height. Where there should have been just empty sea if

they had been on course, was a deserted coastline with endless sand-dunes stretching inland until they merged into green meadows that were dotted with small peasant huts. Still the aircraft was losing height and turning to follow the line of the coast.

'*Ya kapitán samolyóta*: This is the captain speaking . . .'

Roscoe listened to the announcement from the flight-deck, according to which there was a small technical problem that required them to land at Vilnius airport in Lithuania, where they would spend a short while on the ground before continuing their flight to St Petersburg.

Below, small dots in the fields turned into grazing sheep. Smoke rose from a chimney here and there, but there was no sign of a town.

'Is this a complication, Jack?' Van's eyes were open, questioning him.

He shrugged, 'Vilnius is in Lithuania. Like the other Baltic Republics it is independent of Moscow now. Relax.'

They were going down. As the plane banked steeply round to line up on the runway below, the airfield did not impress Roscoe as belonging to a capital city, even of a small Baltic state. It had more the look of a deserted military strip, probably one of those abandoned by the Soviet Air Force when the Lithuanians kicked them out of the country. There was a control tower, several hangars and a few other buildings but no aircraft parked on the ground and no sign of people or cars. The runway itself appeared intact but had a lot of grass growing between the concrete slabs. The pilot left it almost too late before deciding it was safe to set down on the cracked surface, with the result that it took a lot of noisy braking to halt the plane within the landing-strip that had been built for smaller and lighter military aircraft.

They stopped within metres of the end of the runway to a final squeal from the overheated brakes. The engines did not have the normal whine descending in pitch but continued turning fast and making a lot of noise. One of the stewardesses came through the door from the flight-deck and ordered Roscoe to follow her to the rear of the aircraft.

'Let's go,' he said to Van. There was no point in arguing, since there was nothing either of them could do.

The other passengers stared silently at them as they walked along the aisle. It must be like this in a hi-jack situation, Roscoe thought: everyone else thinking, thank God they haven't picked on me . . .

Another stewardess had opened the rear door. Here the noise from the triple fan-jet engines was painfully loud. A current of biting cold air blew in through the door, ruffling Van's long blonde hair. The drop to the ground was a long way down. A battered yellow truck appeared in their field of view, man-oeuvring jerkily towards the aircraft as though it were the driver's first time at the controls. At the back was a crane of the type used for maintenance of street lighting, with a man standing in the bucket, gripping the handrail for support.

It stopped immediately below the open doorway. The bucket was elevated to the level of the aircraft door, where the man standing in it spoke to the stewardess, using what Roscoe presumed was Lithuanian.

In Russian the stewardess ordered, 'You get in with him, please.'

Van looked at Roscoe questioningly.

'I don't think we have any choice,' he said.

'*Právilno*,' said the stewardess, adding in Chicago-style English: 'You guys don't got no choice.'

'What about my luggage?' Van asked. 'It's still in the hold.'

'Fuck it,' said the stewardess helpfully.

'Let's go.' Roscoe clambered over the rail into the bucket and helped Van, who was wearing a tight skirt and high heels, to climb in after him. Intended to hold one man, the bucket was a close fit for three bodies. The cabin door slammed shut. Hardly waiting until the truck could get out of the way, the plane turned and lumbered back down the runway with engines screaming as they spewed a stink of kerosene into the cold air. It rose soggily into the air, wings rocking as it cleared the first line of low dunes with a few feet to spare.

The bucket banged onto the bed of the truck at the bottom of its lift, jarring their spines. Van unblocked her ears and said, 'You should have warned me about this, Jack. It would have been less alarming.'

'For me too,' said Roscoe.

A flash of fear showed in her blue eyes. 'Wasn't this a part of the plan?'

'It's a part of somebody's plan,' he said.

The truck moved jerkily in first gear across the hard-standing to a hangar. At ground level the dilapidation all around was more apparent: huge piles of blackened, rusting equipment occupied the centre of burned patches of concrete. All the windows were broken and doors torn senselessly off their hinges. Great lakes of stinking diesel fuel were seeping into hollows in the ground between piles of rusting bombs that lay open and presumably defused in the open air. Inside the dark interior of the hangar an old and very dirty East German Trabant saloon was parked.

The heavy motioned them to get out of the bucket. On the ground he frisked Roscoe head to toe, and patted Van down, paying particular attention to the inside of her thighs where the tight skirt gave him a problem. Then he raised a hand in some kind of signal and climbed into the cabin of the truck without a word. Transmission whining, the truck drove off, still in low gear, and disappeared between two buildings, leaving Roscoe and Van apparently alone on the deserted airfield.

Van swore, looking at the back of her legs. 'I laddered my tights climbing into that damned contraption.'

Roscoe laughed. The sound echoed off the blank walls of the empty hangars.

'What's so funny?' she snapped.

'You worrying about your clothes when . . .'

'Damn you,' she said. Her voice was trembling as she clutched his arm. 'I'm not worried about my clothes, Jack. I'm just trying to focus on something I can handle – like a hole in my stocking – so I don't drown in an ocean of fear.'

'Now stay cool,' he said, puzzled.

'No, you stay cool.' Roscoe could hear that she was near to tears. 'I'm nearly wetting myself with nerves, Jack. What the hell have I got myself into?'

In the expensive woollen two-piece, with her pale blue eyes and the long blonde hair that never seemed to need a brush, Van looked like an ice princess – Grace Kelly in *Rear Window*. Roscoe stared at her incredulously.

Courage, he knew, was a finite attribute. Men who had risked their lives a hundred times under fire could suddenly use up their lifetime supply and lie sobbing on the ground, unable to stand up. Was that happening to Van? Had that night on the Turkish border used her lifetime's courage?

'Sorry.' She took a deep breath and put his mind at rest by a smile. 'I had to get that out of my system, Jack. I'll be OK now.'

'You had me worried.'

She looked around the deserted airfield.

'Relax,' he said. 'If it was the other side that diverted the Aeroflot plane, we'd be standing here surrounded by men with guns.'

'You're right. I don't know why I lost my nerve. Perhaps I'm out of practice at the spook game, Jack. Or maybe I've grown up, I don't know. Somehow when you're twenty-five and think you're invulnerable, this kind of game is exciting. Now . . .'

For the first time Van looked at Roscoe with some warmth in her eyes. 'Now I just want us all to get safely home: Peter, me – and you.'

Roscoe realised that he had been concentrating on his plans so intently that he had had no mental energy to spare for wondering what would happen if they went wrong. Van's moment of fear was infectious. He shuddered. If he had miscalculated, he would pay the price – but so also would Van and Bergman.

'I never asked you about yourself,' she said. 'When you burst into my life yesterday, I was too busy thinking about myself and Peter. How have things been, these last few years?'

Roscoe did not want to think of Maria and the cottage on the banks of the Dordogne. At that moment the ancient Trabant wheezed into life, saving him from answering. It pulled out into the daylight, coughing black fumes from a broken exhaust pipe. At the wheel was a middle-aged woman dressed in drab civilian clothes. Her hands on the wheel were scarred with toil. They were the ugliest hands Roscoe had ever seen on a woman.

Van recognised the face with difficulty and only because of the country they were in. 'Colonel Zingaris,' she said to Roscoe out of the side of her mouth.

'I remember the name,' he said.

'*Montez derrière, s'il vous plaît.*' The order in French to get in the car, delivered in a rich contralto voice, filled in the blanks in Van's memory. Loreta Zingaris had been a top-flight KGB swallow, one of the best ever to emerge from the training school at Verkhonoye. Her speciality had been seducing French politicians of Cabinet rank during Charles De Gaulle's Fourth Republic. Now all that remained of the woman whose beauty had milked so many secrets from the Elysée Palace was the voice. The face was heavy and lined, the body thick-set and ugly and the once sparkling grey eyes that had teased her targets into shedding their responsibilities as quickly as their pants, were dull and listless.

So far as Van remembered from her days in Movements Analysis, Colonel Zingaris had disappeared from view after her last mission in the West. It was thought that she had been sentenced to a long spell in the Gulag on her return to Moscow in order to expiate the cardinal sin of knowing too much about some matter of State or other.

'*Monsieur Roscoe,*' she said. '*Et vous, madame – dépêchez-vous, je vous en prie.*'

They got into the back of the Trabant. The seat was muddy and torn. It looked as though Zingaris carried dogs more often than humans in her car. Mingled with the smell of two-stroke oil from the broken exhaust was a strong odour of wet fur and rotten meat. There were chewed marrowbones rolling around the uncarpeted floor and a lot of dog hair everywhere.

'I think I'm going to be sick,' said Van.

'Be my guest,' muttered Roscoe. It could not have smelt much worse. He turned to look behind the seat and found himself staring into the eyes of a huge black Doberman, coiled up like a snake in the small space.

'*Ne craignez rien, elle ne mord que sur ordre,*' said Zingaris: don't be frightened, she only bites on command.

She drove off the airfield through one of the many gaps that had been torn in the boundary fence and bumped on the Trabant's worn-out suspension along a track leading to the shore, at the end of which she stopped the car and said in English, 'Now wait.'

'For what or whom?' asked Roscoe, receiving no reply.

He tried to get comfortable on the broken seat. Beside him, Van was shivering, so Roscoe took off his anorak and put it over her shoulders. The Doberman bitch was sitting up and breathing on the back of his neck.

The featureless beach was deserted as far as the eye could see. Under a leaden sky the grey sea stretched westwards towards Scandinavia. The only sign of human habitation was a rickety metal jetty that ran fifty metres out to sea, with a small fisherman's cabin at the end.

Zingaris would not reply to questions but was looking increasingly nervous. Roscoe could not take his eyes off her hands drumming on the steering wheel. The skin was deeply cracked and scarred from heavy manual labour and the fingers ended in fleshy pads where the nails had been torn out and had not regrown. On one hand three fingers had been broken and set crooked, with joints deformed and arthritic.

After half an hour had passed, Zingaris took a length of dried sausage and some black bread from the glove compartment. With a pocket knife she sliced the bread and sausage, passing two impromptu sandwiches back for them to eat

Van's keen eyes were the first to see the dot coming towards them, just above the indistinct horizon where grey sea merged with grey sky. It grew rapidly and turned into the unlikely shape of an old wide-bodied helicopter, skimming the waves to keep below the coastal radar. It had no national markings but long-range tanks added on both sides of the cabin.

As they lifted off in Plotnik's Huey, Roscoe looked down to see Loreta Zingaris on the beach, counting a wad of notes that Plotnik had tossed out to her. She stuffed the money into a pocket and hugged the Doberman, then picked up a piece of driftwood and threw it for the dog to fetch.

'What the hell's going on, Jack?' Van asked. 'And who's the Action Man at the controls?' She had to shout above the noise of the engine and rotors.

Roscoe looked at Plotnik sitting in the left-hand driving seat, up front. 'He only answers questions if both your grandmothers were Russian. At a guess, I'd say our side has lost control of Pulkovo Airport because things are hotting up in St Petersburg and this was the safest way of making sure we get to the Villa Orlova in one piece.'

'What do you mean, things are hotting up?'

'Like a revolution,' said Roscoe. He had to put her in the picture at some point; it might as well be now. In the stripped-out cabin the noise level was such that neither Plotnik nor his co-pilot could overhear.

Van's eyes were wide with alarm.

'It's more exactly a *coup d'état* to put the Romanoffs back on the throne. But I think the guys who are calling the shots want to ship us and your uncle back home before the first of those shots are fired.'

'And they'll trust us to keep our mouths shut?'

Roscoe shrugged, 'So far as they know, we don't know anything about the restoration. Let's keep it that way.'

His words were lost in the roar of twin turbo-shaft engines as a sleek, fast helicopter gunship dived out of the low clouds and buzzed them so close that the Huey, buffeted in its rotor-wash, nearly went submarine.

Roscoe identified the intruder as a MIL Mi-28 – the ultra-fast, heavily armoured tank-buster, Nato code-name Havoc. The weapons racks on its stubby wings were empty but the single 30 mm. calibre gun on the armoured mounting beneath the nose could have knocked the Huey out of the sky with one burst. The Mi-28 was a killer-bird, developed by the Russians after they had lost too many of its predecessors to shoulder-launched SAMs in Afghanistan, where the war against the *mujahedin* had bled the Red Army of men, machines and morale as Vietnam had bled the US Armed Forces for so many years.

The pilot and weapons-operator, seated in tandem and not side-by-side, were staring across at the Huey. As the distance narrowed, Roscoe saw Plotnik's hard face break into a grin as he gave a thumbs-up to the other pilot and got the same gesture in reply.

'And these are the good guys, Jack?' shouted Van. 'I hope I don't meet the others.'

The gunship edged closer to take station a few feet away from the Huey's rotors. The turbulence it caused made the

Huey buck and bump unpleasantly. Then the turbulence grew worse as a second Mi-28 took up station equally close on the other side and the exhaust noise from the unmuffled turbo-shaft engines made further conversation impossible.

As they circled over the Villa Orlova the helicopter escort peeled away and sped back to base for refuelling; even stripped of most of their weaponry, the round-trip halfway to Lithuania had been at the limit of their fuel range.

Roscoe pointed out to Van the house and a few landmarks; she might need to have an idea of the lie of the land at some point before the operation was over. There were cars parked all over the grounds of the villa. The gate in the boundary fence was open, with some vehicles even parked between the fences. In the stiff onshore breeze a flag which Roscoe had not seen before fluttered from the tall white pole in front of the villa, replacing the Russian flag that had been there on his previous visit. The new one bore the black Romanoff double-eagle on a red-and-white ground.

'Here's to Romanoff Roulette,' he pointed at the flag as Plotnik flared the Huey and settled the skids neatly on the H painted on the ground beside the flag-pole.

'Here's to what?' Van asked. Her ears were adjusting as the scream of the Huey's motor died to a whine.

'Romanoff Roulette,' he said. 'It's another great life-or-death game from those wonderful people who brought you Gulag and Iron Curtain!'

Van grinned and squeezed his arm to show she appreciated the gesture. 'I'm OK now,' she said. 'Whatever the name of the game, let's get in there and win!'

Roscoe was wishing that he had made a different joke; the loser at Russian Roulette ended with his brains permanently ventilated, and the penalty for losing a game of Romanoff Roulette was probably the same.

. 5 .

'I'm sorry, General,' smiled Van. She looked as cool and self-possessed as if she were sitting in her office above the shop in Geneva. 'There's simply no way I'm going to identify that man as my uncle.'

'You haven't even talked with him yet,' growled Medvedev. 'The arrangement was that you ask Sir John questions pertaining to family knowledge, proving to London's satisfaction that he is who we say he is.'

Roscoe noted that the tic under Medvedev's eye had grown worse. For an operator as tough as the general to be showing signs of stress, meant that the pressure must really be building up. There was a lot of background activity at the villa, people coming and going, footsteps clattering up and down the uncarpeted stairs. Several times Plotnik had been called out of the meeting; he was looking more lean and hungry than ever. Only Sir John seemed aloof, with an expression of faint amusement on his face at the stand-off between Van and Medvedev. So far he had not even said hello to his niece.

'I've no intention of talking with him,' said Van. She avoided looking at her uncle across the large table in the dining-room in the Villa Orlova. Whatever she was feeling inwardly, to the men watching her she looked cool and totally self-possessed.

'I came here for one reason, General,' she said. 'To obtain Peter Bergman's release. Until I meet him face to face, I don't recognise anyone.'

'That's all under control.' Medvedev was trying to sound soothing but it didn't work; bluster and bullying were his usual techniques. 'It's just a matter of paperwork, I assure you.'

Van peeled off her gloves and laid them on the polished walnut surface of the table beside her handbag. She examined her nail varnish which was immaculate. 'When the paperwork is done, I'll do my bit, General Medvedev – but not before.'

Despite the stench in the zoo, Ossetin had spent long hours sitting on a chair outside Bergman's cage, watching him eat the rations that Plotnik had left behind.

'Enjoy each mouthful, 712,' he whispered. 'When that food is gone, you'll get no more from me. So if your crew-cut friend doesn't hurry back, you'll starve to death.' He seemed to find the thought very funny.

Bergman was aware that, after six years of malnutrition, his body had no reserves of fat on which to draw, so the process of starvation would not take long. The one hunger he could indulge was for knowledge; he read and reread the pile of newspapers that Plotnik had left. Apart from a few snippets of information gleaned from Plotnik the previous year, this was the first news he had had since . . .

He tried to recall the last headlines he had seen. At the time of the ambush on the Turkish border Mrs Thatcher had been the British Prime Minister and the phrase 'Gulf War' meant the all-Moslem confrontation between Iraq and Iran. Then too, the USSR had looked set to last for centuries, whereas now . . .

He sat on the bed reading newspapers and clutching the nearly empty ration-pack. They were the only physical manifestation of reality to which he could cling in this new nightmare. As he read, he went over and over in his mind the conversation with Plotnik:

'Take me with you now, Colonel!'

'I can't, Bergman. The paperwork has to be sorted first. But I'll be back and that's a promise.'

How insanely Russian! thought Bergman. I have to wait, locked up in this shithouse at the mercy of a lunatic like Ossetin while the paperwork is straightened out by some clerk back in Moscow . . .

He blinked. Ossetin had gone. He was standing in the doorway arguing with a short, chubby woman wearing thick glasses and some kind of a uniform. She was holding a rag over her nose and mouth and peering from one cage to another. Behind her walked two men in camouflage fatigues holding AK 74s, one of which prodded Ossetin hard enough in the kidneys to knock him sprawling on the filthy floor.

To Bergman it was like a slow-motion dream. He wanted to shout out, 'I'm over here!' but that might have shattered the dream and stranded him once again in the nightmare of reality.

A warder was kicked into the zoo by a third Spetsnaz man and fell in a heap beside Ossetin on the filthy floor, a bunch of keys in his hand. On hands and knees he shuffled to the door of Bergman's cell and opened it. He tried to smile at Bergman but had forgotten how; the result was more of a silent snarl, showing broken, yellow teeth.

He held out one hand, like a man trying to calm a nervous dog by letting it sniff his scent. '*Etáp dlya tebyá*,' he said. '*Etáp!*'

The word *étape* in French means a stage in a journey. In Gulag slang it came to mean being transferred from one camp or prison to another. Bergman cowered away from the guard, fearing some kind of trick.

'He's not coming out,' said the guard.

'Mr Bergman!' Ekaterina Borisovna took the almost useless mask away from her face. She gagged on the stench and spoke in English to the filthy scarecrow figure whose eyes stared at her from sockets set in a gaunt face. 'I work for Colonel Plotnik, Mr Bergman. He sent me to bring you home.'

A woman's face and a woman's voice, speaking English? Bergman's eyes were wide with disbelief.

'You remember Colonel Plotnik?' she asked, wondering whether he was mad.

'Yes,' said Bergman. 'I remember.' The English words felt

odd on his tongue after so long not using the language. His accent was like Coetzee's: Ah rimimbuh. He corrected himself: 'I remember the colonel.'

'I've come to take you away, Mr Bergman.'

He wanted to laugh out loud but feared that if he started he would be unable to stop. So he took six silent steps out of the cage where he had lived for a year and stood in the open door-way. Ekaterina took his arm and led him into the watch-room. The outside door was open, guarded by another man in cam-ouflage fatigues. The smell was less overpowering here.

She held out a clipboard and a ballpoint pen to Bergman. 'You have to sign here and here. I'm sorry but there are regula-tions. Everything must be signed for.'

In a daze, Bergman signed his name. It was hard to control the pen with unaccustomed fingers.

'And here. And here.' She turned the pages, indicating the spaces for signature.

He signed again: Peter Bergman, Peter Bergman, Peter Bergman . . .

Ossetin – unshaven and with a faint wispy moustache – was goggling in disbelief. His eyes darted from Bergman to Ekaterina and back and his mouth hung open slackly.

Another form. 'Sign at the bottom for your belongings,' Ekaterina requested.

Bergman held the pen poised. 'Belongings? I don't own a single thing.'

'Never mind,' she said soothingly. 'Just sign, Mr Bergman. All the forms must be completed. That is the regulation.'

She tore the bundle of completed forms off her clipboard and thrust them into Ossetin's hand.

'The prisoner is now my responsibility,' she announced.

Ossetin nodded dumbly. The paper in his hand meant noth-ing to him. He wanted desperately to call Moscow for instructions but the only telephone line had been down for weeks, ever since some peasants had cut it for fencing wire a hundred miles away. Clutching the wad of signed and stamped forms, he slumped slowly down against the wall until he was sitting on the floor.

'Come!' Ekaterina pulled gently at Bergman's arm.

He took the first step into the outside air and the second, still wondering whether he would wake to find himself back in the cage. But nothing happened so he took the third step and realised that he was awake and sane despite everything he had lived through.

Reverting to his father's tongue because it better expressed what he was feeling, he muttered, '*Ich bin durchgekommen!*'

'*Na jah,*' Ekaterina agreed. '*Du bist durchgekommen. Jetzt wird alles besser gehen.*'

Bergman felt exhilarated to take full-length strides after the months of cramped pacing inside the cell: five steps in one direction followed inevitably by an about-turn and five in the other.

He let the woman guide him. The night air was chilly and made him shiver. Ekaterina tried to hurry him towards the waiting helicopter. There were two armed men standing beside it – not the slouching, drunken camp guards, but alert young men in camouflage battledress and blue airborne berets, with keen eyes that missed nothing. Bergman took in the fact that the AK 74s in their hands were pointing not at him but at Ossetin's men who stood in a sullen line, muttering to themselves, hands clasped on their heads.

He laughed aloud at the thought that the armed men were there to protect him, Peter Bergman. His lungs had been accustomed for so long to the warm and fetid stench of the cell that the intake of clean, cold air hurt them like a blow delivered inside his ribs, jolting his heart. He took another, deeper breath. The pain felt good because it was real.

'Come, please,' urged Ekaterina Borisovna.

Bergman shook her hand off, refusing to hurry. 'What's your name?' he asked.

She hesitated. 'Ekaterina. Ekaterina Borisovna Antonova.'

'Beautiful name,' said Bergman. He stood under the starry sky and breathed the painfully cold air for the sheer pleasure it gave. He flexed his arm muscles and did some knee-bends. Although weak from hunger, he was fit and free!

'Please, Mr Bergman . . .' she urged him.

'I have to say goodbye to a friend.'

'Then please be quick.'

She watched Bergman look up and orientate himself from the Plough which was clearly visible through a break in the clouds. He turned to the west where Wu lay and raised one hand in salute: 'Do svedánya, Wu!'

'Which one is Wu?' To Ekaterina's eye all the caged beasts in Ossetin's human zoo had looked alike. 'Some special friend?'

'Very special,' said Bergman. 'Without what I learned from him, I shouldn't have been able to stand by now, never mind walk and talk. As it is, I feel that, after a few good meals, I could run a mile.'

'I am so sorry that we cannot bring your friend with us,' said the stocky little woman who had delivered him from Ossetin. 'Our orders are clear. You alone may leave.'

'On úzhe svobóden,' said Bergman: he's already free.

The first few flakes – not of snow but the airborne frost which precedes it – were drifting through the still, dry air. It must be exactly a year ago that we escaped, Bergman thought.

'Please,' repeated Ekaterina Borisovna. 'We must go.'

'Where to?' Bergman roused himself to ask. He was not meaning to be difficult; after six years with never a single reason to hurry it was hard to understand her desire for haste. Also, it was delirious to voice a question after six years of not having the right to ask for or about anything.

'Ty idyósh damói,' said Ekaterina softly. 'You're going home, Mr Bergman.'

.6.

Dawson's room at the Bolshoi Hotel smelled like a cross between a bushfire and a hospital ward. The ash-trays were full of half-burnt pipe tobacco; two empty kaolin and morphine bottles and a box of Zantac pills stood on the night table.

'Gippy tummy,' explained the invalid. He avoided using words like *ulcer* and *colitis*. His normally pale face was a corpse-like grey, with beads of perspiration standing out on his brow. 'My guts play up at times like this.'

'Tough,' said Roscoe.

'You were supposed to call me when you got to Pulkovo, Jack.'

'I didn't get there. The plane was diverted, didn't you know?'

Dawson gestured weakly at a Sony multi-waveband radio on the bedside table. Roscoe turned it on loud and pulled a chair close to the bed.

'Did you get the girl?' Dawson asked.

'She's at the villa right now.'

'Thank Christ for that. You're cutting it fine, you know.'

'What's going on, George?'

'St P. is a hotbed of rumours,' said Dawson. 'The general

consensus is that anything could happen between now and Christmas.'

'Are people talking about a restoration?'

Dawson tried to laugh but had not the energy. 'They're talking about every possibility under the sun, my dear Jack. Some say the Communists will regain power because they are the only people with the experience of government – never mind if they can sort the mess out. Some think the Army will march into the Kremlin and declare a military take-over. There's talk of a Pamyat coup and an American invasion – take your pick.'

Roscoe nodded. 'That sounds like Medvedev's work. Grigori always liked confusing the enemy by feeding us conflicting intelligence.'

'Just so long as we're not around when whatever happens, happens.'

Roscoe was glad that he had not counted too much on Dawson's help. Poor old George did not look as though he could stand up to pee, let alone run interference.

'We should be in a Go condition within the next twenty-four hours,' he said. 'How do we get the money in and Sir John, Bergman, Van and me out?' He held up four fingers to remind Dawson of their deal. 'Four bodies, right?'

'By sea.'

So Coetzee was right after all, thought Roscoe. 'An RIB crossing the Gulf?'

Dawson gestured feebly. 'No fear. Dear Madeleine might risk losing four live people in a rubber boat but she won't take any chances with one million quid in used notes.'

'So how?'

'You'll find out.'

'And how do we communicate, George?'

Dawson scribbled a VHF frequency on a piece of paper. 'Got it? The code-word is *collect*, repeated three times at fifteen-minute intervals.'

'VHF? Is that a good idea, George? Curvature of the earth and all that?'

'From a transmitter at the villa, we've been assured it will work.'

Roscoe thought of the faint smudge of the Finnish shore

visible from the Villa Orlova. Was someone already waiting over there to hear him say, 'Collect, collect, collect'?

'Can I tear up this piece of paper?'

Roscoe nodded and watched the man in the bed pop the pieces into his mouth and chew. 'That'll do your stomach good,' he commented. 'What are you doing now?'

Dawson was heaving himself out of bed. He sat wheezing on the side of it, trying to get his breath back and looking 110 years old. 'Getting the hell out of here,' he said weakly.

Van looked at her watch. Roscoe had left four hours ago. Her uncle had been taken away under escort soon afterwards and Plotnik had left long since. During one visit to the lavatory she had heard Medvedev's voice booming angrily at someone upstairs but could not make out what he was saying. She felt deserted. For some illogical reason she had taken her Brazilian passport out of her handbag and slipped it into the waistband of her skirt where she kept touching it with her fingers as though it was a talisman.

A tray of *zakuski* – cold Russian hors d'oeuvres – lay untouched on the walnut table in front of her. She ate some pickled herring and gherkins, scooped up a large helping of caviare and washed it down with Narzan mineral water.

Twice she had been prevented by the armed girl soldiers on sentry duty at the main door from leaving the villa for a walk in the grounds. As far as she had been able to see, the huge house itself was temporarily divided into several different areas of access with makeshift curtains hung across corridors to screen them off from each other.

It was on her third walk along the corridor that she saw a familiar figure on the other side of a curtain hanging askew and called out, 'Anton?'

The Prince turned. 'My God,' he said. 'Look who's here.'

He came through the curtain, ignoring the levelled AK 74 of the protesting girl soldier, and kissed Van on both cheeks.

She smiled with relief. Anton Romanoff had been one of her first clients and regularly appeared in her shop with some mysterious pre-Revolutionary heirloom which he said belonged to some elderly relative who had fallen on hard times.

'Is Roberto with you?' he asked.

The question startled Van. Her life with Roberto Perreira seemed in another universe. He and Prince Anton were old skiing buddies.

'What are you doing here?' she asked.

The girl sentry was shouting something to the sergeant at the end of the corridor.

'Oh my God!' Van clapped a hand to her mouth as she recalled Roscoe's briefing. 'They're using you for Tsar! No, they can't be, Anton. You're about a hundredth in succession, as I recall.'

'Was,' he said with a wan smile. 'Recently I've lost a number of cousins, moving me up to Number One.'

'You must be crazy, getting mixed up with these people, Anton!'

'Well,' sighed the Prince, 'to begin with, there wasn't much choice.'

'They kidnapped you?'

'Sort of.' A puzzled look spread over the Prince's face. The several holes in his memory were confusing; he had lost track of time and had problems remembering the names of the people he had met. 'I was drugged on what felt like intravenous gin. And then when I sobered up, I had the strong impression that chucking in my hand at this particular game would be inadvisable.'

'I know what you mean.' Van was thinking that this was the first time she had seen Prince Anton not looking bored to death.

'I'm a gambler,' he smiled. 'This is the big game of my life. I reckon the odds are about the same as skiing down a slope below an avalanche that's waiting to happen, but I've done that plenty of times and got away with it, so maybe I'll survive this time too.'

'I hope so, Anton.'

He shook his head, still confused by where he was and what she was doing there, then enlightenment dawned. It was a false dawn. 'Of course,' he snapped his fingers. 'They brought you in to sort all this stuff out.'

He took Van's arm and led her behind the now unguarded curtain and into the room from which she had seen him coming out. It was dominated by an enormous reproduction of the painting *At The Finland Station* in which Lenin, disguised as an engine-driver, was haranguing a crowd from the footplate of a locomotive at the start of the Revolution. But what took Van's eye and held it, was a mass of Tsarist regalia that covered the large table in the centre of the room – the fruit of one trip by Plotnik's recce and infiltration team through the sewers of St Petersburg and into the store rooms of the Hermitage. There it had lain for decades – some of it since before the Revolution. In the general confusion of 1992 there was no money even to heat the Winter Palace building, let alone keep up with the cataloguing of the Hermitage, so it would probably not be missed for months.

Van moved round the table, touching different items with a soft, caressing hand, evaluating them with eyes and a brain that did this job faster than a mainframe computer. She lifted one of a matching pair of ornamental gold-encrusted blue Easter eggs, about six inches high. When the tiny replica of the Imperial crown on top was pressed, a spray of miniature portraits in hand-painted enamels fanned out of a slit beneath it, showing the Tsar, the Tsarina and their children.

'Fabergé?' asked the Prince.

'Yes.'

'Easter presents for the Imperial royal family?'

'Yes.'

'What would you give me if I brought that into your shop in the Grand' Rue?'

'A lot,' said Van thoughtfully. She was reading the inscription on the underside of the egg, between the hallmarks. Easter 1917! Dear God! she thought, these two eggs are the only genuine things in the whole room. Every piece of gold and jewellery must have been filched from the stockrooms of the Hermitage at some time during the last seventy years and copied, the copies put back and the originals quietly sold in the West – either by the Soviet Government or some private entrepreneur. They had missed the two Fabergé eggs because they were made of semi-precious materials: Karelian birchwood and lapis lazuli.

The Imperial family had commissioned the court jeweller, Carl Fabergé, to devise ridiculously expensive eggs as gifts for their friends, starting in 1885. As collectors' items they had become extremely valuable because only fifty-four had ever been made. To keep track of the costly materials used, Fabergé maintained stock ledgers detailing the size and weight of precious stones and metals used in each artefact, complete with a water-colour sketch which made authentication easy. Van had a facsimile edition of the stock books among the reference volumes in her office and had spent hours poring over them. She was certain that the two eggs she was looking at had never been seen in the West.

It was a relief for her to be doing something as familiar as working out the price of a work of art. The Forbes Collection in New York had purchased the 1900 Cuckoo Egg when it came up for sale in 1985. Van remembered the price of $1.76 million. She had herself attended the auction in Geneva the same year of a little Fabergé toy that had been separated from its egg. It was a tiny clockwork model of Catherine the Great in a sedan chair carried by two blackamoors, less than three inches high, which came from the estate of Charles Clore and had brought 1.5 million Swiss francs under the auctioneer's hammer.

Prince Anton was saying something to her but Van did not hear him. Her mind was grappling with the date engraved on the eggs. Easter 1917? In the confusion of famine and the First World War, millions of people were dying in Russia. Even the Romanoffs had thought it was time to reduce their conspicuous consumption so they commissioned for Easter of that year two eggs of less precious materials which were made but never delivered to the Tsar because by Easter he was in prison, waiting to be shot. These were the two eggs she held in her hands.

Value? she asked herself.

Prince Anton lifted a State Crown off the table and placed it on his head, admiring himself in the overmantel mirror. 'Quite comfy. It looks heavier than it is.'

'Crowns do,' said Van distantly. She was doing sums in her head. Say five million dollars for the pair, to be on the safe side . . .

She put the eggs down as they heard Medvedev's huge bulk crashing down the stairs, two at a time. He hurtled into the drawing-room like an enraged bear and slammed a fist into the girl sentry's mouth, knocking out two teeth and throwing her across the room to collapse against the opposite wall. A smear of blood stained the pine panelling. Recovering her balance, she scrambled to her feet and straightened up immediately at attention.

'What the fuck's going on here?' Medvedev bellowed.

Prince Anton did not bother to turn round. 'It's quite OK, General,' he said coolly. 'Miss Bowles-Haddon is an old friend of mine.'

'Don't worry, Grigori Sergeyevich,' said Van coldly. 'The secret is safe with me.' She looked him levelly in the eyes – for once they were visible, he was so angry.

'There are, after all,' she added, 'plenty of other things I have to keep stum about, when this is all over.'

Without a sound Plotnik appeared in the doorway behind Medvedev. His steely grey eyes took in the scene at a glance, noting the blood trickling from the sentry's mouth.

'What the hell do you think you're doing?' he shouted at Medvedev. 'If there's any disciplining of my troops to be done, it's done by me and no one else! Get that!'

Medvedev said nothing. The two men glared at each other for several seconds. It was Medvedev who turned away.

'This damn place is a fucking whorehouse,' muttered Plotnik, calming down. He nodded at Van. 'You come with me, please.'

'Where are we going?'

'You'll see.' He strode out of the room, expecting her to follow.

.7.

Bergman looked around the room. It was the same one in the Spetsnaz sick quarters that he had occupied after his near-death in the snows the previous year. Everything seemed the same – even the snow flakes drifting down outside. So much so that it was hard to be certain that this was not a delusion or some kind of short circuit in his mind. He asked several times to talk to Plotnik, only to be told that the colonel was too busy to visit him for the time being. In between the medical tests, Bergman enjoyed his first hot bath in twelve months. The sores that covered his body were cleaned and dressed, then hidden by the luxury of freshly-laundered pyjamas. After shaving himself, he saw in the mirror the face of an appallingly thin stranger.

After several hours in the sick bay he was watching through the barred and double-glazed window as an open jeep pulled up outside. Plotnik got out and threw a triumphant arm-pumping clenched-fist salute in the direction of the window. Behind the jeep was a black civilian car with a curtained rear compartment into which Bergman could not see.

Plotnik strode along the concrete path to the main entrance

of the sick bay and appeared in the doorway of Bergman's room a few seconds later. 'You lucky bastard!' he grinned.

The two men embraced. 'By God, you need a few good meals,' said the colonel, slapping Bergman's thin shoulders. He pulled back, the lines of tiredness in his face buried in the grin of pleasure. 'You made it after all, fella. You're going home.'

Bergman stared at him, unable to believe the words 100 per cent.

'It's really happening,' said Plotnik, reading his mind. 'This is no dream, Bergman. And brace yourself. You've got some visitors. Smarten up, my friend. There's a lady who's come a long way to see you.'

From the corridor came a sound that Bergman had not heard in six years: a woman in a hurry, heels clicking on the tiled floor. The door opened and Plotnik stood aside to reveal Van standing in the doorway.

Inside Bergman's head all the memories rushed back: the moon over Ararat, the ambush, the shouted *Go! Go! Go!*, the mortar shells exploding closer and closer . . . Then the thousand doubts that had taunted him when morale was low, evaporated in an inarticulate yell of triumph: Van had survived! His sacrifice had been worthwhile.

'Steady!' called Plotnik. He shouted along the corridor for a nurse and caught Bergman in his arms as he fell, unable to breathe from the excitement and excess of emotion.

Van stood unmoving on the threshold of the room, staring at the almost skeletal man in bright blue hospital pyjamas, cradled in Plotnik's arms. Was this the person she remembered as Peter Bergman? Even the photographs that Roscoe had showed her in Geneva had not prepared her for his emaciation. Only the piercing blue eyes were the same as she remembered and they stared at her from dark sockets as though he were a madman.

'Peter!' Van made herself smile for his sake but her voice sounded false in her ears.

Her first split-second reaction made Bergman see himself as she must be seeing him. With an effort of will he pushed away the vertigo and Plotnik's supporting arms to stand straight on his own feet. I am not the scarecrow in the shaving mirror, he told himself. I'm not a *zak* who answers to a number any more. I'm Peter Bergman again!

'It's me,' he croaked. His throat was dry so that he had to swallow to get the vocal chords to work.

'The outside may be pretty rough, baby,' he tried to grin at Van, 'but inside I'm still there.'

Van heard the door close behind her as Plotnik dismissed both himself and the nurse who had come running.

'Peter!' she said again. 'Oh God, Peter!' This time it was her own voice. She walked slowly towards him as she had in a thousand dreams. His arms reached for her and hers for him.

It was like embracing a tall child, he was so thin.

She felt them come, hot and burning, the tears that had been bottled inside her for so long. Her knees felt weak. She wanted to say his name a hundred times. She wanted to hold him and be held. She wanted to keep her eyes shut and just revel mindlessly in the fact that he was alive.

'Hey!' He shook her gently. She was surprised that a man so thin could be so strong, now that his momentary crisis was over.

'No crying,' said Bergman gently. His eyes were shut as he stroked her hair and breathed the air that smelled of her. 'It's called letting the side down, remember?'

Unaware how he had used the past to keep sane in Perm 39B, Van marvelled. 'You remember me saying that?'

Then she laughed, sobbing at the same time. 'To hell with the bloody side,' she said. 'If I want to weep now, I'll damn well weep.'

They sat on the bed to talk. Van wanted to touch Bergman – to hold hands and feel her flesh confirm what her eyes told her – but after the first embrace he kept some space between them.

At first he listened to her but it was hard for him to concentrate for more than a few minutes on what she was saying. Then his thoughts drifted off, always coming back to the question of how to be sure that this was all really happening. It did not make sense when Van told him that Jack Roscoe had set everything up for his rescue. The fixation to which Bergman had clung for six years was stronger than what she was saying. He shook his head to clear her words out of his brain. Van was wrong; it was all Roscoe's fault . . .

And then the door opened and Roscoe himself stood in front of Bergman, a lopsided grin on his face and one hand outstretched in greeting. 'Hi, Peter!' he said.

Bergman could see Van's mouth opening and closing but there was a roaring in his ears that stopped him hearing her. He had repeated to himself so many thousand times the mantra *KILL ROSCOE! I'M GOING TO KILL ROSCOE KILL ROSCOE KILL ROSCOE!* that seeing the object of his hatred standing in the doorway had the power of a hypnotic trigger. Like a sleepwalker he glided towards his target. Sensing something from the fixed stare in Bergman's eyes, Van stood up and made a movement to come between them.

Eyes fixed on Roscoe, Bergman motioned her to stand aside. 'You bastard!' he said. 'I've been waiting six years for this moment.' It was what he had always said in the dream.

'Peter,' said Van urgently. 'Listen to me. I've been trying to tell you . . .'

Bergman shook his head. After all the practice in Perm 39B it was easy for him to switch off sights or sounds he did not want; that was how he had managed to stay alive and sane.

He glided towards Roscoe flat-footed, his hands horizontal knives – *shu-to* was the name Wu had called them. Bergman had planned the moves a thousand times in his dream: a series of kicks and jabs on nerve centres to cause excruciating pain and ending with one slashing blow to Roscoe's windpipe – and then the gut-warming pleasure of watching his enemy choke to death.

Always in the dream Roscoe had fought back. Instead, the real Roscoe stood still without trying to defend himself, his dark eyes watching Bergman come closer.

'Hold it, Peter,' he said calmly.

Bergman did not hear. He saw the mouth open and close but the only message in his brain was *KILL ROSCOE! I'M GOING TO KILL ROSCOE KILL ROSCOE KILL ROSCOE!*

Van caught at his arm. 'Peter, you must listen to me.'

Bergman slid through her grasp like water through open fingers. She reached again for him and missed again.

'Jack,' she screamed. 'Do something!'

But still Roscoe waited.

Before Van's horrified gaze Bergman moved like a dancer of death, his right foot swinging gracefully upwards in the round-house kick known as *ma-washi-geri*. He pulled the blow at the last moment in order not to snap Roscoe's neck vertebrae and end it all too soon. The ball of his foot connected with Roscoe's chin, jerking his head back hard enough to slam him back against the doorjamb with a thud that cracked the wood from the plaster. Stunned, he slumped to the floor.

Van grabbed at Bergman's collar and found herself turned around, lifted and thrown bodily onto the bed, out of the way.

'No,' she screamed again. 'No, Peter!'

Bergman blinked. This was all wrong. Why was Roscoe lying there in the doorway and not fighting back? In the dream he had always fought for his life. In the dream Bergman had fol-lowed up the first attack with a triple punch *sanbon-zuki* and finished his enemy off with the move *shuto-uke-nikite* and that last oh-so-pleasurable knife-hand blow to the throat.

The mists of fantasy thinned. Van was standing in front of him again with her arms stretched wide.

'Peter,' she said. 'You must listen to me.'

She talked slowly and clearly, making Bergman listen when she could see his concentration wavering, filling him in with what had really happened in Turkey and how Roscoe had worked for years to trace him, losing his job as a result.

Bergman's brow was furrowed with concentration as Van's message slowly percolated through. How, he wondered, could I ever have believed that Jack Roscoe would betray anyone? In a dawn of comprehension he saw that the whole elaborate fantasy of revenge had been merely a way of giving himself a specific reason to stay alive, and nothing else.

As the fire of anger left his eyes, Van felt like a lawyer who had just saved her client from the gallows.

Bergman pulled Roscoe to his feet and slapped his face a couple of times, not in anger but just hard enough to sober him up. Roscoe squeezed his jaw tenderly. It did not seem to be bro-ken. Then he felt Bergman's arms go round him in a vice-like embrace of steel and whipcord.

'Thank God that Van was here, Jack!' said the voice in his ear. 'You don't know how near you were to dying, just then.'

Roscoe was laughing now – with relief and happiness. 'Kill me and you don't get out of here, you stupid Canuck,' he said, punching Bergman in the ribs.

'And if I let you live, *soutpiel*?'

'You'll sleep tonight in the best hotel room in Helsinki. That's a promise.'

.8.

It was a grey morning. The grey-painted British frigate hove to within a cable's length of the line of pencil-like yellow buoys bobbing in the grey waters of the Gulf of Finland. There was a light sea running, whipped on by the north-easterly wind pregnant with a whole winter's burden of snow. Like a threat it delivered occasional flurries of sticky white flakes that clung to the superstructure and made the deck slippery.

At the stern of the frigate, the white ensign was furled. All radars were switched off in order to reduce to a minimum the vessel's electronic signature as read by passing satellites. Preserving radio silence, the Aldis lamp on the bridge flickered its message landward into the cold, clinging sea-mist.

The young naval linguist-coder standing beside the captain on the bridge had his binoculars trained on the almost invisible launch heading towards the British vessel from landward. Painted a dark green-grey, the approaching craft was hard to distinguish even through lenses, its position betrayed only by the rhythmic splashes of white as the bow crashed through the wave-tops. A series of brighter pinpoints of light brought the reply in dots and dashes.

The coder translated into English as he went: 'Request you . . . move across . . . to our side of frontier . . . for the hand-over . . . message ends.'

The captain looked at Madeleine Wharton. 'An error of navigation, ma'am?'

She was wearing the nearest she had ever come to a disguise: a WRNS commander's uniform with dark blue trousers showing beneath a dark blue duffle coat. 'A very small one,' she said. 'If you please.'

'Don't log it,' ordered the captain.

The quartermaster rang slow speed ahead on the electronic engine room telegraph and the grey ship on the grey sea inched its way between two of the yellow buoys and into Russian waters.

As he stepped out of the shelter of the bridge superstructure Dawson regretted that he had not accepted the offer of foul-weather clothing. His thin, city-dweller's overcoat was pierced by the biting wind. Despite being stuffed with pills by the ship's surgeon, he was still feeling ill. He slipped twice on the icy deck-plates and caught his balance with difficulty. Waiting for him at the top of the gangway were Baker and Charlie, clad in oilskins and with faces concealed by woollen mufflers.

Below them, at the foot of the gangway just above wave-height, Able was similarly dressed for the weather and anonymity. All three men were unarmed, on Madeleine Wharton's orders. Apart from two lookouts on the bridge, Dawson and the three SBS men had the otherwise deserted deck to themselves for a few minutes.

From out of the snow-haze came the muted roar of powerful diesel motors. The Russian patrol boat curved into sight with two Spetsnaz marines balancing, knees bent, on the bow and stern as it rolled on the swell to draw alongside the frigate's gangway. Dawson noted a tarpaulin-covered .50 calibre machine-gun mounted on the roof of the cabin and another on either side of the cockpit.

He could hear the throbbing of another pair of marine diesels coming from a second boat invisible in the mist, somewhere on the other side of the line of buoys. According to the sonar operators on the frigate, the British vessel had been shadowed by a Finnish patrol launch since leaving Helsinki.

The twin engines of the Russian boat were thrown into reverse with a flurry of foam, then cut to a low throaty purr. With a practised ease the man on the bow threw a line to Able who eased the launch into the steps until the two Russian marines could hold it steady alongside with their boat-hooks.

Dawson walked gingerly down the gangway which was groaning against the ship's side with every roll. With one hand he held tight to the rail. In the other he clutched the handles of two regulation black leather briefcases with OHMS embossed in gold letters on the flaps. In each was half a million sterling.

The Russian marine at the stern of the launch stretched out his free hand to help Dawson aboard. At the chart table in the cabin sat Medvedev and Roscoe. Sir John, who was looking as old and ill as Dawson was feeling, lay huddled in a cloak on one of the cracked and scuffed imitation-leather bench seats. Van was on the bench facing him. Beside her Bergman was swathed in blankets and sitting awkwardly, arms cuffed behind him on Medvedev's orders.

'Morning, George,' said Roscoe in a tight, clipped voice. His blink-rate was rapid and he was sweating from nervous tension. He wanted to get the whole thing over as fast as possible.

'The general would like to count the loot before you take delivery of the body,' he said.

Dawson opened the first briefcase, up-ended it and tipped the banded bundles of used £50-notes onto the table. He was feeling queasy from the motion of the deck beneath his feet as the launch rose and fell on the swell. In addition, he had to cope with the smell of hot engine oil and diesel exhaust fumes in the stuffy, over-heated cabin.

There were two Spetsnaz marines on duty in the cockpit outside, armed with stubby little Makarov 9 mm. sub-machine guns. It occurred to Dawson for one moment that if Medvedev chose to, he could simply order the launch's helmsman to sheer away into the haze with all of them and the money – and there was nothing that George Dawson or anyone else could do about it. Have faith in Madeleine Wharton, he told himself: she usually gets what she wants.

'The frigate's captain doesn't like being this side of the frontier,' Dawson muttered to Medvedev. 'So if we can speed this up . . .'

'Shuddup,' growled the general, throwing another bundle back into the briefcase. 'If I lose count, I start again *s'nachála do konzá. Ty pónyal?*'

He gestured at the bottle of vodka open on the chart table. Dawson sat down on the bench seat beside Sir John and let Roscoe pour him a glass. It was moonshine for the crew, distilled in Plotnik's sick bay. To Dawson's palate it tasted raw as paint-stripper. He coughed, choked and waved away the offer of a second glassful.

'Is OK.' Medvedev finished counting and placed both briefcases under the table. He waved a hand at Sir John. 'You can take him away.'

'I've been betrayed,' said Sir John bitterly. He raised a haggard face to Medvedev. 'Your people once gave me their word, General, that I would never be handed back to the British. Don't you realise what'll happen if I open my mouth about what you're up to at that blasted Villa Orlova?'

'He is mad,' Medvedev winked theatrically at Dawson. He poured and swallowed a glass of spirit in one smooth gesture. 'Sir John suffers from delusions of grandeur, among other problems.'

He laughed, eyes hidden beneath the bear-like brows. 'The poor fellow thinks he's Napoleon, or something – keeps rambling on about Tsars and revolutions, Roscoe'll tell you.'

'I'm going to spill everything about what's going on back there – as soon as I get to London,' threatened Sir John peevishly. It was the only card he had left in his hand.

'Come on,' said Roscoe. He handed Sir John across the gap between the deck of the patrol launch and the foot of the gangway where Able took his other arm. For a moment the old traitor was held in mid-air, supported by the two men. He would have liked to drop into the sea between the two vessels and drown but had neither the strength nor the courage to break free and throw himself into the water. His feet touched the gangway and the moment of opportunity was past.

'Come along now, sir,' said Able in his best copper's voice. He put an arm around Sir John's shoulders and coaxed him up the slippery treads of the steep gangway. 'Got a nice cup of English tea waiting for you in the wardroom, they have. You'll feel better with that inside you.'

Dawson followed them up the gangway. Halfway up, he stopped and looked back. Through the cabin windows he could see Medvedev taking something out of a drawer in the chart table.

Roscoe had his back to the general, helping Van cross the widening gap between launch and gangway. 'You can take the cuffs off my buddy, Grigori,' he said. 'He's hardly going to attack anyone now, is he?'

He turned round to help Bergman across the gap between boat and gangway – to find himself looking down the muzzle of a Tokarev 9 mm. automatic.

'Don't be a hero, Jack,' growled Medvedev. Behind him, the blanket-swathed figure of Bergman stood, covered by the Makarovs of the two Spetsnaz marines. His mouth was still open in the beginning of a shout of warning that was too late, Medvedev had moved so fast.

'Just get aboard the frigate and go home, Jack.' The bear-like growl was menacing.

Roscoe balanced on the gunwhale. 'Not without Bergman, Grigori,' he said. 'That was our deal.'

'I need a hostage,' said Medvedev. 'The girl and you know too much about what's going on back there. If you want to see your Canadian pal again, you both keep your mouths shut, OK?'

Before Roscoe could reply he felt the point of a boat-hook rammed hard into his back just above the kidneys. For a split-second he thought he had been stabbed or shot. Then, losing balance, he fell face down into the near-freezing water at the same moment as the skipper of the launch opened the twin throttles and spun the wheel to veer away from the looming side of the frigate. Lungs full of salt water, Roscoe sank in a whirlpool of foam from the two powerful propellers. He felt himself driven down and down by the thrust of the propellers.

His heart was near bursting from the effort when at last he fought his way to the surface and managed to swim, despite the cold that reached into every organ, sapping both will and strength, to where Van was crouched on the foot of the gangway. She clung with one hand to the last stanchion and reached far out for him to catch her hand. Half-lifting and half-pulling him, she got Roscoe onto the foot of the platform where he lay with his head hanging over the edge, retching and vomiting as she thumped his back and ribs to drive the icy seawater out of his lungs and stomach.

Inside the cabin of the launch, now almost invisible from the frigate, Medvedev poured himself another glass of vodka. He was feeling pleased with his morning's work: so long as Bergman was his hostage, Roscoe and the girl would keep their mouths shut. As to Sir John? He was known to be a congenital liar and no one believed anything a returned traitor said until it had been checked a thousand times. By then it would be all over.

Knocked to the floor of the cabin by one of the marines, Bergman lay, unable to believe that he had been retaken prisoner, literally a few steps away from freedom.

Aboard the frigate, Dawson was barged out of the way at the head of the gangway by Roscoe, who was soaked to the skin and furious. Lungs heaving from the effort, he ran all the way to the bridge, slipping and sliding on the slush.

'You've got to give chase,' he pleaded with the captain. 'They've got one of our people on board that launch in direct contravention of the deal we agreed.'

'I'm sorry.' The captain really meant it. He pointed to the telegraph repeater in front of him which indicated Slow Astern as the frigate inched between the buoys and back into Finnish waters.

'I warned you, Jack,' said Madeleine Wharton. 'You nearly ruined everything with your moonlighting.'

Roscoe had not noticed her standing behind the captain in the dim lighting of the bridge. He felt both arms gripped and pinioned behind him – and did not need to look round to know he was being held by Baker and Charlie.

At the rear of the frigate, Sir John Bowles-Haddon's plaintive whining was drowned by the pounding of boots as a deck party of ratings approached at the double under a chief petty officer, heading for the helicopter hangar at the rear of the ship. A minute later came an explosion of noise when the twin Rolls-Royce Gem engines of the frigate's Mark 8 Westland Lynx anti-submarine helicopter burst into life.

Sir John was being difficult, refusing to go any further. Roscoe was manhandled past him and shoved into the large cabin of the Lynx. Bundled in after him, Sir John turned to Roscoe a face that looked as though he was going to burst into tears.

'They promised me a cup of tea in the wardroom,' he said, his chin quivering. 'It's not much to ask for, is it, old boy?'

Roscoe did not hear. He sat shivering uncontrollably and staring through the Perspex of the cabin windows towards the Russian shoreline. The haze and the snow flurries were clearing in patches. A chance ray of sunlight picked out the gilded domes of the Villa Orlova and the mirage effect in the cold air made it seem to float like a fairy castle in mid-air. Somewhere in the mists between him and the villa, Peter Bergman was being transported back to a new prison. His entire plan had come to nothing.

PART 7
ENDGAME

.1.

Lirian was braving the intermittent flurries of snow on the shore below the Villa Orlova when the patrol launch zoomed out of the sea-mist and swung in to the jetty. He smiled with relief at the sight of Medvedev scrambling ashore clutching Dawson's briefcases. It meant that very shortly he could be driving back into the city with his five per cent commission.

Whatever was being hatched inside the cordon of sentries which guarded the upper floors of the villa – and he had been careful not to make too many enquiries – Lirian had an instinct that quite a number of pawns were going to end up dead before Medvedev and Plotnik had finished their game of Real Chess. As an experienced gamesman, Anastas Romanovich Lirian intended to remove himself from the board before then.

'How did it go?' he asked, meeting Medvedev at the end of the jetty.

'Brilliantly.' The general took a deep breath of fresh air to drive the fug of the cabin out of his lungs. He stamped his feet on the wooden planking. 'Good to be back on dry land. Whoever said that Russians are half-Viking was wrong in my case.'

He lurched and fell against Lirian who caught his arm and held it, smelling the drink on Medvedev's breath. He knew the general had the Russian ability to consume huge amounts of alcohol and stay apparently unaffected mentally. To be as unsteady as this, Medvedev must have swallowed a lot of moonshine on the boat.

The two men walked side by side up the rise to the villa. Snowflakes were floating gently down, melting as they settled on the wet ground between the birch trees which had lost most of their leaves and seemed to have shrunk in order to make themselves a smaller target for winter's onslaught.

'Look!' said the general, grabbing Lirian's arm. 'Did you see that? An arctic hare.' He chuckled with pleasure.

'There! Just watch that cute little bunny run for cover between the trees.'

Lirian squinted through spectacles that kept misting over. 'I didn't see a thing, General.'

'You're shivering,' said Medvedev as they neared the house. 'You might as well come upstairs and have a drink while we settle up, Anastas.'

'I'm not cleared to know what's going on up there,' Lirian reminded him.

'Quite right,' the general growled. 'I was so carried away with the success of the handover that I forgot. But all the same, you'll have to wait while I get someone to type out a receipt for you to sign.'

'If you don't mind, General, I'll wait in my car.'

Lirian sat inside the Mercedes, staring at the pieces laid out on his travelling chessboard. It was the eleventh game of the Fischer-Spassky confrontation at Reykjavik with Fischer leading 6½ to 3½. Unable to concentrate, he put away the chessmen after fifteen minutes and wondered what was taking Medvedev so long. Like a worry bead, he fondled the antique white king in carved ivory, regretting that he had to leave the car and the chess set behind. They were his alibi: as he crossed the frontier that evening, the car with rear curtains drawn would be speeding along the motorway Moscow-bound, its number carefully logged at each GAI checkpoint directly into the Interior Ministry computers.

Medvedev came out of the house, having changed into a thick sheepskin coat and a fur hat. He was carrying two of the guns from Plotnik's collection, one under each arm.

'I'm going to shoot myself some supper,' he announced to the group of drivers waiting with the VIP cars.

Lirian had the impression that Medvedev had continued drinking while inside the house. The drivers looked the other way as the general started singing the aria from 'Boris Godunov' where the Tsar addresses the assembled boyars. He stopped after a few lines and said in a puzzled voice, 'Why can't I remember like I used to?'

'Does it matter?' asked Lirian.

'Yes,' said Medvedev vehemently. 'It bloody well does. Was the time I never forgot anything. Once I could have sung the whole fucking opera from memory. Now . . .'

He lurched into Lirian and belched loudly. 'You never knew I was going to be an opera singer, did you, Anastas?'

'No, general.' Lirian did not care, either.

'Well, I was. My teacher said I had the best bass voice she had ever trained – as good as Shaliapin, so she said. It didn't stop me being passed over by the wogs like you who ran the auditions for the Bolshoi, did it?' Medvedev leered into Lirian's face.

'The receipt,' Lirian cut into the alcoholic ramblings. 'If I can just sign that and have my five per cent commission, Grigori Sergeyevich – I'd like to be on my way before the weather gets worse.'

'Fucking Plotnik,' growled Medvedev. 'I ask him for a typist. He says I've got to wait half an hour. Bloody cheek the man's got! Before Gorbachev loused everything up, no goddam brown job told the KGB to wait half an hour.'

'You could sign the chit later for me, as a favour,' Lirian pleaded.

Medvedev laughed and took a swig from a silver hip-flask. He thrust it at Lirian who refused curtly.

'My dear Anastas,' the general said expansively, 'no auditor is ever going to be able to say that Grigori Sergeyevich Medvedev faked a single receipt. So you'll have to wait. And since you've got to hang about, you might as well make yourself useful by carrying my second gun. Be careful where you point it, it's loaded.'

Keeping the Purdey over-and-under shotgun for himself, Medvedev passed to Lirian the more lethal weapon, a Mannlicher-Carcano rifle better suited to stopping a stag than a hare, albeit a large arctic one. Then he stomped off into the trees, leaving Lirian to follow.

The delay made Lirian uneasy but he had no intention of leaving without his money. He hurried after the general, holding the Mannlicher awkwardly in both hands.

'Look!' Medvedev bent and pointed to the spoor. There were fresh droppings in the snow. He picked them up and rolled them between finger and thumb.

'Still warm, Anastas . . . Somewhere near, my supper is waiting.' The general grinned at Lirian and sniffed the pellets. 'Did you know that our little furry friend crapped these in his burrow last night and had to eat them again in order to digest his dinner properly? Only the second time around does he crap them outside. Interesting, isn't it?'

Lirian was dressed for central heating and shod for carpets, not to go hunting in the mud and slush. He shivered.

'I'm telling you this for a reason, Anastas,' the general growled. 'The hunter must study his prey until he knows everything about it – how it lives, how it thinks, how it feels. Only then can he be sure of bagging the quarry he's after.'

'You're wasting your time telling me this,' said Lirian. 'I am not a hunting man.'

'Nonsense, Anastas,' Medvedev disagreed. 'Any man with lead in his pencil has the instinct to hunt and kill – even a crafty Armenian bazaar trader like you. It's just a question of the right situation bringing the suppressed male instincts to the fore. Then the most civilised man in the world reverts to the primeval hunter/killer that lurks inside us all.'

He held up a hand for silence and stepped carefully between fallen branches that might crack beneath his weight, motioning Lirian to do the same. Soon they were out of sight of the villa, isolated in a world of whirling snowflakes and bare-limbed silver trees.

They came to a clearing in the trees where the hare – or another – sat sniffing the wind on a pile of leaves no more than twenty feet away, its pink nostrils and long white ears twitching.

On a completely snow-covered landscape it would have been invisible in its winter coat; against the pile of wind-driven leaves it stood out clearly.

The hare was upwind of the two men but its radar-antenna ears were nervously scanning in all directions. Slowly the general brought the Purdey up to his shoulder, avoiding any abrupt movement. He sighted, squeezed the trigger and fired one barrel. Too late, the hare leaped into the air, a vivid red splotch marking its fur. It fell to the ground, back legs twitching, as Medvedev lowered his gun with the second barrel unfired.

'Go and pick up my supper,' he ordered.

Lirian hesitated.

'Are you frightened?' Medvedev asked.

Lirian shook his head. 'I dislike hunting. It's so messy.'

'Messy but necessary, Anastas.' Medvedev sounded sad. 'These things must be done. Having others do them for us is no different, morally speaking – for the responsibility of the act remains ours. Or is it just that you are afraid of getting some blood on your expensive Savile Row trousers?'

Lirian had taken three paces forward when he felt the still warm and smoking muzzle of the Purdey against his neck. Medvedev jerked the shotgun sharply upwards and tipped Lirian's astrakhan hat forward. It fell off his head and landed on the slush-covered leaves.

'This,' growled Medvedev, 'is exactly how hunting accidents happen. An eager friend, unused to field sports – not even properly dressed – runs forward to collect the game, unaware that the huntsman is about to fire the second barrel. Then bang!'

Lirian froze, his glasses askew. Knocked by the hat falling off his head, they hung from one ear. He wanted to put them straight but both hands were busy holding the heavy Mannlicher.

'Is this your idea of a joke?' His voice was harsh and strained. 'Put down the gun, Grigori Sergeyevich. Please.'

'You think I'm a fucking idiot.' Medvedev's voice was a low mumble. 'You've taken me for slow-thinking Russian bear all the years you worked for me, Anastas. But I saw through you from the start. I know what you're up to. When you go into the forest, my little Armenian carpet-seller, the first thing you should learn is not to take liberties with a bear – especially a Russian one.'

'General . . .' Lirian kept his voice steady. Another man, he thought, would have ducked, swung round like people did in films, and used the weapon he was holding to knock Medvedev's shotgun out of the way, then shoot the general or club him in the face before he could fire. So be it, other men fought with their muscles but he had lived always by his brains. Being threatened by Medvedev was a situation he had foreseen, although not in exactly these circumstances. His counter-move had been prepared long ago.

Lirian's hands were moist with perspiration, his lips dry. He licked them and said in the same steady tone, 'General, I have an insurance policy.'

Medvedev laughed, 'I doubt they'll pay up.'

'Not that kind,' Lirian hurried on. 'This one's flesh and blood – your flesh and blood.'

'Impossible,' growled Medvedev. 'I don't have any family.'

Desperate to make his pitch while there was still time, Lirian hurried on. 'When I first came to work for you, I did some research on your personal life and discovered that in 1969 you had a liaison with a musician in the Bolshoi Opera orchestra. She looked Russian but she was Jewish. Her name was Gutman – Ludmilla Abramovna Gutman. Am I right so far?'

'Go on.'

'In the same year this Gutman woman was sentenced to twenty years' hard labour in a camp for anti-state activities. When she was arrested, you could have fixed her release but you didn't intervene because you were on the fast track for promotion and it would have compromised your KGB career. Right again?'

'Go on.' A prod from the Purdey reinforced the command.

'She died seven years later in a camp in the Buryat Republic on the Mongolian border from untreated pneumonia. The precise date was . . .'

Medvedev's laugh cut Lirian short.

Lirian stumbled forward, knocked off balance by a savage prod from the muzzle of the Purdey pressing against the base of his skull.

'You're all the same, you blacks,' the general sneered. He used the word *chórniy* meaning anyone who was not ethnic Russian. 'Crafty sods, the lot of you. Are you trying to get some leverage on me with that old blot on my copybook, Anastas? I'm disappointed in you. I'd have thought a shit-hound of your breed would dig deeper than that.'

'Listen, General.' Lirian blinked at the featureless panorama of out-of-focus trees and whirling snow in which he found himself lost. Putting his spectacles back on so that he could see clearly again seemed the most important thing in the world but he dared not risk the movement in case it was misinterpreted.

'My insurance policy is not your affair with the woman,' he said hoarsely. 'It's her child. The Gutman woman gave birth in the camp to a girl – your daughter.'

'You're lying.'

Lirian spoke fast, paring the facts down to the bare bones. 'At age eighteen, the orphanage where she was brought up sent this daughter of yours off to the KGB school at Verkhonoye where they trained our swallows. There she became a *lástochka* – a KGB whore, General.'

'Crazy story!' Medvedev snorted derisively. 'I think you're trying to sell me that little tart of yours with the big boobs and blonde hair – as my fucking daughter!'

'I changed her name, Grigori Sergeyevich. Her real name is Nadya Grigorievna Gutman – Grigorievna meaning daughter-of-Grigori. Right now she's gone underground – only I know where. Your only hope of contact is through me.'

Encouraged by Medvedev's silence, Lirian risked holding up one hand in a plea for time.

'I can prove all this.'

He stumbled in the leaves and half-turned in eagerness to keep Medvedev's attention, his head pushing the barrel of the shotgun sideways. The general – his reactions slowed by all the alcohol he had consumed – failed to relax pressure of his forefinger on the Purdey's second trigger as the gun moved. Part of the blast went into thin air but enough of the shot and expanding hot propellant gases caught Lirian's head point-blank, vaporising the ear plus a large chunk of neck muscle, scalp and skull. The impact spun his whole body round several times, both arms outstretched in a parody of a Cossack dancer. The Mannlicher flew from his hands and landed in the slush at Medvedev's feet. Blood, skin, hair and bone sprayed a red spiral trail, marking his reeling progress across the snow and leaves to where he fell in an ungainly heap beside the shot hare.

Medvedev lumbered across the clearing. It surprised him to see his victim staring up at him, inert but wide-eyed and apparently conscious.

Lirian could hear his life-blood pump-pump-pumping out of an artery. Cold – not the cold of the wind and snow but the black eternal cold of outer space – was creeping up his legs, reaching for the bowels. He felt them empty but there was no pain as such. His sight was slightly blurred, the intact rose-tinted spectacles still hooked improbably round the left ear. When Medvedev's blurred outline loomed above him, he summoned all his will.

'General!' The rasping whisper came from the back of Lirian's throat. His left hand was raised in a plea for attention.

'Can you hear me?' he asked faintly. A ghastly smile twisted one side of his white and bloodless face.

Deafened in his remaining ear, he could not pick up Medvedev's reply but spoke to the blurred and menacing shape standing over him. 'I hadn't finished telling you . . .'

Medvedev knew from his battle experience in Afghanistan that a wound which killed one man instantly allowed another to linger for minutes, maybe hours. Either way, Lirian was not long for this world.

The general would have liked to grab Lirian by the balls and tear the rest of the story out of him slowly, but it was too late for that. He knelt down in the slush beside the dying man. Hearing gone, Lirian saw Medvedev's face loom into focus. The hand he could still control grasped something which he realised was Medvedev's sleeve. He clutched it tightly and groaned. The cold was past his diaphragm now, reaching inside the ribcage for the heart muscles. He summoned all his will to push it back for long enough to complete a few more sentences.

He could see Medvedev's mouth opening and closing. From this low angle, he could also see the general's eyes, livid with anger. There was one last thing he still had to say. Like a marathon runner making a final lurching dash for the tape, he desperately marshalled his remaining energy. His hand let go of Medvedev's sleeve and fell to the ground.

The cold was reaching right into Lirian's brain now, like an icicle slipping between the soft grey matter. His vision closed down to a pinpoint of light. It was the iris of Medvedev's left eye which seemed to Lirian a bright star surrounded by the swirling, infinite darkness of the vortex into which he was being sucked relentlessly down and down.

It was hard, very hard to keep talking – but words were his only weapon against the man who had killed him, so he forced them out: 'The proof, General . . . is that my little Nadya has a birthmark on the inside of her left thigh.'

The dying man's rasping voice grew fainter. 'She says her mother had the same. Perhaps you remember such a mark . . . just below your mistress's cunt?'

'You clever little bastard!' The anger cut through the frozen air like a whiplash. With a bellow of rage Medvedev grabbed the astrakhan lapels of Lirian's coat in one hand. He stood up, lifting the dying man with him, kneed him in the groin and smashed a backhand across the white, bloodstained face. And another and another. He continued shaking and kicking the body and punching the head with his free hand until the rest of Lirian's brains had spilled out through the hole in his skull to end a mess of grey mush among the birch leaves and the melting snow.

Only then did Medvedev let the body fall. Breathing heavily, he rinsed Lirian's blood off his hands and coat with handfuls of slush. He picked up the Mannlicher from where it lay on the leaves, reversed it and used the butt to pound Lirian's empty skull into a formless pulp of bloody bone before slumping to the snowy ground, drained of energy and purged of anger. He wished now that he had killed Lirian outright and not given him time to talk. He could have dismissed the whole story except for that one detail. If it were not all true, how could the little hustler have known about the birthmark? Medvedev felt an immense yearning to see the face of the girl who, he had just learned, was his daughter.

It was not her face watching him. Standing between two tree-trunks was the figure of Plotnik, arms crossed and legs astride.

Medvedev wondered how long he had been standing there. Snow had settled on the peak of his forage cap and on Plotnik's shoulders, which meant that he had probably arrived soon after the first shot . . . So what?

Plotnik strode across the clearing and pulled Medvedev to his feet. 'A hunting accident,' he said.

'I found our leak,' Medvedev laughed weakly. 'Fucking nigger had been shooting his mouth off to the British.'

He took a swig from the hip-flask and waved an arm at the inert form lying in the wet leaves. The other arm described a wild arc which included the villa and Plotnik's base. 'He told them about the Romanoff restoration, our plans – everything. But I took care of him.'

Plotnik looked down at Lirian's unrecognisable face. 'You did,' he said unemotionally. 'You did a very thorough job of it too, Grigori.'

.2.

The Cessna Citation executive jet had been chartered from a Luxemburg company; the Finns had drawn the line at an RAF Transport Command flight from Brize Norton landing at Helsinki Airport. Both pilot and co-pilot of the Citation were blond Icelanders who had done jobs for the Service before. They continued the pre-flight checks without showing any interest in their passengers.

The charter craft was parked on the hard-standing of Helsinki Airport, on the opposite side from the passenger terminals. Over the whine of the twin fan-jet engines came a loud moan from Sir John, seated on the toilet in the rear of the cabin. He had vomited down the front of his shirt – and both looked and sounded genuinely ill. The cubicle door was jammed open by Able's large-booted foot.

As the RN Sea Lynx took off with an ear-shattering roar and headed back for the frigate which was already steaming westbound into the Baltic proper, the pilot of the Citation announced without turning round, 'Two minutes. We expect clearance from the tower to taxi in two minutes from now.'

Roscoe had intended sloping away with Van the moment the

Lynx landed on Finnish soil, only to find himself hustled on board the waiting Cessna firmly jammed between Baker and Charlie. For the short run between the two aircraft all three SBS men had worn civilian clothes with knitted black Balaclava helmets that left only their eyes showing. They peeled them off now and sat with as much expression as three dummies in a shop window, effectively blocking the way to the cabin door. Charlie was sporting a fine pair of black eyes from the head-butt he had received at Pulkovo Two.

In the club seat opposite Roscoe, Van was sitting numbed by the suddenness of Medvedev's double-cross. Beside her Dawson was shifting uncomfortably. He needed the toilet soon but Sir John seemed to have taken up permanent residence there.

'You're out of line, Jack. Way out of line.'

Only Madeleine Wharton, thought Roscoe bitterly, could deliver such Humphrey Bogart dialogue with perfect diction and no sense of the ridiculous.

'I want the rest of my money,' he said. 'I did the job.' His teeth were still chattering despite the dry clothing which Able, Baker and Charlie had rustled up for him out of their personal luggage during the helicopter flight.

'I stipulated delivery in London.' Madeleine's voice was as cold as Roscoe felt. 'That's where you'll be paid.'

'I'm entitled,' he argued. 'I've delivered Sir John. I want to be paid here and now.'

Whilst he was unsure what could still be done for Bergman, one thing was certain: with each hour that passed the chances of finding him again and getting him alive out of Russia diminished. Once Plotnik and Medvedev launched their revolution, Bergman the hostage would become a disposable nuisance. It didn't bear thinking about.

'Even if I had the money here,' said Madeleine Wharton, 'I should not authorise payment of one penny to you until we land in London – and that's on condition that you are still with us when we get there.'

Money was less important than speed, Roscoe decided. He rose from his seat. 'I've got some business here in Finland,' he said. 'I'm not a member of staff under your discipline. I'm getting out.'

Madeleine's mouth tightened; the last thing she wanted was an argument in front of the SBS trio and with the two Icelanders listening in. 'You can't get out here, Jack. The Finns don't want you. To be exact, they don't want any of us. We are officially not here.'

'I've a valid passport,' argued Roscoe. 'They won't stop me.'

There were two police cars with flashing blue lights parked outside. Madeleine looked from them to the airport buildings on the other side of the field. Dawson noted the danger signal; no one in the Service had ever seen the DG lose her temper because she always looked away or out of a window at the crucial moment when her emotions were obvious.

'Let him go,' she said to Dawson without looking round.

Dawson nodded to Baker and Charlie who subsided into the front club seats, allowing Roscoe to pass between them but stopping Van when she tried to follow with an apologetic, 'Sorry, Miss.'

Roscoe stepped out of the low doorway and walked down the integral steps. Before he had taken five paces on the ground, a Finnish policeman was hustling him into the back seat of one of the patrol cars beside a hard-faced man who introduced himself as Inspector Koskelainen of the Security Police.

He listened to Roscoe, took one look at his passport and said, 'I think you should leave on that aircraft, Mr Roscoe.'

'I'm a civilian.'

'I don't care if you're a dog, just go away.'

'I could ask for political asylum, Inspector. Then you'd have to let me in.'

'. . . and you'd be the guest of the Finnish Government for a couple of weeks while your case is examined. Is that what you want? I can promise you the application will be rejected – on my personal recommendation.'

'Shit!' said Roscoe. 'Look, I'm a private citizen. I have nothing to do with the other people on that aircraft. They gave me a lift here, that's all.'

'You haven't understood,' said the inspector. 'We don't want you people in Finland.'

'I'm a tourist,' Roscoe pleaded.

Koskelainen noted the number of Roscoe's passport in a

small notebook and handed it back. 'Be a tourist someplace else,' he said flatly. 'Try New Zealand or, better still, the Falkland Islands. It's summer down there.'

Nadya Gutman lingered by the American-built Baldwin locomotive on the footplate of which Lenin had sneaked back into St Petersburg in 1917, disguised as a fireman. It was a tourist attraction placed inside the new Finland Station, built after the Luftwaffe had modified the original structure in 1942.

Her passport was a well-used German one in the name of Hildegard Sommer, with stamps from half the countries in Europe, both east and west. As instructed by Lirian, she had cut her hair short, dyed it a nondescript brown colour, and rubbed in some cooking oil to make it look greasy and unwashed. She was wearing no make-up or nail varnish and her nails were cut short and grubby. Her clothes were the sort an experienced Inter-railer would choose: worn jeans, trainers and an old anorak. A well-used down sleeping bag from KaDeWe, the Berlin department store, was tied on top of her backpack. Her Berliner accent was as authentic as the sleeping bag; two of her compulsory lovers at Verkhonoye had been German. Heavy-framed spectacles completed the transformation. The thick lenses plus the brown-tinted contact lenses she was wearing were equivalent to plain glass.

The final announcement was being made for the departure of the express to Helsinki.

Where was Anastas? Nadya looked around one last time and hurried towards the barrier, her backpack slung over one shoulder and bumping against her hip. Her protector had briefed her on exactly what to do in the event that he missed the train but she felt insecure without him. Their relationship was a peculiar tangle of emotions and mutual needs that she had never been able to unravel.

At the platform barrier there was some kind of identity check going on. Nadya joined the queue and saw three blonde girls standing to one side, looking unhappy. They were guarded by armed militiamen who kept their eyes on the huge, bear-like man standing by the ticket-collector. When Nadya recognised Medvedev, her pulse quickened. She wanted to turn away and leave the queue but one of the militiamen was watching her, so she shuffled forward, making herself breathe deeply as a way of keeping control of her nerves. When it was her turn, she held out her ticket, a much clipped and stamped Inter-rail pass, valid for two more days.

General Medvedev took it and growled, 'Passport!'

Nadya held it out. He checked the entry visa and looked from her face to the photograph several times before returning the document with a growl of: 'You can go.'

Nadya muttered, '*Danke schön,*' and plodded wearily along the platform, disciplining herself not to look back. Halfway along the train, she heard a commotion and turned. One of the three blonde girls who had been hauled out of the queue was screaming in protest as a militiaman held her arms while a female colleague lifted the girl's skirt in full view of passers-by to examine the insides of her thighs. Men were stopping and staring until a bear-like bellow from Medvedev threatened to arrest everyone in sight. A second later everyone was walking past the extraordinary sight with eyes averted, seeing nothing and hearing nothing. It was a moment that epitomised seventy years of the dictatorship of the proletariat.

'They're looking for drugs, I guess,' drawled a Texan voice above Nadya's head.

She looked up. The second-class compartment was full of American college boys, crowding at the windows to see what was going on. From their grins, they seemed to think the body-search was funny.

'Can I join you guys?' Nadya asked in English with a German accent.

'Be my guest!' The Texan opened the door and hauled her backpack aboard then stretched down to help her up.

'Come right on in,' he said. 'There's no spare seat, but I guess a coupla the boys'll squeeze up to make a place for you.'

'Thanks.' Nadya looked back as she scrambled aboard. The third girl was in tears, having been made to lower her jeans while the militiawomen gave her the same search as the other two.

'Real Iron Curtain drama going on over there.' The Texan was staring back down the platform. He had an expensive camcorder in his hand. 'My pa's the Chief of Police back home. I've a mind to shoot off a few frames and show him how the Russkies handle these things.'

'I wouldn't do that,' said Nadya quickly.

'Maybe you're right,' he grinned at her and pulled up the window as the train started to move. Nadya sighed with relief and sank back onto the uncomfortable seat.

'Where you from?' one of the boys asked.

'Berlin,' she said. 'And you?'

'Houston. Say, what's going on now?'

The train jerked to a stop. Luggage fell off the rack. It was several minutes before they were moving again. In the warmth, surrounded by the easy-going friendliness of the American boys and after a few puffs of what they were smoking, Nadya was lulled into a false sense of security long before the door of the compartment was thrown open two hours later by General Medvedev. He was accompanied by two of the armed militiamen and one of the uniformed women.

Medvedev was backing a hunch by working his way through every compartment on the train and checking all the female passengers. In the lining of Lirian's travelling chessboard he had found a first-class ticket for this train. So far he had checked the identity of over two hundred women passengers. If necessary he intended holding the train at the Finnish border until he had examined every female on board in even approximately the right age-group.

'*Ty!*' he beckoned at the girl in glasses. '*Idí syudá!*'

Nadya sat tight. I understand no Russian, she told herself. I'm a German girl from Berlin. My name is Hildegard Sommer. I was born on . . .

'Outside!' growled Medvedev in English.

Before she could move, the Texan boy who had invited Nadya into the carriage stretched out one long leg which ended in a cowboy boot, barring the doorway.

'Now hold your horses, Ivan,' he drawled. 'This lady's with us.'

Medvedev ignored him, staring at Nadya. From the smell in the carriage, he knew that he could have nicked the lot of them on the spot for smoking hash bought from one of the Azeri pushers who worked the Finland Station. One of the boys slid open the small ventilator window and dropped a paper bag outside.

No, Medvedev told himself, holding the green German passport. Lirian would have trained the girl better than to get herself mixed up with riff-raff like this, liable to get her arrested for the wrong reason. And anyway the German girl travelling with the Americans was too dowdy, he thought, to be the Armenian's little tart. He had never looked at her properly, just taken her for granted as another man's sexual property. But now that he thought about it there had been something in the way she looked at Anastas with those hazel eyes of hers that recalled Ludmilla Gutman.

Ah, Ludmilla! She had been so beautiful that even after all these years Medvedev could still recall her face superimposed on the monotonous flat countryside rushing past outside the carriage.

He threw the passport back at Nadya and slammed the door, leaning against it to fight a momentary access of despair. Through the glass he heard the Texan drawl, 'That's the way to handle those guys, Hildegard. I took an option in Psychology last semester. Seems a lot of what the media term police brutality is victim-precipitated – triggered off by the way guys cringe when they get arrested. It's like they're inviting trouble. Before I came over to Europe, my pa told me, "Son, if you get yourself arrested, you just look the guy in the eyes and refuse to back down. That way, you'll get away with most things." Believe me, it works even in Russia.'

'You're very kind,' said Nadya. 'I'll remember that.'

General Medvedev sighed and moved on to the next compartment, and the next and the next – with the hopelessness growing inside him like a cancer.

Plotnik's boffins had hacked their way into the Ministry of the Interior's files for him to check Lirian's claim. It was true: 49578923 Prisoner (female) Gutman, Ludmilla Abramovna, born 23 August 1938, had been sentenced to twenty years in a labour camp under the catch-all Article 58 of the Soviet Constitution (date of incarceration, 2 May 1969). Sent two thousand miles to the east, she had been passed medically fit for heavy labour on the construction of a dam near the Mongolian border where she had given birth to a daughter in the camp hospital four months later. Father was listed as unknown but the child's patronymic was given as Grigorievna, meaning: daughter-of-Grigori.

It was a long time since Medvedev had thought of what it must have been like for his lover in the camp. The old guilt resurfaced, pricked out with new questions. Why had she never contacted him when she knew she was pregnant? Had she not hoped that he would help her for the child's sake? Maybe her pride had kept her silent? Or perhaps she had known too well his overriding ambition and decided not to humiliate herself uselessly one more time? Or again . . . maybe keeping his child's existence a secret had been her only weapon against him?

Revenge, thought Medvedev. Lirian was having his now all right. 'You bastard,' he said aloud. 'You motherfucking Armenian bastard . . .'

Recalling with pleasure the feeling of hitting that already dead head and literally beating the brains out with his fist, he rubbed the knuckles grazed raw by Lirian's teeth.

'*Izvenítye, generál?*' Thrown against him by the rocking of the train, the militiawoman peered into Medvedev's eyes, thinking he was ill. The fire of rage burning there made her recoil.

'He's mad,' she whispered to the man beside her when Medvedev had moved on. 'Stark, raving mad.'

'He's also a general,' he murmured without moving his lips. 'Just do what he says and keep your arse clean. Don't get us involved, for God's sake.'

At the border, Medvedev stepped down from the train, admitting defeat. It had only been a tenuous lead. His mood of hopelessness was gone, replaced by a sullen anger that Lirian had caused him to waste nearly a whole day of his very tight schedule.

On the platform at Helsinki, Nadya said goodbye to the American boys who were bound for the Eurohostel on the island of Katajanokka. She had said she was staying with a Finnish girlfriend but promised to join them for dinner in the self-service restaurant of the Happy Days complex on the

Pohjoisesplanadi where they had heard the food was good and not expensive by Helsinki standards.

Nadya had no intention of being there. She waited until all the passengers from the St Petersburg train had left the station before opening the luggage locker whose key was hidden in the sole of her right trainer shoe.

Inside were two toilet bags. She had bought one of them as a small present for Lirian on a trip abroad; the other was brand-new. Nadya unzipped the first one. It was full of unsigned traveller's cheques in dollars, Deutschmarks and Swiss francs. She zipped it up again and stuffed it inside her anorak. The other bag contained identity papers, some genuine, some forgeries. She replaced the dark blue Canadian passport with the other papers and started reading the long handwritten letter. After the first few lines her vision blurred and it was hard to read on.

A woman passer-by picked up the open bag which Nadya had let drop to the ground. She handed it back to her with a mild scolding in her halting English: 'You should be more careful with your papers, you know.'

Seeing the unhappy, lost look on the girl's face, she asked, 'Are you ill?'

Nadya shook her head. Even if she could have trusted herself to speak, it would have sounded too stupid to tell the woman that she – an experienced KGB-trained prostitute – was reading the first love-letter she had ever received.

.3.

It was late afternoon when Roscoe and Van landed on the right side of Helsinki Airport. Thanks to Madeleine Wharton and Inspector Koskelainen they had lost half a day.

The immigration officer was a plain-looking woman of about Roscoe's age. He charmed her with a wide smile as he handed over his passport. She smiled back, ticking off details on the immigration form.

'Purpose of visit, Mr Roscoe?' she asked.

'Holiday.' He kept the smile in place.

'At the end of November?' She looked up enquiringly. 'Not many tourists come to Finland in the winter months.'

'Cross-country skiing,' said Roscoe.

'You didn't bring your skis?'

'I hire them.'

'And there's no snow yet.'

'In the North,' said Roscoe. 'I thought maybe in Lapland I could do some cross-country stuff – towed by reindeer, that sort of thing.'

'Ah yes.' The rubber-stamp thudded down. 'The Lapps have plenty of snow already. Have a nice stay.'

Roscoe watched from a distance as Van walked through, using her British passport. She was still pale from the shock of what had happened on the launch but seemed to have got a grip on herself otherwise. He hoped she was all right but had no intention of being seen with her until he was sure that Koskelainen had not fed his passport number into some computer. It never occurred to him that she might be the one who was being followed.

Once she was in a taxi, he changed some money into Finnmarks and took the shuttle bus into town, getting off at the main station. He bought a plastic mac and strolled through the drizzle to the Pohjoisesplanadi, Helsinki's answer to the Champs Elysées. There he headed for the Tourist Office, browsed through skiing brochures and picked up a copy of *Helsinki This Week*. At the counter he asked about train times to Savonlinna and Joensuu and where to hire cross-country ski equipment up-country.

Coming out, his attention was drawn by a couple of buskers performing in a bar opposite. They were not very good but the dark-haired girl singer had a vivacity that reminded Roscoe of Maria and the way he had let her down. He dawdled along the Esplanade, mixing with the crowd of mainly young people who did not seem to notice the rain which was turning to sleet. He bought some large-scale maps of Finland and downed a beer at a bar in the Happy Days complex.

Satisfied that no one was tailing him, he took the Metro north to the Hakeniemi stop and walked to the hotel whose address Coetzee had given him. The name had been easy to memorise, with so many double vowels and consonants that the neon sign on the façade looked as though a child had designed it at random from a bowl of alphabet soup. It was a good place to stay: unpretentious, in a quiet street, looking onto a small park. The only shock was in the room prices which were astronomical.

Van met him in the lobby with the news that she had got no reply from either of the telephone numbers which Coetzee had obtained from Larsen. At one, after listening to an unintelligible recorded announcement in Finnish, she had left Roscoe's name and the name of the hotel.

He unpacked, had a shower and slept for a couple of hours, to be woken by Van. She was looking excited. Two men followed her into the room. They could have been Inspector Koskelainen's brothers. They had the same hard faces and unfriendly eyes that made Roscoe wonder whether Finns ever smiled at strangers. Both men were dressed in thick anoraks with the parka hoods unzipped and thrown back.

'Jack Roscoe?' said the shorter one. His booming bass voice came from a barrel chest between a pair of wrestler's arms.

'That's right.' Roscoe's heart sank.

'Hi!' A hand like a shovel shot out and enveloped Roscoe's. 'I'm Arvo Kunnas and this is Pekka Manninen. *Anciens du Premier Regiment Étranger d'Infanterie – à vos ordres!*'

'*A moi, la Légion!*' Roscoe subsided on the bed with a relieved grin; the Legion had come to the rescue. 'Come in. Am I glad to see you boys!'

They closed the door and gave Roscoe and Van a lesson on Finnish beer. There were four strengths: the first was not worth drinking, the second was average, the third no longer existed and the fourth – of which they had brought along a supply – was lethal. One bottle put a man over the legal limit for driving.

Roscoe also learned that Lars Larsen had come up trumps. The extrovert Arvo Kunnas was a boat-builder who had a yard in Kotka, a port only a few miles from the Russian border. As he said, it was a good business to be in, in a land of 188,000 lakes – although Finland was affected by a peculiar recession of its own. 'Our country has lived for twenty years by building Western-style quality hotels, conference centres, airports and roads for the Russians. Now they are broke, they buy no more and so we have much unemployment in Finland.'

Pekka Manninen, the taller of the two blond men, was a slowly-spoken fisherman with an unkempt beard and eyes that were shy of Van although they met Roscoe's levelly enough. He left the talking to his friend whenever possible. It took a while to winkle out of him that he had a boat in the port of Naantali, to the west of Helsinki. It was a small herring boat, far too slow for what Roscoe had in mind.

The third beer was affecting Roscoe's concentration. He put the bottle aside and opened the window to breathe some cold air. Behind his back, a quizzical look passed between the two Finns.

'You better level with us, Jack,' boomed Arvo. 'What's the problem? Larsen said something about an old Legion buddy in trouble. We'll help if we can, but what kind of trouble is this guy in?'

'Russian trouble,' said Roscoe. 'He's on the wrong side of the border.'

'He is Russian citizen?' asked Arvo warily.

'No,' said Van. 'He's Canadian.'

Arvo laughed in evident relief. 'Then the border guards won't stop him leaving, unless he's set fire to the Kremlin. He can come out by train or in a car at the Nuijamaa or Vaalimaa crossing-points. No problem. What did he do, overstay his visa because of some girl trouble?'

'By about six years,' said Roscoe.

'Huh?'

'He's been in a special camp in the Gulag and the Russians are so fond of him, they don't want him to leave.'

'So?' Arvo looked at his friend. The two Finnish faces went blank and unfriendly again.

'I want your help to get him out.' Roscoe looked from one to the other.

'Impossible,' they said in chorus.

'If I can get him as far as the border,' persisted Roscoe, 'can I count on you guys from there on?'

They laughed.

Arvo spread one of Roscoe's maps on the bed to explain the realities of life.

'You got to understand our position geographical, Jack,' he boomed. 'Since a thousand years we Finns are fighting either the Swedes to the west or the Russians to the east. Right now the Swedes are the good guys and Swedish is our second official language. All same, since the 1948 Peace Treaty was signed with Moscow, our government is most strict to make no nuisance along the eastern border. You live next door to a crazy bear, you don't poke sticks through the bars, right?'

He took another draught of beer and hunched forward over the map, drawing a thick thumbnail along the border. 'On the Russian side of the frontier, Jack, you got a forbidden zone fifteen to twenty kilometres wide, all the way along the border.'

'Can you go round it?'

A shake of the head. 'It's 1289 kilometres from south to north! They got ski troops, helicopters, dogs, minefields – the lot. And if you get your pal through all that shit, you are in the Rajavyöhyke.'

'What's that?'

The two Finns looked slightly embarrassed. 'That's our forbidden zone,' grunted Pekka. 'On Finnish territory it is, but no one goes there without special permit.'

'Tell me about it.'

Arvo sighed and started his fourth bottle. 'This thing is not something we talk about, Jack. Even many Finns don't know it. In the Rajavyöhyke – the zone is four kilometres deep – you may not light a match, shine a torch, use binoculars, take photograph or even raise your voice! The penalty for any of those things can be two years in prison, right?'

Roscoe nodded soberly. He had known that getting to the Russian side of the border would be difficult but had not expected complications like this.

'How do you know so much about this Raja . . . this forbidden zone?' Van asked.

'I have a sister who lives . . .' Arvo's thumbnail scored a groove in the map no more than twenty miles from the Villa Orlova. '. . . just about there.'

'You visit her?' asked Van.

'In summer,' Arvo admitted. 'But to do that I need local police permit, Jack. Even I who am Finnish citizen cannot pass the night in own sister's home. We Finns are very law-abiding race, but such things make Marja – my sister – real angry.'

Roscoe stuck his head out of the window and took several deep breaths of the cold outside air.

'I'm sorry,' said Pekka in his slow voice. 'We would like to help this buddy in trouble, Jack. But I don't think there is a single thing we can do until he is on our side of the border and clear of the Rajavyöhyke. Then, of course you can count on us to make sure he is not picked up and handed back.'

'What about by sea?' Van interrupted.

The two Finns looked as though it was news to them that most of the planet's surface was covered by water.

'Sea?' asked Pekka, scratching his beard doubtfully.

'Yeah,' said Roscoe. 'The wet stuff your boat floats on, you know.'

'Tell him, Pekka,' boomed Arvo.

'The trouble, Jack,' said Pekka gloomily, 'is that the border goes right out to sea, like so.'

He traced it on the map with hands that were scarred by cuts which had healed slowly, forever wet with salt water. 'It's policed day and night by Russian and Finnish patrol vessels. The net is so tight not even a herring can slip through.'

Roscoe saw in his mind the line of yellow buoys and recalled the slick efficiency of the Spetsnaz crew on board the launch that had kept the rendezvous with the Royal Navy frigate. His spirits sank.

'Let's just worry about the Russians,' he said doggedly, staring out of the window for inspiration. 'You're not going to tell me that the skipper of a Finnish patrol boat will hand us back to the other side?'

Pekka did not reply. Roscoe turned around. 'Well, would he?'

The big Finnish fisherman shifted unhappily. 'Jack, these things you don't understand. But yes, when an illicit boat is intercepted out of sight of land with no witnesses, it does happen so.'

'You're kidding!' Roscoe exploded. 'The Finnish Navy does the Russians' job for them? What kind of a country is this?'

'It's a country of five million people,' said Arvo coldly. 'And we live next door to one hundred fifty million Russians who used to own this little land of ours. So you work it out for yourself. The reality of life here is tougher than you think, Jack — never mind the climate. Until a year ago, even those refugees who made it right to Helsinki were put back across the border if picked up by the Finnish police, right? Their only chance was to get to a Western embassy and claim asylum. If our Security

Police got them first, they were handed back to be locked up in a mental home over there for several years – or maybe worse.'

The big fisherman was looking gloomier than ever. 'Jack, I tell you,' he said in his lugubrious voice. 'I have cousin who is skipper of Finnish frontier patrol boat. He says their Standing Orders are like Ten Commandments. The First Commandment – you might say it is . . .' He broke into Finnish.

Arvo translated: 'Thou shalt not poke sticks into the bear's cage, Jack. Nothing else matters, right?'

'I don't believe all this.' Roscoe's frustration was making him angry. 'The Cold War is over everywhere else. Why is it still going on up here?'

Arvo finished his fifth beer. It did not seem to have had any effect on him.

'We know the Russian mentality, Jack,' he said. 'Right now, there are a lot of very disturbed guys sitting in the Kremlin. All those former Soviet Republics have shit on Moscow. Right? So the Bear would sure like to have an excuse to kick arse and make himself feel better. It's natural. Trouble is, whose arse? The former Soviet Republics have more weapons than people, all left behind by the Red Army. But Finland would make a convenient victim: we're next door, we have a very small army and we don't belong to Nato. Moscow could kick us – how you say? – kick us to buggery and probably get away with it.'

'Why would they want to do that?'

Arvo laughed. 'It would be a good way of distracting the population from so many internal problems – like your Mrs Thatcher used the Falklands War, you know? So for the time being, Helsinki makes sure our eastern frontier stays nice and calm. If anything, it's sewn up tighter than it was – and it will stay that way until the political temperature in Russia cools down.'

Roscoe exhaled in a loud groan. 'Thanks for the briefing,' he said wryly. 'Now let me buy you guys some dinner in return.'

'Tell us about yourself, Jack,' said Arvo as they made their way down to the dining-room. 'What's your job when you're not rescuing old buddies from the Gulag?'

Musician? Spy? Soldier? Roscoe never knew what to reply. 'You might say I was once a professional poker of sticks into bears' cages,' he answered. It was a poor joke, but the best he could manage. 'What do you call that in Finnish?'

'A fool,' boomed Arvo.

'A dead fool,' said Pekka quietly.

. 4 .

A mile away from the alphabet soup hotel, in a bedroom on the fifth floor of the Holiday Inn, Nadya was standing by the window, looking out at the lights of the city and feeling lonely.

She had had a busy afternoon shopping on the Pohjois-esplanadi and neighbouring streets, buying mainly clothes, jewellery and accessories. Twice she had been within seconds of bumping into Roscoe but neither of them would ever know.

She had skipped lunch altogether but had no appetite. The dish of mixed hors d'oeuvres that she had ordered from room service lay beside a plate of fruit on the dressing-table and both were untouched. Looking out of the window, she saw below her the mournful grey Baltic town coming to life as evening fell and the twinkling lights pierced the snow-haze, reflecting in the water of the harbour inlet below her window.

Nadya was feeling more alone than she could ever remember. From birth to age eighteen she had lived in dormitories. At Verkhonoye there had been no solitude and even on her assignments abroad before Lirian discovered her she had always been closely controlled – swallows were well rewarded but never given the freedom to fly away. Now she was completely alone for the first time in her life and it was disturbing.

If Anastas were here, she thought, what would he tell me to do? Work first, he always said, and play afterwards. Well, there's a lot to do, working up my new identity – so let's get on with it, Nadya.

She corrected herself immediately. Not Nadya, not Hildegard but Renata. That was her new name.

She took the documents that Lirian had prepared for her out of the second toilet bag and spread them on the small correspondence table. It was hard to concentrate because the mood was wrong. After half an hour of more day-dreaming than concentration she gave up and took the letter from her new handbag, to read it one last time.

My dearest Nadya,

If you are reading this letter without me beside you, you will know that I made all the right moves and yet lost the game. That happens in chess as in life.

My only regret is that I shall not look again upon your dear face, nor see the beauty of your body, nor hear your beloved voice that is the only music I have ever known. Believe what you like of me, Nadya, but know that I truly loved you.

If I could have proved it physically, would things have been any better? No, although some beautiful young women do love far older men, I do not think you are such a person! In any case, Nadya mine, I should not have wanted you to compare me to the other men who have used your body. Somehow I hope you consider my love the purer for that.

Nadya put down the letter. Consider my love the purer . . . Whatever did he mean?

Anastas had never made love to her physically but he had enjoyed watching her walk around naked and getting dressed in the clothes he gave as presents. She supposed that he had gone into the bathroom afterwards to masturbate – it was one of the syndromes they had learned about at the training school –

but since he had never wanted her to help in whatever relief he needed, she had not enquired.

As other men are given sexual prowess, I was prodigiously gifted to play a game – which is a fairly ridiculous thing for which to thank God. I shall have something to say to Him about that very shortly.

In life I have been no angel as you know. My motives for taking you away from the trade for which you were trained were purely selfish to begin with, I admit. I little imagined that by doing so, I was making myself vulnerable to love for the first time in my life!

Consider my love . . . The phrase would not leave Nadya's consciousness. She stopped reading and wondered again, had he loved her? Had she loved him? She had accepted his obsession with her because it made for a better life than that of a swallow, but had she actually loved him?

Perhaps I did, she thought. What I felt when I knew he was dead was different from any other emotion I ever felt. Maybe it was like that when my mother died, I can't remember . . .

Do I love you as a man loves a woman – in all but the physical act – or as a father loves a daughter? I think the latter, for it was your helplessness, the way you were so totally in my power, that engendered all my feelings for you. Truly I do not know the answer myself, Nadya mine, for I have nothing with which to compare my emotions for you. In any case it is futile for those of us who do not conform to any norm, to try and pigeon-hole ourselves or our emotions by using other people's labels.

Know that you gave me great joy in many ways. All I can give you in return you will find enclosed with this letter. There is enough money in the unsigned traveller's cheques to last you for a couple of weeks. Sign them immediately and use them for all your needs. In the West, always travel first class and stay in good hotels. That way, no one will ask you questions. A room has been reserved at the Holiday Inn for you in your new name: Renata Witzig. Also today, buy yourself a completely new wardrobe, my dear. Get rid of all your clothes, luggage and possessions immediately.

That had been fun: shopping – buying anything that took her fancy, from Italian shoes to a fur coat. But it had been lonely too, after so long with Anastas always there for Nadya to ask him: 'Does it suit me?'

I have given you a Canadian identity for the same reasons I created one for Molody/Lonsdale and so many of our illegals: Canadians are welcome anywhere in the world so you can choose where you want to live! Also, there is no such thing as a Canadian accent – or rather there are thousands of accents in Canada, a land of new immigrants. The way you speak English now will pass without comment until you absorb a little transatlantic twang! A bonus of being Canadian is that you can go freely into the United States.

Renata means reborn. You can put together the legend of your ancestry from the enclosed documents. Everything is there: from your birth certificate to the death certificates of your parents. The real Renata Witzig was a Swiss-born Red Cross nurse who died in the Sudan while doing famine-relief work. She never visited North America. You are a good liar – trained by the best teachers! – so I am sure you will develop an impenetrable legend for yourself, my dear Miss Witzig.

As soon as you get to Canada, you must claim the funds from the two Swiss accounts which I set up for us. Identify yourself by the number on your new passport and the code-phrase: 'Nadya is Reborn.' What could be simpler? The accounts are joint and several, which means that you do not need a second signature. You will be surprised at the sums on deposit in Miss Witzig's name!

You will be free and rich! You are already beautiful! What more could I wish you? May I make one request, which perhaps sounds very stupid? When and if you marry – and I hope it is for love as well as riches – will you say a prayer for the soul of Anastas Lirian on that day?

Yes, she thought, I'll do that. I'll say: '. . . and God bless Anastas without whom . . .' She shuddered. 'Without whom my life would have been hell.'

> *A few warnings I bequeath you, my dearest Nadya. Do not be tempted to keep the passport used on the train from St Petersburg – it could be traced. And all your life, beware of any relationship with a Russian. Of the whole nation, avoid Grigori Sergeyevich Medvedev like the plague. It was Medvedev who caused your mother's death and mine. Believe me when I say that he would kill you also, given the chance.*
>
> *I should have liked this last letter to be more poetic, more romantic, more loving – but there it is. The clock is running and I must make my move.*
>
> *With my undying affection,*
> *Anastas R. Lirian.*
> *PS Now burn this letter immediately. Do not be tempted to keep it.*

The word *affection* had been crossed out and replaced by *LOVE!*

Nadya had cried the first time she read the letter in the railway station. This time, although her thoughts were sombre the letter was not a cause to weep, but more like a boundary post marking the end of the past and the beginning of the future. She was, as Lirian had written, free for the first time in her life, alone and in a strange country – literally with the world before her. It was both frightening and very exciting.

There was a knock on the door. A bell-boy handed to Nadya a parcel of lingerie – the third delivery of clothes which she had bought that afternoon. She dumped the parcel on the bed with the two others and went into the bathroom, where she used a match to set light to Lirian's letter.

She flushed the ashes down the toilet pan. One unburnt piece floated back to the surface. On it were the words *Medvedev who caused your mother's* . . . She saw in memory the general's angry face, shouting at her on the train. It made her shudder. What would have been her fate if he had seen through her disguise? Hauled into the corridor and stripped by the militia-woman, her birthmark revealed, would she have ended her days back in a camp like the one where her mother had died? She knew too much to believe the popular myth that they had all been abolished.

Nadya flushed the last obstinate pieces of paper away and sat on the edge of the bath for a long while before setting fire also to the photograph she had taken illicitly of Anastas Lirian one spring day in Gorky Park. It was badly framed and crooked; she had been holding the camera sideways, pretending to photograph some children feeding a squirrel, in order not to alarm him. In the picture Lirian was watching her with a gentle smile on his face that would have surprised anyone who had known him professionally.

Anastas would have been so angry, she thought, if he had known about the picture and even angrier that she had been so unprofessional as to carry it with her on the train, tucked inside her bra. As his face was consumed by the flame Nadya dropped what was left of the photograph into the water. She wondered what Toronto was like. According to some of the documents in the toilet bag, she was the owner of a duplex in a condominium overlooking Lake Ontario.

She stood up and stretched, repeating aloud her new legend and erasing the old: 'I am Renata Witzig from Toronto . . .'

She rehearsed it by picking up the telephone and talking into the mouthpiece with what she thought might be a passable transatlantic accent: 'Hallo, I'm Renata Witzig from Toronto . . .'

When she had finished the script she hung up the phone and removed her silk Japanese kimono dressing-gown. It was new, but her underclothes were not. She unhooked her bra and dropped it with her pants into the waste bin beneath the vanity unit. Looking at herself in the full-length mirror, she saw that she was beautiful. Her hair, shampooed in the hotel's hairdressing salon, was restored to its natural colour. The urchin style did not suit her face but her hair grew fast and would soon be long enough for her usual style. But perhaps she should change that, to be on the safe side? Yes, Anastas would have insisted on that . . .

She cupped her breasts and slid her hands down her smooth belly, turning sideways on as she had turned for him to admire her. He had never spoken when she was naked in front of him, just followed her adoringly with his glittering eyes.

Her beauty was flawless, apart from the one small birth-mark on the inside of her thigh. Every man who had seen her naked, had desired her – even Anastas in his way. She wondered what the Texan boys would say if they could see her as she really was. Her Plain Jane act had really fooled them! They had been so polite and protective of her on the train journey, treating her like a sister, she thought. That had never happened to her before. It was rather nice. From now on she would only go to bed with men she really fancied.

She recalled her first mission as a swallow. The target had been a middle-aged politician in Bonn. He had sweated on top of Nadya for a few minutes while two men photographed them through a fibre optic tube inserted in the wall. The incident had been no more disgusting than the advances of the other old men with whom she had had to make love during her training. It was something she would never have to do again.

Nadya gazed at her reflection in the glass, wondering. She leaned forward and moved from side to side, studying the movement of her breasts as they swung beneath her. Would some Canadian or American millionaire fall in love with her body?

'You're day-dreaming, Nadya,' she accused herself in Russian.

Immediately she corrected both language and name: 'I am Renata Witzig from Toronto. I was born on . . .'

In any case, she warned herself, it would not be a good idea to aim for a millionaire, for such a man would use private detectives to check her story. She must be careful and choose a husband only moderately rich. That would be safer. And would she be able really to fall in love? Would she ever forget the lessons and the tricks she had learned, the films that all the girls had been forced to watch of themselves whoring with young men and old ones, to the accompaniment of Lydia Furtseva's dispassionate voice criticising sexual technique like a sports coach discussing the moves in yesterday's game?

She shivered, mentally brushing up all the crumbs from her

memories – the good and the bad – to dump them in the toilet with the ashes of Lirian's picture. She would start the future by spending a few days in Helsinki getting used to her new identity before trying it out in Canada.

The cistern had refilled itself. Renata Witzig pressed the lever and watched the last traces of her other selves disappear down the swirling vortex.

.5.

'Jack?'
        'Yeah?'
    'Can I come in?'

Roscoe padded to the door and found Van standing in the corridor wearing only a thin silk peignoir over matching pyjamas. In London he had bought an instant wardrobe at Marks & Spencer on Oxford Street to replace the clothes borrowed from the SBS men, but it had cost Van a small fortune in plastic money to replace her missing luggage and clothes at the Gatwick Airport boutiques while they were waiting for the return flight to Helsinki.

'I'm cold,' she said. 'Do you mind if I get into bed with you?'
He hesitated.
'Don't get the wrong idea. It's not your body I'm after.'
'It can't be my brain,' Roscoe grunted.

He had spent the dark hours in a nightmare timescape, running hopelessly up immense sand-dunes in a vast egg-timer, trying to reach first Maria and then Bergman before they were sucked down and buried for ever beneath the shifting sands of time. He felt Van shiver beside him and pulled the duvet over her as she snuggled down in the bed.

'What's the plan for tomorrow?' she asked.

Switching out the light, he played for time. 'I'll tell you in the morning.'

'This is like old times,' she squeezed his hand. 'We made a good team professionally – you and me.'

'That was different,' he said. 'Then we had back-up.'

Van sensed the doubts in Roscoe's mind and the effect on his morale of Medvedev's last-minute volte-face. 'We're better off without the Service, if that's what's worrying you. We're experi-enced Intelligence officers, Jack – as good as they come, or better. And we can count on each other one hundred per cent, which is more than one can say for some of our former colleagues.'

He lay silent.

'What was the first thing,' she asked rhetorically, 'on the List of Operational Essentials that we were taught?'

'Intelligence.'

'We've got it,' she said. 'Nobody's more up to date than us about what to expect on the other side of the border. Next?'

'Authority for Decision.'

'We make our own. What's left?'

'Funding and Resources,' he said grimly. 'I've got most of my ten thousand sterling left but it's not enough to fart with. To run a clandestine op costs money, you know that.'

'It's ironic,' she said, 'but if I'd thought faster, back at the Villa Orlova, we'd have several million dollars to play with right now.'

She told him of the roomful of faked regalia in the Villa Orlova and the two Fabergé eggs which she could have slipped into her handbag while Medvedev and Plotnik were busy slang-ing each other.

'Are you sure?' he asked.

'It's my job,' she said. 'Of course I'm sure, Jack. If I can grab those two eggs next time round, we'll all be millionaires, several times over.'

Roscoe was silent for several minutes, then: 'We're supposing Bergman's still being held there, at the villa or in the Spetsnaz base nearby.'

'Oh, he's there,' said Van.

'How can you be sure?'

She rationalised with: 'At this stage in preparing their coup to put Anton on the throne, Plotnik and Medvedev are not going to waste time and transport taking Peter back to some camp in the Gulag, are they? They've got more important things to think about.'

'Medvedev could have put a 9 mm. bullet in his head,' Roscoe objected, 'before they even got back to shore.'

I might as well tell him, thought Van. She gripped Roscoe's hand tighter in the darkness. 'I know Peter's alive. I always knew somehow that he hadn't actually died that night on the border. But I told myself he was dead, so I could get on with making a new life. The alternative was too hard to handle, do you understand? I'm not like those Vietnam wives and girl-friends who went on fighting for their missing husbands and lovers, year after year.'

She paused for a moment. 'I have to say this, Jack. I admire the way you went on fighting for Peter, even when it cost your job. I wish I'd had that kind of courage.'

Roscoe did not speak, so Van lifted his hand and brushed her lips against it.

She was dozing off when he put the light on and climbed out of bed, grabbing some hotel notepaper on which to make lists before the whole intricate web of timing and logistics fell to pieces in his mind.

'Can you write a cheque right now for, say ten thousand ster-ling?' he asked.

'No problem. I could double that if you want.'

He filled her in with the details as he wrote, then looked at the sheet of paper. The columns were headed *ME* and *VAN*. He tore the sheet in two and passed one half to her. Outside the window, a grey dawn was rubbing its eyes and trying to sum-mon the will to get out of bed.

'I'll handle the seaborne logistics,' he said, 'while you look after the landward side of things.'

The journey by taxi to Arvo Kunnas's boatyard in Kotka seemed to take an eternity. Roscoe used the time to work out how much he could safely tell the burly Finnish ex-legionnaire.

He had the choice of divulging everything or nothing. Since he had no duty of secrecy to anyone, it was better to give Arvo the full picture.

He kept the driver waiting and walked through a forest of boats winterised on stocks and under tarpaulins to find Arvo busy using an oxy-acetylene cutter on the bent fin of a shark-like steel-bodied hydrofoil of his own design. Watching him was Pekka Manninen, still looking as gloomy as ever.

The buckled plane dropped free, sizzling on the wet ground. Arvo turned off the oxygen, reducing the cutter flame to a smoky flare. He pushed the mask back from his face and nodded a welcome to Roscoe before picking up the metal with his gauntleted hands and tossing it into a puddle to cool it down faster.

Arvo's office reminded Roscoe for a moment of Coetzee's old base back in the Transvaal: spare parts rubbed shoulders with half-drunk mugs of coffee on a carpet of overdue bills. Over mugs of coffee which Pekka laced with *akvavit* Roscoe swore both Finns to silence and sketched out his plan for them.

'What makes you think this guy Plotnik will leave the border completely unguarded?' Arvo asked.

'I know my man.' Roscoe sounded one hundred per cent certain. 'Just about the last thing he'll be worrying about on the day is trouble from the west. Any real threat will come from the opposite direction, i.e. Moscow. Plotnik has to spread his troops thin on the ground. He'll calculate that by the time the world has realised the border troops have been withdrawn, the *coup d'état* will be over. There's virtually no risk in having the border open for a few hours; it's the sort of inspired gamble that a soldier of Plotnik's breed likes. But those few hours give us our window.'

'Hold it,' objected Pekka. 'Does this Spetsnaz colonel command all the troops along this stretch of the frontier? I seem to remember they're doubled up with MVD border patrols which are not under his command.'

'Don't worry,' Roscoe grinned. 'The MVD troops are there to catch refugees, smugglers, that sort of thing. We'll be moving too fast for them to do anything about it, except jump out of the way. Our weapons are speed and timing.'

The two pairs of cold blue eyes thawed as he got into his

stride. Brief excited exchanges in Finnish passed between them; the idea of stealing a march on the Russians while their big neighbour's eyes were closed for a few hours, appealed to both men. Pekka knew from his cousin in the frontier patrol that the Russians had several times over the years withdrawn all troops from the border for manoeuvres, so Roscoe's guess made sense to him.

Arvo spoke for both Finns: 'It's about time that Pekka and I did something more exciting together than just get drunk at the weekend. You know, Jack, I think this plan of yours could work. But by God, you will need a fast boat.'

He leafed through a pile of boating magazines and jotted down a list of possibles on an oil-begrimed message pad.

'Top of the range is a Birchwood TS 54, lying on the west coast, not far from Naantali where Pekka comes from. It has two 1,000-horsepower MAN diesels – plenty of power to play with.'

'What's it cost?' Roscoe blinked at the asking price of £350,000.

'OK,' continued Arvo. 'Next we have a Searay Sundancer, lying at Mariehamn. Twin 375-horsepower Caterpillar diesels. Asking price: 159,000 pounds. No?'

'Cheaper,' said Roscoe.

'A Hunton Maverick 34. Decca navigation equipment, VHF radio, colour television, stereo, central heating, microwave, ceramic hob and fridge . . .'

'I'm not thinking of living on it, Arvo. One trip across the Gulf of Finland is all . . .'

'She's powered by two Mercruiser 454 Magnum engines and has Kiekhafer trim tabs. The owner guarantees she will do seventy knots in the right conditions. Asking price is eighty-five thousand pounds, Jack.'

Roscoe stroked his chin and realised that he had forgotten to shave that morning. All he had in his pocket was Madeleine Wharton's £10,000 and a cheque of Van's for the same amount. 'Twenty thousand sterling,' he said. 'Say thirty thousand dollars. What can I buy with that, Arvo?'

Arvo put down the magazines. 'Not much, Jack. Power boats are rich men's toys. And another thing I didn't tell you. I would say all these boats are out of the water, under tarps, maybe with the motors stripped down or taken out for overhaul. In Finland people don't go to sea for pleasure in the winter. So how soon do you leave for Russia?'

'Like today. And tomorrow is maybe when I need the boat.'

'No chance.' Arvo shook his head.

Through the drizzle-spattered window Pekka's gaze alighted on the hydrofoil. He nudged Arvo in the ribs.

'Goddam,' said Arvo. 'Why not? It will be some kind of a test for my boat, hey? If you help me, Pekka, and we work all night . . .'

He pushed aside Roscoe's money with: 'We are all in this thing together, Jack. *On est tous des légionnaires ici.*'

But Roscoe insisted, 'If anything goes wrong, I want you to be covered by a signed bill of sale so that, on paper, it's my boat. And you must have the money in your bank account to back that up.' The least he could do was give Arvo a dorsal 'chute in case there was a snafu.

He spent the next two hours picking the Finns' brains and trying to cover all the possible contingencies that might crop up in Bergman's rescue. It was midday when he arrived back at the alphabet soup hotel in Helsinki to find Van the less-than-proud owner of an ancient Alfa Romeo 1600 convertible with 120,000 kilometres on the clock. The white bodywork was patterned with rust, the hood was torn.

'. . . and there's something wrong with the carburettor,' she said, 'so that at each red light it's like being on the starting grid at Brands Hatch. If you don't keep revving up, she'll stall.'

'Was that the best you could do?'

'You try, Jack Roscoe,' she said. 'You just try and buy a convertible sports car in the middle of the Finnish winter. Every garage I rang thought I was crazy, including the man who sold me this heap of rust.'

She kicked the wing and a shower of mud and rust fell onto the slush in the gutter. 'And as for getting insurance to take a soft top into Russia . . . I leave you to imagine the problems. It cost more than I paid for the car and I had to sign a piece of paper saying that the car will be locked up and guarded every night.'

She had been given a booklet in English entitled *What To Do*

When You Break Down In Russia. Roscoe flicked through it. Most of the advice could be summed up in one word: don't.

They went into the dining-room. Roscoe had the feeling that the late lunch might be their last meal for a long while. He drank a lot of coffee and ordered a double portion of ham and eggs from the kitchen followed by generous helpings of several different cheeses from the buffet table. Nothing had any taste; he was too busy going over in his mind all the arrangements.

The question in his mind, as always when setting out on a clandestine operation was not 'Have I forgotten anything?' but 'What have I forgotten?'

.6.

They checked out of the hotel and drove eastwards out of the city with Roscoe at the wheel. As Van had warned him, the throttle seemed to have only two settings: *fast* and *stop*. Roscoe would have liked to strip down the carburettor if he had had any tools. Several times he stalled at red lights. At the city limits Van navigated them onto the dual carriageway leading towards the Russian border. There was a sign reading: St Petersburg 433 kilometres. Most of the long-distance traffic was made up of heavy trucks.

It was now that they found the heater did not work. Luckily Van had purchased a pair of bulky *après-ski* anoraks. They put them on and tried to keep warm as Roscoe overtook transporter after transporter loaded with top-of-the-range Volvos, BMWs and Mercedes.

'Someone in Russia,' said Van, 'has to be making a lot of money to pay for them all.'

Arvo had warned Roscoe that traffic would be heavy because the next day was a national holiday: Independence Day.

'*Självständighetsdagen*,' he had called it in Swedish.

And Pekka had joked in his gloomy voice: 'Try saying it in Finnish – *Itsenäisyyspäivä.*'

'Independence from whom?' Roscoe had asked.

'From the Russians, of course,' they had told him.

The weather worsened as Roscoe drove east. Sleet mixed with snow was settling on the ground and hardening, making driving dangerous. Near the frontier Roscoe deliberately drove off the international highway and into the forbidden zone of which Arvo and Pekka had talked: the Rajavyöhyke.

Within two hundred metres a Finnish border guard lieutenant with the same unfriendly eyes as Inspector Koskelainen was curtly examining their passports and the papers for the car and redirecting them back onto the main road. The two guards behind the lieutenant were wearing white cotton snow-camouflage smocks and trousers over their uniforms. They were armed with automatic rifles and looked alert and fit, unbothered by the foul weather.

There was a long file of trucks waiting on the Russian side of the border-crossing at Vaalimaa. Roscoe walked through driving sleet to the head of the queue, braving the bored looks of the truckers dozing in their cabins, eating and listening to the radio while they waited their turn. He parted with ten US dollars to a green-tabbed border lieutenant for the privilege of jumping the queue and drove into Russia with a salute and what might have been a smile.

On the verge were notices in several languages warning drivers not to divert from the main road and not to leave their cars in the event of breakdowns, but to stay in them until help arrived. There were also less obvious notices further away from the road which warned of mines. Roscoe dawdled along at the speed of the slowest trucks, taking everything in.

He nearly missed the turning that led to Plotnik's empire. Unmetalled, it was designed to be even less conspicuous to traffic approaching from the west than from Vyborg. Roscoe clamped on the brakes and slewed the Alfa off the busy highway onto the grass verge, reversing back until he was level with the turn-off. He opened the driver's window to see better and got a faceful of freezing slush as a German truck swished past. It was hard to be certain that this was the right place; from where

Roscoe sat the alleyway between the trees looked like a fire-break or a loggers' road at best. There was a gap in the central reservation right opposite the turning.

He decided to back his hunch, took advantage of a brief lull in the traffic to bump back up onto the road and accelerated across both carriageways, skidding past the No Entry sign and fish-tailing down the icy track for a hundred metres until he could straighten out the Alfa.

Roscoe heaved a sigh of relief at the first bend as the sandy soil gave way to a well-made road surface. It was the right road after all. Remembering the police checkpoint just after the first tight bend he changed down with a prayer, 'Don't stall on me now, you bastard!' He had no desire to be arrested by the wrong people.

His right foot stamped on the pedal and they accelerated round the bend in a controlled skid. Alerted by the sound of the overrevving engine, two GAI traffic policemen ran out of the wooden hut beside the red-and-white boom calling on him to stop.

'Duck!' Roscoe shouted at Van.

He gritted his teeth and lined up the centre of the car's bon-net with the mid-point of the barrier. At the last moment he ducked his own head below the level of the dashboard, close to Van's. They heard the boom tear across the bonnet and smash into the windscreen before breaking in two with a crack like the noise of a light howitzer. Windscreen and roof were torn off in an explosion of wood from the barrier mixed with glass, metal and canvas from the Alfa.

Roscoe sat upright in the now topless sports car and jammed his feet on the brake and clutch pedals. Somehow he freed his right hand to shove Van's head back beneath the dashboard. The next few seconds' timing was literally life-and-death. If he slowed too soon, the armed police behind him would still have time to loose off a few shots. If he slowed too late, Plotnik's men at the blockhouse on the next bend would welcome them with a far more lethal hail of nickel-clad death.

Alerted by the noise, they were waiting and ready as he skid-ded round the icy bend and into view: a Spetsnaz lieutenant and two men in white snow-camouflage fatigues with AK 74s in their hands. From the blockhouse itself, the muzzle of a heavy-calibre machine-gun followed the progress of the car with the damaged hood flapping at the rear like a giant bat from hell.

Roscoe kept his foot on the brake pedal and raised both hands off the wheel, high in the air where they must be clearly visible. To stop the car he chose the simple expedient of letting it skid off the road and into a tree. With a hiss of escaping steam, the radiator cracked and the car settled lopsidedly on the side where the bent wing had punctured a tyre.

An AK 74 trained unwaveringly between Roscoe's eyes, the nearest guard jerked his head. '*Vydíte!*' he said: get out!

A second man grabbed the door handle. With a creak of bent metal the door was pulled open and Roscoe stepped gingerly out, hands still held in front of him. As soon as his feet touched the ground, he was spun round and slammed against the car, his head pushed brutally forward and down onto the damaged bonnet. For a second of excruciating pain he thought his nose was broken. Blood filled both nostrils and ran across the Alfa's scratched and dented white paintwork.

Roscoe's hands were grabbed and twisted behind his back, the anorak wrenched off and thrown on the ground. He felt handcuffs click tight on his wrists. Someone kicked his legs apart and away from the Alfa until he was leaning on the car at nearly forty-five degrees. Only then was he frisked very efficiently from head to toe. One by one all the items in his pockets were slammed onto the blood-smeared bonnet of the Alfa.

On the other side of the car, Van was being dealt with a little less violently by the other armed guard.

Roscoe swallowed blood and spoke in Russian: 'Now may I stand up?'

'*Nyet*,' said the lieutenant.

'This is a test exercise,' Roscoe bluffed. His blood-filled nostrils made his voice sound as though he had a heavy cold. 'Colonel Plotnik asked me to check up on how good you guys were.'

'Load of crap,' said the officer to the guard standing behind Roscoe. 'If he doesn't shut up, kick his balls in.'

The jeep from the villa did not arrive for a quarter of an hour. Within minutes Roscoe and Van were suffering muscle cramps from the uncomfortable position and shivering with the biting cold. Each time Roscoe asked permission to stand up or tried to talk to Van, he got a Kalashnikov muzzle rammed painfully into his kidneys and the threat of worse if he did not shut his mouth. The same thing happened whenever he raised his face from the now freezing metal of the car bonnet. The only good news was that his nose stopped bleeding.

If there had been any doubt that they were in the hands of Plotnik's men, it would have disappeared during that interminable quarter-hour of pain and cold. From time to time he heard other vehicles passing, wheels swishing through the deep slush. Judging by the noise and the occasional sideways look he could sneak, they were all civilian cars. Business, it seemed, was hotting up at the Villa Orlova. Off the road surface, among the trees, the snow was lying and building up fast.

'Mr Roscoe?'

He stood up warily and turned to find a bespectacled female Spetsnaz NCO getting out of the passenger seat of an open jeep, her face half hidden in a fur-lined parka.

'Ab I glad to see you,' he said, teeth chattering and nostrils blocked.

'It isn't mutual,' said Ekaterina Borisovna. She stared at his bloody face and rain-sodden hair.

'Did they beat you up?' she asked in English.

'Doh, doh,' he said. 'I'b a compulsib blood dodor.'

'You have only yourself to blame,' she said, unamused. 'You're not supposed to be here, Mr Roscoe. Nor the girl.'

Ekaterina looked for a moment at the wrecked Alfa before going into the blockhouse to talk with the lieutenant. Van was allowed to go with her to get warm. Roscoe stood massaging the cramps out of the muscles in each leg by rubbing it with the other foot. The cold metal of the cuffs was burning the flesh of his wrists and he was still shivering uncontrollably; his new quilted anorak lay in the mud and slush. He could hear Ekaterina talking in Russian over the telephone inside the blockhouse but was unable to pick up what she was saying.

Roscoe looked around cautiously. One of the guards was still watching him with a sly grin, as though he was waiting for an excuse to put the boot in.

Plotnik's men were good – very good, Roscoe thought admiringly. There was a second blockhouse on the other side of the roadway fifty metres away, which he had not seen the first time he had driven past. It was completely hidden in earth and greenery. In it was what looked to Roscoe like the muzzle of an anti-tank rocket-launcher, trained on the Alfa. For all he knew there were other concealed guard posts. In any event, the interlocking fields of fire of the two blockhouses would take care of any likely intruder up to and including the size of a main-battle tank.

The ride to the villa was uncomfortable in the under-sprung jeep. It was freezing cold, even when Van draped her anorak loosely over Roscoe's shoulders. With his hands still cuffed behind his back, unable to hold on or brace himself, he was nearly hurled out of the open vehicle at every bump. The armed guard sitting between him and Van laughed his head off each time this happened.

At the villa Roscoe saw a familiar bulky figure getting into a stretched Volga limousine and called out, 'General Medvedev!'

The car stopped level with the jeep and Medvedev looked across at Roscoe and Van as though they were two strangers he had never seen before.

'Grigori,' Roscoe shouted. 'For God's sake, have them release me. I only crashed the barrier as the quickest way of getting back here.'

'Roscoe, you're crazy,' growled Medvedev. 'You had a break; you threw it away. Some people don't know when they're lucky.'

Roscoe grabbed what might be the only chance he was going to get. He threw himself out of the stationary jeep. Off-balance and unable to break his fall, he landed on a knee-cap. A stab of pain shot up the leg. He rolled upright and hobbled across to Medvedev's car.

'I have information for you,' he shouted.

Medvedev waved back the Spetsnaz guard who was coming after Roscoe, looking angry. 'Let him speak to me,' he growled. 'That's an order.'

Roscoe saw himself in the gleaming coachwork of Medvedev's car. With blood all over his face and shirtfront, he looked as though he had been dragged through a sewer and beaten up.

Medvedev confirmed the impression: 'You look like shit, Jack!'

'Grigori,' said Roscoe urgently. 'You have to know this. I was hijacked by Madeleine Wharton and packed off, back to London. Whilst I was there, they grilled me about your plans for the Romanoff restoration. I didn't tell them a thing but I learned enough to be certain that the Service knows all about your plans for a *coup d'état*.'

'Why are you telling me this?' Medvedev's face was expressionless.

'I don't owe any loyalty to the Service,' said Roscoe desperately. 'You know that. Also, we have a deal, Grigori. I want Bergman out of here before it's too late.'

'If London knows about our plans –' Medvedev poked a menacing finger at Roscoe through the open window, '– it's because you told them, Jack. I warned you what would happen.'

'No!' shouted Roscoe. 'They knew already, I tell you.'

'Lock him up,' Medvedev bellowed at Ekaterina.

'Grigori,' pleaded Roscoe. 'I'm not stupid. I wouldn't come back here if . . .'

Medvedev's window slid smoothly up. Inside he said something to the driver. The black Volga rolled past, leaving Roscoe standing in the slush.

He let himself be herded back into the jeep by the guard. 'Where are you taking me?' he asked Ekaterina dispiritedly as the jeep lurched forward.

'You'll find out,' she said. 'And please, Mr Roscoe, don't pull any more tricks like that or you'll end up getting hurt.'

'Let me talk to Plotnik,' Roscoe begged. 'At least he'll want to know what I have to say.'

'The colonel is busy,' she said. 'Everyone's busy, Mr Roscoe.

I'm afraid you have to be locked up because no one has time to deal with you right now.'

Van was looking distinctly unhappy.

Roscoe shrugged away the pain in his wrists and muttered to her, 'Don't worry. Everything's going according to plan. I could have done without the nose job but crashing the barrier was still the best way of getting back here in a hurry.'

'You could have fooled me, Jack.'

. 7 .

'Hold still, Jack.' Van was mopping the dried blood from Roscoe's face with a small handtowel soaked in cold water. They had been locked into a room in the Spetsnaz sick bay. With barred windows and a locked steel door it made a good temporary holding cell.

'Is my nose broken?' he asked.

'I never played nurses,' she shrugged. 'It's swollen as hell, that's for sure.'

'And tender,' he said, gingerly exploring his nose which felt twice its normal size.

'You look a real mess,' she decided.

Roscoe stood up and sniffed; his nose needed a rebore. He ran cold water over his swollen wrists to reduce the livid weals from the too-tight handcuffs. From the washbasin, he could see through the barred window. A long line of white-painted trucks and armoured personnel carriers was parked opposite under camouflage netting that sagged beneath the weight of snow building up on it. Beyond it, harder to see in the early twilight and drifting snowflakes, was a parked column of fast and lightly armoured BMP armoured fighting vehicles, armed with Sagger anti-tank missiles and 23 mm. cannons. It looked as though the forces for the coup were under starter's orders.

A command jeep with a long whip radio antenna drove up to the waiting column of transport. Plotnik sat in it, conferring with a group of officers over a map for several minutes. Then he drove off fast, showering slush over the men with whom he had been talking.

By placing his face flat against the window glass and squinting sideways Roscoe could see the main door of the sick bay. As he had guessed, Plotnik had stripped the base staff to a minimum; there was only one guard in sight and he was no Special Forces veteran like the ones who had given Roscoe a hard time at the roadblock. With his pasty face and spectacles, the young recruit stamping his feet to keep warm in the snow looked more cook than commando. He was toying with the fire selector of his assault rifle as though he had never handled one before.

'We'll wait until the big boys have gone,' Roscoe said. 'Then we'll kick up a row and jump the guard when he comes to see what's going on.'

'You make it sound easy,' said Van.

'I'll be lying down moaning on the floor to put him off his guard. You stand behind the door and hit him with that metal stool as he comes through.'

'Couldn't we swap roles?' Van protested. 'I'm out of training for this sort of thing.'

Roscoe gripped both her shoulders. 'You can do it,' he said. 'Has to be that way round to put the guy off his guard. We won't get a second chance.'

He sat down to eat some of the black bread and cold soup that had been left for them on a tray. 'I advise you to do the same,' he said, chewing each mouthful. 'It tastes pretty basic but it's nourishing.'

Bergman's initial bewilderment at being screwed out of his liberty by Medvedev's double-cross, had changed to a determination to escape or die in the attempt rather than ever be sent back to Perm 39B again. From his room at the rear of the sick quarters he had not seen Roscoe and Van brought in. As night fell and his calls and banging on the door produced no reaction, Bergman assumed that the sick bay was momentarily deserted. As far as he was concerned, any chance of escape was the right one.

Opening locked doors was one of a thousand tricks he had learned in the Gulag. He folded back two prongs of the fork on his meal tray and bent the other prong to make a lockpick which he worked into the doorlock and felt his way through the mechanism. Luckily it only looked strong; like many things manufactured in Russia, the quality of workmanship inside the heavy casing was poor. With a thud that sounded loud in the silent building the bolt slid back and Bergman pushed the door ajar, to slip through and into the dimly lighted corridor.

Moving like a ghost, he explored the next room and the next. He found a master-key hanging on a rack in the duty office and used it to speed up his hunt for outdoor clothing and food. Outside, heavy engines were revving up as the last trucks left the base, heading for St Petersburg. The only guard was the one on the main entrance.

Bergman had drawn blanks through most of the building when he heard shouting in what sounded like Roscoe's voice. Looking through the glass observation panel into the room from where the noise was coming he saw, rolling on the floor as though in agony, the man he had thought drowned in the icy waters of the Gulf of Finland. Roscoe was clutching his belly and groaning, but otherwise he was very much alive. Mystified, Bergman unlocked the door and stepped into the room. 'Jack,' he said, 'what the hell's . . .'

A creak of the door hinge alerted him to the weapon that was coming down fast, aimed straight at the crown of his head.

'In such a case –' Bergman heard Wu's calm voice in his mind, '– an interesting move is *kani-basami* – the crab scissors. I show you how.'

Bergman moved fast. Before the steel leg of the stool could connect with his scalp, he had thrown himself down and sideways, his legs scissoring horizontally to wrap themselves around his assailant. As Van crashed to the floor and lay winded, the stool beside her, the unreality of the situation sank in and Bergman exploded in the first real laugh he had had for years.

The sentry arrived on the scene to find all three of his captives lying on the floor, the two men laughing helplessly and Van wheezing as she got back her breath.

'*Shto sluchayetsa . . . ?*'

Before the guard could finish the sentence, Bergman swivelled and kicked his feet from beneath him. Within ten seconds the man was unconscious from the pressure of Bergman's thumbs on nerve centres at the base of his neck.

'Is he dead?' asked Van.

Bergman shook his head. He still felt weak from all the laughter. 'He'll wake up in twenty minutes and wonder what happened.'

'We have a very short window of opportunity,' Roscoe finished Bergman's briefing. 'Four hours at most, I think – just as long as it takes Plotnik to grab control of St Petersburg and have Archbishop Alexei crown this new Tsar they've got lined up. Then I estimate they'll run for cover back here until the Western media pack hits town and gives them an umbrella to keep Moscow's troops at bay while they carry out their next step, whatever that is. By the time they get back here, we have to be on the other side of the border.'

Bergman had kept alive by trusting no one – not even Wu – to make a decision for him. He felt good now to know that Jack Roscoe had it all worked out: for once someone else was driving and he was a passenger, except . . .

'What happens,' he wondered, 'if there's bad visibility across the Gulf and your Finnish pals can't see the signal flare?'

'Then we go out overland,' said Roscoe. 'It's a twenty-mile slog on skis, maybe more. Do you think you can handle that, Peter?'

Bergman grinned wolfishly. 'I could run up Everest, if it was the only way home.'

They left the sick bay by a fire door to the rear and avoided using the network of roads through the base in case Plotnik had left some flying pickets behind. The entire Spetsnaz complex was a ghost town. Under the street lamps only the criss-crossing wheel tracks in the slush showed where all the vehicles and men had gone.

In places snowdrifts slowed them down. They started jogging because none of them had been able to find any protective clothing to keep out the sub-zero wind. There was a thin crust of ice on top of the snow which Roscoe reckoned made skiable conditions if they had to go out overland. Over one shoulder he was carrying his holdall which Bergman had unearthed with Van's luggage in the doctor's office. With only the memory of the jeep-ride that afternoon to guide him, he heaved a sigh of relief as they came in sight of the floodlit gate to the grounds of the Villa Orlova.

It was unguarded and the house itself completely deserted. In the kitchen there was a roster pinned up on the wall, according to which all stewards and cooks were to report at 23.00 hours the previous evening for guard duty . . . which explained the sentry's incompetence, thought Roscoe.

In the smoking room, seated in the deep, comfortable chairs on either side of the tiled stove, were two men: Leonid Blok and Prince Anton, dressed in his coronation robes. They were both dead.

Roscoe did not bother looking for a pulse. Blok appeared to have been killed first without a struggle but the carpet around Prince Anton's chair was kicked awry, he was missing one shoe and a small drinks table had been knocked over. There was broken glass on the floor and a nearly empty bottle of vodka lay near the chair as though the Prince had used it for a weapon.

'When?' asked Bergman.

Roscoe lifted Prince Anton's inert hand. There were traces of skin and blood under the nails, indicating that he had put up some kind of a fight for his life, despite being pinned in the chair by the bear-like bulk of General Medvedev.

'Rigor mortis sets in after about six hours.' Roscoe moved the arm which was still limp. 'Maybe earlier in a warm room like this. So if it's six a.m. now, these two were killed sometime around midnight. I'd guess the deed was done straight after the staff left the villa.'

Van could not take her eyes off the grotesque purple death-mask of Prince Anton's face, with its bulging eyes and protruding tongue. When Roscoe closed the dead men's eyes and threw a couple of floor rugs over them for decency, she expelled a long breath as the distorted features vanished from view.

'Poor Anton,' she said softly.

'Who are these guys?' asked Bergman.

Roscoe had a sick feeling that he had made a major miscalculation – and that it would be a good way of spending the next few minutes if he could work out exactly what was going on. He repeated the question, trying unsuccessfully to work out what the murders meant in the overall panorama of events.

'On my left,' he said, like a wrestling referee, 'you have the late Prince Anton Nikolaevich Romanoff, known as the Pretender to the Throne of All the Russias. He should have been crowned Tsar just about now, according to the timetable I was using. The other man I don't know.'

'And who stiffed them?' Bergman called from the next room, more interested in the guns displayed on the library wall than in two corpses.

'That I can tell you,' Roscoe answered. 'I recognise the *modus operandi* of the guy who double-crossed us on the boat – General Grigori Sergeyevich Medvedev.'

Roscoe divided the responsibilities. Bergman was to find some protective clothing and choose a couple of light automatic weapons to take with them; Van's job was to grab the Fabergé eggs and a day's supply of food and drink from the kitchen, in case they had to go out overland. Roscoe himself headed upstairs to find the highest window on the western side of the villa, there to ignite the magnesium fishing flare that should be visible on the far side of the Gulf – if the snow held off and if there were no fog.

If, if, if . . . There were a thousand complications with which he did not want to bother Van or Bergman.

Had there been enough time for the two Finns to repair Arvo's hydrofoil and get it back into the water? And how long could they wait to find out without throwing away the chance of getting away overland? Despite all Bergman's bravado, Roscoe hoped it did not come to that.

In the attic he blundered by mistake into the windowless computer room and found himself staring at a dozen unattended computer screens flashing the message 'TRADING

SUSPENDED' above totals of figures in dollars, Japanese yen, sterling and Deutschmarks which meant nothing to him.

Downstairs Bergman picked two of the smallest guns from Plotnik's collection: an Uzi machine-pistol and an ugly but lethal little Heckler & Koch MP5K, less than thirteen inches long. He used the butt of the Uzi to break into the glass cabinet and find ammunition.

In the smoking room Van kept her eyes averted from the two inert shapes beneath the rugs. She hunted through the pile of regalia for the two eggs which had been thrown aside with some unwanted robes and checked the hallmarks to make sure she had been correct. The clincher was finding between the tiny punched indentations, the initials H.W. Henrik Wigström had been Fabergé's senior workmaster, so that tallied. A further thirty-second examination convinced her the eggs were 'right'. She weighed them in her hands; they were not much heavier than duck eggs. From the next room came the snick of Bergman testing the action of the Uzi and chambering a round.

By nightfall, thought Van, Peter, Jack and I will be either very rich or very dead.

.8.

Tourists sleeping in the immense 1500-room Moskva Hotel overlooking the park around the Nevskiy *lavra* were awoken by the scream of twin Isotov turbo-shaft aero engines as Colonel Plotnik's MIL Mi-28 gunship came in low, hugging the river to land inside the central courtyard of the monastery.

Plotnik checked his synchronised wristwatch: he was two minutes ahead of schedule. Precisely on time, almost every man and woman in his command had deployed at the strategic points of St Petersburg in a scaled-up copy of the way he had taken over Kabul at the outset of the Afghan War in December of 1979. With a minimum of overt presence on the streets, every important building was in their hands. That there had been almost no bloodshed and only a few outbreaks of firing to disturb the sleeping populace, was due to perfect timing, superb training and Plotnik's planning.

'You've got it!' he shouted to the pilot in the rear cockpit, meaning: take the controls.

'I've got it,' came the calm reply in his earphones.

Plotnik unbuckled himself and pulled off his helmet as the Mi-28 hedge-hopped over the low monastery buildings, flared and settled neatly beside the other helicopters and vehicles parked in the courtyard, out of sight of the curious, bleary eyes in the huge hotel across the park.

The colonel jumped down from the weapons-operator's position in the front cockpit. He hit the snow-covered ground on the run and kept running all the way through the cloister and into the cathedral itself. In the dim lighting he could see a group of men standing at the high altar.

'Why are the television lamps not on?' Plotnik shouted. With no live audience, the video coverage was the sole justification for setting up the coronation in St Petersburg itself.

'Power cut!' someone answered.

Plotnik had men at the power station and switching centres for just that eventuality. Also, in the gloom he could see the glowing viewfinders of the television cameras. The hairs on the back of his neck prickled.

'What's wrong?' he asked, striding up to the group standing by the altar.

Medvedev separated himself from the others.

'What's the hold-up, Grigori Sergeyevich?' Plotnik asked. 'I want to start moving out in . . .'

Someone threw a switch and the television lamps came on, blinding Plotnik. He shielded his eyes and looked round. 'Where's the Prince?' he asked.

It was Medvedev who spoke. 'He had an accident.'

Plotnik saw the scratches on Medvedev's face. 'Were you hurt too?'

'Less than him,' growled Medvedev grimly.

Plotnik's eyes flicked right and left, trying to see a single familiar face, aside from Medvedev and the archbishop. 'I didn't hear anything over the radio about an accident. Where did it happen and when?'

He backed away towards the edge of the pool of light around the altar and loosened the flap of his holster, only to feel the muzzle of a weapon thrust into his back by one of the men he had mistaken in the gloom for camera operators.

'Don't move, Colonel Plotnik,' ordered a hard voice he had never heard before. 'You're under arrest for treason.'

Plotnik raised his hands away from his body but not too high.

Someone reached from behind, removed the Makarov automatic from the holster on his belt and threw it onto the floor
where it skidded away into the shadows.

'You set me up, Grigori,' said the colonel.

Medvedev chuckled, pleased with his night's work.

'When did you change sides?' Plotnik kept talking.

'I never did.' Medvedev could not resist taunting the man he
had outwitted. 'From the start, this is how I planned it.'

'And you, Archbishop Alexei?' Plotnik turned to the priest
clad in his everyday robes, not the ceremonial garments for a
coronation. 'You were in it with him, all the time?'

'The Church,' said Alexei smoothly, 'must survive, Colonel.
To do that we have to side with the strongest.'

'All that crap about kissing crosses,' muttered Plotnik, bitterly incredulous at his own stupidity. 'You really took me for a
ride, priest.'

'Like the Pope in the Second World War,' said the archbishop,
'I must think of my Church first and my personal conscience
second.' He raised his left hand in a blessing, as another man
might have said sorry.

'In a different century,' he intoned, 'we might have been allies.
Today belongs to men like Grigori Sergeyevich, I'm afraid.'

Plotnik's shoulders slumped. His hands fell, a picture of
dejection.

'*Vnimánie!*' shouted Medvedev: watch out!

He was too late. Plotnik's gesture of despondency was con-
verted into a body-turn as smoothly flowing as an Olympic
gymnast's. His right elbow smashed into the nose of the man
standing behind him, driving the bones upwards into the brain
and killing him instantaneously. Before he fell, the colonel's
left hand had grabbed the Kalashnikov assault rifle that had
been poking in his back. Plotnik hit the ground, rolling fast
towards the shadows, banking on the men in the lit area being
blinded when they looked for him. He came to his feet in a
crouch and took out the three fake cameramen he could see,
each with a single shot. An AK 74 stuttered behind him. There
was a scream of bullets ricocheting off the stone walls. Plotnik
whirled in a crouch, firing one short burst to drop the man who
had missed. In the arched nave the noise of gunfire echoed

backwards and forwards deafeningly. Screams of agony from two gut-shot men mingled with the shouting of contradictory orders.

In the babble of confused commands, all in Russian, one voice stood out. Plotnik homed blindly on the woman calling in English, 'This way, Colonel. Over here!'

He vaulted over some seating and hit the floor beside Ekaterina Borisovna Antonova among a pile of bodies of his men – all unconscious or dead. In the poor lighting, Plotnik saw a large dark stain down the front of Ekaterina's fatigue blouse. The pale face and staring eyes told him she had not long to live. It was amazing that she had found the energy to shout.

'You go, Colonel,' she gasped. 'Just leave me one grenade!'

Plotnik unclipped a fragmentation grenade from his webbing harness and thrust it into her outstretched hand.

'You'll get promotion for this!' He patted her shoulder and headed for the door in a crouching run.

'. . . to the rank of angel,' she murmured, pulling the pin and staggering to her feet.

Plotnik was hardly through the doorway into the cloister when he heard her body fall against the heavy wooden doors behind him. In the centre of the courtyard several men were standing over the body of the Mi-28's pilot which was lying in the snow. Plotnik fired a short burst that dropped them, all but one. A bullet from that man's weapon tore through Plotnik's shoulder muscles, missing his carotid artery by an inch and slamming him back against the double doors.

Despite the pain, he managed to loose off another short burst one-handed to take out the man who had shot him. On the other side of the door, he could hear voices.

Someone shouted, 'I can't open the doors. The damned woman's wedged her arm through the bars for the locking beam.'

'Pull it out,' bellowed Medvedev.

'If I do,' shouted the first man, 'I'll kill us all. She's holding a primed grenade.'

There was a scream of pain from Ekaterina and Medvedev's voice: 'I'm holding her hand closed. There's no danger. Now open the door.'

'I can't. Her arm's still jamming it shut.'

'Then break her fucking arm,' roared Medvedev.

The doors began to heave to and fro, each movement marked by a fresh scream of agony from the woman whose broken arm would not let go.

'*Yob tvoyu mat!*' Medvedev shouted furiously. 'Shoot her arm in half, motherfucker! And get this bloody door open!'

Plotnik was gunning the controls as the sustained burst of automatic fire shattered the flesh and bones of Ekaterina's arm, severing it at the elbow. Medvedev's men burst into the courtyard to be blinded as he switched on the twin landing-lights of the Mi-28 and started the take-off routine. They would have done better not to shoot. Gritting his teeth with pain, Plotnik used his injured arm to hit the feed selector button for the Gsh 30 mm. cannon mounted on the pod beneath the gunship's nose. It fired a single anti-personnel shell that pierced three bodies to explode against the ancient stone wall, releasing several hundred white-hot flechettes, miniature arrow-heads that burrowed at supersonic speed into all the living flesh within range, shredding arteries and vital organs.

In the suddenly empty courtyard, Plotnik released the weapon controls and turned pilot. He bumped his craft forward and lurched into the air, operating the aircraft controls awkwardly with one hand and his knees. Airborne, he skimmed over the roof of the cloister and circled to gain height. In the courtyard below, black figures were running across the white snow towards the other helicopters. This time Plotnik selected HE feed for the nose-pod cannon. He wheeled and dived on the frantic scene in the courtyard below, firing eight of the Mi-28's sixteen wing-mounted AT-6 anti-tank rockets and adding a burst of high-explosive shells from the 30 mm. cannon for good measure. The fireball consumed the men and machines in the courtyard, billowing briefly high above the monastery roof. The blast wave rocked Plotnik's craft as he fought for control and clawed upwards towards the low cloud base.

It was strangely peaceful once lost in the cloud, lit by the directionless diffused first light of dawn. Plotnik's world shrank to the familiar layout of the essential instrument panels in front of him. The shock of being wounded made him want to lie down and forget the betrayal. The noise of the engines, muted by his helmet, was lulling him to sleep.

He roused himself with the thought that there were people down there in the waking city who would pay with their lives for their loyalty to him, if he did not do something about it fast. He opened the oxygen supply valve to his helmet mask, held it over his mouth for a moment and breathed deeply until his head cleared.

Lucid again, Plotnik took a field dressing from a leg pouch and jammed it over his wound. It hurt and was bleeding alarmingly. He guessed that a vein was nicked. He searched his memory for the stand-down code, then decided to do it in clear so that the other side heard as well. That was the only way to avoid misunderstandings.

Trading height for speed he came out of the cloud a mile north of the column of black smoke rising from the monastery. On the opposite bank of the Neva, approaching the bridge that led to the *lavra*, was a column of armoured vehicles: light tanks, mobile rocket-launchers and APCs, halted and waiting for the order to cross into the city. Medvedev's preparations had been thorough.

Plotnik swallowed the bitterness that it was ending this way. At two hundred metres' altitude, just below the cloudbase, he keyed the mike for a multi-frequency transmission.

'*Ya polkóvnik Ivan Ivanovich Plotnik, kommanduyushchi Voiská Spetsiálnovo Naznachéniya . . .*' he called to his troops listening below and to anyone else who was monitoring the Spetsnaz frequency. The transmission was automatically picked up by ears-in-the-sky and bounced to voice-activated recorders at listening stations in Britain, Japan and North America.

'*Treniróvka zakónchena! Povtoryáyu: treniróvka zakónchena!* The exercise is finished, I repeat, finished. All Spetsnaz units will return to base in good order. If armed resistance is encountered, do not return fire.'

Plotnik's mood changed abruptly as, from the direction of the tank column, he saw the heat-trail of a SAM-11 missile heading his way. A warning bleeper screamed in the cockpit. The ECM panel lit up automatically, listing his options and flashing *RELEASE CHAFF: RELEASE DECOY FLARES*. Plotnik ignored the message; he had his own methods.

He waited until the missile was too close to manoeuvre, launched two of the anti-tank rockets as heat-emitting decoys, turned the Mi-28 on its side and dropped like a stone, putting all his faith in the upturned exhausts of the Mi-28 which reduced its heat-signature to nearly zero at that angle. The missile wavered, locked onto the two rockets and swooshed past the helicopter so near that its slipstream hit Plotnik's craft like a metal fist. Invisible in the overcast, it detonated in thin air a few seconds later on reaching ceiling height.

Angrily, Plotnik keyed the mike again. 'Correction! If armed resistance is offered, blow the bastards to hell — and that's an order!'

He flew deliberately over the tank column now wending its way across the bridge, daring his enemies to fire again. The mobile missile-launchers' tubes were pointing skywards. They tracked the narrow, ugly Mi-28 like gun dogs following the flight of a game bird overhead but they did not open fire.

Grigori Medvedev was not a man who believed in leading from the front like Plotnik. He had stayed well back inside the church as his men scrabbled over Ekaterina Borisovna's still-moving body to get after Plotnik. As a result he suffered only the smell of burned meat in his nostrils when Plotnik carbonised the men in the courtyard.

His voice came over the integral earphones of Plotnik's helmet now: 'Ivan Ivanovich, come down and land. There is nothing you can do. Land your craft and surrender immediately.'

'Up yours, Grigori!' Plotnik pulled the commo jack out of the control panel and left Medvedev talking to himself.

A glance at the fuel gauge confirmed that his pilot had refuelled at the last landing before the monastery. There was sufficient fuel for an hour's flying, maybe more.

A warm wetness was running down the skin of Plotnik's chest. From the rate of bleeding he estimated that he might last for an hour at most without proper medical attention. With luck he and his craft would flare out together.

But Grigori was wrong, he thought. There is one last thing I can do to hit back at all the people like him who screw the poor fools like me, all over the world.

.9.

The Villa Orlovà had been scoured for a pair of binoculars without success but Bergman had discovered in the smoking room something even better: an antique brass telescope with a compass on its calibrated mount.

Roscoe carried it out into the snow-covered garden and set it up on the tripod. Lower down the slope, Van and Bergman were hurdling through the knee-deep drifts, heading for the boathouse at the end of the jetty. On the highest window ledge of the house one of Pekka Manninen's magnesium flares burned brightly.

As though in answer to Roscoe's prayers, the wind had dropped and it was not snowing. But how thick was the snow haze over the Gulf? he wondered anxiously. Would it mask the light of the flare?

Roscoe read off the reciprocal bearing of the course he had given Pekka. Scanning the horizon in that direction, he strained to detect the slightest irregularity in the monotony of grey – and saw nothing.

He straightened up and rubbed his eyes. There was a minute anomaly in the murk. He stared at it and saw nothing again.

Then he looked away and picked up, out of the corner of his eye, a tiny pulsing white dot in the expanse of grey sea. He glued his eye to the telescope on the new bearing and groaned with relief on finding that he was looking at the bow-wave of a boat cutting fast through the low waves.

It was Pekka, heading straight for the flare.

Roscoe felt like shouting, '*A moi, la Légion!*'

A huge elation filled him. With Van's help he had brought off a rescue operation of which the Service or the CIA – with all their resources – would have been justifiably proud. He had beaten Colonel Charlie Beckworth and Delta Force who had failed to rescue the American hostages in Tehran. He had done what Bull Simons had failed to do when he led the abortive Special Forces' operation to release the American POWs at Son Tay.

'We've done it,' he shouted at the boathouse where Van and Bergman were waiting.

A roar of twin turbo-shaft engines made him throw himself flat as Plotnik, attracted by the flare, diverted from his base, skimmed the ridge of the villa and landed the Mi-28 clumsily with one hand, less than ten metres away.

Roscoe got to his feet, clawing for the Hockler which had slipped round behind his back.

'Don't shoot!' Bergman had recognised the man slumped at the controls. He was running back up the hill towards Roscoe, shouting, 'That's Colonel Plotnik!'

Just in time, he barged Roscoe sideways so that the burst of 9 mm. parabellum bullets from the Heckler impacted harm-lessly on the snow-covered ground.

The rotors slowed and Plotnik levered himself painfully out of the front cockpit, grimacing with pain and clutching the spreading red patch on his battledress fatigues.

'Thanks, Bergman,' he said with a tight-lipped grin. 'That makes us quits,

'What's happened?' asked Roscoe.

The wounded man echoed Anastas Lirian's summing-up. 'I made all the right moves,' he said tiredly, 'but against the wrong enemy.'

Van had come up behind them, unable to follow what they

were talking about. She looked round to see the rescue boat circling back out to sea, wary of the armed gunship on the ground.

'For Christ's sake,' she screamed above the rotor noise. 'Look behind you, Jack!'

Roscoe spun round, weapon ready and looking for a threat close to but seeing nothing.

She pointed seaward. 'Look!'

Roscoe took off fast, with Van in pursuit. They ran along the jetty waving at Pekka who throttled back when he recognised Roscoe and Van. The hydrofoil settled in the water. Warily the big Finnish fisherman nursed Arvo's ultra-streamlined boat inshore and brought her alongside the landing-stage.

As he slid the throttles of the twin diesel engines to idle there was a loud *whoomp!* from the top of the mound which made everyone look round. The magnesium flare, blown back into the bedroom by the draught from Plotnik's rotors, had set fire to the curtains and bedding. Flames were erupting from the open windows and licking at the decorative wooden lintels of the villa.

'Make quickly, Jack,' called Pekka. Despite the freezing air, he was sweating with excitement.

'Come on, Peter,' yelled Roscoe, one foot on the boat and one on the jetty. 'Let's go! Get down here right now!'

Bergman had cut open Plotnik's uniform to expose the wounded shoulder. He threw away the sodden, bright-red field dressing and was bandaging a tightly rolled wad of lint and gauze over the wound, trying to get some pressure on it to slow down the rate of bleeding. He gave no sign that he had heard the shouted order.

Roscoe thrust the machine-pistol into Van's hands and said, 'You get on board while I fetch Peter.'

He left her scrambling aboard with Pekka shouting urgently something about a weather forecast and a storm heading their way.

'I'm not coming with you, Jack,' announced Bergman as Roscoe ran up.

He pulled Plotnik's fatigue jacket back over the shoulder, causing an involuntary groan from the colonel who was sitting on one of the Mi-28's stubby wings that served as weapons pods, saving energy and breathing deeply to fight the pain.

'Colonel Plotnik and I,' said Bergman calmly, 'are not ready to leave yet.'

'What the hell are you saying?' It was hard for Roscoe to make himself heard above the noise of the rotors and the fire which was rapidly gaining a hold on the tinder-dry ornamental woodwork of the house, cracking and roaring as the wood split and exploded with the heat.

'You heard.' Bergman did not even look round.

Down at the jetty, Pekka was revving the engines to make the point that he wanted to get away very soon. Roscoe grabbed Bergman by the shoulders to make him come by physical force. He found he was holding thin air and looking down the muzzle of Bergman's Uzi.

'You're crazy, Peter,' he said.

'You go,' said Bergman. The cold blue eyes watching Roscoe were devoid of feeling, as was his voice. 'I've got some unfinished business to clear up. Plotnik's going to give me a hand.'

Roscoe could have cried with frustration. 'Damn you, Peter,' he screamed. 'D'you know what I've gone through to save your worthless skin? This is the only chance you'll get and you're throwing it all away. You're insane!'

'I was never more sane in my life,' drawled Bergman with an infuriating smile.

He turned to Plotnik and snatched up the map-case Velcro'd onto the knee of the colonel's flying suit. Eyes closed for a moment's rest, Plotnik was swallowing a handful of dextroamphetamine tablets.

Unfolding the large-scale map of the area, Bergman ordered Roscoe, 'Show me exactly where you planned to cross the frontier, Jack — if we had to go overland. And where is this farmhouse you're using as the emergency RV? OK, I've got it. Now you get Van out of here and I'll catch up with you guys later.'

'Peter!' Roscoe pleaded desperately. 'Whatever crazy idea you've got in your head, just listen to me for once, please.'

Bergman's Uzi slammed into Roscoe's chest. 'Get out of here, will ya?'

Roscoe grabbed the Uzi. A burst of fire splattered the snow

between the two fighting men, narrowly missing the tail rotor of Plotnik's helicopter.

'I warned you,' said Bergman coldly. He slipped below Roscoe's guard, spun round and back-kicked him in the chest.

'Get the hell outta here,' he shouted. 'I can look after myself.'

The two helicopters were following the nap of the earth, dodging between low hills rather than going over them and appearing above someone's radar horizon. From time to time, Plotnik ranged ahead to get his bearings, leaving Bergman to lag behind in the Huey which they had taken from the Spetsnaz maintenance bay because Bergman was familiar with the controls. Stripped out for repairs and devoid of armament, it lumbered after Plotnik at half the speed of the colonel's Mi-28.

In addition to attacks of weakness from all the blood he had lost, Plotnik was also having problems due to the tandem design of his aircraft. The Mi-28 was a two-man craft designed to be flown from the rear cockpit where the pilot had a switchable multi-function display projected onto his helmet vizor, giving information from the FLIR forward-looking infra-red camera, a low-light television camera and satellite-linked navigational aids which included a moving map display that automatically followed terrain and showed the craft's position at all times. The front cockpit, where Plotnik sat, was intended for the weapons-operator and had only secondary controls for the aircraft and a small selection of the navigational aids, so the colonel was having to navigate by compass and the occasional landmark.

'How're we doing?' Bergman had to repeat the query before he was answered.

'Fine. ETA five minutes from now.'

Until then they had kept radio silence, avoiding chit-chat that would have enabled direction-finding of their transmissions. The landing itself had been discussed in a few words: Plotnik was to stay airborne and give cover while the Huey was on the ground.

It was eerie for Bergman to see how small was the camp that had been his whole world for so long. The compound was lost in the immensity of whiteness. The two bunkers – Ossetin's zoo and the guards' quarters – were small concrete boxes. It did not seem possible that so many men could live in them.

Bergman shut down his memory banks and landed the unmarked Huey a few metres from the entrance to the bunker. Thinking this was a rations delivery, a guard stomped a trail through the drifts to open the large side door of the cabin and found himself looking down the barrel of Bergman's Uzi. His point-blank view lasted for less than a second before a single 9 mm. bullet pierced his brain and exited neatly through the occipital bone at the rear of his head.

Bergman stepped down and took in the scene. Plotnik's Mi-28 hovered above the guards' quarters. Several of the staff were outside, looking up at the unusual sight of a gunship overhead. Deafened by the noise of the two sets of rotors, they had not heard the shot. Bergman ploughed through the snow and sprayed them from a range of ten metres with a sustained burst from the Uzi. He felt no compunction as they dropped into the red patches on the white snow and disappeared from view: the world was cleaner without them.

Magazine changed, Bergman went after Ossetin who was inside the airlock, leaning over the desk and shouting excitedly into the telephone which had been repaired that morning.

'Ossetin! Look at me!'

Bergman called out his name to make the commandant look up, then shot him through the head as he would have put down a mad dog. He tore the phone cable out of the wall. Two more guards appeared from the tunnel leading to the other block. Alerted by the noise of the shooting, both were armed with old Kalashnikov AK 47s.

Before they could open fire, Bergman shot one dead and wounded the other, kicking the groaning man to his feet with the order: 'You die later. First you open the cages and release the prisoners.'

Nursing his shattered right hand under his left armpit and moaning with pain, the guard chose to live a few more minutes. He staggered from cell to cell releasing the filthy bearded *zaks* inside. There were six in all.

'Where are the others?' Bergman asked.

None of the skeletal, dazed men replied. None of them even looked at their liberator. They stood outside their cells waiting for orders and kept their eyes firmly on the ground in front of their feet as they had been trained to do.

'Come on,' shouted Bergman. He hit a couple of the prisoners with the stock of the Uzi to try and shock them into replying and repeated, 'Where are they?'

The guard mumbled, 'All dead. We had no food to give them, these last few days – since we were cut off by snow.'

Bergman tore open the man's padded *bushlát*. There were no signs of malnourishment on his body. It was well fed and flabby from years of excessive drinking – obscene to Bergman's eyes in comparison with the haggard scarecrows of which he had been one. He took one pace back and fired a single shot into the man's head.

None of the *zaks* moved as the body slumped to the ground in front of them.

'Let's go!' shouted Bergman.

Obediently they shuffled forward in the direction he was prodding them. He had to help them board the helicopter by heaving each man bodily over the long-range tanks and through the door. Lastly he pulled the door shut behind himself.

'Now sit!' he shouted, and they sat on the floor, heads bowed, obedient as well-trained dogs.

Plotnik waited until Bergman was airborne before launching two rockets. The first entered the door of the bunker which Bergman had left open. The second hit the outside oil store which ignited with a *whoomp!* There was a secondary explosion as the armoury went up. It was the end of Perm 39B.

The smoking mess of shattered concrete was like an oversized tomb that had been desecrated by vandals. Bergman felt absolutely no emotion as he circled once over the wreckage before setting course for the border rendezvous.

.10.

'Never have I seen the Gulf of Finland like this,' Pekka muttered into his beard. He was talking not of the flat calm which foretold a big snowstorm on the way, but of the absence of patrol craft on both sides of the frontier.

He took one hand off the wheel and gestured at the empty sea, relying on the power steering to hold the hydrofoil on course. Behind the boat, the spreading wake led the eye back to the glowing point on the far shore that was the burning Villa Orlova.

'Not a Russian vessel in sight,' said Pekka.

'Nor one of yours,' commented Roscoe.

Pekka shrugged. In the same gloomy voice, he explained, 'The sixth of December is our national holiday, Jack. I told you, *Itsenäisyyspäivä* – Independence Day. So my cousin swapped duties. It was not hard – other guys like to be at home with their families. My cousin will keep his launch in harbour so long as it's possible.'

They were travelling fast on the planes, the hull completely out of the water. Beneath the roar of the unsilenced engines, the vibration of wave-tops hitting the underside of the hull at speed was a sustained, unpleasant buzz. It travelled up the legs and threatened to shake the brain loose inside the passengers' skulls each time they forgot to keep their knees bent as shock absorbers and stood straight for a moment.

As the hydrofoil swerved through the line of yellow buoys that marked the frontier, Van decided that power-boating was just about the most uncomfortable method of surface travel imaginable. She felt nauseated by the noise and vibration. She was also angry at what she took for Roscoe's incredible weakness of will in giving way to the fantasy of a sick man and leaving Bergman behind.

Ahead lay a low coastline of a thousand creeks and inlets, all of which looked identical to the passengers. Eyes narrowed against ice particles in the slipstream that knifed across the top of the low windscreen, Pekka seemed to have no trouble picking out some kind of landmarks on the featureless coast. As they were entering the creek which he said would lead to the farm belonging to Arvo's sister, his keen eyes spotted a distant dot in the snow-haze, out to sea.

He gestured one-handed. 'Look there! Finnish patrol launch of my cousin. Good timing, huh?'

'Will they see us?' asked Van.

'My cousin's great hero is your Admiral Nelson.' Pekka winked and Van realised that despite the gloomy tone of voice, the big fisherman had just made a joke.

Throttled right back to tick-over, the hydrofoil settled into the water and became a boat again. Slowly it nosed a passage through the thin sheet of ice that edged out from both banks of the creek and would soon make the waterway impassable until the spring thaw.

On the landing-stage beside the small boathouse, Arvo was waiting anxiously. 'Where's the guy you were going to rescue?' he asked, grabbing the painter which Roscoe threw ashore.

'It's a long story,' said Roscoe. 'He's coming overland.'

Arvo's face fell. There was an angry, tense exchange in Finnish between him and Pekka, and then more explanations from Roscoe which ended in Arvo hustling him and Van under the covers of a sledge hitched to a two-seater snowmobile.

'I am sorry,' he apologised, 'but inland the whole area is over-looked by watchtowers. You must not be seen.'

They had been airborne for half an hour when a hand tapped Bergman on the shoulder. He turned to find the solitary black prisoner staring through the plexiglass screen at the snowscape rushing past below.

'*Kudá idyóm?*' the black whispered.

'*Idyóm damói!*' shouted Bergman. 'We're going home!'

The black shook his head. Tears of disbelief ran down his emaciated face and trickled into his wispy grey beard. Another face appeared over his shoulder, repeating the question. It was the tall American who had been taken prisoner in Vietnam, twenty-seven years before.

'Home!' shouted Bergman. 'I'm taking you all home with me!'

Before Bergman could grab the man, he walked to the door, slid it open a few inches and stepped out into space. None of the four scarecrows sitting on the floor even looked up.

Bergman circled over the small smudge in the snow. The trees were too close together for him to land, even if there had been any point. He climbed back to height and pushed the speed up as high as he dared, searching for Plotnik's craft ahead of him.

'*Vnimánie!*' The colonel's urgent voice was loud in Bergman's phones. 'We have company, Bergman!'

Instead of one dot against the greyness ahead, Bergman saw three. The two more distant ones became a pair of fast-movers – Mig-29 fighters closing on Plotnik's craft.

Plotnik spun the Mi-28 in a tight circle, heading back to cover Bergman's unarmed Huey. Without any radio warning, the two fighters opened fire. A stream of 23 mm. uranium-depleted shells made a cone of fire around Plotnik's craft.

'*Yob tvoyú mat!*' Bergman heard him swear into his now open mike.

The Mi-28 danced out of the line of fire and turned far more tightly than the Migs could follow. Dedicated to a ground-attack role as a tank killer, Plotnik's machine also carried two air-to-air heat-seeking missiles. He launched the first at the lead fighter as it flew past, saw that it was going to miss and sent the other one after it. The first missile exploded harmlessly three hundred metres below and behind the fighter, whose pilot heard the explosion and thought himself safe just as the second missile ended its brief flight inside the Mig's starboard engine exhaust. The wingman peeled off and vanished into the low cloud, made wary by the fireball that had been his leader and which was now consuming itself and falling slowly groundwards.

'Nice shooting, Colonel,' called Bergman.

'Goddam!' swore Plotnik. He wished he had the multi-function display available in the pilot's seat. His gunsight radar was useless for the moment; it showed a blank screen apart from the blip that was Bergman's Huey.

'The Mig'll be back.' The colonel's voice was faint and slow. 'Question is: how good is he?'

'Does it matter?' Bergman asked. According to his map, they were less than twenty miles from the frontier and dead on course for the RV point. If they could just keep airborne as far as the border . . .

'It always matters,' chuckled Plotnik weakly. He was circling above and behind Bergman's Mi-8 – where he thought the threat would come from. His fuel gauge showed approximately three minutes' flying time remaining. The ECM screen in front of Plotnik lit up as the surviving Mig's radar re-acquired the two helicopters.

At the same moment, Bergman shouted, 'I see him! Six o'clock – above and behind you, Colonel.'

'*Yevó vízhvu*,' Plotnik laughed: I have him visual. He changed to English in case the Mig pilot was listening in. 'He's coming for you, Bergman. Definitely second class, this guy – going for the pigeon first. If he was good, he'd take me out and then get you afterwards.'

The Mig-29 was using air-brakes to slow its dive on the slowly moving transport helicopter. From the angle at which he was attacking, it looked to the pilot as if Plotnik's weapons pods were empty. Out of the corner of his eye he was aware of the Mi-28 flipping over sideways as he came level with it. Too late, he saw the remaining anti-tank rockets. If he had let Bergman go, there might still have been time to save his own life but he was short of combat experience and held course for the easy target below, as the colonel had guessed he would.

Plotnik's machine was side-slipping, losing height level with the incoming fighter. At the last moment, the dying man at the controls swung the Mi-28 into a power-dive like the weight on a pendulum. Down it went and up – straight into the approach of the oncoming Mig.

To Bergman watching below there was no doubt that Plotnik was in control all the way. He saw the Mi-28's last rockets fired ahead of the Mig to distract the pilot at the same second as the first 23 mm. shells from the Mig tore through the thin skin of the Huey's cabin, shattering the plexiglass dome into a thousand pieces. When the collision above him was inevitable, Bergman closed his eyes to avoid being blinded. He re-opened them as a huge pressure-wave hit the Huey like a kick from God's boot, slamming it sideways and down until it was lower than the highest treetops.

Bergman fought for control and altitude. There was the noise of a crazy rip-saw *shash-ash-ash-ash!* as the rotor-tips tore a passage through the top branches of trees and a whine of protest from an overheated bearing in one of the engines mounted above the rear cabin, which had been damaged by shell fragments.

A violent shaking made the Huey almost impossible to control. Bergman tried reducing throttle but that made the vibration worse, so he opened the throttles wide instead. The shaking was less but so many oil-pressure gauges were now in the red and warning sirens screaming that he knew they were not going to stay airborne for long.

. *11* .

The farmhouse where Arvo's sister Marja lived was a tiny log cabin consisting of a kitchen/dining-room, two small bedrooms and a bathroom. She was a small, bustling rosy-cheeked woman who welcomed the visitors without hesitation. Her children had been taken to play at a neighbour's house, Roscoe learned, and Marja's husband had died in a fishing accident at sea two years before. She managed to make ends meet by running the small farm herself, refusing obstinately to leave the home where her children had been born.

Two miles away – so she told Van – she could have made up the family budget by letting one of the bedrooms to holiday-makers during the brief summer season, but here in the Rajavyöhyke that was forbidden. She communicated in a mixture of Finnish, Swedish and English. As far as Van could make out, she was helping them that day as a gesture against the authorities who made her life so hard.

Roscoe sat at the one big window facing the border, waiting and feeling impotent. Arvo had wrested the MP5K from him and thrown it into the creek, saying that any firearm found in the Rajavyöhyke would result in a prison sentence. He was nervous about Van and Roscoe even being there and refused permission for either of them to go outside. The open snowfield which led to the border, a few hundred metres away, was under surveillance from a Finnish guard-tower which loomed above the trees to the south.

'The calm before the storm,' droned Pekka from the doorway. He sniffed the windless air and smelled more snow on the way.

'How is your buddy going to get here?' asked Arvo for the tenth time. Prepared to take a chance himself, he was now regretting that he had embroiled his sister in the rescue plan.

Roscoe shrugged. 'I don't know.'

'You must have some idea,' Arvo persisted. 'If the snowstorm comes first, a man will lose his way and die out there.'

'If Bergman gets here before the snow,' Roscoe pointed out, 'those guards in the tower are going to arrest him before we can smuggle him away. He needs the snow for a smokescreen.'

He had run out of curses for Bergman's obstinacy which had seemed to have cancelled out all his hard work in setting up the rescue operation. Now he felt just numb and tired.

Arvo swore. The words were Finnish but the meaning was plain. 'This could make big trouble for Marja, you know.'

Van was sick with worry for Bergman. She pushed away a cup of coffee untasted. 'You should have stopped him, Jack,' she said for the hundredth time.

'I tried,' said Roscoe.

'Oh sure,' she said scornfully. 'Bergman's just been released from a camp. He's weak and half-starved and you let him get the better of you?'

'He learned karate from some pal in the camp,' said Roscoe. 'You saw the way he took out the guard in the sick bay.' It didn't sound like much of an excuse even to his own ears.

Their squabbling was interrupted by an urgent hiss from Marja. She was standing in the porch where the family's skis were stacked. 'I hear machine,' she called.

Roscoe followed her and Arvo outside. By staying on this side of the house, he was out of sight of the guards on duty in the watchtower. In the dead calm he could hear the noise of a helicopter which seemed to be in trouble. It was hard for him to estimate distance to the sound in a world blanketed by snow.

Apparently reading his mind, Marja held up one finger. 'One kilometre, Mister Jack. One kilometre other side of border. No more.'

The distant engine noise cut. There was silence and then the faint sound of a large object smashing through branches – but no explosion.

'That was Bergman,' decided Roscoe. 'I'm going in after him.'

He ran back into the porch and started buckling on a pair of skis but the bindings were different from those he was used to and would not fit his boots.

'You not going anywhere,' boomed Arvo. He stood against the outer door, arms folded across his barrel chest, barring the exit with his bulk. 'Already you are causing enough problems here, Jack. Across the border I cannot let you go.'

'You heard the helicopter crash,' argued Roscoe. 'Bergman may be injured. We can't leave the guy out there, Arvo. Not when he's come so far.'

'We don't know it was him,' Pekka pointed out reasonably. 'Also, we don't know who else is out there. That is Russian territory, Jack.'

Skis or not, Roscoe was going. 'Get out of my way,' he shouted.

Arvo stood his ground. 'Jack, you can't do this thing to my sister. Marja will lose her home if there is any trouble, I am telling you that.'

'He's right, Jack,' Van sided with Arvo. 'I feel just as sick as you, but there's nothing we can do until Bergman walks across the border.'

Considered by many to be the ultimate sniper rifle, the Haskins M500 is made by an eponymous Arkansas gunsmith in very limited numbers.

Originally produced for a small handful of the best Green Beret snipers, only two had ever come into the hands of Her Britannic Majesty's armed forces. They lay on the table in the crowded hut which was perched atop the watchtower overlooking Marja's little farmstead. The matt grey finish of the adjustable skeleton stock, the fluted barrel and the muzzle brakes that deflected propellant gases rearward to diminish the kick – all these features combined to make the most lethal rifle in the world look like an oversized child's space gun.

Able had unpacked a box of twenty .50 calibre armour-piercing shells. Designed for a heavy machine-gun, each cartridge held an oversized charge which expelled the 1.5 ounce bullet from the muzzle of the Haskins with five times the energy of a standard 7.62 mm. Nato round – and consequently extended accurate range and penetrating power.

On the observation platform outside, Baker and Charlie, wearing borrowed Finnish frontier guard uniforms and black Balaclava helmets, were clamping monopod mounts onto the lowest of the three horizontal safety rails. Fitted with a x 10 telescopic sight, the M500 could hit a man in the eye at half a mile – and thanks to the explosive bullet, kill and maim at twice that range. The only drawbacks were that it was single-shot and had to be reloaded by removing the bolt after each round was fired and that its weight of twenty-three pounds necessitated mounting on a firm support like an Olympic match rifle.

Inside the hut, Inspector Koskelainen checked his watch. It was a nervous tic. There were days when he did not like his job one bit – and this was one of them. He turned to Madeleine Wharton as the ranking British official present. She was dressed like him in quilted white snow trousers and a thick sweater.

'There is to be no firing at Russian personnel,' said Koskelainen, 'whatever the provocation. And no killing on Finnish territory, either. Is that understood?'

'Perfectly,' she said. 'My men are professionals.'

Koskelainen had said his piece for the record; she had said hers. What was actually going to happen would be re-written like all history by the politicians. The Finn just wanted all the foreigners – Russian, British and the rest – to get out of his country and not treat it as their own backyard.

'If it's any consolation, Inspector,' Madeleine continued, 'I don't like this business any more than you do. The only justification is that it avoids unpleasantness on a far grander scale.'

Koskelainen looked to the north-east, where the weather was coming from. He was hoping that the blizzard which had been forecast would arrive before men got killed. They might die anyway, but that would be by the hand of God and General Winter, nothing to do with Oskar Koskelainen . . .

Outside, Able was reading off distances from a small Pentax optical rangefinder and passing them to his two men. Satisfied, he ran through the drill they had practised so many times on ranges and in real life.

'You fire first,' he said to Baker.

He turned to Charlie. 'You wait for the sound of his shot. Whilst he's reloading, you select your target and fire. And so on. I pass the shells to each man in turn.'

Baker took the first watch, lying on the icy boards of the platform beside his rifle. A spare anorak covered his head and prevented frost from his breath or body-heat crystallising on the eye-piece of the scope which had been rezeroed that morning.

Like hunters everywhere, the other men settled down patiently to wait. Charlie stuffed his hands deep inside his anorak pockets to keep the fingers supple. George Dawson brought out three mugs of steaming coffee and passed them round. Half a mile away a column of smoke rose from the chimney of the farm, vertical in the still air.

'Your pal Roscoe's still safely inside the farmhouse with the girl and the others,' said Able, lowering his binoculars.

'Let's hope he stays there out of harm's way,' prayed Dawson.

'If he does, fine,' said Able. 'It's the others we're after, boss.'

'Poor buggers,' said Dawson. 'After what they've been through, they're probably half-crazed anyway.'

Medvedev's frantic phone call had set wheels in motion in Moscow which had turned cogs in London. Men sitting safe in offices by the Thames had taken decisions which ended in Medvedev's voice being patched through a scrambled radio link to the British frigate steaming in the Baltic, in whose wardroom sat Madeleine Wharton, busy analysing that morning's developments in St Petersburg from as close as she could reasonably get to the scene of action.

And George Dawson's watching brief in Finland – to prevent Roscoe causing an international incident – had changed with the arrival of the Sea Lynx bringing his boss to take command and the three SBS men to do her bidding. The pristine white snowfield to the east of the little farmhouse, with its twin lines of frontier posts, was to be a killing ground.

Dawson wondered what secrets could be locked inside the handful of escaped prisoners from Perm 39B. Or was it just that the men had to die because they were on the wrong side of history and governments did not like to be caught out in old lies?

'Ours not to reason why,' muttered Able.

'I've got a funny feeling about Roscoe, boss,' he added, sipping the coffee. 'We got to know him pretty well out on the moor – which was the point of the exercise. When our man gets the bit between his teeth, he goes berserk. His code-name was Dog so we called him Mad Dog.'

'That's Jack,' agreed Dawson. His stomach pains were getting worse. 'He's a romantic who acts first and thinks afterwards.'

'Sarge!' It was Baker, lying on the ground beside his loaded rifle. Squinting through the sight, he said, 'There's a movement in the tree line.'

Charlie threw aside the anorak that had been covering his M500 and lay down beside it, nestling the stock into his shoulder. He adjusted the sight minutely and confirmed: 'It looks like there are . . . I'm counting: one-two-three-four-five-six men. One's clean-shaven. He's got some kind of a weapon and he's pulling and shouting at the others to get a move on, by the look of it.'

Dawson was looking the other way, at the farmhouse. He grabbed Able's binoculars and saw a group of people obviously arguing in front of the tiny building.

'No, Jack,' he said uselessly. 'For God's sake stay out of it.'

He saw a man in a yellow oilskin jacket – it was Pekka – throw an arm up in the direction of the watch-tower, pleading with Roscoe to go back into the house. Roscoe landed a blow on his chin that knocked the big fisherman to the ground and started running awkwardly through the knee-deep snow with the other man in pursuit. They were both heading towards the distant figures on the other side of the frontier.

'George!' It was Madeleine Wharton's voice from inside the hut. She sounded cool and controlled as always. 'Come back inside. There's nothing you can do now.'

Bergman squinted across the snowfield. He saw the line of

red-and-green posts on the Russian side and the matching blue-and-white ones, two metres further away on Finnish territory. Was it only a year since he had almost made it to the border, thanks to Wu? This time, thanks to Jack Roscoe, he was going to make it all the way. And thanks to Plotnik, he was bringing out the other survivors from Ossetin's earthly hell. That made him feel extra good.

Bergman's lungs were bursting. He knew that he was almost at the end of his depleted reserves of energy. Somehow the knowledge that he had only to get as far as the border for Jack Roscoe to take over, gave him a last shot of adrenalin and the energy to take a look around instead of just stumbling blindly onward.

He saw the Finnish watchtower looming over the trees to the south and picked up some movement there. That's pretty damn close, Jack, he thought. I hope we don't all end up arrested by the friendlies . . .

Behind him in the woods there were voices calling in Russian and dogs barking.

'*Paidyómte!*' Bergman shouted at the men with him . There was no need for silence. 'Come on, you guys! Move your arses! *Daváitye! Daváitye!*'

Despite his blows and encouragement, the half-starved prisoners could not move faster. That he had brought them so far was due to his willpower, not theirs. Left alone, they would have lain down in the snow and waited for their pursuers with dogs to catch up.

They were halfway between the tree-line and the frontier posts when the first man fell. Bergman stooped to pull him upright when he heard the second whip-crack and another man dropped, his head transformed into a faceless red cabbage staining the snow all around.

A voice Bergman recognised was shouting, 'Leave them, Peter! Run, for God's sake, run!'

He looked west to see Roscoe standing halfway between the farmhouse and the border. He was tearing Pekka's yellow oilskin off him and pulling it on as he ran through the snow in an awkward jumping run, lifting his feet high with each step.

'Help me, Jack,' Bergman screamed. 'Help me!'

On the top of the watchtower a pinpoint of light showed from the muzzle of Charlie's M500. Bergman heard the same whip-crack as the bullet, travelling supersonic, missed his ear by a couple of inches. Until that moment he had thought the shooting was coming from the men in the trees behind them.

He aimed his Uzi at the tower and fired all the rounds that remained in the magazine. At that range it was useless; no more than a gesture of rage. He threw the empty weapon away in the snow and kicked the black prisoner who seemed to be more alive than the others.

'Head for that guy over there!' he yelled, pointing at Roscoe. 'Go on, man. Run for your life!'

He grabbed the two remaining prisoners, one in each hand, and forced them into a shambling run for the last couple of hundred metres to the frontier itself, relying on their uneven progress – the falling, the slipping and sliding, the lurching forward and back – to put the men on the tower off their aim.

Roscoe was nearly at the border now. His breath was rasping in the freezing air. He heard the muted cracks coming from the tower and saw the muzzle flashes and the men falling around Bergman. A line of pursuers was beginning to emerge from the treeline behind the runaway prisoners, trapping them between two fires.

'Come on!' Roscoe shouted again through cupped hands. 'Leave the others, Peter! Save yourself!'

He ran through the Finnish line of posts and between two of the red-and-green Russian ones further on. The black man stumbling towards him stretched out both his hands.

On the tower, Able spoke, the binoculars glued to his eyes as he passed the next round to Baker. 'Hold it, Charlie. Don't fire. Mad Dog is over the border. Traverse left twenty degrees. Target is one man in a yellow anorak. Got him?'

'Yes, Sarge.' Charlie's voice was deadpan.

'Take him out, Charlie,' Able ordered. 'Shoot the Mad Dog first and then go back for the others.'

The crack was loud on the platform. Bolted to its tripod, the Haskins hardly jerked and Charlie watched the man in the cross hairs fall. Confident of his skill, he traversed right, reached without looking for the next round and reloaded.

There was a roaring in Roscoe's ears, like the noise of the pebbles on the beach at Samos, dragged back in the undertow. To get through the snowdrifts he had been using a kind of hurdler's stride. He was not surprised when the black running man appeared, hurdling towards him as he had at Kolwezi, moving effortlessly through the knee-deep snow.

'Come on, man,' he challenged Roscoe, white teeth gleaming in a black face. 'You can do it.'

It was harder than Roscoe had thought to keep on running. His body seemed hollow yet heavy. It wanted to lay down in the soft white eiderdown all around. But the running man was reaching out to him. 'Here,' he shouted, holding out a hand. 'Come to me.'

Roscoe grinned with happiness. They were going to be buddies after all. The first time they met in death – that day at Kolwezi – had not been personal. There was no hatred in the black face.

He reached for the black hand above the white snow and felt the running man lift him up and up into the air. There was a strange emptiness in his chest.

'Don't matter,' said the running man. 'You see, Jack? Dying is easy. For you an' me, it's living that's hard.'

Van's anorak was over Bergman's shoulders. He was shivering uncontrollably in reaction to his own adrenalin as the first snowflakes of the coming blizzard settled on his hair – and was so exhausted that he lacked even the energy to keep his eyes open.

She stood between him and Madeleine Wharton. 'You have no jurisdiction over this man,' she said repeatedly, refusing to back off and let them take him away. 'Peter Bergman is a Canadian citizen, so take your hands off him or I'll make sure you really have an international incident to worry about.'

She was still shaking with the mixture of rage and fear that had fuelled her sprinter's dash to the border, stepping in Roscoe's tracks but stopping beside the blue-and-white post, willing Bergman to her as the last man dropped beside him and still he kept coming – weaving and bobbing and rolling the last few yards through the snow to make an impossible target.

As he collapsed on Finnish territory, lungs bursting and heart hammering in his chest, she had thrown herself on top of him, defying the men with guns like an insane hunt protester protecting an injured fox, screaming through the tears her challenge that echoed in the empty valley: 'You'll have to kill me first, you bastards!'

Now she was using other weapons to save Bergman's life: nerve and coolness. In the background, Dawson stood near the three SBS men whose faces were concealed in Balaclava helmets. He looked like a man of eighty, staring haggardly out across the snow to where Roscoe's body lay. He neither spoke to Van nor even looked at her.

'You killed those men in cold blood,' Van accused Madeleine Wharton.

'It had to be. There were reasons of state.' The Director-General of SIS was willing the younger woman to back down.

'Reasons of state, my arse!' said Van. 'I know why the security services insist on evidence being given in camera at a spy trial. It's not to keep vital knowledge from the enemy, is it, Miss Wharton? If there are grounds for a trial, the enemy already knows. It's to keep the population from finding out just how criminally inept you people really are.'

She threw out an arm embracing all the men who had died, including Jack Roscoe. 'Those poor bastards in the snow out there only had one state secret between them. I'll tell you what it was: the knowledge of your failures, the CIA's failures, the KGB's and God knows who else's. You're all in this together. Don't talk to me of reasons of state, because I know the truth.'

It was a stalemate. The Sea Lynx departed after Madeleine Wharton's final warning: 'Vanessa Bowles-Haddon, I am formally reminding you that you are still bound by the Official Secrets Act.'

There were other threats too, to which Van's reply was, 'I despise you. Now go away and leave us alone. But I warn you, if anything ever happens to Peter Bergman, I'll dedicate my life to bringing you low, Madeleine Wharton! By God, I will. So don't forget that.'

In the premature dusk that heralded the oncoming blizzard, Inspector Koskelainen and his Russian opposite number were in a hurry to get their men back under cover before the storm struck. The bodies could stay where they lay; in a short while they would be impossible to find until the spring thaw.

Koskelainen and the Russian had known each other for years. They had seen other cover-ups but none so blatant and bloody as this one. After shaking hands at the line of posts they trudged away through the snow to their respective sides. For once there were no bilingual reports to be written, signed and countersigned because officially nothing had happened.

.12.

'*Grigori Sergeyevich! Kak mnyé priyátno!*' Boris Yeltsin stood up, walked round his large desk and kissed General Medvedev on both cheeks.

The armed sentry in ceremonial uniform closed the door softly. Medvedev was wearing his high-collared general's uniform. Three rows of medals were pinned above the left breast pocket and jingled slightly as he moved. A long piece of sticking plaster covered the deep lacerations on his cheek.

The President's private office in the Kremlin was immense, designed by Stalin to impress his visitors, and kept virtually unchanged by its successive occupants ever since. The dim lighting came from a hundred crystal wall sconces. Through the bullet-proof window the view was of the golden onion-shaped domes of the Kremlin churches against a dark, snow-laden sky.

The two men stood in the middle of a carpet which Lirian would have recognised as a priceless nineteenth-century silk-weave Tree of Life pattern from Kazakhstan. It was so large, and the knots so small and intricate, that it had taken eighteen years to complete and ruined three women's eyesight before it was finished.

Yeltsin pumped Medvedev's arm. They stood for a moment body to body as though posing for photographs. With the President's eyes hidden in pouches of fat and Medvedev's invisible below his bristling eyebrows, they were like two blind giants about to start a wrestling match.

'You realise,' said Yeltsin in his habitual tight-lipped mumble, 'that your achievement will never be publicly acknowledged, Grigori? Only inside the Kremlin walls can I say how I appreciate your brilliance in dreaming up The Revolution That Never Was.'

Yeltsin led Medvedev to a pink silk-covered sofa in one of several conversation areas. On the low table of Karelian birchwood inlaid with amber and mother-of-pearl was a samovar, gently bubbling. The President opened the tap and poured scalding black tea into two glasses set in gold enamelled holders which had been used by Peter the Great.

He passed one to Medvedev with the instruction: 'Tell me about it.'

'There's not a lot to tell,' growled Medvedev. The details, he had decided, were his property. There was nothing on paper even in his own office. 'Like every con man, I set out to invent a plausible cover story. I knew from contacts in the Pamyat movement that the idea of a Romanoff restoration was many people's idea of how to solve our country's current problems.'

'What was Plotnik's game exactly?' Yeltsin interrupted. He placed a lump of sugar between his teeth and sucked hot tea through it.

Medvedev felt a moment of genuine sadness. 'Ivan Ivanovich was a man living in the wrong century, Mr President. Charging across the steppes at the head of a regiment of sabre-waving Cossacks, he would have won honour for himself and glory for his country.'

Yeltsin understood the problem. 'You took a risk, Grigori Sergeyevich. Men like that hear inner voices.'

Medvedev defended his decision: 'I chose Colonel Plotnik deliberately because he was the ideal man for the part. At Frunze where we were cadets together, he was first at everything – except political theory where he came bottom of the class. He won the Sword of Honour and most of the prizes.

Then in Afghanistan our paths crossed again. It was Plotnik's troops who were dropped in to secure the airport and vital communications on the first night of the war.'

'A hero, in short.'

'. . . and one who commanded his own small private army – big enough for a modern revolution. In a sense, it was Plotnik who made everything else in my fake revolution credible.'

Yeltsin had still not decided how the meeting was going to end.

Eager for praise, Medvedev continued, 'But Plotnik was not stupid. Towards the end he began to smell a rat. I had a hell of a job inventing reasons to keep the poor bastard on the run the whole time for those last few days – so he didn't have time to sleep, let alone think.'

You don't have to tell me you're clever, thought Yeltsin. 'And that old CIA stooge, the banker?' he asked. 'You're not going to tell me that a hard-headed Boston businessman was carried away by dreams of glory? Why did he swallow everything you told him?'

Medvedev shifted warily on the sofa. 'He was like so many *émigrés*, Mr President. Over the years we have exploited their fantasies often. With Old Man Blok, I followed the basic pre-cept of disinformation: you tell the target what he wants to hear. He had dreamed since childhood of returning to Russia under a Tsar. I promised to make his dream come true, that's all.'

Yeltsin was smiling. It could have meant anything.

Medvedev fingered the plaster on his cheek. 'Young Blok was, if anything, easier to con. He thought my fake restoration was going to be the Big Deal Of All Time, with the Blok Corporation ending up richer than many governments from all its commissions.'

Yeltsin nodded. Like the smile it could have meant anything. 'You put nothing on paper, Grigori Sergeyevich?'

'Nothing could be put on paper.' Medvedev gave his eyes an outing. 'The beauty of the plan, Mr President, was that – for obvious reasons – nobody could ask me to confirm anything in writing.'

Yeltsin picked up a folder lying on the table beside the

samovar. He ran his eyes over the confidential single-sheet memorandum from the Minister of Finance. The bottom-line total of hard-currency funds on deposit with the PanBaltia Bank ran into billions of dollars – greenback hostages for the depositors' sympathy, every one.

He pointed to Medvedev's rows of decorations. 'The country owes you a reward, Grigori Sergeyevich. One more medal is hardly enough for the man who has kept Russia afloat for another six months! And I owe you a personal debt as well because the success of your scam will give me time to hold elections and hopefully to outmanoeuvre those bastards in Parliament who are trying to inch their way back to the power they lost two years ago.'

Yeltsin's eye was caught by a white telephone flashing on his desk. 'How can I reward you properly?' It was a rhetorical question. 'I have no precedent for such a situation, my dear Grigori. Yosef Vissarionovich whose desk I have inherited . . . Now, what would the great Stalin have done with you? I know and you know that he would have had you shot for being too damned clever, wouldn't he?'

He pointed to a fake book-case on the wall. 'Behind there is what the staff still call Stalin's Shithouse. It looks like one: a small, white-tiled room with no washbasin or lavatory, just a single tap in the wall and a drain in the middle of the floor. It was built for killing in, not crapping in.'

Like a jolly grandfather playing with a small boy, he made a pretend pistol with two fingers, pointed it at Medvedev and said, 'Bang!'

Despite his self-control, Medvedev's palms were moist with nerves.

'This samovar is also interesting.' Yeltsin leaned forward to demonstrate. He placed his glass beneath the ornamental tap. 'I turn the tap with my glass underneath. Out comes tea from the main boiler, which I am going to drink.'

He took a sip and put the glass down on the table. Taking Medvedev's glass he observed, 'You're sweating.'

'It's hot in here,' said Medvedev.

Yeltsin concentrated on the demo. 'Now, if I press down at the same time as I turn the tap, I activate an internal lever which operates a small valve inside. What comes out of the tap now is not from the main boiler but from a separately filled small cylinder inside the main tank. It's like an indirect hot-water heater. Ingenious, isn't it?'

He raised his glass and waited for Medvedev to do the same. When both glasses were empty he said, 'It was Lavrenti Beria's idea when he was boss of the KGB. He used it several times as a mechanical variant of cutting the apple in half with a knife poisoned on one side of the blade.'

'It makes very good tea,' said Medvedev, putting down his glass.

A second telephone was flashing on the President's desk. Yeltsin stood up and stretched. 'How would you like to be President in my place, Grigori Sergeyevich?'

Medvedev stood. For a moment he felt dizzy. Then he reassured himself; the central heating was turned up too high and the two cups of scalding tea were making him sweat. He pulled the high collar away from his neck to let some body-heat escape.

'Not at all, Mr President,' he said earnestly. 'I work better in the shadows. The limelight is for other men like yourself.'

Yeltsin had thought of rewarding Medvedev with Beria's old job. Now he thought it might be safer to put this deceptive old bear somewhere more visible. 'I need a man with your brain as Minister of Defence,' he decided.

Medvedev bowed his head in gratitude for the appointment.

'And I have a small present for you.' Yeltsin took from a drawer in his desk a green German passport. The photograph inside jogged Medvedev's memory vaguely.

'It was found in a garbage bin in Helsinki,' said the President. 'Very law-abiding people, the Finns. Someone handed it in to our Consulate. They found that the number appeared among those listed on the St Petersburg-Helsinki train you checked last week. I thought you might like to keep it as a souvenir.'

Yeltsin's voice was sympathetic. 'The passport was one of a batch issued by the KGB years ago to Anastas Lirian, so it was almost certainly used by the girl you were looking for.'

Medvedev looked at the face of Hildegard Sommer and wondered where Nadya Gutman was now. The only certainty was that he would never see her again. The taste of success turned to ashes in his mouth; from beyond the grave, Lirian had won that game after all.

Bergman walked alone from the Canadian Consulate on the Pohjoisesplanadi to the Holiday Inn. Van had wanted to come with him but he had decided it was time to begin looking after himself.

To be among noisy crowds for the first time in years was a confusing, almost frightening, experience. Bergman bought a glass of beer in a bar and left it half-drunk, panicking when the gay barman mistook his customer's emaciation for that of an AIDS victim and became too friendly.

It was hard for Bergman not to keep looking over his shoulder in the street. He kept taking the temporary travel document out of his pocket and rereading it. The slim piece of card meant that he existed again in a world where identity was a matter of having the right piece of paper.

Van was waiting in the foyer of the hotel. She stood up as he came through the revolving glass doors. 'You look tense, Peter,' she whispered. 'Take it easy. Everything's fine.'

'I'm OK,' he said, blinking rapidly. 'Tired, is all. I hafta get used to people talking to me again.'

When he had calmed down, they walked to the reception desk and filled in a registration form. As they waited for the clerk to issue their room cards Bergman noticed the attractive blonde girl who was checking out at the cashier's counter next door. Her bags were on a porter's trolley beside her. He read the labels.

'Well,' he said, tapping her on the shoulder. 'That's a coincidence. You're from T.O.?'

Renata Witzig turned. 'Am I?' She tried to place his accent but could not.

'Toronto,' said Bergman. Surely every Torontan understood T.O.?

She looked blank.

'I grew up in Etobicoke,' he said. 'I haven't been back home for a long while. I guess the old place has changed, huh?'

Renata could not place the stranger's accent but guessed he

was making references that should mean something to her. Flustered, she dropped her dark blue Canadian passport on the floor. Bergman picked it up and handed it back to her.

'You bet,' she said uncertainly. 'It's changed a lot.'

'Especially downtown, I guess?'

'I'm sorry, I can't talk to you.' She turned away. 'Goodbye!'

'Well!' Bergman turned to Van with a wry smile. 'I must be looking pretty rough if I frighten off the first attractive girl I try to pick up.'

'You're looking just great,' said Van.

'Luggage?' asked the reception clerk.

'We don't have any,' said Bergman. 'Is that all right?'

'Perfectly, sir. The lifts are over there.'

'Where do we get the room keys?' Bergman had not seen an electronic room card before.

The clerk eyed him warily, thinking: no luggage, doesn't know about card-operated locks . . .

He was reassured by Van. Confident and poised, she smiled, 'It's OK. I'm his keeper.'

.13.

Close but not touching, they walked along the harbour wall above the brightly painted fishing boats bobbing at their moorings on the dark blue water. The first snows of winter had thawed quickly along Finland's west coast. In the low-angle morning sun the colourful wooden fishermen's cottages around the little port of Naantali had the simple charm of a child's painting.

Van was glad she had accepted Arvo's advice to take Bergman for a short holiday in this quiet corner of Finland until he was ready to handle the hustle and bustle of big cities. Jan Coetzee was due to fly into Helsinki that morning and would be joining them for a few days to strengthen the links with Bergman's past.

Pekka Manninen gave the two strollers a gloomy nod as they passed him mending nets on the deck of his sturdy little herring boat. He was planning to buy and restore a fully-rigged Baltic schooner with his share of what they called 'the loot'. In a rare moment of expansiveness he had told Van the previous evening all about his hero Gustav Erikson, the Finn from Mariehamn who had owned the world's last fleet of working clippers and had ten tall ships among the thirteen that sailed in the last-ever Grain Race of 1939.

Van wished Bergman would open up to her like that. She did not understand that he was still trying to reconcile what had happened on the border with the fantasy of suspicion and revenge that had obsessed him for six long years.

They passed a small granite war memorial to the men of the town who had fallen, fighting against the Russians in the winter of 1940. Bergman stopped and looked at the indecipherable Finnish wording.

'Can you read Finnish?' Van asked.

He grunted, 'They all say more or less the same thing: "Greater love hath no man . . . *morts pour la patrie . . . caídos por la patria . . . im Krieg gefallen* . . . our glorious dead." Glory, my arse! The reality is guys die screaming when they're gut-shot or barbecued alive. War is shit!'

'So why did you and Jack become soldiers?'

Louder than her voice was that of Roscoe when they were both cleaning boots in the showers at Castelnaudary. Bergman listened to it for a moment, then said slowly, 'Jack had dreams of glory. That's why he joined the Legion. At Kolwezi he found out what war was all about.'

He gestured at the granite column. 'Hell, most of the poor guys whose names we read on memorials got hit before they knew what was happening. The difference between them and Jack is that he *chose* to do what he did.'

'Coming across the border to get you?'

Bergman shook his head; Van did not understand Roscoe's sacrifice. 'Jack didn't run out across that snowfield in a bright yellow jacket to get me. He ran in a dead straight line for one purpose – to give 'em a target they couldn't resist shooting at. By deliberately drawing the fire, he gave me those extra few seconds to make it to the border and you. Greater love . . . How does the rest of it go?'

'Greater love hath no man than that he lay down his life for his friend.' Van remembered hearing the text read by her uncle Neville at her father's funeral service. She turned her face away so that Bergman could not see the tears she was shedding for Jack Roscoe.

Silence and the plaintive calling of the gulls. Behind her, Bergman's voice was low. 'Any reading material you get in the Gulag you devour a thousand times, y'know? One Christmas Wu gave me a present. From somewhere he had stolen part of a play by Shakespeare, in English. God knows how it got into Perm 39B, but there it was – just a few pages some guard must've been keeping to wipe his arse on. It was Cassius's speech at Caesar's funeral, all about *honourable men*. Can't say as I understood it too well but of course I pretended for Wu's sake that I was pleased. Now Jack really was an honourable man.'

He looked back at the monument. The dew-glistening column of stone seemed to burn in the almost horizontal sunlight. He saluted a memory, whether Roscoe or the men on the column it was impossible for Van to decide. She thought there were tears in Bergman's eyes too and left him in privacy, to sit waiting a little further along the harbour wall. Winter's fingers were reaching inside her clothing but Bergman gave no sign of feeling the cold.

She had tried several times to lead the conversation around to his plans for the future. So far he had not seemed to grasp that owning a half-share in her Geneva shop as well as one of the Fabergé eggs made him a multi-millionaire, free to do anything and go anywhere he wanted.

Bergman walked up, absorbed in watching the white gulls diving for fish scraps floating in the blue harbour water between the red and white and yellow boats. Colours, he thought, colours are life. I lived for so long in a world without colours . . .

Van thought how all his movements were strangely graceful and flowing. He seemed to have an inner peace, like a gyroscope spinning around a still centre.

'Listen to me,' she begged. 'Do you realise that you and I are worth around seven million dollars between us?'

'You and I,' Bergman corrected her, 'are worth a whole lot more than that, sweetheart.' The echoes of his laugh travelled around the harbour wall and came back to them.

Money, he thought, is nothing, compared with being able to watch a white gull swoop out of a blue sky or smell the thousand age-old scents of a fishing port.

'And don't say you don't want your share,' said Van, thinking he was going to refuse.

She was wrong. Bergman's silences were his way of finding space for the present between the memories which had filled his days for so long. Squinting against the light, his eyes followed another gull wheeling against the sun. How different was this sunny fishing port, so full of colour, from the grey gloom where Jack Roscoe's body and Wu's and Plotnik's lay in the snows, far to the east . . .

The bird swooped and grabbed a fish, fumbled it and screamed. Bergman wished the fish good luck and godspeed. Then for the first time he saw Van clearly, her face turned to him, lit by the low, golden sun. He saw the way the long blonde hair bounced on her shoulders as she turned her head, the way her body moved in the red anorak and white trousers. Colour, he thought. I want to drown in the colours of sunsets and sail to far horizons.

Returning his look, Van asked softly, 'What are you going to do with your share of the money, Peter? Do you have plans?'

'I've got plenty of plans.' He traced her eyebrows with one finger, and the line of her nose and her lips, marvelling that he was still alive to touch her and enjoy her beauty. 'I had all the time in the world for dreams.'

'Will you tell me about them, Peter? Or are they private?'

Bergman's cold blue eyes were set so far back in their sockets that she could not tell what he was thinking, or even whether they were focused on her or looking through her to sights that he alone could perceive. There was an impression of such strength radiating from this man who had suffered so much, that she knew there was no point in trying to break his barriers down. Either Bergman would open the door into his soul of his own accord or he would stay out of her reach for ever.

'Will you?' she prompted.

Bergman took a deep breath. He had deliberately dammed all emotions except hatred long ago in order to conserve energy, but now it was time to start living again – living and feeling. 'First thing I'm gonna do, is satisfy an ambition Jack and I had – way, way back.'

He smiled slowly, recalling memories of crazy things they

had done together. 'We fucked up that time, so I'm going to sail around the world now, for both of us.'

'Great idea.'

'I want to be clean,' Bergman said. 'I lived for so long in the stink of excrement, Van. I want to smell the wind and taste the spray of salt water on my lips. Do you understand?'

She nodded. 'Will you come back?'

Bergman knew what she meant. He grinned briefly. There was a spark of contact there, she was sure.

'If I don't meet that little bastard Wu on the way,' he said. 'If he doesn't swoop down on me, sitting on a blue-and-white surf-board atop some giant wave and take me down with him to a watery grave – then I'll be back.'

All her life, Van had hated asking for something she could not have. She swallowed her pride now to ask, 'Do you have to do this thing alone, Peter?'

He did not answer. She sensed that time had a different dimension for him; it didn't necessarily mean he was hostile.

Bergman's thoughts in any case were not what she would have guessed. He was thinking: I never knew Wu. I never knew Plotnik. And I never really knew what made Jack tick. All my life I was running too fast to slow down and get to know anyone thoroughly – or let them get to know me. Now is about the right time in this man's life to know one person really well . . .

'Y'ever done any sailing?' He was looking at the boats, not at her.

'Dinghies,' she said swiftly. 'The estuary at Salcombe with my dad, every summer holiday since I was old enough to handle a jib-sheet. I can hold a course, cook a meal on one burner and I'm very cool in a crisis, Cap'n.'

Freedom brought so many choices, Bergman thought. He could understand why some released prisoners committed crimes just to get back inside. If Van came with him, he would not meet Wu and the others, but there was no hurry for that. It would happen soon enough.

'If you're free,' he said, 'I'll be needing a crew.'

'Just one?'

'Right on.'

'I'm free.'

'We might be away a long time.'

'That's OK.'

He sighed. 'Could be, we find a place that's good to live – and don't come back ever.'

Van wanted to touch Bergman's face but thought it was too early for that.

'Either way,' she said, keeping her voice neutral. 'That's fine by me.'

There was a long pause during which she realised that she would have to get used to Bergman's silences.

'I've sure got a lot of living to make up for,' he sighed.

As Bergman's fingers intertwined with hers, Van felt a great flush of happiness fill her body. It welled up and up inside her until she had the sensation of being lifted off the ground, literally treading on air. With cheeks flushed and eyes sparkling, she returned the pressure of his fingers, knowing that everything was going to work out. Now that he had made the first move, she could make the second.